CITY OF GOD

A STONE OF THE HEART

SEASON'S END

SPEC *(a play)*

W . W . NORTON & COMPANY

NEW YORK / LONDON

CITY OF GOD

T O M   G R I M E S

The text of this book is composed in New Baskerville
with the display set in Madrone
Composition and manufacturing by the Haddon Craftsmen, Inc.
Book design by JAM DESIGN

Library of Congress Cataloging-in-Publication Data

Grimes, Tom, 1954–
City of God / by Tom Grimes.
p.   cm.
I. Title.
PS3557.R4899C58   1995
813′.54—dc20   95-1730

ISBN 0-393-03789-4

W. W. Norton & Company, Inc., 500 Fifth Avenue, New York, N.Y. 10110
W. W. Norton & Company Ltd., 10 Coptic Street, London WC1A 1PU

1 2 3 4 5 6 7 8 9 0

for Jody

Observe now the city of confusion in order that ye
may perceive the vision of peace, that ye may
endure that, sigh for this. Whereby can those two
cities be distinguished? Can we anywise now
separate them from each other? They are
mingled, and from the very beginning of
mankind mingled they run on unto the end of
the world.

—from "On Psalm 64," St. Augustine

CITY OF GOD

< X X N >

Fade in ....

The fires are framed by darkness now, the bodies of helicopters swooping above them turning into black phantoms as evening's last light goes out of the sky. In the distance beyond the
phantasmal stilts of searchlight beams, a low grid of sprawl oozes
out from the city. Lines of traffic slither along loops of beltway.
Past power plants, malls, and torched residential districts. Past
toxic waste recycling stations and armories. On toward constellations of glowing, clustered subdivisions. Nearby, windows in office
towers brighten like candle flames. Small trash fires surrounded
by shadowy rings of huddled figures are scattered along the street
below. Ghost buses with iron-gated windows pass by, sizzling images advertising liquor, radio stations, crisis hot lines, cable TV
sex, and designer-brand ammunition affixed to each side, their
bright interiors empty except for the driver in bulletproof vest and
riot helmet. At an intersection a mercury vapor lamp arcs over the
curb, draping a tank and its crew in a urine-colored cone of light.
Cars, the few that appear, ignore traffic signals.

Down the elevator and out through the building's pristine
atrium comes Julia, heading home after a day in Hate Crimes. It is
late. The spray of the indoor fountains is the only sound. Everyone
has gone home except for the reception desk guards, and janitors
who hang suspended by harnesses from the domed glass ceiling,

misting Rapunzel ferns that spill down alongside terraced restaurants and automatic teller machines, the codependency temple and health club, the combination hair stylist, mind gym, and take-out koan shop.

The far side of the shatterproof glass doors brings a charged, mucosal air teeming with invisible grit. Ahead, beyond the plaza's commissioned sculpture—four working televisions carouseling above a rusted flatbed covered with dirt clods, charred hay, and human-shaped rib cages made of wrought iron—Mish, the East European refugee and head of nighttime security, waits for her, speaking into a walkie-talkie. As Julia comes close, he rehangs the radio on his belt clip and waves her on, checking to his left, the direction they will be walking. Then he turns back to her, smiling, nodding, saying hello in some derivative Germanic tongue she doesn't understand, though he never seems bothered by this. It is their ritual, the ground of unknowing on which they meet.

Raising the elbow nearest him so that she may take his arm as she says, "Hi, Mish," he nods, mumbles a syllable, then glances over one shoulder before they begin.

On the street Julia finds herself wishing that everything—the slimy mist; the prismatic halos surrounding the flying-saucer-shaped streetlamp casings; the dark figures in stained overcoats, their brows glistening with an unhealthy sweat, others slack-jawed and nodding out inside their unbuckled rainboots and mismatched athletic shoes—would glide into cinematic slow motion, allowing her to separate herself from it. To watch it, like television.

Instead, several in the crowd approach. Some with a palm upturned. A few simply reaching out for a body to fall against or cling to. One of the bodies leans in drowsily and Mish puts the point of his nightstick to the man's shoulder and nudges him back. A dim, unmoored consciousness tries to work its way into the man's eyes and project itself. But the effort amounts to only a small waking.

Then he totters backwards, while she and Mish move on.

As they weave through the shuffling maze of bodies, another man, bare-chested and shoeless, goose-steps along the curbside, raving. A passing car—tinted windows, sonic boom drumbeat thumping inside it—slows. One window opens. An arm emerges and flings a grease-soiled fast food sack, a tattered rain of food bits, emptying cartons, and crushed ice spattering a small circle of bodies after the bag bursts in midair. There is some complaint from the street crowd, a confused then gradually angry bleating. Syncopated fuck yous, cries of "douche bag." It becomes almost playful, a rallying cry, until two of the bodies that have stepped into the gutter and chased the car, hurling bottles which shatter on the pavement in its wake, bump into one another. One is clubbed swiftly to the ground. Mish's only reaction is to squeeze Julia's arm a bit more tightly.

The guard ahead at the parking lot gate, part of the illegal immigrant Mafia which accepts jobs most naturalized citizens will not, hustles a few loiterers past the lot entrance, then waves Mish on. Julia feels like a parcel some nights as they pass her along, fearful not really for her but for her safety, the aura of her, her wrappings and packaging. Get it there undented, collect your money, and go home. Or maybe it's just that she has no idea what they're saying to one another as they exchange grips on her arm. She feels ignorant, a bit helpless. They move in two worlds; she needs somebody to walk her to her car.

Which is now brought up from underground by a young man in a knitted cap and fatigue jacket. Death's-head patches are sewn onto its sleeves beside small American flags. Spelled out across the back in tie-dyed script are the words "Born to Kill." He steps away without acknowledging her, not even a glance. Ever. He isn't stoned. There's no rubberiness in his movements, or a crack hangover turning the whites of his eyes into a sunset of burst blood vessels. He's never tried to look crazy at her like the young gang-bangers do in court, either. This guy looks right through her, as if she isn't even there. And to him, Julia realizes, she is and she isn't.

The fool on the sidewalk is another matter. As Julia rolls her car toward the exit, he stands in front of her headlights as if he were some badass cowboy. Inside the car—its gauge faces beaming, processed air caressing her face—Julia feels safe. The radio scans the airwaves, passing through traffic reports, call-in fortune telling, suspicions about the undulations of the week's jet stream. There is programmed heavy breathing, a suicide methodology seminar, easy-credit terms for death row residents, end-of-the-world rock. When she looks around, there is no sign of Mish or his refugee-in-law cousin, and the young man in the cap is long gone. The guy stands there, staring, and the city's night fear is back in Julia's stomach, a tiny detonation of acid hollowing her just below her ribs. The impulse to roll down the window and ask him to move quickly reveals itself to be futile and dangerous. Exhaling, she whispers, "Christ." But as if someone has suddenly changed the channel of the television she's been watching, Mish springs into view, materializing like a comic-book superhero, comet tail of color trailing him in from the corner of the frame. He blindsides the guy shoulder high, body-checking him into a small herd of trash cans stacked three deep near the curb. The clatter of the cans tumbling, lids crashing to the ground and warbling, is muffled inside the car. Then Mish, nightstick flashing as he clears a breach in the river of bodies before waving her on, seems unreal to her as well through the windshield glass, as if he too were a part of the sounds of the radio—electronic, plugged in—which seem to possess the texture of dreams.

Julia eases the car forward, the too-stoned or permanently spaced bumping into her fenders and doors before pinballing backwards. She glances once more at the downed man and sees him struggling to get to his feet among the scattered cans. Dazed, he slips, falls, then spins on his ass when he hits the ground. She looks away, the front end of the car dipping as it enters the street. But even this is cushioned inside the vehicle. The street begins to pass beneath her with accelerating swiftness, her speed dissolving into a feathery lightness until she has the sensation of floating. She glides past stoplights, deserted intersections, the collapsing shells of squatter-occupied high-rises until, locking into cruise control, she ascends from the downtown streets through a thin band of fog and rushes out over the city, its coruscated sprawl receding in the rearview mirror as she banks away from it at the crown of the free-way's entrance ramp. Her breathing slowly returns to normal. The car swoops into the thinning caravan of late evening traffic. And, for the night, she leaves behind the fires and helicopter search-lights, which fall away from her in the distance. . . .

Same time, same Bat channel. Only . . . there is no Bat signal to project against the smog-glazed underbelly of inner-city clouds. No Daily Planet building. No superhero to summon by telepathy, secret decoder ring, subliminal advertising, voice mail, or wild-eyed bike messenger. And all the pay phones are busted, defaced, poleaxed, tommy-gunned, or else not able to connect you to your calling card company's network. All there is, down among the car carcass graveyards, trashed playgrounds, graffiti-smeared project walls, and row house temples of worship Julia is rushing from, is a single squad car. Granted, one equipped with bulletproof glass; a revolving, computer-controlled, roof-mounted, .50-caliber ma-chine gun; steel-reinforced, mine-resistant undercoating; and two officers packing semiautomatic assault revolvers. Hit an arm, rup-ture a spleen. The weapons deliver a body-shattering kick, bullet impact rending and tearing organs and muscle. Still, the car is no nuclear-warhead-hardened bunker, and the two guys inside it are no futuristic cyborg law enforcers. They bleed.

And up alongside them in baggy, sky-blue nylon pants, the cuffs tucked inside Velcro-strapped air pump sneakers, a wool nightcap with dangling pompom on his head, and an autographed, hoop-god warm-up jacket slinks skinny-assed, nineteen-year-old Do-Ray, solo. Solo, but not quite alone. Rap Master Coda's exhortations to "bring home the hate" are thumping inside his head and chest, his heart pumping like some hip-hop rhythm section.

Ray doesn't know who Coda is, exactly. Seems no one does. There's just this bootleg tape-slash-CD making the rounds, underground. Black jacket cover, no photos of Coda or his DJs, no band promo info or fan-club address. Hell, the tape don't even have a distributor's label, at least not no major name like XXN. Minus Five's video arcade was the only place you could score a copy, and even then Ray had to beg Minus Five to sell him one, at primo prices too. But the tape is like beyond hip, leaves old-style gangsta rap behind at light speed. Coda's stuff ain't about boastin' and bangin'. It's flat-out, get-down political—like, enough of this foolin' around, time for some genocide. The white man can run, you know, but he can't hide. And Ray definitely digs where that attitude is coming from. Right up front Coda tells you that the eternally cool thing, the thing which gets you divine respect, plus the rank of disciple in this great, vague clique called the Discordia Sect, ain't just listening but *doin'*. That's why Coda ain't into distributors and mainstream recording labels. As he say, "the money will come/once the killin' gets done." And killin's a street thing. And Ray knows about street things.

See, Ray's wasted a brother before. O.C., Orange Crush, one of his own homies. Big fucker. Always in Miami Dolphins duds. Wore a helmet and linebacker pads just to check out a movie or hang in the crib with the tube on. Bottle of o.j. in his hand as if it were put there permanently by the process of natural selection. Then he had to go and dis Do-Ray's Raiders cap, calling its pirate insignia pussy bullshit, which drew cries of ooh and ouch from the other dudes on the stoop. Ray didn't help his own case any when he said O.C.'s Dolphins logo was for people too stupid to know fish can't play football. After blowing air through his lips and shaking his head like, why do I even got to be dealing with you, O.C. just said, "A dolphin ain't no fish, fool."

So, that's it. Ray got his older brother's gun (Big Henry, R.I.P. home, '69–'91) and waited for O.C. after football practice. Standing at the end of the alley just past the bus stop, he watched O.C., duffel bag in hand, board the evening bus, then bolted for the door and climbed on himself. Pupils glazed from the Train '99 he'd been sipping to give him the crazies and make shooting O.C. feel soft, slippy, and movie-like, Ray imagined O.C.'s flesh tearing in slow motion, fake blood pouches bursting inside his jersey like on TV. He followed O.C. down the aisle as the bus began to move, the heads of the passengers on either side of him staring past their own reflections in the windows at the darkening streets outside. O.C. smiled for an instant when he took his seat, even started to say Hey, Ray, happy to see his friend. So the gagging stench that poured out of his bowels, hot liquid running down his thighs when he saw the dazed hate in Ray's gone-wild eyes, didn't even seem to be his. The first bullet entered his sternum. And even though it was genuine, 100% Grade-A blood—O.C.'s blood—Ray stood vengeful and gangster tough over his friend's body, squinting just the slightest bit as he pumped the trigger. The second shot entered O.C.'s open mouth, paralyzing his expression, eyeballs locking like slot machine images, their sockets pooling with blood. A moment later, a thick clot of it, viscous and cherry-black, snaked down O.C.'s tongue and rolled onto his chin, as if a chunk of his brain had dropped through his sinuses into his throat.

Ray hopped from the stopped bus, cut through an alley, walked a few blocks, then trash-canned the pistol after wrapping it in a paper bag. He tossed his gloves through a sewer grate, then headed for a discount electronics outlet up the avenue where he hauled out three Walkmans, a couple of cellular phones, and some computer software, stacking it all under a cement sidewalk bench on which he sat and took five for a smoke before returning to attempt lugging out a boom box the size of a compact car. Finally, the manager saw the two gun-drawn cops he had summoned and decided it was safe to flip the alarm. At fourteen Ray did a gig in juvey hall—for shoplifting. O.C. became a statistic, lost and seemingly forgotten. No better place to be when the Man was looking for you, Ray thought, than under his nose.

But now, five years later, to be creeping up on a pair of them, even if it is for Allah and High Mystic Rap King Coda, for all the brothers and baby sisters of the devolution-revolution, Ray simply a soldier helping to bring an end to the genocide being perpetrated against his people—yeah, even so, he's never shot the Man before, not even in a drive-by. Killing the Man is stepping into a whole new world. It's messing with the order of things.

So what if he's dreamed of revenge a zillion times? Imagined the whole white world rocketing into space like one big screaming fireball, with him, little Do-Ray, the first black superhero, straddling the planet, giving the entire exiled, oblivion-bound, swine race the finger. Feeling justified, vindicated, and morally cleansed like Rap Master Coda said he would when he turned his white-man-inflicted sense of worthlessness around. When he stopped venting his rage, hate, and guilt on his own color. When he rid the earth of this sex-drained, techno-death-worshipping scum. Yeah, Ray knew all that. Still you don't just shuck four centuries' worth of fear that easy.

Or forget the time your mother got all tense and sharp-tongued, years earlier. Out driving in the car. Ain't done nothing. Do-Ray just a little peckerhead, hardly see over the fat dash of that gas guzzler. All of a sudden, while he was in the middle of asking some dumbass kid question like, why does milk gotta be white, his mother told him, for no reason he could get a handle on, to be quiet. Ray saw her check the rearview mirror as she eased the car over to the side of the road. A blue uniform showed up in the driver's-side window a moment later, evil-looking nightstick and finger-darkened revolver handle riding its hips.

There was no face at first, not until his mother had turned over her license, her hand trembling. Then the eyes appeared. Appeared and looked briefly at his mother, then past her at him— know-nothing, no-account Ray. And the eyes needled some wordless sense that Ray had done something unredeemable, rendering him worthless for all time, into him, the Ray who understood it was best to turn his little homeboy's eyes toward the ground and keep 'em there. And so he did. He did until he couldn't even look in the mirror without wanting to wipe this thing called him out of existence. No, you don't lose this sense of worthlessness overnight, no matter what Coda, Allah, or any other all-seeing, all-knowing, all-chillin' prophet says. No way.

So as Ray slides out through the doorway of the condemned building he's been perching in and walks up alongside the squad car, his breathing gets twisted inside his chest, punchy and erratic, as if there's a fist stuck where his Adam's apple should be. His arms and legs go lead pipe heavy when he sees the backs of the cops' heads through the rear windshield, the low burbling of their voices enveloping him. They strike Ray as innocent. Of what, he's not sure. Maybe something which they don't even see or understand, making them, perhaps, worthy of mercy. He nearly allows this feeling to carry him past them, down the empty street. But he knows that if he does he'll feel, in the wake of his cowardice, their contempt. So his pace quickens. Fuck mercy. Be redeemed in another life, motherfucker.

Ray doesn't even want the cheap wine buzz now, doesn't need it to carry him slo-mo and ugly through the killing the way he needed it when he wasted O.C. A soundtrack clicks on in his head. His actions merge with celluloid fantasy, his terror vanishing as the moment becomes a movie.

He comes abreast of the passenger-side window. His gloved hands unsheathe the truncated rifle barrel strapped to his chest when the cop nearest him looks out, his eyes meeting Ray's. They don't pick up the gun at first. It's just a simple turn of the head, a reaction to something stirring near the blurry edge of peripheral vision. When the cop scowls, hate rushes through Ray. Any sense of compassion he had vanishes.

The first C-4-tipped shell hits the window and rocks the car, its passenger-side tires lifting off the ground. The plastic explosive in the cartridge bursts on impact, dappling the windows and doors with small bright stars and kicking back a shower of sparks. Holes open in the passenger window and Ray can hear shouting—panicked, angry, terrified—inside the vehicle. The second round rips through the interior of the car and blows out its far windows, glass leaping from the door frames and fanning out over the street. This time no voices are heard under the clacking of metal as Ray reloads, just a deep, hoarse whining. He fires again, this blast taking off the steering wheel top. Then he realizes that the whining sound is the cop nearest him trying to breathe. As the gun's report echoes down the street, it becomes quiet enough for Ray to hear the man gasping for air. The spooky thing is, the sound seems to be coming not from his mouth, but from his chest.

Ray peers into the car and sees that the man's head has fallen back against the security grating behind him. His jaws are open, part of his throat torn away. What's left is a thin, bloody, faintly pulsing stalk. His shirt ripped open, a fractured bone juts out from the skinless stump of shoulder, his flesh from sternum to ribs peeled away like a skinned onion. The man's insides gleam, slick and reddish-black in the streetlight. For an instant, Ray thinks he sees the man's heart dangling by a partially severed artery, beating arhythmically outside his ribs. His own heart clutches.

Then a staticky babble tumbles from the car's mangled radio and Ray begins firing wildly, rocking the car with rifle blasts. His fear of bad spirits makes him manic, and he becomes obsessed with the notion of obliterating the bodies. Destroy the grounds of his transgression, destroy the sin.

One shot vaporizes the first cop's head. Ray moves around the car and does the same to the second, blowing the back of his skull off with one round, decapitating him with the next. There is neither praise nor condemnation from Allah, no rap wisdom from Coda, no black superhero fantasies to buoy him. It's just little Do-Ray up against his own demons, alone.

Only he isn't quite alone. He doesn't know it, but he's got company. . . .

The first flash produces a brief bright glimmer down among the grid of streets, sparks floating around the detonation like fireflies, then dying out to black. From the helicopter's height it could be harmless fireworks exploding, or another minor conflagration. Flames burrow into the city's sprawl—undulating, wind-whipped badges of orange, black-tipped light. Someone with a metaphysical tilt of mind might be tempted to read something infernal into the landscape: the garish light of the commercial strips, the flame-puffing refinery stacks and reactor cooling sleeves, the vandal fires burning like lost souls amid great patches of wasteland darkness. Someone. But not chopper pilot R.F.U. "Crash" Tillinghast, nicknamed not only to acknowledge the lad's talent for surviving them—he has totaled two whirlybirds in his brief, undistinguished, often sleep-deprived and hungover tenure, so far—but also to pay homage to the screeching, reverb-indebted guitar riffs of his heavy metal days with Coma Orgasm, whose debut CD included the ballad "Serial Killer's Lament," a slash-and-burn version of "Hitler Got Rooked, Man," and a live cover of "Sonic Baboon" featuring "Crash"—then known as R.F.U. as his standard answer to rock mag interview questions about his life, mental state, health, or what he had gotten the night before was, invariably, Real Fucked Up—performing slide dobro wizardry during which the drug-addled guitarist slit his wrists, then continued playing until a medical emergency team rushed from the wings to perform onstage surgery, backed by a drum solo. When the band disbanded for the usual reasons—drug overdoses, sexual battery and attempted murder charges, the bassist's conversion to a religious sect which believed in the abolition of income tax—R.F.U., the group's sole non-felon and governor's nephew, took several megahits of Ecstasy, time off, flying lessons, and two years plus one major haircut later emerged as Wing Private Tillinghast, chopper cop.

Pirouetting over the urban DMZ and pyre-brightened ghettos, and grooving on the fact that "Hey, dude, from up here the city looks like the inside of a huge stereo receiver," he turns the whirlybird belly up and slices through pink bands of smog that are sucked over the Plexiglas bubble by the updraft of the chopper's propeller. Tuned to WXXN's weeknight pro football doubleheader, the last thing R.F. has on his substance-abused mind is an inclination to lay any sort of metaphysical polyurethane or while-U-wait apocalyptic laminate over his view of the inferno below. To him, the disappearing curtain of sparks that follows the flash is merely and literally "far out." No cause for alarm or investigation.

The second flash, though, much closer as both cockpit and interest-piqued R.F. shoulder their way earthward, is nastier. No

electron particle fizz or swirl of sparks. No rosebud-shaped glim-
mering of flames. Just a silvery-white burst.

R.F. punches in computer grid coordinates and flips down the
frames of his night vision goggles. City, night sky, the copter's dash
and computer monitor all go greenish-black, grainy and underex-
posed as reconnaissance photos. The helicopter's heat-sensing de-
tection device begins picking something up. Searchlight off, R.F.
slows the sweeping fall of the chopper, righting the aircraft as he
manipulates graphics appearing on the monitor, the Nintendo
skills of his extended childhood a strong factor in his appoint-
ment to the force's Night Wing Security Division. The nose of the
cockpit lifts slightly, body and tail swaying before recovering their
headlong forward motion. Then, cloaked in darkness, the bird
streaks toward its target.

On the computer screen, though, there isn't any video-game
landscape. No cartoon supervillain, or chopped and channeled
buddy-movie roadster in distress. Just a lone squad car, the shit
being blown out of it by a thin figure moving around the front
end, firing repeatedly. Raising the chopper's tail, R.F. opens the
bird up to full throttle, hurtling down into the halo of unhealthy
city light, over a blur of residential rooftops. Radioing for help, he
locks his flight path into the canal of a sidestreet leading to the
source of the explosions, drops the landing rails to car-top height,
and, prop blades kicking up a squall of street trash and dust
around him, lets out a howl as the besieged squad car and Do-Ray
appear up ahead.

He switches off the computer and takes manual control of the
ship. Night goggles up. He'll work with streetlight. He even turns
off the evening's football game, preferring the chromosome-dam-
aging rock broadcast by the local college station for a battle soundtrack. Down the road, the squad car and its assailant are still scale-
model size but growing, prodding R.F. to dig the fact that like,

check it out, he's sort of flying through this giant zoom lens which makes them keep getting bigger, you know. Until, moments later, he realizes he's been seen.

The bursts of light cease. Something is flung toward the vehicle. And the thin figure which had been circling the car, still a shadow at seventy-five yards, begins running, headed for a large, vacant lot, an expanse of ditches and rubble, on the far side of which stands a haven of housing projects and darkness. Well, too bad, R.F. thinks. No magic mushrooms or video-game bad guy's extra lives for you. He zeroes in, forgetting about the critically injured fellow officers in the car, or the possibility of other colleagues arriving on the scene. He did radio, didn't he? Although, what's short-term memory to an ex–mall rat? Fuck it. He concentrates on two things. One: What are his chances of hooking the guy by the collar with one of the chopper's landing rails, like a hawk snaring a field rat and carrying it away into the night—to the sound of applause, of course; nothing's real anymore unless it's a movie, even if the movie only takes place in your head, right? And two: When is the department going to trust him with the front-end-mounted .50-caliber machine guns they've been promising?

More concerned with the bullet-spanked squad car, the officers inside it, and the propeller-driven crystal ball winging toward him six feet above the ground is McKuen. As his unmarked car screeches around a corner, he doesn't notice Ray booking double time for the chain-link fence and empty lot beyond it. He's too busy avoiding a head-on with the helicopter doing a hundred at haircut height—not exactly what one expects to find on a deserted sidestreet. McKuen's car spins out, tires laying huge black brushstrokes across the pavement as the belly of the copter roars by, close enough to make the car shudder. When it comes to rest, McKuen looks up and spots Do-Ray vaulting over the fence top, helicopter and demented wing pilot angling after him. The bird swoops past the fence, landing rails clearing the spiky tips of chain link by milli-inches, then hurtles off into the night sky.

The figure in the lot stumbles as he lands, but keeps his forward mo going and comes up sprinting. McKuen, detective first class, black male, Vietnam vet, and midlife-crisis candidate, pulls along-side the torn-up squad car. No need to get out. McKuen takes one look at the massacred figures in the car, then inches forward to inspect the sheet of paper stuck to what's left of the front wind-shield. A decree of some sort. A manacled black fist clutching an automatic rifle. The only word McKuen can make out in the dim light is "Discordia." He leaves it for the crime scene squad, then he's moving again, smashing through a section of fence, posts popping out of the ground as chain link drags over the roof of the car like a metal veil.

The helicopter, climbing toward the cloud-dimmed moon like some hallucinatory Santa's sled, pivots in midair, metal tail whip-lashing behind it, then charges earthward toward Do-Ray, search-light glaring. McKuen accelerates, bouncing over potholes, head-ing for the widening shaft of light ahead. Ray's shape grows larger inside it, the chopper above him a dark silhouette until, with all three of them converging, McKuen loses both Ray and the copter in a whirlwind. Pebbles, glass shards, the odd nail and empty alu-minum can pelt the car from all sides. The helicopter's search-light blazes through the reeling debris, a huge silver-white disk blinding McKuen like some divine, after-death beacon. It's sort of like driving through a cocaine hallucination, everything bright and spinning, only he isn't in love with himself and the concepts of pain and danger still carry some weight.

The chopper's propeller blades clap concussively above the roof of the car. A moment later, the deafening sound fades. The wind lifts, the grit cloud around the windows thins and settles to the ground. McKuen sees Ray, who has lost his cap, sprinting for the fence on the far border of the lot. Two long swift steps later the kid, using a schoolyard hoops move, lands midway up the ten-foot-high barricade. Two more and he vaults the top, near the rear entrance of the projects. By the time McKuen slides to a stop and hustles out of the car, Ray disappears down a narrow alleyway between the brick towers, only the white soles of his sneakers flashing in the last bit of streetlight, before blinking away into darkness.

The fence links ring lightly as McKuen clambers over them, and he loses the faint patter of Ray's footsteps in their flat chiming. When he hits the ground and begins running, dark-eyed walls of the abandoned projects loom over him, the blown-out and rock-shattered windows surrounded by halos of charred brick. His chest constricts, wrenching his breath down to short dry bursts. In the distance, the city's traffic washes by faintly, its incessant hiss punctuated by the stray siren or horn. Otherwise, there is total silence but for his breathing.

A deep loneliness plunges through him. Less fear or despair than revulsion for the act of hunting this other creature. Or maybe his loneliness means stop. Give up the chase. Maybe that's what the heaviness in his legs is telling him. Stop. Because in the world he inhabits just this side of information-laden cyberspace, there is no point. He catches this kid, then what? A confession? An admission that the killings were done in the name of God or race? Some convoluted rhetoric about justice?

Yet, he continues running. There is a brightening at the end of the alley. His breathing starts to come back. The kinks and stiffness bleed out of his joints. He picks up speed, the walls flashing dimly by in the dark. And for a moment he has the sensation that he's outstripped the drag of his own flesh, as if he were flying.

He emerges from the dark into the broad expanse of the projects' plaza. It is a dream world populated by the walking dead, and he attunes his senses to Ray's trail, which can be detected in the druggy attentiveness of the settlement's inhabitants. He walks past a number of people living in cardboard boxes. Others glide by him, ragged sleeping bags and dented aluminum cookware strapped to their backs. A family congregates around a small fire, a torn sofa and matching armchair pulled close to it. Behind the couch is a set of bunkbeds, one of the women tucking in children. A man crawls into the burnt, overturned shell of an automobile, blanket and knapsack dragging on the ground beside him.

McKuen steps around people lying on mattresses. The ones on their feet ebb away from him, wary but also curious, as if he were somehow untouchable. McKuen detects faint traces of Ray in their sleepy-eyed skittishness. The kid's fear lingers, charging the air the way ions crackle before a thunderstorm.

McKuen scans the faces of the towers surrounding the plaza. A light here or there in one of the windows, plastic trash bags tacked to the casings to keep the wind out. Squatters. Inside because they have the guns, unlike the ones out here. McKuen knows what the insides of their cells look like. Swastikas, centerfolds, pictures of presidents and movie stars taped to the walls. Faucetless sink, roach-infested stove. Maybe a kerosene lamp. Beside the make-shift bed—usually a few sleeping bags thrown across a plywood board set on cinderblocks—are piles of race-baiting propaganda sheets, assault rifle manuals, the holy book of choice, the yellow-ing copies of fan magazines.

The figure McKuen is tracking is just passing through. This is the dead zone, the forgotten city within the city. No safe houses here. No terrorist cells or revolutionary front's home office with twenty-four-hour-a-day answering service. Just inner-city cancer, a spreading dark. Even the fires McKuen steps past barely light the place. And for a short loop of dreamy, film-like time, he feels like he's a LURP again, back in Nam running the nightly recon patrol outside the perimeter.

The sensation passes when he notices the first faint stirrings of commotion in a dark knot of bodies. A pipe is being passed among them, but there's a subtle shift in the group's posture, an unease. McKuen's breathing tightens when he sees a pair of shoulders begin to zigzag through the swarm of bodies. Then he's running too, shoving aside the zoned and the lost as if they were some kind of fleshy jungle overgrowth.

Beyond the crowd, the towers intersect, closing off the end of the plaza. A metal door at the base of one flies open, the "Condemned" sign hanging from it clattering as the door booms shut. McKuen sprints across the pavement, the door and the darkness behind it approaching like the kind of movie image that segues into flashback: McKuen chasing a VC through the underbrush; McKuen the rookie cop pursuing a black kid and shooting him due to a judgment error, the revenge by the boy's brothers, though never proven, ending his marriage by taking his wife's life.

But for now there is no guilt-plagued past haunting him, just a stitch pain under his lower right rib. Machine pistol unholstered, he stops and leans against the base of the building, breathing deeply. No light leaks from inside the door as he inches it open. No sound. Only a damp fecal chill. He waits a count of three, heart rapping against his sternum, then swings into the doorway and fires into the darkness. When he springs out of his crouch, he is across the threshold and in.

The dark erases his body, his shallow breathing seeming firmer than his flesh. He finds the clammy surface of a wall and presses his back against it for a sense of definition, of limits, then turns his head and tries to make out any sort of shape or marker in the darkness. But there's no texture, no gradation of shadow, just pure black. And a dripping, something sewery, catacomb-like. Rainwater leakage or a form of underground regurgitation creeps over his shoes, chilling his feet. He wants to move. Only toward what? The thin stream of warm air snaking through the dank blackness? Ray's heat and fear, a whisper of his presence perhaps, resonating in the dark?

McKuen slowly adjusts to the idea that he has surrendered his eyesight. Once he does, the shifting microclimates and murmurings of the space reveal themselves, and he knows Ray is there. He begins to move, fingertips creeping spider-like across the slick surface of the wall. Some part of him—body, mind?—can't give up the security of the wall. Yet another part—maybe his soul—isn't daunted by the prospect of letting go. It seems to need no sense of borders. But what keeps him inching forward in the dark is his knowledge that whoever he's chasing is as scared as he is.

His fingertips bump up against something silky, something warm, something human. An instant later, he leaps from the wall and, in the middle of the abyss, fires. When the echoing claps of the gunshot recede, he hears feet slapping against the floor, and what sounds like someone smacking a wall with the palm of his hand. Then the squeal of rusted hinges, a booming echo, and, on the far side of it, footsteps again, fading.

McKuen goes after the sound. The footsteps blossom again when he finds the door and goes through it. He uses his toe to locate the bottom step, then reaches for the banister rail. Once he has it, he counts. Sixteen steps turn, sixteen turn, his rhythm accelerating as he ascends. By the time he reaches the fifth floor, his wind practically gone, he takes steps he can't see two at a time. Several flights later there is a second booming. It reverberates as he rises into it and finds another door. He shoulders it open and the city's sickly air seems to restore his soul to his body. He feels disoriented, as if he were still ascending. When his dizziness subsides, the huge roof begins to compose itself around him. Ventilating ducts. Crumbling water towers. Exposed steel beams where a section of roof has caved in or burned, and ledges leading to other buildings. But no Do-Ray. Just the heaven-turned face of the city, its fires and uncountable lights beaming like bodiless souls. . . .

. . . .This is XXN. . . .

The hiss and gurgle of the automatic cappuccino machine lactating milk into a waiting espresso cup—double portion, naturally—has little chance of rousing Christian Nicholas Wolf ("Nick" to his friends, which number zero) from sleep. Roosting warm and redolent a mere condom's length from his pillow, the coffee's aroma does nothing conscious-tickling enough to stir him. So all bets on his waking shift to his stylish but, given Nick's prowess for snoozing, meek alarm clock. Which, of course, has never had any success in the past.

As usual, it takes the combined voices of his left-on-all-night television, his electric mantra dispenser (set to go off ten minutes after the espresso maker), and his loyal administrative assistant Dan to wake him. The boy has phoned, endured the Dadaist thirty-second answering machine message—Nick's suicide note being read over Gregorian chants—then recited, as instructed by Nick himself via office memo, lines 26–32, Act II, Scene 2, of *Romeo and Juliet,* to wit: "O speak again, bright angel, for thou art as glorious," etc. Yes, all this to entice the slumbering and ever tardy public defender into a state where opening his eyes actually seems like wish fulfillment, an activity Nick regards as his sole reason for living.

"I'm up, I'm up," he says, grabbing the receiver.

"Civilization's grateful. But listen—"

"Call me back in five."

"Every day you do this—"

The connection is broken on Nick's trusty and admittedly infatuated aide. Nick had barely hired the intelligent but unskilled boy when the twenty-year-old, clad in head-to-heel leather, platinum slave bracelets, and stiletto-toed lizard-skin boots, appeared in Nick's cramped office cubicle and announced that he would preserve himself in as near a virginal state as possible (eyes lowered, the boy acknowledged his sordid suburban adolescence) until his rule-flouting, blue-eyed, inexplicably and, some claimed, hazardously employed prince accepted heterosexuality for the erotic dead end it is. Nick smiled. He was touched, but uninterested.

Sitting up in bed—eye shades removed, double cappuccino in hand—Nick's eyes alight immediately, as always, on the unpaid-for 52-inch television screen hanging directly across from the foot of his convertible couch. On-screen, two near-naked fashion models rub themselves with vegetable shortening, then proceed to wrestle before a black-robed judge while an unshaven male vocalist bemoans his lost innocence and unfulfilling superstardom. Nick watches, sleepily, on the prowl for any cultural trends or items to be mail-ordered which may have escaped his attention during unconsciousness.

As the caffeine slithers through the corridors of his nervous system, Nick's attention turns. No, not to the financial world, since he is, like the majority of his generation, penniless. Given the state of the global economy, his penury is hardly unusual. So the way Nick sees it, his determination to continue spending money he doesn't and indeed never expects to have actually should be considered heroic.

His laissez-faire attitude toward debt, particularly his own, devolves from his rich kid's childhood. The security of one-day-to-be-inherited wealth coddled him throughout his errant youth. But of late Nick, erstwhile heir and lifelong familial black sheep, has refused to acknowledge that any hope for prosperity is long gone, dead, amscrayed. You see, Wolfie *père* disowned the boy, in his will describing his sole offspring as "a faith-shaking blow to the idea of procreation." The testy septuagenarian went to his well-manicured, though seldom visited grave choosing not to entrust responsibility for the family's fortune to Nick, the self-made failure. Who, at this moment, is heeding the advice of his adoptive parent, the television, as his thoughts turn to the weather.

Granted, there is a window. The only one to grace Nick's two-hundred-square-foot studio apartment, it is a mere foot from his bed. So he could get up and look through that, barred frame, grime-tinted panes and all. But watching the always stunningly erroneous five-day forecast implied for him a profound, if baseless and ultimately moronic faith in the future. Besides, he is unabashedly smitten with the station's new pseudo-meteorologist. He owns both her exercise videos, which he drunkenly replays in slow motion on lonely weekend nights. Calls her 900 number when he should be perusing *Kent vs. the United States* for a precedent which will get his latest thirteen-year-old serial killer a trial in juvenile court rather than direct teleportation to the death chamber. Loves her despite the recent haircut, which has caused a drop in her ratings. And, basically, understands that his obsession with her could not possibly provide any clearer indication that he desperately and without question needs to get laid.

Speaking of which, his piss-hardened member is beginning to get a tad painful inside his silk boxer shorts. Considering the thing's long-standing resilience, companionship, disease-free reconnoiterings, and undeniable faithfulness (he'd kiss the little guy, and probably more, if he could), Nick doesn't want to keep it waiting, much as he'd like to loll in the sack and imagine slow-boning his favorite climatologist, while she gasps, groans, and recites the daily pollen count and misery index figures.

The day's forecast: gloom—with a light wind chill.

Cappuccino machine reset for refill with the push of a button, Nick tosses aside the bedspread and slides off the mattress. Tiptoeing across his plushly carpeted cell—not much space or natural light, but it's comfy and lacks none of technology's amenities, all possible information and nutrition funneled in by cable, radio wave, laser beam, telepathy, or delivery person working for minimum wage plus tips—he flips on his laptop PC and punches up the day's docket. Standing before the glowing screen he shivers. God, it's damp. Never any sun. Then goes off for his tinkle.

A quick brush and floss, some close-up hairline, eyeball, and tongue inspection. All seem okay. His disease paranoia *may* be a bit groundless or neurotic. He does have several unprovable theories that viruses are being targeted by zip code, income bracket, and impoliteness to telemarketing operators, then transmitted per instructions of industrial spies. Or else spread by bottled water, junk mail, and automatic teller machine transactions. But then again, he's a media baby. Since when does "reality" impinge on existence?

He returns to his "it's a desk, it's a dining table!" home/office work station—laminated black Formica glued to a sheet of particle board, collapsible black canvas and aluminum sling chairs all around. A second cappuccino steams screenside, right next to his freshly poured three fingers of morning Scotch. Top-shelf stuff, of course.

No matter what his profession, Nick would most likely need a morning bracer or two, plus the usual afternoon and evening doses of substances he is fond of abusing. But the mind-numbing hopelessness and tedium of working for the Public Defender's Office allow him to rationalize his dependency. His lack of satisfaction with his station in life, his perceived victimization—each strikes him as being utterly American, circa the year 2000. He's entitled to feel fucked over; it's his right as a consumer. Nick does wish at times that he could muster some libertarian zeal for the job, go kick some butt for the rights of the underprivileged. It's just that in a culture built on glitz, getting excited about people who are poor, inept, violent, and always guilty is a bit of a stretch—especially when *they* don't like you. Nick knows most clients resent him for the simple reason that his presence in their lives is a form of charity, pity, disdain. Aw, can't afford a lawyer? Here's a schmuck who failed out of three law schools before nailing a degree from a university located in a strip mall. A few of Nick's colleagues work in the office by choice, very few, and then only briefly. Nick has no choice. Like his clients, no one else, no one respectable, will have anything to do with him. And for hating his job, doing it poorly, and on occasion not doing it at all, he's underpaid.

Through the voluptuous eddyings of smoke unspooling from the tip of his cigarette Nick stares at the keyboard, taps open a folder, and watches as the first of his day's symbols appears. The letter "A" inside a perfect circle. Skinhead symbol for Anarchy. Found scrawled in bold black strokes, presumably made by the charred end of a torch, on the office walls of a "liberal" weekly. Three college students were stomped to death, welts from chains and baseball bats covering their bodies.

Scrolling forward as he takes a hit of Scotch, Nick scans a synopsis of his seventeen-year-old defendant's past. High SAT scores. Little League. Parents part of the downwardly mobile middle, their union jobs gone, replaced by sixty- to eighty-hour-a-week gigs in the low-paying service industry. The boy was once co-captain of his high school debate team, though Nick decides to squelch this tidbit. Not exactly the type of arguably fascistic material he wants on the record, given the unhappy meeting of Aryan philosophy and public speaking skills in the past. That chick in Hate Crimes—what's her name? Julia?—would eat it up.

Drifting like the smoke from his cigarette, Nick stares past the PC screen and projects her face onto his memory monitor. Cute, actually. A little heavier than he likes. But considering he's about to qualify for a doctorate in self-abuse and possesses neither the capital nor the unromantic inclination to buy a Third World bride through a P.O. box in the classifieds, he's willing to overlook a few pounds. He leans back and directs scenes from the movie of their love affair in his head. Him grabbing her by the arm as she tries to stomp off in disgust. "Come on, forget it," he says, laughing off his sleazeball courtroom tactics. Then she conks him upside the head with her briefcase. How can she not love him? He's such an *asshole!*

His cigarette ash snaps off at the filter and lands in his lap, alarmingly close to his pecker. While brushing them off his thoughts return to his white supremacist defendant. Since the boy's humble beginnings—NRA membership at fourteen, summer internship with an ex–soldier of fortune who ran successfully for alderman—he has gravitated (been seduced, recruited, and brainwashed by, Nick will argue, though he doesn't for a minute believe it) toward extremist groups. Narrow-minded, xenophobic authority figures. Comrades in hate. Nick will contend that the boy was pressured into it. He was looking for an identity. A sense of community. Nick stares at the symbol on his computer screen which the boy has surrendered to, the way they all do to eradicate themselves. Nick has seen all the symbols. The hooked and ansate crosses. Inverted pentagrams. The axe-like symbol for anti-justice. Pick a symbol, kneel before it, submit. Turn your hate for yourself over to a greater hate. An infinite hate. Something eternal. Hate is purity. Destruction is order.

Nick figures his client will do eight to ten on a reduced charge, then come out and run for Congress. Hell, a decade from now, prison time served for a hate crime might even turn out to have been a good career move. Every war has its heroes. Next.

He scans a few more files. He's ready to eighty-six the last one, but finds himself lingering. An Asian kid. Orientals usually keep a lawyer or two on retainer and don't need the Public Defender's Office. The Tongs, the Golden Triangle Boys. All known for taking number-one care of their soldiers. The gangs are ruthless, closed to outsiders, and operated solely for profit. Even the Viet Ching, without question the most *diddy mao* of the bunch. The gangs are a marriage of nihilism and Adam Smith. Plus a few easy-to-remember gang pledges: Cross the gang, die by a myriad of swords. Cross the gang, die by a myriad of thunderbolts. Etc. Strong middle management, medical and dental, lifetime (short though it may be) job security.

So Nick assumes *he's* defending the kid, who was caught holding a warehouse full of stolen electronics equipment, porn videos, alimentary paste noodles, and automatic assault weapons, because the kid was dicking someone. This thought doesn't exactly endear him to Nick, given Asian gangs' tendency to show up in drop dead black designer suits and wraparound shades, then reduce their enemies to spring roll stuffing with AK-47 fire.

Nick decides to suggest the kid turn some names. He'll emphasize the boy's sense of cultural alienation in a plea-bargaining session. Recount his childhood flight from Cambodia. Explain the American Dream nature of the youth's (all right, criminal) acquisitiveness. But we're talking crimes against *property* here, Judge, not genocide. Not hate. By this point, Nick has reimagined the kid as scholarship material, a boon to the community. Though he wonders if maybe he couldn't just fax in his defense—it would be a lot safer—when the speaker phone rings.

"Speak to me," he says, voice-activating the machine. He slouches, bare legs stretching out underneath the table to cross at the ankles, Scotch in hand.

"Are you—"

"Dan!" Nick exclaims, as if the call were some grand and unexpected reappearance by his assistant. Meanwhile, Nick sends his work files off into computer chip cyberspace, then brings up his latest virtual reality landscape with the touch of a single outstretched fingertip. On screen, the laser graphics universe appears—devastated cityscape just like the city outside, only vicarious, safe, a playground for the era's new eroticism: fear. "I'm only dimly aware of your petulant silence," Nick says to his assistant. "This is the beauty of electronically extended consciousness. Human relationships become almost totally dispensable. Notice I said 'almost.' Call me a romantic."

Nick scans the video inferno's topography for a leaping-in point. Some choice rabbit hole through which to plunge into cyberspace in search of—what else?—the captive, designed-to-your-fetish, virus-free virgin.

"Face it," he adds, "there can't be any emotional human bonding in a world with call waiting." Tapping a few command keys, Nick calls up video nemesis profiles, a grid of the imaginary city, and his previous best score in the game. "For better or worse, we're all just cable stations in each other's basic service contract. I know I'm quoting country-western lyrics again, but this is what passes for wisdom in a telemagazine culture. Treasure it the way you would your stamp collection."

During the boy's silence, Nick "arms" himself for the game's hunt, stuffing his video knapsack with lightweight machine pistols, exploding breath mints, low-cal gourmet K-rations. A Walkman. A rocket launcher. Rockets, naturally. One long-distance calling card. A neutron device equipped with a selective programming capability. A musette bag for said nuclear device. And a tube of cherry-flavored Chapstick. "So, why so quiet? Don't love me anymore?"

"Are you ever coming to work?"

"I am at work. I am at my *work* station. Here in my home/office. I don't see how I could possibly be more *at* work if I was 'at work.' Listen to me. I. Inhabit. My. Job. I live and breathe the law. If I want to urinate, my kidneys have to file a writ of habeas corpus. The quote-unquote 'office' is nineteenth-century detritus. Dickens. What am I, a factory urchin? You're assisting a legal Robin Hood here. I steal prison time from the rich and give it to the poor."

"How much have you had to drink?"

"Don't go pro-life on me. I hired you for your cynicism."

"You hired me because I was the only person crazy enough to work for you."

Nick lights a smoke, then pours another three-finger bracer, despair creeping over him as he sinks back in his chair. Closing his eyes, he allows himself to float, to drift and not fight this blackness that is his true mother. All the symbols and insignias of his city-assigned charges pass before his mind's eye: stained-glass swastikas, the "Mark of the Beast," 666. Hate as revelation. Hate as God.

"Come on," Dan says. "I think you should come into the O. Be social."

"I am social. Isn't this being social, what we're doing here? Talking. Linked by microwave transmission." Nick drags on his cigarette, then exhales.

"I'm wearing heels and a leather skirt," Dan jokes.

"Forget it," Nick says, moved by the kid's affection and—yeah, okay—lust. He opens his eyes, and sends a cigarette ash winging toward the desk's surfeited ashtray, assessing in a glance the passing emblems of his life's disorder. Just the usual morning funk. No need for alarm, extreme unction, or a call to one of the city's suicide hotlines.

The truth is: Nick lacks the *faith* required for true pessimism. And he knows it. The quality is simply absent in him, unlike his clients who seem to possess it in disturbed abundance. Fanaticism. The search for meaning. He finds the trait touching. So naive. The idea that "meaning" should not only exist, but be comprehensible to man. Maybe "meaning" *begins* with everything man *doesn't* know. Ever think of that?

To Nick, it's all illusion. So sit back, enjoy the ride. Have a drink! And tap into techno-reality—the illusion you can trust. The illusion that *reveals* its limits.

Nick already has to piss again, the coffee and Scotch windsurfing through his system in record time. "Look, I'll be in for my . . ." He punches his calendar up onto the screen. Appointments are noted by crime—assault, manslaughter—with footnotes added: premed, serial, drug-induced, hate-motivated, sex crime, race killing. He sees that he has an eleven o'clock hearing scheduled for his eight-year-old mass murderer. ". . . eleven o'clock gig in juvey. Until then you're my eyes and ears around the office. No other orifices are being offered." Spirits lifted somewhat by the booze—though, hmm, maybe one more nip just to be sure—Nick checks his clock and sees that eking out a thirty-minute ride through cyberspace isn't beyond reach. He might even be able to fantasy-fuck the video virgin if he stops pining over the human condition and hurries. "Gotta go, Boy Wonder. Techno-sex calls."

"You'll never make your eleven o'clock."

"Yeah, well, the wheels of injustice, etcetera."

"Yeah, well, I suggest you ditch the music videos, which I'm sure are playing in the background—"

"Your powers of deduction are uncanny. Here, let me turn down the television volume so you can enlighten me."

"Turn on the news."

"New theme song?"

"Just do it."

"I love it when you talk dirty." Nick reaches for the set's remote control.

On screen are flashing siren lights, a bullet-scarred squad car, and the inevitable microphone-bearing news anchor. Yellow "Do Not Cross" police ribbon is wrapped around the area surrounding the vehicle.

"I hope you haven't bothered me for another cop-killer story," Nick says.

"Just watch."

A viewer warning appears in electronic typescript at the bottom of Nick's screen. "The following material may be too graphic for some viewers. Discretion is advised." XXN-TV.

"Right," Nick says. "Look away if upset by cannibalism. Give me a break."

"You're drunk."

Watching the screen, Nick senses something missing. "What happened to the music?"

The neo-rap cut that had been playing softly in the background has vanished. Even the news anchor's dutiful monotone falls silent as the camera moves in tight and pans the two decapitated bodies inside the car.

"You roust me for police murder?" Nick says. "This is even stale by network standards."

"Not everything is pop culture."

"Yes it is."

"Not murder."

"Especially murder." Wound tight from the booze, Nick's tone reeks of condescension.

"You're not just drunk. You're a prick. The world *does* go on outside your room, you know."

"Cop murder, revolution, consumer goods. All part of the same illusion."

Nick takes a sip of Scotch as he looks at the television. The newscaster's muted voice explains that the decapitated police officers are believed to be part of a citywide series of executions. Scrawled on the white sheet is the word "Discordia."

"Name-of-God murders," Nick says.

"There's talk of martial law, locking down the city."

"Except during the Christmas shopping season. Now we get the two-week jump in security alarm sales, and practical shooting lessons."

"I think it's going to be worse than that."

"Apocalypse has a pleasant ring, doesn't it? There's a lot of stress involved in leading a meaningless existence. Get my drift?"

"Uh-huh." Dan doesn't sound enamored, just tolerant.

"The end of the world is kind of appealing, like the new summer blockbuster."

Before the inevitable montage of wedding album photos, merit badges, and citations yields to a final image of two bloody silhouettes, followed by the synthetic foods commercial, Nick clicks back to music videos. Meaninglessness with a beat. He tosses the channel changer onto the bed, then swivels toward his computer. On screen, virtual heroism is waiting. Absolute escape. Even if it's temporary.

"No, I'm afraid the forces of darkness roll on, undeterred." He taps a keyboard button, then finishes by saying, "I only listened because I liked the music."

"Supposedly it's by some guy called Coda. Tapes were released to XXN after the murders."

"Audiotapes?"

"Yeah. New-wave rap stuff. Go-out-and-kill-people type lyrics."

"So they do executions instead of music videos. It's a novel promo technique, but dispiritingly predictable. This end-of-the-millennium barbarism is really tired. And frankly, I have a little trouble with a revolutionary signed to a major recording contract."

"That's the thing. The tape's not for sale."

"Yet. They'll be splicing this news footage into his TV advertising within an hour. Then he'll receive a suspended sentence when he volunteers to do an anti-violence PSA."

"I don't think so. The tapes arrived with a note renouncing copyright."

"Really?" Nick holds off on lighting a new cigarette. "So everybody, and anybody, owns it?"

"Yeah."

Nick has to lean back to let this millifact sink in. "Hmm. No merchandising as an approach to merchandising. Radical. I could be into it."

"No one knows who Coda is. But supposedly there's a kid named Darren Adams, nicknamed Inch, down in homicide on another beef. The buzz is that he may be tied to this thing called the Discordia Sect. Maybe even to these executions."

"How long has he been there?"

"Couple of hours."

"Whose clock is he on?"

"Guy named McKuen's."

"Mr. Serious. Great."

"You know him?"

"By rep. Tell you what." Nick lights his last pre-shower cig. "Raise McKuen on the phone, tell him I'm coming in. Push my eleven o'clock in juvey back three-quarters of an hour."

"We don't know that this kid Adams has asked for a lawyer."

"They all ask for lawyers. Cops just don't hear them. I'll see you in an hour."

"I love you."

"And get me a bagel," Nick adds. "I'm starving here."

He hangs up, inhales several hits of vasopressin, a hormone reviver good for clearing alcohol-induced brain fuzz, then downs the last watery dregs of his Scotch. Heading for the shower, he flips back to the news, watches for a moment, then walks out of the room, the screen's images flickering in his absence . . .

"People are happier when the lines between TV and reality blur."

XXN

What is only the ghost of sunlight—the hazy daytime sky a perpetual gauze of toxins and streaming pollutants—yields no more than a cinereous brightening. But it and the layered mur-murings of the subdivision plugging itself in for the day—car en-gines turning over, footsteps and muffled conversations bleeding through floor and ceiling, water sluicing through pipes inside the walls—lift Julia out of the final, buoyant atmospheres of sleep.

Beyond her bedroom door she hears the cooing of a sultry femi-nine voice. It is accompanied by an exotic, soft-core porn Muzak, flaccid and sinuous as a condom. Among the folds of her mock Shaker comforter, one hand comes across a magazine and the case for her reading glasses. The pair itself has fallen off during the night and slipped between the pillows.

Her digital clock says she has ten minutes before she should get out of bed and get a move on; twenty to thirty before she abso-lutely must. So her head falls back. And soon, not by design but a dreamy curiosity, her fingertips begin to find her own body. To slowly rediscover and fall in love with it. Places she just generally washes, pinches in fat-finding despair, checks for the cyst, lump, or tumor she expects will appear one day, and otherwise ignores. She takes a stranger's delight in their softness, her own gorgeous architecture. Some voice not her own begins whispering her name, some hands not her own ravishing her.

It's about time, too. She never planned on celibacy. But the en-tire male race, including her ex-husband, suddenly seemed to sink into a state of catastrophic undesirability. They were all either needy or domineering. Julia finds it scary to feel this way. She's not a feminist. Ideology is the last thing she needs, another sham panacea. Although, that's about the only thing left. Nationalism, racism, pessimism, television. Confused about life? Uncertain as to the state of the global village? Blame it on someone and hate them for it. Be the first in your cellblock. Don't miss our end-of-the-mil-lennium special.

Only now, Julia is on the downside of arousal. Half-horny, half-distracted. Serves her right for trying to bring in a pair of hands from the outside world, a stranger's voice. She can't even get laid in her fantasies anymore.

Through her fast-fading desire, heat ribboning out of her as her lust unspools, comes the chill of loneliness, a numbing sadness. The kind that overtakes her when—reading, cooking, seated among a roomful of people, standing in front of a mirror, it doesn't matter, the recognition isn't fussy—she realizes that she is going to die. Her. Julia. Whoever that is. The unaging voice that runs without pause inside her head? The Julia drifting through this body, connected to it by pain, decaying reflexes, ruined flesh? The seldom ravished Julia?

She floats on this sense of her own extinction, the enormity and blankness of it. Then a deep breath carries her back into the flow of the world and she realizes that now she's really depressed, and late. Way to go, Jule.

On the heels of her own failed self-abuse, what, she wonders, does she say to her son? Slumped on the couch, morning paper in one hand, channel changer beside his hip like some video culture gunslinger, he is tuned to the lingerie channel. Twenty-four hours a day of lace-trimmed bras, femme fatale garters, and orgasm queen stockings. Ball scores and rock concert 800 numbers flash across the bottom of the screen, along with instructions for ordering prophylactics, intercourse accessories, and live, personalized sex fantasies via your local cable and phone company. With a potential skull-and-crossbones hot-stamped on every stranger's sex fluids, Julia is torn between lecturing Paul on how degrading this is to women and encouraging him to stay home and masturbate.

Paul is fourteen. Julia can't decide whether this means he's old enough to make decisions on his own. The banks evidently think he is. Pre-approved credit card applications began arriving the month he was accepted into private prep school.

"Morning." She leans over from behind the couch and kisses the top of his head.

"Hi."

He isn't embarrassed by the on-screen preening and mock erotic ecstasy. His shyness about sex faded months ago. Now they each treat the models as products, although Julia's not sure if this is an indication of mental health. True, it shows a lack of fanaticism. But whether it's a complete surrender to decadence, she doesn't know. Ambiguity is not a good quality in a prosecutor of hate crimes. Everything should be simple, binary. Guilty, not guilty. Her case load includes mutilations, executions, mass killings, torture. Nothing subtle about it. Evil versus good. Don't blur the distinctions.

Paul, on the other hand, seems unconscious of any sense of ambiguity, and is somehow inaccessible to despair as well. He lacks urgency, vitality, kind of like television. He's distracted a lot. The only thing that fascinates him is his fetish for high-tech military paraphernalia. Not just the guns, missiles, rockets, and tanks. He's into the boots, the riding crops, the dark shades. Uniforms. The thrill of submission and domination. Master/slave, pain/non-pain. Clean, binary, unambiguous.

His wardrobe is an Armageddon-survivalist's fashion statement. Mud-and-leaf-toned fatigues. Calf-high lace-up boots, buffed spotless. T-shirts bearing various apocalyptic slogans or illustrations, one featuring a rock star's crucifixion. Band members and various U.S. pop-historical figures—ex-presidents, celebrated murderers, evangelists—encircle the martyred youth who hangs from a cross, his tattered loincloth cut out of an American flag. Shirtless, his pectoral muscles and fitness center abs are highlighted by air-brushing and body grease. The band's name, spelled out in thorns, sits on the recently rape-charged hero's crowned head. Today, Paul is wearing a sleeveless bulletproof vest he picked up at a used clothing store.

"Can I have a piece of the paper?" Julia asks.

"Sure."

"Anything interesting?"

"I don't know."

She tugs at the braided, shoulder-length rat's tail hanging over his collar, the rest of his blond hair buzz cut. He doesn't respond. As she reaches down to the coffee table, she notices the latest nuclear holocaust best-seller at his feet. He's into apocalypse. The plot synopsis of this one? Brown-skinned, satanic-fundamentalist armies do battle with a multicultural U.S. counterinsurgency force. The American fighter pilot hero's name is Jack. Shirtless, his pectoral muscles and fitness center abs are highlighted by. . . . No need to travel to the mall for a copy. Paul simply calls it up on their PC, places his order, and hits "print." Laser type begins spewing unbound chapters of the dispos-o-lit, cover art and all, seconds later. On recycled paper, of course.

When Julia isn't afraid for him, or overcome by a sense of helplessness toward her grown, almost gone son, her own estranged flesh—his once divinely small weight, even his heartbeat, still echoes inside her—she's almost afraid of him. Rage is a low heat in the boy. The culture of blame, of spent and degraded hope, has nurtured his undirected, end-of-the-empire sense of anger, dread, and confusion.

A poster that reads simply "1999" hangs on his bedroom wall. Valentine-red numbers burn through a glossy black background. It's hypnotic, almost pulsating. And to Julia, daunting, a spooky icon. One that seems to promise unspeakable horror. But Paul seems tuned into the image in a way she isn't, and could never be. She watches him, frowning as he reads, and understands that her son is hers to a point, but in a deeper, maybe truer sense, a child of his time, of the world.

"Want some breakfast?" She heads for the kitchen, in need of a caffeine surge before a televised dose of the day's horrors, followed by a quick shower.

"I had a shake," he answers, turning the sports section page idly, his boredom unvarying, the one near absolute in his life. "Made you coffee. Vanilla almond chocolate pinto bean."

"Funny."

He pretends to ignore her. " 'Thank you,' she said."

"Thank you. You're beyond an angel."

"Right. Angel-*plus*."

"Angel, the sequel."

"Angel, the next generation."

In the small kitchen off the living room, Julia opens one of the subdivision's standard-issue cabinet doors. The prefabbed cheapness of the room, the near weightlessness of the plastic coffee mug, the bleak parking area outside the one kitchen window, its snaking driveways leading toward the security checkpoints of the garden apartment compound, all of it feels makeshift and failed. Maybe it's only the residue of her botched orgasm, but she's blue, and nothing here is going to pick her up. The acrylic lid of the auto-drip coffee maker is water spotted, the tap water so full of chemicals—pesticide runoff, ground poisons, sulfuric rains—that it stains dishware, eats laundry, turns white fabrics ash gray. She doesn't even want to consider what it does to skin over the long term.

"Who's doing what in the world?" she calls to Paul.

"Sixty-two teams made the second round of the playoffs."

"Uh-huh."

"The terminally ill can withdraw IRAs without penalty for trips to Disneyland."

"Yeah." She never knows what's actual and what he's inventing, which is their game. She's also amazed at how he perks up when she moves away from him. "What else?"

"White supremacists have started a clothing company called Aryan Jeans."

She groans softly at that one.

"And a toy company—"

"I don't want to hear it."

"—Goys-R-Us."

"How about some news news?"

"McNews, News-Lite, or Robo-News?"

"I'm ignoring you."

As skim milk cools her coffee she sips at it, taking in more air than liquid, while giving a dying houseplant the once-over. Long-shot odds on recovery. She fingers a near-dead leaf. Behind her the TV blurts out a crazed eight-second spot for XXN's new sit-com, *Functional Family!*

"I found the cure for cancer in chemistry class today!" Billy blurts at the dinner table. Then the announcer's voice comes on in overdrive: "Can Billy leave his family, even if it means saving millions of lives? Decide tonight—7 City/8 Sprawl time!" The station programmers kindly allow an hour of TV grace for commuter traffic. After a split second of silence some neo-rap hit's bass line and drumbeat kick in.

"Hey," Julia calls over her shoulder, "I thought we were going to get some news?" She continues flipping through the mail she didn't get to last night. Save-the-environment brochures. Membership application to the Television History Book Club. Pizza delivery coupons. And three copies of the same upscale fashion catalog, one to Paul, one addressed "Resident," and one for Julia herself. Recycled chinos, guaranteed worn by the homeless, are selling for seventy-five dollars a pair.

"This *is* the news."

Turning, Julia looks into the living room and sees two blood-slicked corpses, each decapitated, being lifted out of a partially exploded squad car. Paramedics, cops, and National Guard troops swirl in the scene's dark background, chopper lights illuminating the foreground sporadically, the bright air glowing like radioactive waste. When the camera cuts to close-up, a sheet of paper can be seen affixed to the car's shattered windshield. On it, the image of a raised, gun-clutching black fist, and the words "Discordia Sect."

"By afternoon it'll be a T-shirt," Paul says.

The hip-hop music is part of the show. A newscaster's voice explains that the music is the anthem of a sect claiming responsibility for the executions. Lyrics and music are by Coda, a.k.a. "The Final Word."

"Tapes containing the song were distributed to XXN late last night," the anchorperson announces.

Coffee growing cold in her hands, Julia watches the montage of bloodied bodies, paramilitary figures, and weapons—stock inner-city inferno footage, now complete with a chart-topping sound-track. The music is synthesized bedlam: shrieks, whip cracks, gunshots; loops of movie dialogue and historic speeches; sirens, Bible passages, blown whistles, prayer. Coda's voice is part gospel preacher, part superlover sex god. Backup singers sound like an angel choir in the throes of orgasm. A drum machine stomps out a beat as the revolutionary-slash-instant-celebrity lays his kill-the-white-race rap down in sixteen-track Dolby Surround-Sound. "The Discordia Sect's Hate Funk Jam." Dig it.

Aw, check it out
1999 be approachin'
400 years the man been encroachin'
Rapin'—get it!
Lynchin'—quit it!
Time the whole white race done bit it!
Homies want a real revolution
CODA's got the final solution
Chillin' here round the end of the millennium
I say it's time we bring about the end of 'em
Hey white boy, think this is idle warning?
Look out ya window, them's your gates
we stormin'
Homes can't stop what you motherfuckers bred
So get one thing through yo'
muthafuckin' head—you dead
Yeah, swing it, c'mon
So go down Moses, and stay down!
Young black man gonna wreck yo' town
MLK go on get out the way
Time this native son offed some ofay
Tired a hangin' round like a dumbshit clown
Black man comin', burn it all to the ground . . .

The end of the song plays along with footage of the murder
site's cleanup effort. Medics, cops, members of the urban militia,
each a potential TV hero coming packaged and dehydrated—just
add blood and stir. "Look, there's a pizza delivery car in the background," Paul says.

"Come on." But it's true. A few reporters and idle police officers are pooling dollar bills.

"Someone must have 'accidentally' dialed the pizza emergency
number. 911-zzah!" After a moment, he adds, "My friend says

cops tip dick." He picks up the remote and flips channels.

"Would you please turn it back on?" Julia says.

"Make me. Force me. Be a single parent. Rule the roost."

"Paul."

"I want discipline, upbringing. A sense of values."

Julia's about to say, "Don't make me repeat myself," when she thinks, Oh God, I sound like my mother. "Fine. Watch what you want."

He flips back to the massacre scene immediately.

But there are no more images. No more horrors . . . for the moment. The newscaster merely caps the report by noting that there have been similar assassinations during the night, footage to follow, and that sporadic rioting is breaking out in the city. Then the station cuts to a commercial.

Julia sits there. Now that it's over, she feels shamefully disappointed. The horror wasn't great enough. Wasn't transcendent. Coda's probably a communications major at city college, another pop star wannabe. Why not execute a few cops to get a CD on the charts? Julia has no trouble accepting this scenario. And this bothers her. Her cynicism runs so deep it numbs. It fits her like the elastic-waistband sweats and old running shoes she's wearing. She's comfortable in it. She's home.

Paul watches for several moments then says, "No school closings. Some revolution."

"Maybe you should stay home."

"Yeah, right. Hurricanes get more respect than this."

"It's early yet. Why don't we wait to see what happens?"

"Low-pressure systems get more respect than this!" Sulkily, he stares at the set.

She can't tell if he's trying to cover up his anxiety, or if she's projecting her own onto him. "You'd stay home in a second any other time."

"Not when you offer. Truancy has to be unsanctioned." His voice turns mock-heroic. "Rebellion has to be earned."

She begins to place a hand on his, then stops. "It's alright if you're scared."

"Ha."

"Your vocabulary always leaps a notch when you're. . ."

"Go ahead. Think of a word that won't make you feel guilty for belittling me."

". . . upset."

"Pathetic," the boy mumbles. He will not look at her.

"I'm not telling you what to do."

"You couldn't."

The TV commercial is the only sound.

"You could put your intelligence to better uses than hurting me," Julia says, finally. But there is no response. He's gone, incommunicado. Sullen, insecure, witty, abusive. She doesn't know which Paul to appeal to. They trade places so quickly. "Look, you've decided that no matter what I say, it's going to be wrong." He snorts softly. "So, since I lack moral authority in your eyes, you decide if you want to go to school or not." Julia rises from the couch.

"Sure, abdicate the position of responsibility," he says, behind her back.

She turns to face him. "I'm accepting the responsibility of turning your life over to you." She stares at his profile, knowing that he doesn't understand what this costs her. Then adds, "Would you like it some other way?," hoping that he will.

Again, no answer. The news logo and theme song return. Paul clicks the remote and skims channels, images skipping from one to another. End of conversation.

Overload is peace. More is less.

This is XXN. . . .

"**R**ay? Ray, baby?" A voice spirals down through the soft flesh of Ray's sleep like wire coil through a wine cork, his slow extrusion from dream riding the tail of a breath that fills his chest. A moment later he opens his eyes and sees his grandmother hovering over him. "Honey, what happened to your face?"

Ray gropes for his just-awakened compass bearings, imagining he could be anywhere on his soul's time line—making a coma comeback, getting his first peek at heaven. Only the ceiling of Paradise shouldn't be peeling, should it? Also, now that his grandmother mentions it, a dappled stinging does seem to be plucking at the pores around his eyes, nose, and lips. His whole face feels as if it has been stuck with pins.

He sits up on the couch. Been there all night it seems, Thunderbird finally unwiring him, lullabying him to sleep sometime around daybreak. A deep wooziness twists through him, his brain brittle as a piece of fossilized sponge. He closes his eyes, head in hands. Purplish-white supernovas whiz by in the darkness. Pressing his fingers to his temples, he opens his mouth and breathes deeply. Slowly, the colors fall away inside him.

"Sweetie, you alright?" His grandmother, Odessa Roberts, stands before him, all sixty-four bathrobed inches of her, barely taller than Ray as he sits perched on the edge of the secondhand couch. She sweeps a cool hand over his sweat-dampened scalp.

"Yeah, I'm alright. Don't be doin' that." He brushes her hand away and stands. A black-edged dizziness pulses inside his head as he starts for the bathroom.

"You frowning and you ain't done dreaming five minutes yet." His grandmother collects the empty wine bottle wedged between the cushions of the couch. "I don't know why you want to be doing this to yourself."

Ray ignores her. But bad as he needs to pee, he flips on the bathroom light and stops in front of the sink to take a look at his face. Not exactly the way he likes to start a day. To see himself he has to look through the Man's eyes. Hate becomes self-hate. So the less he sees of his reflection, the happier he is.

Bloody scabs dot his face. Tiny little fuckers, about the size of salt crystals, which make him look as if he were getting over the measles. He picks at one. It's still soft. Rubbery surface with a jelly center. A good bit of sting lingers around it. He squeezes and the skin breaks, opening up a trickle of blood.

Images wing across dim, telescoping reefs inside his head. At first he thinks they're just hangover visions, the sweet-wine blues. Then he sees the squad car, its front end sweeping past him as he circles it. Concussive gun blasts rock its body, figures inside flying apart like scarecrow stuffing. He sees himself step into a constellation of sparks. He isn't sure if this is memory, or if he's imagining the scene, directing it like a movie. But he is aware of the sparks lighting on his face, weightless as angels, as if he could still feel them.

He pushes away from the mirror. There's something strange

and unfamiliar about his features. He can't figure out what it is, except he feels lighter, and the suicide fantasy he indulges in whenever he gets a look at himself turns out differently this morning. It begins as it always does. An all-white SWAT team, their schoolboy faces shielded by transparent visors, surrounds a condemned tenement building and begins firing from the rooftops when Ray bursts through a doorway, filled with last-stand bravado. His body is impaled on the pavement by volleys of automatic weapons fire. Lying there, arms outstretched, palms up in the time-honored pose of crucified surrender, he has the sense that his outlaw soul—despite all he's been, despite all he's failed to be—is saved. Pure. Nobler than those of his assassins.

But today, his body begins to levitate. The wounds covering his bullet-torn corpse unmake themselves, disappearing like sleight-of-hand celluloid miracles, completing his I-told-you-so resurrection. Female backup singers cakewalk out of row-house doorways. Gangbangers, rap heroes, graying R&B granddaddies, OD'd bop saxophonists, even tuxedoed swing-band rhythm sections fall in line behind them. At the head of the parade, it's Grand Marshal Ray. Reborn, reincarnated, God-is-love Ray. Good old Second Coming Ray! Ray II, the sequel. Crowds, klieg lights, crane-mounted cameras, microphone booms. Resurrection as music video. *White kids* wear Ray T-shirts, Ray caps, Ray warm-up jackets. They even buy Ray-monogrammed condoms and "Save the 'Hood" decals from sidewalk vendors, as Ray glides forward into full close-up, looks out at his oppressors, and, "live" on XXN, *forgives* them.

Only this morning, he doesn't *feel* like forgiving them. Fuck 'em's what he *feels* like saying. Then he realizes he has, the night before. *That* was his resurrection. *That* was *him*, exploding out of those cartridges. He looks at the scabs covering his face and sees them suddenly not as a scarring, but a baptism. That's what he stepped into last night—himself. Hard to believe it's actually him he's looking at. He's even smiling. There's a big old fat-assed smile on his face. Ho! Goddamn.

"What are you laughing at?" his grandmother calls.

"Who's laughing? I ain't laughing," Ray says, mock-innocent, his lifelong funk gone, vanished, vamoosed, as if it never existed. He tucks his lips together and boxes himself in the mirror. "C'mon, motherfucker." He makes the sound of body punches landing.

Then he unzips his fly and lets loose, shooting straight for the center of the bowl where the water is deepest, the resonance loudest. He even has a little chat with his pecker. "You done good, dude. *We* done good. Ha!"

"Close the door when you peein'." His grandmother walks past the door. "Don't wanna hear that tinkling while I'm having my tea." She backpedals, poking her head into the bathroom. "And who you talking to?"

Ray waves her away, closing the door. Finished, he zips his fly, then peels off his T-shirt and holds it up to the light. A veil of rust-red stains forms a V down the center of it, outlining the area of the shirt that his zippered jacket leaves exposed. From collar to breastbone the camouflage-green shirt is darkened as if he had passed through a mist of blood. "Damn." He remembers peering through the squad car's blown-out window, a thin fountain of liquid spurting from one man's torn-up body. Coda's do-it-yourself execution instructions didn't mention nothing about bloody T-shirts though, which Ray figures come under the heading of evidence. He looks into the mirror. His skinny torso doesn't show any marks or abrasions, although he still is not pleased. His arms and chest are as smooth and unmuscled as a child's, virtually unaffected by the iron he pumped every now and then, whenever the mood struck him. It isn't the body of someone who has just killed two cops.

In his bedroom he finds the basketball warm-up jacket he wore the night before hanging in his closet. He doesn't remember placing it there, doesn't even remember coming home really. It's like he isn't just hungover but disconnected from himself, spacy. The blood on the jacket is there, though, no question. And folded up inside the lining's pocket is one of the Discordia Sect flyers he had made up. The black figure on the Xeroxed sheet is built like one of those dudes in TV workout-machine ads. Ray checks his body again in his dresser mirror. Uh-uh. He reads his own words off the flyer, most of which he clipped from Coda's lyrics. "I am the beginning and the end, the Alpha and the Omega. Check it out, fools. This is not a warning. The war is on." Not knowing what the Greek words mean gives Ray a sense of their gravity. Scare the shit out of whitey, maybe for once get taken seriously, him *and* his race. Still, he wonders if the rest of the mofos in the Discordia Sect, whoever they are, are built as puny as him. Fuck it. He takes one of the T-shirts his grandmother has pressed and laid, neatly folded, in his top dresser drawer. Then he balls the bloody shirt inside the jacket and carries the bundle out of the room, tossing it onto the couch.

In the kitchen his grandmother is sitting at the table, Bible reading. Fifteen minutes every morning before heading to work. At forty-five she already looks old. Thick rolls of flesh ring her neck, dark blue-black pouches hang beneath her eyes like bruises. She keeps her nails nice—manicured, polished—but her right hand is permanently curled into a half-formed fist from holding the handle of a hot-stamping machine all day long for minimum wage. Only a generation older than Ray, she strikes him as being from another world. Shaking her head, she would say she didn't see no sense in what they was doing whenever Ray asked her about Malcolm or the Panthers. Look where they wound up. Look where MLK wound up, Ray would backtalk. But she'd only shake her head some more and say it ain't the same thing. Slaving away at some dumb job, and proud that she got one. Listening to Aretha or maybe Big Joe Turner on New Year's Eve. Keeping television out of the house like it was the devil. Ray just didn't get it. Why, he always asked her. Why?

Looking at her seated at the table, a brokenhearted love that makes him want to go out and kill the whole white world is unleashed inside him. He wants to go over and tell her to put the book down, look at him. Him, reborn Ray. Tell her you don't need no white man's savior. You got me. Ray. Black superhero Ray.

But he has no words to explain his metamorphosis. He can't pass his deliverance on to her. He can't do it for others. They have to do it for themselves.

He looks around for his cap, then remembers losing it as he vaulted the fence, crazy helicopter motherfucker overhead. He spots his old Raiders cap, the one O.C. hated, beside the scratched-up, rusted fridge, and the same old loathing for his life comes on him again. Everything in it secondhand, cheap, ruined. He wants to get out, lose himself in thinking about last night, feel the rush and pride of killing all over again. He chugs some juice, puts the container back in the fridge, then slides behind his grandmother. He leans down and places a kiss as light as one of the sparks that christened him on the crown of her head.

"What's that for?"

"Felt like it." Buttoning his jacket, he heads for the door without looking back to see her staring at him.

"Ain't you gonna eat?"

"Ain't hungry."

"What about your face?"

"It's my face."

"When I'm a see you again?"

But Ray has grabbed the bloodied shirt and jacket, and is out the door.

The courtyard's deserted. Just garbage, boarded-up windows, spray-painted threats and boasts. Quiet. Sun's just up. Too early to knock on Inch's door, tell him what went down with the C-4 Inch had scored for him. Still, how can people be sleeping and shit? Get the fuck up, he wants to yell. I liberated your asses!

Bopping down the steps Ray lights a smoke, then tosses the match in the direction of one of the stumpy, branchless trees that line the yard. Limbs hacked off, joints tarred over so the branches can't grow back. You know niggers. Only be startin' fires in 'em and shit. Busted glass everywhere. Smoked-down roach ends, crack vials. Initial-carved benches ringed by condom wrappers.

On the street, a car with its insides burned down to the seat springs straddles the curb, front end crushed against a lamppost, windshield smashed. "Bring the Hate" is spray-painted on its hood. Walking toward the corner, Ray feels something besides the longing to get high rising in him: calm, a sense of peace. The notion that he done good. It's strange. And new. And it feels alright.

He ditches the shirt and jacket in an alleyway Dumpster, then searches his pockets, but doesn't come up with much. Smoked up all his rocks. Only has a piece of scouring pad with some crack residue clinging to it left. Might be enough for a buzz. He hangs a right and heads for Minus Five's virtual reality arcade, see if Five'll front him a little extra base. Play that new virtual reality prison game while he waits for the world to wake up, and tune into what he's been up to. Maybe they'll even put his ass on television. Check out *Ray's* action for a change. Impress Inch, Minus Five, and all the other motherfuckers. *I acted, homes.* Know what I'm sayin', cuzz . . . ?

McKuen's living room TV is tuned to something primetime and familiar. Heat lazily billows into the room; warm light streams from a shaded lamp. McKuen's shoes are off, evening paper on the coffee table. The carpet beneath his feet—a discount warehouse closeout—is sweetly soft. Here in his VHA-mortgaged home, his wife sitting across from him in an American Colonial-style armchair, McKuen feels that all is divinely right within his world.

Except for his wife's face, which he can't quite picture, now that he looks closely. And the front door, which opens onto the world at large, is troubling. Despite its alarm sensors, menace seeps in around its edges, something violent and unstoppable.

His sense of helplessness balloons the instant he notices the lock is not tripped. He tries getting to his feet but his movements are syrupy, rubber-limbed. His wife floats at the periphery of his vision as the door swings open. Tumbling into the bright room, for that's how they seem to move—spilling, oozing, a dark sludgy mass, fecal and repellent—are five bodies clad in rags, and armed.

In the dream, McKuen is able to look down and watch himself struggle toward them. He rounds the coffee table as two figures descend on his wife, from whom he's separated by a dream-field muteness. His warning is futile, and she is swept out of sight.

Then McKuen is engulfed by the others and driven to the floor, their flesh smothering him, and he vanishes inside his own fear.

He wakes, his heart filling his chest. He tries to sit up but the surface beneath him is shifting and amorphous, more dream-quicksand. He finally manages to throw his upper body forward, face coming to rest inches from his knees, and finds himself praying. As the dream fades and his heartbeat slows, he realizes he's on a cot in the station's interrogation room where he had retreated in order to catch a few zzzs.

As for his wife, she is still unreachable, a spirit from another life.

McKuen thought the past would grow lighter, lose its pull as he drifted from it after her death, the way gravity diminishes when two bodies move away from one another. Instead, his wife's presence seems to grow heavier the longer she's gone.

There is a light rapping on the door. Office sounds blossom inside the room as it opens. Cochrane's head appears, a smile on his face. He derives some twisted sense of pleasure from his role as the grizzled homicide detective. American icon, existential hero. The moral touchstone in a world fallen beyond the pale of redemption.

"Yeah, what's up?" McKuen lowers his face into his hands and rubs the sleep-creases from his skin. The night before he had been winding down a double shift when he picked up the radio alert from Wing Private Tillinghast, demented chopper pilot. Now, another full shift later, with execution footage just beginning to hit the talk show circuit—live-via-satellite discussions featuring experts in terrorism, urban violence, ritual killing, cults, religious sects, as well as rap musicians, their agents, friends of next-door neighbors of the deceased, and members of Celebrities Against Violence—McKuen finds himself in the position of having logged only thirty minutes' sleep in the past day and a half. A fatigue that seems too deep and pervasive to be human has attached itself to his body during his nap. His blood feels like molasses.

"Your client," Cochrane says, referring to the kid McKuen brought in to question about the executions, "is whining about needing to use the john."

"So? Let the kid use the john. What's the problem?"

"The problem is, this 'kid' has a rap sheet long enough I could drive home, fuck my wife, nap, shower, go out to *eat,* and still be back before the thing is printed up. You run a DNA check on this kid, you're gonna find his *chromosomes* are wanted in fifty states. It's time for the officer in charge to get off his ass."

McKuen nods, and the door closes.

The kid, Darren Adams, known to friends as Inch, is pacing when McKuen opens the holding room door. Maybe he is innocent. The stone guilty ones go straight to sleep. Step out of the room for five, come back they're nodding like junkies. This kid is beyond edgy. Either he figures he's going to be nailed for something nastier than what he hoped, or he really does need to piss big time. But he doesn't say. Instead, he stops pacing and waits.

"Come on."

The boy is across the room and past McKuen with stunning speed, despite his slight limp. McKuen can't remember the boy favoring one leg when he picked him up earlier. Maybe the nap has sharpened his attention to detail. Or it could be the light. A dying, grayish-blue light like the kind thrown by off-the-air television signals, when television did go off the air. In the sickly daylight everything looks worse. The bleak office corridors. The city outside, its alternately charred and pristine spires making for a hallucinatory contrast. Even the boy seems unhealthy, decrepit. His face is slicked with a light, oily sweat, his clothes stiff with vintage grunge. When he speaks, McKuen notices his teeth are speckled with brown stains and rot.

"Took you long enough," he says, looking back as he stays half a step ahead of McKuen. Scared as the kid is, he's going to dish out some attitude. A true hard case simply would have pissed on McKuen's interrogation room chair, yawned, then kicked back and closed his eyes, wishing there was a TV. This kid's style is pure tough-guy emulation, no idea what the fuck he's doing, which McKuen finds refreshing, even sweet.

"I got tied up."

"Yeah, right." Darren Adams nods, trying to decide how antagonistic he can be.

McKuen watches as if the boy's thoughts were sliding across the back of his baseball-capped head in electronic lights. He's convincing himself that McKuen, along with being less of a prick than he could be, is also a brother, meaning he's trustworthy—maybe.

"Tied up." Darren snickers. "Probably feedin' your ugly face."

"Actually, I was sleeping."

The kid's pace slows and he throws up his hands. "Sleepin'!" In the office, several heads turn to look down the corridor. "Man. . . ." The kid whines, totally at ease. He's not sure why, he's not even thinking about why. Which is perfectly cool with McKuen, who is.

"Yo." McKuen beckons with his index finger and indicates a cul-de-sac off the corridor. Barred, soot-caked windows open onto brick wall. There's a caged lightbulb, a paint-chipped green door. "This way."

"Hiding the bathroom. Sleepin'." Darren hisses. "Shit."

McKuen stops him. "I'm giving you three minutes, hear? Not out in three, next time you see your dick's gonna be in a lost and found column."

"Yeah, yeah."

McKuen stops him again, firm palm to the shoulder. "You getting comfortable here?"

The kid's eyes scrunch up. "What?"

"You like it, I'll arrange a stay."

"Man, I ain't scared a the joint."

"It isn't a threat. It's an offer." McKuen knows the kid isn't lying. What did he have to go home to? A two-room apartment, pulverized crack vials dappling the ground outside like silver gunshots. But he does know that the boy wants to do all he can to avoid the Vietnamese gang that's looking for him for robbing one of their cousin's convenience stores.

"Trust me," McKuen purrs. "Allow me to take you under my

wing." He puts an arm around the boy's shoulders and begins walking him toward the john door. "You don't know anything about the two decapitated cops, right?"

"No, man. I tol' you."

McKuen puts a fingers to his lips. "Shh. I believe you. You are going to tell me about the C-4 that we found in the cartridges, though. And this flyer left on the car." McKuen holds up a copy of the Discordia Sect flyer which had been left on the annihilated squad car. Darren Adams is uncomfortably silent.

"I tol' you, I don't—"

McKuen stops and this time puts the finger on the kid's lips. "It's all right. You're confused. I see this all the time. Right now, all I want you to do is take your piss, don't take more than three minutes, then come back out." He holds the boy a moment, and looks into his eyes. "Lemme ask you something. You like VC food? Vietnamese stuff? Chopsticks?" The boy stares back, silent but definitely digging what McKuen is saying. McKuen takes his finger from the boy's mouth and gently taps his shoulder with it. "Repeat after me: 'Oh, that C-4. I thought you was talkin' about somethin' else.'"

The boy shuffles his feet. "Yeah, maybe."

"Yeah, maybe what? Maybe you bought some off my Viet Ching friends and passed it on to somebody who *does* know something about the two decapitated cops I found?"

Darren Adams looks away, then says, "Yeah, maybe I know somethin' about it. But I ain't repeating that shit, though. That's stupid."

McKuen is silent, then says, "Go ahead." He releases the boy, giving him a slight nudge forward.

Watching him limp toward the door, a sadness for the boy blows through McKuen, leaving him feeling wasted and hollow. The kid is going to tell him what he wants to know, and maybe even help himself in the process. To what end though? To survive for what?

Stepping into the homicide office proper, McKuen raps on Cochrane's desk. "I'm going for coffee. When the kid in the bathroom comes out, do me a favor. Put him back in Number Two, gently please."

Cochrane shakes a cigarette from the pack sitting beside his ashtray. "I'll watch the dipshit. If he gives me any crap, though, I'm gonna put my cigarette out in his asshole."

A clerk reaches up as McKuen walks past his desk. "Some dweeb from the Public Defender's Office called while you were power napping." The guy hands McKuen a scrap of paper. Scratched on it is "Wolf, 11 A.M." "He wants to talk."

"Tell him to talk to my publicist." McKuen crumples the paper.

"I'm only telling you," the clerk says in his wake.

Steaming cup of vending machine coffee in hand, McKuen is assaulted by a near-lethal combination of aftershave and whiskey breath as he reboards the elevator. Showing him an inordinately large number of teeth, considering they are two strangers meeting in a public space, is a white dude in a monogrammed dress shirt, elegant pinstripe suit, and tasseled European loafers. Nestled under one arm is a slender oxblood attaché case. He gives McKuen a little wave.

The guy looks like some deranged and, given his presence on the precinct's grungy elevator, lost junior CEO. Or the young senatorial type. Deep financial bloodlines, a few unprosecuted date rapes in his past. The usual private university degree and hushed-up real estate scandal. It's odd to actually see one in the flesh, offscreen. No limousines, flags, microphones. No black-suited security figures, or corporate logos hovering in the background. McKuen wonders if he's hallucinating from sleep deprivation because this guy is the flipside of his nightmare—a KKK Imperial

Wizard in designer duds, the aging preppie as massa of the techno-plantation.

McKuen steps close to the soft strands of dun-colored hair and lightly freckled skin. Another race, another country, another life, he thinks. Sure, he and the guy may cross borders every once in a while, by mass-market default. Gathered in their separate cells around the same televised ball game. Slicing past one another on fiber-optic lines. Maybe even pouring a Coke out of a can the other recycled. The illusion of inhabiting each other's world is there like a TV left on, images flickering the way votary candle flames once guttered in drafty churches. But illusion is all it ever was, is now, and ever shall be. Or is it?

Turning to face the elevator doors, McKuen glances at the indicator panel and sees his floor button's halo glowing. He feels the need for a slow double take. Against hope, Nick is still there. Even more than just there. In some way, he is supra-real, the way celebrities and figures embodying evil incarnate are.

Nick looks at him as the doors close, then extends his free arm toward the instruction panel. "Floor?" he says, eyebrows arching, fingertip awaiting direction. His smile has segued into an expression of cheerful, accommodating patience.

"That's fine," McKuen says.

" 'Hm. Homicide, huh,' I say, retracting my arm, giving you the once-over."

The elevator jerks into ascent.

"Don't you find elevators Victorian? Ropes, pulleys, gears, friction. The phallic implication of the shaft. The fear of plummeting into some bottomless well if a cable snaps. You step on an elevator, you surrender yourself body and mind to industrial-age time warp. People get weird. Or"—Nick's index finger springs into midair—"they rise above the situation. Mentally. They pretend to think non-elevator thoughts. Literature, nature, God." His tone drops an octave. "But we know they're not thinking these things. They're only waiting for the ride to be over. They're waiting to be released."

The elevator stops unexpectedly. They're both silent, eyes on the floor light indicators. Nick inhales and exhales deeply. "You ever notice the inordinate amount of sighing on elevators?" He shakes his head in disappointment. "We're trapped in here—with our bodies, with our own mortality. Where are the teleportation devices and molecule unscramblers they've been promising, huh? When are they going to start letting us fax ourselves?"

A telephone rings. Nick opens his briefcase and whips out a cellular phone. "Yeah, talk to me." He's briefly silent. "Yes. Yes. No. Yes. Good. Listen, I've got someone else here." He turns toward McKuen. "You want to get in on this? Poll-in-progress about the executions." McKuen shakes his head. Nick shrugs. "Not interested," he says into the mouthpiece. "Sure. Listen, do I get paid for this?" He mumbles something, clicks off the phone, then sighs deeply.

"They could alleviate all this angst with one simple stroke—install televisions. Multiscreen wherever possible. Keep us in the flow. But will they? No. You know why?" A whisper. "Elevators are a form of mind control." Upright and normal-voiced again, he warns McKuen, "Do yourself a favor. Ride them as little as possible."

McKuen sips his coffee, eyes raised to watch the floor indicator light begin to skip from digit to digit again. Beside him, Wolfie's knees are shaking, fidgeting away nervous energy. "Then again," McKuen says, eyes still tracking their climb, "the tension between up and down, opposites, does add depth to the idea of existence. Doesn't it?" The floor arrival tone sounds.

"Wrong!" Nick shouts. "Tension's out, plenitude's in. Tension is sin, death, chaos. Plenitude is Being. Eternal flow."

Trailing McKuen, Nick strides into a hallway which announces in no uncertain terms this city ain't working. Peeling, turd-colored paint, every third lightbulb turned out to save electricity, fatigued cops dragging cuffed prisoners through the moldy bureaucratic maze with brutish impatience. McKuen turns a corner and heads toward the recently enlarged homicide quarters, Nick in pursuit.

"Get with the program. On/off, good/evil, light/dark. Archaic concepts. Sleep? Sleep is not off. We've known that for a century. Death isn't even off anymore. It's just another mode of processing information. Media. Extensions of man. They syndicate us, rerun us, mass-produce us. *They* make us inexhaustible. *They* make us immortal. Information is the Second Coming. Information . . . is the City of God."

McKuen flings his empty coffee cup toward a huge, open-topped recycling drum made of an unsettling blue plastic. Standing in one beverage-spattered corner like the statue of some discredited saint, the container exudes a kinship with pollutants, industrial poisons, and toxic waste. Yet it seems somehow cheerful, almost happy. Pasted to it, a decal shows an extended family of elfish cartoon figures energetically ridding the planet of nonbiodegradable litter. Below that, the National Centers for Disease Control's 800 number.

"Personally," Nick adds, "I'd be much happier if I were rechargeable."

McKuen stops and turns in Homicide's doorway. "You ain't getting the kid till I got what I want out of him. So forget it." Leaning close, he jabs Nick with one fingertip. "You dig, dipshit?" But he doesn't wait around for Nick's answer.

Nick follows McKuen into the office, sweeping past puzzled cops. "I'm going to compose myself here. Brush off my lapels, apply pressure to my hemorrhaging sense of manhood, clear my throat, then ask, How did you do it? Legendary powers of deduction? New police technology? Or did you simply channel my identity? Then you come back with something snappy and crude like, Who else could get his head so far up his own ass, except a schmuck from the Public Defender's Office? But in time you'll develop a grudging affection for me. Sure, you have a prickly exterior, but you're alright underneath. Crusty but tenderhearted. Otherwise, why would the audience care about you? By the final scene, when I suggest something improbable, you'll love me. I guarantee it." Nick grabs McKuen's arm and spins him around. "But for now, you get me a sitdown with this kid in thirty seconds, or I'm going to see to it that your ass is written out of the movie. Are we conversing in a common tongue here? Miranda the motherfucker, and back off!"

Cochrane emerges from the corridor on the far side of the room, Darren Adams ahead of him in the pustular light. Nick spots them over McKuen's shoulder.

"Hey, you asked for a lawyer, I'm here," he shouts. "Talk to them, you'll never see sidewalk again."

Cochrane grabs the kid by the shoulder and holds him. "McKuen, you want to start at least *pretending* to be a cop and get this leech out of here?"

"Fuck you," Nick says. "Sit your ass down or *you* can explain to our mayor why you're holding a seventeen-year-old without legal representation." He turns. "McKuen, you're the one who believes in good/bad, crime/punishment. You want to live in the nineteenth century? Perpetuate the illusions of innocence and justice? Fine. Make a statement about content and meaning. Spring the kid! Now, do you dig, chief?"

A plainclothes cop near the TV curses loudly. With no further prompting, people converge on the tube with such deep instinctive thoughtlessness that the migration seems entirely shorn of volition. The entrancement is profound, total. It can't even properly be called a conditioned reflex. The TV has been playing in the background all along, a constant stimulus. Even the boy, who seems to have been forgotten by Cochrane, shuffles toward the cluster of bodies surrounding the screen.

McKuen watches, feeling like the last uncloned man in a pods-from-outer-space flick. Moving past silently glowing computer monitors, unattended fax machines, and wild sproutings of rubber-sheathed coaxial cable, he experiences a sense of dislocation. Around him the familiar ruin of the phantasmal city is trickling away to dust, being timeworn into nothingness. And in the midst of it, these imperishable waves. Information's ebb and flow, constant as the once-undying seas.

McKuen eyes Nick, but the public defender is too involved with the tube to notice. The others huddled around the set stare as infinitely replenished images break from one to the next in a fractured streaming.

On-screen, another execution is in progress. Hooded figures drag two uniformed police officers, handcuffed and blindfolded, down the center of a deserted street. Burned-out, graffiti-scarred houses line it. Empty bottles twist and kick along the curbsides, shoved forward by the wind. A large rat waddles across the hostages' path.

A newscaster's voice breaks the silence to explain that the televised material is being fed into the studio's monitors by unauthorized live remote. "We have not yet determined how this has been accomplished, but believe it to be the work of terrorists. I repeat, this transmission is live and uncensored. And from the look of things, I would say we're in for some unpleasantness. So determine for yourselves what, if any of this, you wish to watch." Electronic type scuds across the bottom of the screen, restating the warning, adding that XXN apologizes for the anticipated violence.

A boom box is set down on the street and turned on. Coda's

"Hate Funk Jam" punches through the TV's speakers. Several hooded figures begin dancing and mock fucking, weapons in hand. Another, dressed in a yellow rain slicker, medieval court jester's cap, and Day-Glo sunglasses, tiptoes to the camera lens. He flashes the Discordia Sect manifesto McKuen saw pasted to the squad car's windshield the preceding night, then chicken-steps out of close-up, cackling. For some reason, this flyer looks slightly different, as if it had been scrawled by a different hand. While Coda sings about the beginning of the end, the first officer is shot through the head. A finger appears, then blurs as it wipes spattered blood from the camera lens. "Oh God," the newscaster mutters. The woman officer is thrown to the ground and shot. The executioners turn and begin walking up the street, dancers following. The one in the jester's cap spasms with raspy laughter. Holding his sides, he stumbles toward the camera, scoops up the boom box, and falls in behind the others, his laughter tailing off into silence as their figures recede. Then the screen goes black, a grainy void hanging there like televised abyss. . . .

"Far out," Nick says.

But McKuen's attention has shifted. Shepard, another detective, is pacing on the far side of the room, jacket off, his sleeves rolled. His holster straps give him the look of a harnessed bull. McKuen edges toward Darren Adams, hissing to get his attention.

Then Shepard fullbacks his way toward them. Hands pull at his shirt. Bodies surge forward with him, forming a human wave, their voices garbled. McKuen steps in front of the boy as Shepard lunges for him. Hit chest high, McKuen and Darren Adams reel backward. McKuen reaches for a handhold, something to arrest his fall, and is whacked on the head. He closes his eyes, darkness spinning through him. When he reopens them he sees bodies tumbling over him. And off to one side, briefcase lying open on a desk top, demonic grin spread across his face, Christian Wolf peering down at him through the short black lens of a portable camcorder.

—In Beijing this morning—
—What famous canine—
—Slowly stir in the cream—
—So you've got this huge unsettled area of low pressure—
—Executions depicted during XXN's "Discordia Sect" coverage do not reflect the station's opinion, and are not intended to represent acceptable public behavior. Viewer detachment is advised.—

She smells lovely. Whether it's the scented deodorant, the lingering bouquet of apple-spiced shampoo, the slow-baking traces of feminine douche Tinkerbelling around her skirt like wood sprites, the aroma of her Number 15 coconut-based sunblock, or Julia's own still-fertile muskiness producing her glorious presence, well . . . that's the wrong question to ask here in the forsaken city.

She bears her sunset girlishness without guile. A virginal white, fabric-softener-softened turtleneck holds her finely boned face above its collar like an exquisitely shaped gem. Intelligence shines in her eyes as she strides into the Criminal Court Building, past dozing cops and impatient prostitutes swept into the hallways during the night, past the misdemeanor possession cases and ten-year-old shoplifters, down along offices marked Fraud, Homicide, and Sex Crimes until she arrives at her own, which says, quite simply, Hate.

A long way from ECAB—Early Case Assessment Bureau—the place where Julia began as one of three hundred Assistant District Attorneys. A twenty-four-hour-a-day clearinghouse for the city's you-name-it, we-got-it assortment of crimes. Misdemeanors, first-time felonies. Assault, weenie flashing, burglary. Barking in public when not a member of the canine species. Trampling people at a heavy metal concert. Black market baby farming. Public admission of a dysfunctional childhood.

She worked the lobster shift, midnight to 8 A.M., her casework crammed into a metal shopping cart under glaring fluorescent lights. A steady din rose from the horde of victims, attorneys, complainants and their families. A case was called and Julia would hastily flip through her basket, looking for the numbered folder. Ninety percent of the cases she handled weren't even her own. Attorneys worked revolving shifts, simply exchanging carts, the folders in them stapled with six, eight, a dozen scribbled shorthand notes updating the case.

Now she dreams about hate. When she started in Hate Crimes, she thought hate was the opposite of love. Then discovered it wasn't. Discovered there are no opposites. Only different channels.

A long gray-carpeted runway unspools down the office's center, separating cubicles which are stuffed with case files, wanted posters with mustaches Magic-Markered onto felons' faces, desktop mounds of junk food. Hookups for viewing virtual reality crime reenactments. Law books. "Dudespeak" versions of the Constitution popularized by the host of a music video show called *Rock for Retards:* "Kay, like free speech and all, I mean, like, just do it, dudes." Family-size and broken-family-size bottles of Coke. Stacks of witness testimony videotape. The odd sleeping bag, spare suit, or electric guitar.

As Julia strides through the office, monogrammed leather briefcase swinging at her side, harried ADAs dash past her, late for court. Others fall briefly into step with her and pass on notes, affidavits, perpetrator rap sheets, lab reports, late-breaking case info, each updating her in cryptic legalese, then peeling off into minor character limbo. The whole scene is meaningless, but has cinematic energy.

"Reinforcements," says Cliff, one of Julia's cubicle mates, glancing up from his desk. Julia sets down her briefcase, and reaches for the plastic-lidded container of snack-wagon coffee Cliff hands to her. "I was beginning to worry," he says, offering doughnuts, bagels, trail mix. Finally, he extends a pouch of chocolate-covered espresso beans.

"No thanks."

He retracts the bag and pops a bean into his mouth. "I didn't know if you were going to make it. It looks like all hell is ready to break out."

Danna, cubicle colleague number two, grumbles. Sleeves rolled, stubby non-filter cigarette clamped with film-noirish swagger between her lips, she is sifting through crime scene photos. A ransacked grocer's shop. Fifty-pound bags of rice slit open, their spilled contents shat upon, "yellow peril" literature scattered about. She leans back in her chair and lets her arms fall to her sides in defeat. Her oversized suit jacket opens. Julia sees she is wearing a T-shirt with the word SCUM—Society to Cut Up Men—silk-screened across her breasts. On the cubicle's TV, a "dramatization" of the prior evening's executions is in progress.

The event, only hours old, is already the subject of magazine article proposals, theater workshop showcases, and editorials lamenting the trivialization of a tragic event. A telejournalist reports that one officer's grieving wife has been offered a six-figure movie option on her husband's life story. Riots are breaking out across the city.

Cliff watches for a moment. "They're talking martial law, curfews."

"Death squads," Danna adds.

"House-to-house searches. Police checkpoints."

"We weren't happy knowing the Third World had something we didn't."

"Did you see anything on the way in?" Cliff asks Julia. "Blockades? Troop movements?"

"Just had to have something new to watch, didn't we?" Danna says.

Silent, Julia rides out the wave of sadness gliding through her. The tube gathers and disperses information, divinely unhurried. As events unfold, it begins its insidious storyboarding—searching for lead characters, exotic images, narrative through-lines, places for commercial interruption, and a catchy logo. But her grief is unprogrammed, preempted by the ongoing carnage. Still, the souls extinguished on-screen seem to sweep through her, leaving in their wake the iron taste of oblivion.

Snakes of smoke crawl around Danna's head. "Big Daddy just had to have another war to fight." Her eyes widen, telling Cliff that as a white male he is automatically implicated.

"Oh, come on, Danna. You've been processing neo-Nazi/Armageddon cults too long." He eyes the mock "Wanted" poster above her desk. The felon's criminal stats read: Suspect: White Male. Height: 5′6″ to 6′5″. Weight: Gives in pounds. Eyes: Yes. Warning: Has penis (small one) and has been known to use it. "Everything evil isn't the result of Caucasian testosterone levels.''

Lou Parsons, senior ADA, pokes his head into the cubicle. Julia looks up and he tilts his head to one side. Slipping his hands into his trouser pockets, he shuffles down the corridor ahead of her.

One of the city's "Big Three" prosecutors, Parsons is job-grizzled, but has a reputation for being fair, politically unambitious, and honest. Tie loosened, collar button undone, he stares out through a graying hallway window. Beyond the ruins of downtown's high-rise cell blocks and abandoned condo towers, he sees street fires, the city unmaking itself in climbing spools of tarry smoke. In his youth, the place had given Parsons his identity, his sense of promise. There was a time when he enjoyed tales of land scam deals, rigged elections, power and water company intrigues, sprawl development kickbacks. All the thieving heartlessness of the city. Its deep greed and rapacious scheming were its magic. At this late hour, though, he feels the city is fated for extinction, the graveyard mists of history.

He doesn't hear Julia come up alongside him. "What's up?" Without removing his hands from his pockets, he nods toward the window. Outside, thick whorls of smoke are draped across the sky, their peaks blending with the smog that obscures the sun. Julia feels that something of the natural world—ocean, mountains, a gentle blotting of plains—should be glimpsed in the distance. Instead, silver-white satellite dishes glow dimly at the edges of subdivisions, the few communal swimming pools she can make out glinting like chips of quartz. On the inner rim of the sprawl, fires are coming faintly to life. Silhouetted helicopters creep across the sky, their shadows vanishing behind eddying veils of smoke. Following the descent of one as it plunges silently, she sees a condo development's guard tower collapse, its long struts crumpling like an insect's legs. Closer in, riot vehicles and personnel transports speed past overturned cars, emergency lights whirling. A delivery truck burns sullenly, unattended. A second explosion erupts, blowing out its sides, flames rippling up around it like wind-whipped flags. Ahead, near the street's vanishing point, human shapes swarm like microbes on a slide. A single bright flash turns the area's light opaque. When the explosion evaporates, Julia sees figures running from its fringes as the riot vehicles approach.

Directly across from her and Parsons, city police appear on a low roof of the Criminal Court Building. Helmeted sharpshooters sprint to points along the parapet and check the street, rifle barrels held upright. An airbus lifts off from the mayor's mansion rooftop just to the west. Its belly tilts slightly as it banks toward them, gaining speed. Righting itself, it thunders past the window, its imperial colors seeming to hang for a moment in the air after the bus has vanished. In its wake, a camera crew harnessed to its open passenger door, comes a news chopper, yard-high lettering identifying it as the property of XXN.

Parsons turns away and starts down the corridor. Julia catches up with him as he nears his office. "Your kid go to school this morning?"

"Yes." She slows her pace. "Why?"

Parsons circles his desk. "Sit down." He points to one of the armchairs, then removes his telephone's wireless handset from its cradle and extends it to her. "I heard a few minutes ago they were closing the schools. Check, see everything's alright. Then we'll talk."

Stunned, Julia can think of nothing but Paul sitting at home, watching television. The day is going too fast for her, the city slipping beyond control and taking her along with it. When Parsons sets the coffee he has poured in front of her, she says, "I can't remember my phone number."

"Press J. I have it on file."

Julia touches the key and hears faint electronic chirping. On the third ring she gives up hope, and a moment later is listening to her own voice on her answering machine.

Parsons pretends something outside the window has flagged his attention. Coffee in hand, he goes to it.

Julia takes a breath. "I'm—it's me. I'm at work. Um, listen. Call when you get in. It's about 9:30 now. I heard the schools were being let out. So, you know." She realizes the message is going on too long, rambling, but she can't give it up just yet. "I'll try you back in a little while, in case you can't get through. Have them page me if I'm not at my desk." Then the hope that Paul would pick up the receiver is gone, and she feels empty, her silence a home for his absence.

"Try the school," Parsons says, not turning from the window.

She dials information, then the number, and gets a recorded message. "The school is closed. There have been no incidents, everyone is safe. Students are being taken home by shuttle bus. There is no need for alarm. Your patience and cooperation are appreciated. Please be patient. For information on the resumption of classes, please tune to XXN. Thank you."

Parsons turns, but Julia is not looking at him. He stares down into his coffee cup.

"Everyone's being taken home. They said there hadn't been any incidents." She mouths the words as if they were charms, things with the power to cast a protective spell over her son.

Parsons is quick to be encouraging. "That's good. They've got it under control." He moves back to his desk, reassured.

"It wasn't exactly a 'they.' I heard a taped message."

"Oh." He drops into his chair, the crispness of his movements abandoning him.

Julia notices, but doesn't mention it.

"Well," he says, "it's probably best you got a tape. They can handle more calls that way." He nods, thinking. "They're taking the kids home, escorting them?" Julia nods. "Good. Good." His gaze drifts to the window and the smoke-darkened sky beyond it. "Barbarity," he says softly. He leans forward, elbows on his desk top. "Look. Your son's going to be alright. You're far enough out of town, most of this won't even reach your area. He'll be fine." He pauses. "But my guess is that this is going to be worse than the last couple of these things. You saw the TV this morning?"

"Uh-huh."

Parsons grunts. "Yeah. Well, I think we've gone past the random violence stage."

"You think it's organized?"

Parsons shrugs. "I doubt it. What I mean is . . . the killing is entrenched. It's dug in and it's not going away. It's . . ." He tosses one hand up and sits back.

One word shapes itself in Julia's mind, coming through with the clarity of a station identification: hate. The new religion. She sees it every day in court. Hate as catharsis, hate as redemption. So what's taking place on the streets isn't unexpected. It's merely the flashpoint of the city's anxiety.

"The scary thing," Parsons says, "is that we're going to have to sift the hard-core killers from the half-zillion kids who think this is an action movie. You know what I'm talking about?"

She knows. Not just gangbangers but an entire generation tuned into pop apocalypse. Rifle-site jackets, "Kop Killer" T-shirts, caps that read "Kaos '99." Apocalypse, the ultimate marketing strategy—provided it doesn't actually come to pass.

"You know McKuen?" Parsons asks.

"Homicide?"

"The black guy. Yeah."

The black guy. Julia feels embarrassed, then realizes that he merely said what she thought.

"Well, he brought in a kid he thinks is connected to one of the executions. Not a doer, just a link."

"He booked him?"

"That's the wrinkle. He has, but not for the thing tying him to the killings."

"Which is what?"

"Titanium bullets."

"Armor-piercing stuff."

"Right. And something else. C-4. There were burn traces of plastic explosive all over the squad car. McKuen retraced the lot he chased the kid through and lucked out. He found two unused shells."

"Kid?"

"Whatever. The one who offed the two in the car. He dropped a couple of slugs. Half-inch layer of C-4 in each one."

Waiting for Julia's reaction, Parsons imagines the intimate surfaces she hides in the office, the frailties and innocence she keeps to herself. He is drawn to her, not by lust, but as if he were being beckoned to a place where he could forget his sadness. A sanctuary beyond the witchery of the city.

Then his vision is gone when, softly but abruptly, she says, "It sounds more like narcotics, or even white supremacist hardware, than gang related. They're into machine pistols. Nothing creative."

"Right."

"So we're going with the theory that this sect—"

"Discordia."

"—is a move from gang violence to organized revolution. Correct?"

"That's the operative theory. But organized?" He sits forward, palms up. "You see what we get through here. You've got people

8 3

killing each other for walking on the wrong side of the street. The rest are dope mercenaries and psychopaths. Who's there to organize? One nut demented enough to believe in revolution? The community's gone. We've wiped it out." He falls back in his chair. "This is anarchy. Or worse." He stares at Julia. "It is organized. But on another level." He allows Julia time to absorb this, for conspiracy's dark sweep to rewire her brain, tuning it to some new wavelength. . . . "You follow?"

"You're saying there's something *behind* what we're seeing?"

"I'm suggesting it. As a possibility. Don't run away with it. Am I certain? Do I absolutely know this is being orchestrated? No. But keep something in mind—the foundations for it exist. Ask yourself: Who benefits by this?"

Parsons's question hangs there, outside the city's unofficial history. The illegal drug sweeps and mass arrests. Racially selective curfew laws. Displaced cold-war operatives and FBI/CIA agents turned loose inside the city's war zones to combat the drug trade, proving indeed that you can go home again. Only if any of this conspiracy theory stuff is true, or even simply exaggerated, Julia knows that it's in part due to some of the city's more zealous patriots, who don't seem to realize that when you return home from a war, you don't bring it back with you.

"So, who benefits? That's always the question. We can only speculate. But I'm warning you up front: things may get weird."

"Weird?"

Parsons holds up one hand. "Flak is going to be coming in from all sides. I'm expecting mass incarceration, street sweeps, you name it. This is going to be swift, but it's going to be ugly. Any straighter, I can't be." He looks directly at her. "So, give McKuen what he needs—"

"I'm with McKuen?"

"Of course. But remember—what he *needs*, not what he wants.

We still have something resembling the Constitution. Think of it from time to time. And don't go for results—go for the truth. This isn't about now, it's about the future. All I'm saying is: worry about the reverberations." Parsons sits back, seeming to dismiss his words with a brusque wave of one hand. "Alright, end of tough-guy speech. Where are we? McKuen pulls in this kid, Darren Adams—"

"—off the C-4 lead."

"—Right. Through the Viet Ching. They run most of it. McKuen has connections from his Nam days with an old ARVN colonel. Golden Triangle type. He oversees—I won't say commands, they're fucking lunatics—the gangs."

"The colonel turns the kid."

"Yes. And not only for C-4 but—this is a nice touch—for knocking over a convenience store owned by one of the gang's refugee cousins. So the kid, who's safe only as long as he's with McKuen, is dead unless he cooperates. And McKuen knows this. So. He booked Adams on the robbery, but what he really wants is the next stop on the C-4 trail."

"Which is whoever tipped the cartridges found at the decapitation scene with C-4."

"Right."

"But why book him on Rob-1," Julia says. "If there's more leverage with the kid thinking he may be *allowed* to walk, what's the point?"

Parsons nods slowly, then bites his upper lip. "I'm going to say one name, one time. Christian Wolf. Legal aid. Asshole nonpareil. Also known as the Person You Would Least Like to Have Defending You. Confessed *killers* have sued this guy for malpractice. You know him?"

"Did he suggest his own incompetence as grounds for a mistrial once?"

"That's the imbecile. The kid hadn't even *asked* for a lawyer. McKuen had him ready to talk, Wolf shows up. It was book the kid, or lose him. So McKuen booked him on Rob-1 in order not to tip his hand." Parsons stands and moves toward the window.

Outside, the city's horizon is painted by charcoal-colored veils of smoke. Blood-orange flame sprints across a strip of landscape, black clouds scrolling away above it until smoke and flame separate, and the fire begins to burn cleanly, purged of crude flammables. He turns away, wondering how far events were going to go this time.

"What do I do with McKuen?" Julia says.

"For starters, get him a warrant for the kid's house. But as the kid now has legal representation, don't mention the C-4. We'll get nothing but grief and the Fifth if we do."

"What am I looking for, then?"

"McKuen did a 'plain-view' search when he picked up Adams. Saw some Discordia Sect material. Xeroxed, like the one left on the squad car. Go with that. As much as I hate to say it, I don't think 'probable cause' is going to be held to very strict standards here. That's why I want the warrant brief and airtight. We're talking precedent. Leave out the VC informant. Go with McKuen's 'plain view.' Nothing else."

"What do I tell Wolf?"

"Nothing. This is Rob-1, let him think it's Rob-1. We'll call the kid for a lineup when we get to it. Meantime, you and McKuen no longer lead separate lives." Parsons slumps into his chair. "So, that's it. When you need me. . . ." He doesn't finish, but instead sweeps one hand over his desk. When Julia reaches the door he says, "Your son."

Hesitating, the knob in her hand, she turns.

"He's probably not the child you imagine." Sensing that no response is forthcoming, Parsons adds, "He'll be alright."

Julia nods quickly, and an instant later is gone. The room fills with her absence. Parsons closes his eyes briefly, then swivels toward his bookcases, reaches for the remote handset, and clicks on the TV. . . .

Cut to:

Minus Five's Video Arcade:

Ray pounds on the locked door until he sees Minus Five's sleepy figure approach through the metal security grill. "Open up. Come on."

"What the fuck I gotta open up early for you for?"

" 'Cause I'm just gonna pound on this door till you do. You know what a pain in the ass I am. Come on, you can go back to sleep once I'm in." Then Ray adds, "I'll clean the place for you."

Minus Five unlocks the door with his good hand and Ray follows him into the front room of the arcade as Minus Five heads back toward the cot in his office.

"I'd be a lot quieter if I had me some rock to smoke, you know." Ray watches Minus Five plug in his little one-cup coffee maker.

"You'd be a lot quieter if you was dead, too."

"You ain't gonna wish I was dead."

"Yeah? Why's that?"

" 'Cause I just liberated your ass."

"Sounds to me like you been smokin' rock already."

"Come on. Five dollars' worth of rock, two quarters—"

"Two quarters?" Minus Five holds off flicking on the office TV to look at Ray.

"For cleanin' the place!"

"You ain't cleaned it."

"You ain't paid me."

"And what about the rock?"

"I pay you. Paid you for that Coda tape."

"Hadda hound your skinny ass for the money."

"You got it though."

Minus Five grumbles. "Wait outside the office. Don't like fools in here." He shuts the metal door, then reappears moments later behind the cashier's window. He smacks down a vial of crack and fifty cents. "Don't forget to clean the place up."

Ray sweeps through the arcade with a broom, emptying ashtrays and picking up empty cans in record time. Two minutes later, the rock toasting away inside the bowl of a pipe, he's off into the back room, and strapped into helmet and gloves for a stoned trip to:

The Elijah Muhammed "To the Max" Detention Center, P. O. Box 1999, Cyberspace.

The following info skitters across the virtual reality monitor in radioactive-green type, though Ray has a hard time reading it.

Prison Population: Most a da black male race, some *cholo maricons* for spice, the odd Caucasian psychopath.

Average Sentence: Life, and then some.

Description of the Joint in One Word: Bad.

Cloaked in perpetual darkness, it rises out of the desert night like a constellation glittering in velvet blackness. Ray's computer-controlled airship glides toward it. Handcuffed, sort of, he watches the ship's radar scan the terrain below. Its heat sensors pick up forms identified as mongrel dogs. Other three-dimensional computer images appear, deep basins which hold something off-the-charts hot. Old nuclear waste sites. The landscape is dappled with them, the dead earth around the shadowy cauldrons cooked brittle as shale. No telling where a prison escapee might fall through and wind up chicken-fried.

Ahead, the penal city rises into the wasteland's sky. Tiered like a ziggurat, its smooth stone-and-steel face is bathed in a cool blue light. The prison rests on the only solid ground within a two-hundred-mile radius. And if that ain't bad enough, check this out. It's surrounded by a moat. And the moat is filled with—name it: reactor core runoff, acid rain, toilet bowl deodorizer, mechanical alligators.

Electrified fences and armed roboguards become visible as Ray's prison-bound ship descends. So does something that sits atop the pyramid, floodlit like a shrine. Clouds of power-plant steam slither past the ship's windows, turning the penal city into a spectral field of searchlight beams, and for a moment Ray can't see shit. Then the ship drops through the radioactive fog and the shrine reappears. It's a giant satellite dish perched above a ring of television screens. Huge letters read XXN. Ray checks out what's playing and sees commercials, sitcoms, cop shows, music videos, and—are his eyes workin' right?—an XXN classic movie channel screening of—ho, it is!—*Birth of a Nation*.

Meanwhile, calculations for Ray's demolecularizing and beaming down are chittering away in cyberspace. Suddenly, his hand and ankle cuffs vanish. He goes to rub one sore wrist and closes what only moments ago were his fingers around a bubbling nothingness. Pretty soon the rest of him is percolating too, though with no sensation of heat. He's simply devolving into electron charges, a loose conglomeration of particles as discrete as those of a television image.

When he rematerializes he's in the open city of the virtual prison. A sewery darkness, sharp with the stench of old urine, immediately wraps itself around him. Chromium-alloy cyborgs patrol the prison's central mall, their sculpted torsos gleaming among the silhouettes of inmates. Ray looks around and sees pillars of light sweeping through the hall to illuminate packs of doo-ragged gangbangers. Other prisoners flash into visibility, then are swallowed up by shadow, as are the dying and the dead who lie on the slick, piss-puddled floor.

Ray's eyes follow the light beams up along graffitied walls, past converging tiers of catwalks. The prison's atrium seems to rise forever. Above him, hundreds of televisions dangle by invisible wires, suspended in midair like legless spiders. Finally, Ray's gaze reaches the pyramid's peak, twenty stories high, where all light beam sources converge. There, barely visible, is, as legend has it, the *only* locked cell in the place.

What the cell contains is the subject of mojo debate. Some say faith divides those who view the cell's presumed contents with reverence from those who claim it's bullshit. But even the naysayers are down with the fact that there is a certain grail quality about the thing. Guesses as to its actual booty range from unlimited pussy, mountains of blow, and vault after vault of cashola, to eternal life, resurrection, and labyrinth's end. Nobody really knows. It all comes down to where you stand on transcendence. You find what goes on inside your own head. Believe in zilch, find zilch. Into the Great Universal One? Step right this way for the collective unconscious's ongoing extravaganza, a Las Vegas for the soul. Whatever. Once you're inside, project as you wish.

The point is: you gotta get inside to win. After that, you're on your own. But it's a long way from the nearest parapet to the central peak of the pyramid. Leap and miss, and it's a long fall back into the city. . . .

Which, for a prison, looks an awful lot like the 'hood. Brothers jiving and fighting. Homes drinking malt liquor. Dudes hustling.

Robocops beating on homies. There's even a half-court game going on way down the other end.

And him? Little ol' Do-Ray? He be speedin'. Dex crystals cut with them crack shavings Minus Five gave him. Little hard on the throat, nasty dry heat. But, you know, two minutes after toke *numero uno*, the "croak" smoked down to a pebble, the bowl of his pipe beginning to cool between his fingertips, which are already losing all but the dullest, dreamiest layers of feeling, sinus drip's sour mucousal balm slithering over his toasted larynx cartilage and scorched glottal membranes . . . who cares?

The prison world moves a little slow, kind of watery and remote, and Ray has the feeling that he doesn't actually occupy it in a true physical sense. He laughs to himself. Shit, every black boy's invisible. But with his nervous system iced by speed, he's invisible *and* insubstantial, plus lost in a corporate virtual reality game. Damn, the white man got his ass every which way.

Including up. 'Cause as Ray stares into the firmament, thinking, This ain't so bad. Little smelly and shit. But I could definitely deal wit' it, the prison as homeboy's crib, he notices way the fuck up where, according not only to rumor but also the game's rules, the mystical cell is supposed to be, a silvery halo. Four spokes of light with a dark center. It looks familiar, but Ray can't put the images together at first. A circle, yeah. And . . . it is. A cross. Beams of light intersecting at right angles like the small crucifix his grandmother wears around her neck.

Except . . . hold on a second. The soft white halo and the crucifix form crosshairs inside a perfect circle. A rifle site. Damn! It *is* the 'hood.

Ray looks around at street level again, bodies cruising past him in brightness and shadow. His eyes readjust and he flags a gray-bearded old-timer who's shuffling by, talking to himself.

"Hey, hey, yo, come here." Ray has to grab the guy by one arm to slow him up, and even with Ray's hand on him the old dude keeps trying to motor. Persistent little sucker. Stoned for like definitely ever. A mess of tics and jitters. Crazy. Crazier than crazy. "Yo, yo, old-timer." Ray points overhead where the cell is. *If* it is. "What's that made out of, anyway?"

"Mirrors."

"What?! Get outta here!" The old guy is already pulling away and Ray is dragged a few steps. "Ho! Where you going? Ain't done with you." Ray makes the guy hold still. "If you so smart, how you get up there?"

"No way up. No way." The guy shakes his head compulsively.

"Gotta be."

"Nope." The guy tries to pull away again.

"You crazy. Fact, crazy'd be a step up for yo' ass." Ray releases him to be swept up by the dim flow of the crowd.

But now that he looks again, Ray does have to admit that the catwalks and parapets do kind of, well . . . stop a good two, three stories below the sucker. Have to be skyin', home, to get up there. 'Cause hard as Ray squints he can't see any handholds, elevator lobbies, ski lifts, or "Watch Your Step" signs anywhere near the rifle site's bright abyss. Just cavernous dead zone. So maybe the OT's right. No way. Give it up, home. Ain't nobody can, been, or meant to get his ass up there. 'Specially not no little gangbangin' nappy-headed fool.

Though some brother, *one* brother, one time, Ray thinks, must have. . . .

"Put your hands on your head and spread your legs." The voice is pure electronic buzz, metallic and hollow. An electric razor with good diction.

When Ray looks for its source he sees a mass of polished chrome sculpted to comic-book-hero proportions emerging from the throng. Stoplight-red eyes; plodding walk; smooth, curiously unendowed crotch. Obviously the product of whitey's techno-fetishism. Sterile death machine as ideal man.

"Don't move."

The same breathless, synthesized voice, only this one comes from behind a group of brothers who have stopped shooting craps to watch Ray get the bejesus stomped out of him. Ray sees a second, identical cybocop approaching. He holds a nightstick made from the same alloy he's made of, and doesn't appear to have second thoughts about using it. It's the 'hood all right.

"Let's see your pass card."

Pass card. What pass card? This is the joint.

"Watch it. He's going to make a run for it."

Ray's gotta admit he has been contemplating doing just that, but he didn't think the idea was floating above his head like a thought balloon. What's the deal here anyway?

"I'm getting a reading," the first one says, beginning to accelerate even as Ray starts slowly, slyly he'd hoped, to backpedal.

The crowd edges away from him. Looking around for help, Ray sees no hint of solidarity. No whispered safe house offers or passage on some underground railroad are made. No limousine chauffeur with one of those airport arrival gate placards, no cars to hot-wire. There's not even a bus to catch. All there is—aw, hey, that's cold, cuzz, Ray thinks. Fools are setting up concession stands and pari-mutuel windows along the sidelines. The action isn't even giving him any chance of surviving, only odds on the various ways the bookies expect his eligibility for food stamps to be canceled, *permanente*. No respect. Ray turns, deciding it's time to seriously beat feet.

"He's starting to change. I'm losing contact."

"Quick, after him! Before he turns into. . . ."

Heads spin, gasps and murmurs rip through the crowd. Bored

homeboys, gangbangers, pimps, hustlers, bespectacled scripture scholars, nodding junkies, and stone crazy killers have metamorphosed—in sympathetic accord?—into a cheering, direction-giving gauntlet of well-wishers. Betting windows clap shut, sideline vendors roll up their umbrellas. Three-card-monte tables are abandoned, boom boxes drowned out. A motley confetti begins to fall. Racing past shadowy bodies, Ray looks up to see it streaming from the parapets above. Brothers are cocking their arms and winging, well, rolls of toilet paper actually—but it's, you know, the thought—into the pyramid's towering abyss, crack vials, bags of smack, blow, fat joints rolled in hash-oil-brushed banana paper, and methadone packets all joining in. Whipped by air duct thermals, they form a great swirling blizzard in which the screens of the TVs are rendered invisible. Just as Ray, thinking this can't be happening, time to check into rehab, get clean, maybe, you know, go to college or something, slowly begins to pass out of visibility himself.

He glances at a necklace of low-hanging television sets not yet obscured by the storm of drug paraphernalia and sees himself televised from a variety of angles—close-up, crane shot, split-screen commentator deal. He ain't got nowhere yet and they're already anchoring the event. Finally made it onto the tube. That's something, ain't it?

Except . . . whoa. Suddenly his tear-assing behind is fading from the screens. He's disappearing, slipping from ghostly mist to transparent afterimage to—Ray begins to feel anything's possible—maybe even immanence. Yeah, I could be down wit' that. And what he notices on the faces of all the brothers urging him on as he streaks beyond visibility—into. . .who knows? hyperspace apartheid, sci-fi dystopia, myth?—is hope. Because it's him, roboguards in heated pursuit. No question. It's Afroman. . . .

As he's the first black superhero, his comic-book adventures not yet collector's items—for that matter, they're largely unwritten—here's some A-man history: Neither faster than a speeding bullet nor able to leap tall buildings in a single bound, he is nonetheless able to dunk like a motherfucker. Can dance too, no question. Fact, left to pop entertaining and ballplaying, Afroman's got a handle on things. Comes to leapin', jivin', fuckin', singin'—call Afroman. Anything else, anything serious though, you're on yo' own.

He's a master of disguise. Hard to recognize, near-impossible to track. Invisible when he's right under your nose. And never where, what, or who you think he is. Just like the joker in the three-card-monte game that Ray, to his own surprise, finds himself overseeing when he rematerializes.

"I got five says you too pussy to lay down a bet. I got ten." He checks the crowd. "Nobody wants to bet here?"

The brothers milling around the upended crate Ray/Afroman is using for a gaming table are too busy calculating their chances of losing to notice the approaching roboguards. As for the guards themselves, they can't believe their computer tracking devices are answering queries as to Ray's whereabouts with, "You got me."

"I got twenty dollars say this dude right here," Ray points to a shy-looking homey, "this little four-eyed, spectacle-wearing dude, probably been to colleges, universities, everything—dental school!—ain't got the pecker to put down fifty, I let his black ass shuffle the cards hisself." Ray checks the crowd's faces, then peeps over their heads to scope out the roboguard activity, cybocops stopping homes, waking winos, and shining their highbeams into black faces, clueless.

"I'll bet."

"Say what?" Ray sees the bookworm holding a fifty in his fist like an ice cream cone.

"I'll bet."

Ray shuffles the cards as roboguards move past him, uninterested. They stop to confer, scratch their helmet heads, then disappear down one of the prison's labyrinthine passageways. Heh-heh. Dopes. And for every second Ray's free, he scores more video game points.

"Sorry, time to go." Ray tosses the guy the fifty, pockets his two queens, marked joker, hustled cash, and . . . well, that's it. Travel light. "Later, homes."

"I don't get to bet?"

The whiny voice stops Ray in his yet-to-be-made tracks. He fixes an impatient stare on the guy. "You wanna bet?" The fellow hesitates, and Ray wonders why he's become so intimidating all of a sudden. "Well?"

Mousy voice. "Yeah."

"What?"

"Yes, sir."

Ray throws the cards down on the table where they fall into line, evenly spaced, amazing the crowd of homies. But he's cool, shows *nada*. He extends an open palm. "Money."

"Sir?"

"Put it here. How you gonna shuffle? Use one hand and your dick?" Laughs all around. The guy gives up the fifty. Ray plucks the middle card off the crate. "What card 'm I showing you?"

"Joker."

"Now, I'm a take it out your face. Where I'm putting it?" Ray palms the joker and drops a third queen from his shirt cuff into its place, facedown.

"In the middle."

"In the middle. Right." Ray sweeps a hand over the cards. "You're on your own."

The little dude steps up to the crate, studies the cards, rubs his chin. Ray studies him in profile, leaning close at one point to peer through the guy's bifocals. The cards shrink to the size of postage stamps.

"You see 'em cards?" Ray asks, incredulous.

"Yes."

"Well shuffle then. Ain't rocket science." He checks around. No roboguards in sight. When he looks back, the guy is still thinking. "I'm a start charging you by the hour you don't get some fingers on them cards."

The guy begins shuffling slowly, no grace, no style. The cats around the table snort and crack up.

"You done this before," Ray says.

"No."

"Tell me no. You a hustler."

More laughs.

"You're making me lose my concentration."

"Look at them hands fly!" Ray pushes them down onto the crate. "Alright. Fun's over. Pick a card." The guy gingerly touches one. "Good." Ray reaches for it, but the guy's fingers leap to the adjacent card and flip a queen. "You lose. Thank you." Ray scoops up the cards, and pockets the fifty without missing a beat.

"There he is!"

Ray looks up and sees a new pair of roboguards. "Uh-oh." He turns and zips down a passageway, dropping the cards in his wake. The alley darkens and narrows, then opens onto a street. Dumpsters, people living in boxes, graffiti. Ray glances back and sees four red eyeballs glowing deep in the passageway's dimness. He runs past streetlamps and some clockers selling crack. Hm. Ray's about to say don't mind if I do when he remembers the tireless technocops on his hiney, not to mention the fact that he's in prison. Should there be streets and dope peddlers in the joint? Maybe this is one of them new, experimental facilities. Ray figures this must be the case when he ducks through an open doorway into a superbright storefront.

"You pay."

"Huh?" Ray looks around and sees snow peas, daikon radishes, mung bean sprouts, glass-doored refrigerators filled with overpriced cans of malt liquor. Damn, these prison designers are good.

"You pay." An Asian woman inside a bulletproof cashier's booth barks at him through an amplified voice box. "Now!"

"I didn't take nothin'."

She trips an alarm and her husband, brothers, cousins, whatever, barrel out of the storage room, wielding crowbars.

"Okay, Okay." Ray drops the fifty on the by-the-pound salad bar, the bill feathering its way onto a bain-marie marked "Hi-Protein, No-Cal Ranch Dressing," then turns and bolts.

"You no come back!" The voice blares from the streetside megaphone as he dashes through the door. Don't worry about it, Ray thinks.

Outside, robo-militia spot him. He hightails it around a corner, down a crowded street, and comes upon a theater marquee. Female names in lights, small box office manned by a stoned-looking hooker past her prime. A sign taped to its window reads, "PR manager wanted. No exp. nec. See Herb." Ray does. Fifteen seconds later he's back on the sidewalk, leaflets in hand, among tourists, degenerates, and runaways in a virtual red light district.

"Say say, whoa, where you going? Got girls here. Titties, asses. Orifices of every persuasion. Come on in here. Yeah, you. Go ahead in." Ray hands a leaflet to an emaciated, eyebrowless white dude wearing an old military topcoat, pajama bottoms, and unlaced high-tops.

"You have corpses?"

Ray hesitates, then says, "Yeah sure, we got corpses! Got every-thing. Skeletons. Mummies. Get your butt in there." Ray pushes the guy toward the box office, whispering, "Come out, get some sun on yo' ugly ass."

Speaking of which, it's kind of dark. Ray steps from under the marquee and looks up as the occasional taxicab cruises by. Beyond the streetlights he spots a couple of twinklings. Office tower win-dows? No stars in this neighborhood. Then he realizes that they're not window lights. They're more television screens, flickering in the firmament. Off in the distance to the west, a brightening. It's the faint outline of the rifle site, glowing softly inside its silver halo. Terminus and beginning, end and resurrection. Staring at it, a vast loneliness sweeps through Ray. He will be forever unfin-ished, solitary, hunted, and without love . . . Man, I could pity my-self big time. I just ain't into it is all.

Fear gets his ass back in gear when he looks down the street and sees his pursuers turn the corner. He begins offering leaflets to passing cars, jaywalkers, bands of Japanese businessmen prowling the street, sex excursion guidebooks in hand.

"Hey hey hey, no need to go any further, no need to take an-other step." Ray slides into the path of one group, palm up. "Say you been laid? Fucked, sucked, flayed, and filleted? No. Uh-uh. Look in your book. What it say?" Ray skims the page with his fin-gertip, reading, to his surprise, a whole lot better than when he was little old Do-Ray. I could be into this Afroman shit, he thinks. "See it? What's that say? Your glasses working or what?"

"Work fine."

"Says 'the finest.' Says 'you ain't been nowhere 'til.' Five stars. One for every orifice you gonna come through. Can't get this shit in Bangkok."

"Bangkok closed. No good." The sex capital, once famous for teenage prostitutes of both sexes, has been decimated by viruses, the only classifications for its victims: dying or dead.

The metallic-smelling heat of the techno-cops cuts through the sour odor of street trash and urine. Ray hears their motors whining faintly. The oncoming street crowd parts, hustlers of every stripe faking casual interest in the ground or some action across the street. Anything to avoid locking eyes with the robo-heat sliding up behind him.

Despite his nervousness, Ray straightens up and smiles, showing lots of yellow teeth, gums the color of medium-rare sirloin. "Howdy, officer. How you doin' there tonight? Got some cybosex specials guaranteed to blow your microchips. Look at this." He flashes a black-and-white photo at the flatfoot. "Lola Lubelightly, direct from gay Paree. Made by Peugeot and everything. Ever seen a face like that? Hundred percent nickel-plated. Got an intake valve could suck a MX missile outta its silo. And eyes? Beautiful. Like headlights." Ray tries to hand him the photo of Lola. Spread-eagled on her back, a guy in an auto mechanic's jumpsuit stands between her legs inserting a long, ribbed-metal shaft marked "Five Speed Transmission."

"Here, take this. Lemme initial it, get you a ten percent discount." Ray pulls a pen from the blazer pocket of a sex tourist and John-Hancocks Lola's gleaming beaver. "Go 'head, get your wires uncrossed, top popped, whatever it is you guys do. Have a nice day."

But Lola's high-gloss pudenda and silicone boobies don't leave Ray's hand. And the robo-fuzz doesn't look any happier—or hornier for that matter—than he did a minute ago. In fact, his eyes seem a more malevolent shade of red, the honeycombed wire mesh embedded in his sockets glowering like tiny devils that carry a mechanical suspicion and hatred of Ray, the white man's loathing for him so deep that it has been passed on to his machine doubles. The gaze sends Ray reeling back to the first pair of state eyes he ever saw, deep cold blue ones hovering outside the car window beside his frightened, long-gone mama. Telling him then the same thing these are telling him now, in a game. The same thing the pair staring out at him from the squad car last night told him before he blew the cops inside it to whatever segregated kingdom-come they were fated for. That for all his disguises and ingratiating, shucking, and jiving hambone masks, he was still Do-Ray, little piece-o-shit black boy Ray, worthless and despised from now till the end of white time. . . .

"You think he's the one?" the second cybercop asks, sliding alongside the first.

They consult a Ray "Wanted" poster. Ray peeks at the laser-printed reproduction, his features computer-sketched down to the last detail. High cheekbones, dark, shifty, looking-nowhere eyes, big old lips. Yup, it's him. Him and ten million other homies.

"Well, customers waiting, gotta go." He darts for the porn house doors.

Inside, the concession stand area smells of buttered popcorn and semen, the lighting like a disease. Ray dashes into the manager's office to give notice, collect his paycheck, and ask if he's eligible for unemployment benefits only to catch Herb, brothel manager and overweight coronary candidate, in the middle of a working lunch. Egg salad in pita, garlic-flecked tabbouleh, Danish flatbread, lox, sliced raw onion, beefsteak tomato from Israel, kreplach, cream soda, and frozen nondairy carob-chip yogurt, all nesting on grease-soaked sheets of recycled waxed paper atop time cards, payroll records, purchase orders for G-strings, K-Y jelly, 10-30 weight oil for Lola, and of course two sets of accounting books. The only light is a halogen bulb suspended over Herb's desk, shaded by a thick cone of jade-green glass. Breathless, Ray locks the door behind him and slumps against it.

"I thought you were—" Herb's query is interrupted by a tubercular cough. Still choking, he extends an arm, pudgy fingers grasping for a carton of king-size super-cool menthols. He clears his throat, then says, "This is some kind of coffee break action I don't know about? Who's working the door?" A lighter the size of a hand grenade appears from his voluminous trouser pocket, and a finger-long flame nibbles at the cigarette's tip until it begins to glow.

"—it's just that, see . . . my grandmother's sick."

"Your grandmother?"

"Yeah well, she called and all, and the baby's got worms and . . . well, not really worms, but kind of a virus kinda thing." The door behind Ray shudders as a deep booming spreads into the room. A hinge flies loose. Metal groans and pings. "So if I could just get my check." Then the blade of a fire axe bursts through the door, nearly Van-Goghing Ray's ear.

Herb drops his cigarette and springs like a jack-in-the-box out of his seat. *"Der Schutzstaffel!* Quick, the secret room."

"What?"

"Meshuggenah! Always a hideout keep. This way."

Herb presses a button hidden beneath his desk. Costume trunks are swept to the side, billboard photos of strippers now cashing in IRA accounts crumple as vault doors open. Inside the chamber, Herb's got some things: Uzis, AK-47s, rows of TEC-9 automatic machine pistols, tranquilizer guns, tasers, tear gas canisters, Remington 66os, Ithaca 12-gauge shotguns, a few Persian scimitars. Ray thinks he even sees a SCUD missile or two.

"Ho, shit."

"All bought wholesale," Herb says, hefting a rocket the size of a canoe. "Enough with the door, my prostate's in my nostrils. Gimme a hand here."

Ray zips across the room, the locked door exploding into a confetti of woodbits and sawdust behind him. When he pulls up alongside Herb, his boss is talking softly to himself, reading the launcher's instruction booklet in a whisper.

"You ever use one of these things?"

"Say what? I thought you was a expert."

"Ach!" Herb tosses the pamphlet aside. "We wing it."

They wrestle the rocket into the launcher's mouth, robo-fuzz streaming through the doorway.

"Okay, pull the trigger."

"It's got a button."

"Pull, push. Enough pishing around. Fire!"

Ray does and the front end of the launcher explodes, smoke drifting away to reveal strips of mangled metal, undeterred cyber-cops, and Herb—face covered with soot, hair frazzled, eyebrows singed, suspenders smoldering like strips of burnt bacon.

One frame later, he and Ray are scrambling for the secret passageway, Herb loading up on supplies—machine guns, flak jackets, a carton of cigarettes, and something that looks like a picnic basket. Amazingly, he no longer shows signs of being incinerated.

In the tunnel's dark, they spiral and ascend, shoe soles pinging dully on the metal staircase, candles guttering in the cavernous draft and shadow. Then onto a catwalk. A pale, ghostly brightening opens beneath them. Ray looks down and sees they are above the chambered hive of sex cubicles. Porn shows are in progress, bodies writhing like mudworms. Strobe lights flash like noiseless bomb blasts. Whips crack, wrists are bound. And hey. . . . Ray stops above one cell. I know those guys.

Ray's Japanese sex tourist buddies are group-fucking Paree's own Lola Lubelightly. Some of her other features are being put to use as well. It seems Lola's rib cage contains a state-of-the-art laser printer and fax machine. And playing at the back of her super-smooth chromium-alloy skull is a high-definition television carrying live-via-satellite action from the floor of the Tokyo stock exchange.

A whistling sound bottlerockets above Ray's head. He tracks it into the fading brightness where Herb's chubby face is ghoulishly visible. "Schmuck, come on. *Vamanos!*"

Which ain't a bad idea. The robo-posse is clattering onto the catwalk, taillight eyes streaming through the thinning dark. Taser cables loop out of the shadows, snapping taut inches from Ray's head, then falling away. When a noose wings past him, Ray knows it's time to book. But as he catches up with Herb, his boss slaps one hand to his chest, groans "Oy," and collapses in cardiac arrest.

Ray rolls the pornmeister onto his back, cradling his perspiration-soaked head in his hands. "Take it easy. You're gonna be alright."

"No, you go on."

"Okay."

"Here, take this." Herb hands Ray the picnic hamper.

Ray checks inside and finds matzoh and cartons of take-out Chinese. "Thanks." Ray extrudes Herb's wallet from his pocket. "I'm a take this too, seein' as how you dyin' and all."

One of Herb's clammy hands claps shut around Ray's wrist, mousetrap quick. "Remember. They hate us equal, though maybe you a bit more."

A laser blast sings off the catwalk's railing.

"So go."

"I'm gone."

Hamper in hand, Ray turns and scuttles away, robo-bullets whispering past, comet-tailing into the darkness ahead. Herb's kamikaze war cry and barrage of Uzi fire is sucked swiftly out of the air as Ray zips through the video landscape, a nightworld of virtual apocalypse, no fear in his heart. He races up a ladder, darts across a roof, barrels down a fire escape. Swims a river, crashes brick walls. Pursued, he reaches into the magic hamper and lays down an oily slick of roast pork lo mein in his wake, wings matzohs like lethal disks, robo-oppressors dropping behind him, decapitated, tangled in soba noodles. The prison reels past, rocked by explosions and firestorms, chopper searchlights clashing like lances in the low sky. Images. The weightless end of the world.

Within striking distance of the pyramid's shining epicenter, rifle site outlines brightly gleaming, Ray swings from cable to cable among the dangling TVs, rising higher still, racking up mega video game points as he vanquishes image after image with his own weightless superpowers. Snuffing these figures, though, is nothing like taking out last evening's real cops. And it's *their* weight, perhaps, that slows his flight when the prison's long labyrinth comes to an end, and he emerges in full sprint onto the pyramid's top level. The rifle site glows just ahead, across an abyss. Hovering above it is the mythical cell, locked inside it who knows what. Maybe even Rap Prophet Coda himself, the final word, spirit-voice of all raging, hope-stripped black boys.

And so, wearing his best high-tops, Ray takes, count 'em, two, three long strides, then leaps. The prison city's abyss opens like eternity beneath him, his fingertips scrape the bottom edge of the halo of light, and then he plunges back into the labyrinth. . . .

Lights go dead. The whine of the video machine dissipates. "Game Over" flashes mutely on the dead screen. Parachuting back into the funk of unwired, non-electronic being, Ray sits quietly before removing the game's virtual reality glove and visor. His buzz is gone, the crack leaving his head feeling craggy and wind-gouged, the speed it was cut with swirling away into some vast sea inside him. He steps out of the cockpit chair, feeling heavy and hollow at the same time.

Behind the bulletproof cashier's window, Minus Five is sipping wine cooler along with his coffee, his eyes on the countertop television when Ray shuffles out of the game room's cavelike dark. The place is still deserted, 9 A.M. the witching hour in the 'hood. Nothing around but bad overhead lighting, mud-smeared tile floor, and flaking plaster walls. Every building in Ray's life—school, projects, j.d. hall, county lockup—bore the same institutional look, each a nearly indistinguishable variation on the same prison.

"I get a sip of that?" Ray asks, pointing to the wine cooler.

"What do I look like, free lunch program? Buy your own." Minus Five's voice is metallic, distant yet blaring on the booth's speaker system.

"I used all my quarters, man. Come on."

"That's not my problem. You broke again, go rob somebody."

"Come on, man. I used 'em in your goddamned machines." Ray stares at the side of Minus Five's head, hoping this will get him to turn his attention from the television. No dice, so he raps on the glass.

"I tol' you already. No. Now shut the fuck up, lemme watch this shit."

Ray looks at the TV screen and glimpses something familiar, though at first he can't place it. A movie he's seen? Rerun of some you're-there-for-the-arrest cop show?

It's *his* handiwork. Decapitated police officers are being hauled out of the squad car by paramedics as riot lights lasso the night air. Ray didn't expect television to pay attention. He'd hoped so, but didn't figure it would happen. Nothing was shown when he offed O.C.; no pictures in the paper, either. Zip. Like it never happened. Not this time, though. Cameras, guys with headphones and mikes, vans marked XXN.

Jump to daylight: the bodies gone, a police tow truck jacking up the front end of the squad car. Fence, empty lot, burned-out projects in the distance. Same place, only ghostly, a postcard from his dreams. The whole thing—the executions, the crazy-assed chopper dude, spinning up stairs in the dark and emerging on a rooftop lit by scissoring columns of phosphorescent air patrol beams, their rifle sites glowing—all of it seems dream-like and far away to him, remote as Afroman. TV only makes it feel more unreal.

"Turn it up so I could hear," Ray says.

"Look. I give you a rock—"

"Thing was a pebble."

"—cut it for you—"

"Fuck, I gave you fi' dollar."

"Gave?"

"I promised you, man. You get it."

"Get you high so's you can go play video games. Then you gotta be comin' 'round bothering me?"

"Just turn the thing up."

"That gonna shut you up?"

"What you think?" Ray goes sulky as Minus Five scowls. "Come on, man. Yeah." Minus Five turns away, setting down his wine cooler then reaching with his only fingered hand for the remote.

A fine-boned black anchorwoman appears on-screen. Ray recognizes her. Started out as Miss Black America, made a bad movie or two, then had a brief singing career as a demure, crossover rapper called "Cafe au Lait," who didn't cross over. Now she's clutching a long white microphone, Discordia Sect manifesto in her opposite hand. Ray feels uneasy. He wishes there was some fat-headed white peckerwood up there, KKK tattooed all over his face. This sister reporting on how evil and shit the executions were, and how they were probably only gonna hurt the black community, leaves him with the sense that he fucked up. Misunderstood Coda's message, misunderstood Discordia '99, stupidly betrayed the one thing which offered him hope.

"Definitely fine," Minus Five says.

"What?"

"A fox of super-divine quantifiability. Without question, a ten on the peter-meter."

"I thought you wanted *me* to shut the fuck up so you could hear this?"

"Before, I needed to hear. Right now, I need to see. But more than anything, I need you to butt the fuck out of my life."

Ray points at the screen. "Some brother finally stood up and done something, all you can think about is your dick."

"Stood up for what? Any *fool* knows it ain't 'bout standing up. It's 'bout gettin' it up."

"Yeah, that's 'cause you ain't never done nothing 'cept lose your fingers to some Jamaican motherfuckers."

Ray focuses so deeply on the television that he doesn't notice Minus Five glaring at him. The action on-screen jumps to other execution sites, something else Ray wasn't expecting. Coda's tape said that the Discordia Sect was all about doing it solo, not getting hung up organizing. It was about acting. It was about taking things into your own hands and being a hero. Coda's bootleg set up a scenario for the executions, suggested killin' times through killin' rhymes. But as far as Ray knew, he was the Discordia Sect. He was Coda's homeboy, the special one. Now there's all this other shit.

As Ray watches, his confusion spins inside him. The anchorlady is talking about rioting. A computer grid of the city lights up, indicating which streets have been engulfed by fire and violence. To Ray, everything seems to be both happening and not happening, as if it were all a kind of unreal chaos.

"Ray."

"I'm trying to hear this."

"Ray."

Ray looks at Minus Five, who has clicked off the set. "What you doin'? They're showing stuff going on just a few blocks from here."

"You want to see it, take a walk. I'm gonna ask you one time, nice. Get your mangy ass the fuck outta here, and don't be bringing it back."

"I done for you, man. Cleaned this place, liberated your ass, everything."

Minus Five hoists a 12-gauge from underneath the register, then sits with it upright in his lap. "Mmm-hmm," he says, nodding.

Ray begins shuffling backwards. "I done things you wish you'd a done," he shouts. Shoulders bobbing, he takes another couple of steps, then spins and heads for the door. Before he reaches it, he one-eighties again. "I done things you ain't *dreamed* a doing!" Ray nods as he glides in reverse. Minus Five simply rests his face in the fingerless stump of his hand. Ray flicks a final, I'm-a-be-looking-for-you finger at him, then whirls out the door.

For a moment the street is a tonic. Low gray sky, smoke in the air. His spirits rise, released from Minus Five's contempt and the arcade's claustrophobic funk. An instant later he's deflated as confusion overtakes him once again, and he realizes how alone he is.

In the direction of the rioting, Ray sees pale spouts of smoke, vehicles the size of insects darting beneath them. Before he is even aware that he's moving, his feet are carrying him toward the scene. Bodies drift past him swiftly, some at a trot, some locked into a purposeful gait. No one speaks. In fact, few seem to know one another. Even the cars sail by in open-windowed silence, drawn forward as if by magnetic force. It's a pure, unfrenzied streaming, the answering of some hypnotic summons or enchantment. There is none of the street-party hysteria that fueled the sporadic, short-lived riots of his boyhood.

He remembers himself dressed in an oversized T-shirt, skinny legs sticking out of a pair of shorts, feet stuck inside unlaced high-tops as he carted off things he didn't need from an overrun restaurant supply store. Two dozen salt and pepper shakers, a case of corkscrews. All of which his grandmother made him return the moment he brought them home. On his way back he stopped to join a bus-toppling free-for-all. Climbing onto the overturned side of it with a tide of others, he jostled for position in order to stomp a window out of its casing. Someone cranked up a boom box to the point where the music's bass line and drumbeat became nothing but breeze-flogged distortion and everybody started dancing, right on top of the bus. A woman twice his twelve years patted him on the shoulder. When he turned, hips broader than his shoulders were already swaying, inches from his chest. Her legs seemed as long as his whole body, faded summer dress riding up her thighs, bare feet planted wide as she wagged her tail, screwing it down slow, palms caressing the insides of her legs as if she were a present to herself. A funky sweetness came off her, the scent snaking directly to Ray's crotch, a deeper sort of dance blooming there as she brushed against him. Then she was gone, spun away by some tattooed motherfucker in a tanktop. Short ponytail, grapefruit biceps, loco green eyes. He slipped a hand around the small of her back, put one thigh between hers, and ran his tongue from her breasts to the tip of her uptilted chin. Ray cruised to the next riot site as if strolling through a carnival, TV cameras covering it all. Although *he* couldn't seem to get noticed, his chant of "bring the hate" ignored by anchormen and film crews who kept shooing him away, concerned only with reeling off on-the-spot assessments and commentaries, packaging the chaos. . . .

This time there's something somber in the air. The event unfolds dutifully, as if there were no anger, no sense of release, because there is no hope. Ahead, a bonfire in the shape of a pyramid unspools coils of lush black smoke. A fuel tanker has been toppled and ignited, flames pooling around it. People creep near the fire's edge and light crude torches. Some of the men strip off their shirts and wrap them around lengths of pipe, which they use to ignite parked cars, storefronts, shabby three-story apartment buildings. The activity is deliberate, workman-like. Only the children seem excited, running along the fire's perimeter, playing tag with it. Ray feels he has drifted into a place of last rites, into the end of something.

Old people are being escorted from their houses. The invalid are carried in armchairs. One skeletal, white-haired man is borne down the steps of his apartment building on a cot, his IV stand trailing in the hands of a teenage girl. Torch bearers trot past him in the opposite direction. Moments later, smoke begins to eddy from the building's windows, draping the street with a dolorous incense. Burrowing through the odor of burning tires is the scent of something Ray can only conceive of as human. Not flesh, but possessions, the sadness of discarded things. In his head he sees neatly made beds, wall crucifixes, drawers full of folded socks. Eyeglasses, amber prescription bottles. Kitchen calendars and piles of newspapers. All of it swept away by fire. The frailty of small, impermanent things.

In the distance, a siren keens faintly and he looks to see where he is. He imagines his grandmother searching for him, her voice ghostly and helpless. Around him, buildings turn into walls of flame. People retreat, the street filling with bodies. A slow exodus gets under way. Women gather up children who are still looking for things to throw into the fire. Old souls on crutches work their way past the inferno's noise. Younger men walk ahead without glancing back. Nothing is taken, nothing rescued or carried away, the procession not a moving forward but a leaving behind, a severing and an end. Against the backdrop of this, Ray tries to make sense of his executions, but cannot. They seem shorn of meaning, fallen into the vacuum of history. Weightless and lost as he feels himself to be.

Overhead, a small cavalry of police helicopters appears, hovering in the rising waves of smoke. They float above him, eerily unthreatening, as if merely witnesses. Ray stops to watch them. Bodies bump against him, then rejoin the funeral march.

An instant later, he is running back past the fires. When a ratcheting drone slices through the noise, he looks over his shoulder and sees two helicopters riding the fire's crest in pursuit. The executions suddenly make sense again. He feels reconnected to something—time, hope, meaning. He's not sure. All he knows is that it feels good, it feels right, to be running, like Afroman. Down past the last burning building, Ray zips through an alleyway, reaches a high courtyard's parapet, vaults it and leaps. And for a moment before he vanishes, he's flying. . . .

Nick tugs on the door handle before the cab has even rolled to a complete stop, but it's locked tight. He's about to mention this to the dreadlocked driver whose head and shoulders are obscured by tumbling coils of ash-gray smoke when a voice booms out of the cab's rooftop loudspeaker.

"Twenty dollars, mon."

Ears ringing, Nick stares at the driver's window. "I said Criminal Court. That's eight blocks."

The guy takes another hit off a spliff, which has been rolled out of the morning's paper. The joint is so long Nick can make out part of the headline which, in the paper's tradition of photojournalistic brevity, is one word: "Apocalypse." Beside it, the daily misery index rises straight as a thermometer's mercury through zones marked suicidal, homicidal, kill everyone, total hell.

The cabbie releases the toke, then croaks, "Twenty-*five* dollars."

"What are these, riot rates?"

Nick watches the dude's dreadlocks sway as he nods his head.

A quick check of the plaza outside police headquarters reveals a wide net of deserted streets. Office towers and municipal buildings ring the square, but the familiar clutter of buses, trucks, and pedestrians is gone. Sidewalks stretch into the distance, lonely as condemned railroad tracks. A pair of police cars streaks along one of the avenues, their sirens filling the air. Others screech up out of the station's underground parking lot as the precinct house continues to lock down. Steel window shutters grind closed, artillery units take up rooftop posts. Not exactly the best place to flag another cab. Nick checks the driver's door and sees that of the dozen credit cards he accepts, two are among Nick's latest acquisitions. One issued by a pizza delivery conglomerate, the other a new venture by a heavy metal band that's diversifying.

"Twenty, and I get a hit off the joint."

Nick waits, watches the guy eye the streets and rearview mirror. A second later the lock buttons spring up.

Inside, Nick plucks the huge roach from the narrow opening in the bulletproof partition. He inhales, filling his throat and lungs with a sensation only slightly different from swallowing burning paper. Steering with one hand, the Rasta cabbie keeps his free hand extended, waiting for the spliff's return. Nick lets smoke burst from his lungs. Hoping to suck down another humongous hit before relinquishing the joint, he says, "So, seen any rioting?"

"Me take the spliff, mon."

"Mmm, mmm." Nick manages to squeeze out a few muted grunts after greedily inhaling a second blast. "Absolutely," he says, choking. "All yours." He leans forward and pushes the severely smoked-down doobie through the aperture, the joint no more than a long spindly ash. The cabbie's dark eyes glare at Nick in the rearview mirror. "Good stuff," Nick offers chummily, then claps the partition shut.

The pot opens dreamily inside him, his brain gradually turning into a jellyfish. The stuff must be warehouse grown, though. There was some organic fragrance missing when Nick raised the joss stick to his nostrils, some lack of the sunbred vividness he remembered from the dope highs of his youth. Today's crops were grown in abandoned waterfront storage space, and windowless aluminum garages near industrial parks tattooed with "For Rent" signs. Indoor sprinkler systems, banks of overhead "grow" lights. Nature as simulacrum. The high itself isn't all that bad. Yet something about it feels sterile, flavorless, distant, like phone sex. Nick is only technically high, high in the abstract. All the poetry of the experience is gone.

Then he considers that he simply may be getting old. He looks out the cab window at the emptied, dream-like streets and thinks, it's quiet here at the end of the world. The stoned cabbie, his driving in tune with the drug, allows the car to drift past stoplights, darkened shops and hotel lobbies, past posters advertising nirvana seminars, easy credit, and missing children. In other quarters of the city, apocalypse is in progress, signing on sponsors by the minute. But in this as-yet-untouched section of the city, this unmoved portion of Nick's soul, all is calm, if not bright.

His thoughts turn to money. Product, marketing plans, distribution, copyright. Nick finds enormous solace in money. On the great haphazard plane of man's inventions, he believes it to be on par with God. Pagan sacrifice, finance charges. Selling indulgences, thirty-year bonds. God's silence, money talks. If we can sell salvation, why not merchandise apocalypse?

Nick stares out the window. Dumpster trash and a few ragged nomads pushing their possessions in shopping carts appear. His mind drifts. He imagines himself being interviewed on television. He speaks with great authority. About what, he has no idea. But that's alright. The world's paying attention. He is photographed rushing from limousines into posh award-ceremony lobbies, mega-blond ingenues on his arm. He is seen with rock stars, movie idols, hip political candidates. He is rich, famous, one of the elect. He has seen the horror and marketed it.

A fine grim mist begins to fall, fire ash swooping lightly down from the skyscraper tops to settle along the curbstones and rat warrens and the grates of overflowing sewers, a snow for the dead. Nick ignores it. Or, rather, feels soothed by it, as if it were a sort of requiem. For his soul is in the throes of a vision so sublime, so omni-everything—not to mention lucrative—that it seems to be the word of God.

Immediately, he is on his portaphone, ringing through to an ex-friend, law school colleague, and person to whom Nick himself readily admits he (a) owes seven thousand dollars, and (b) is no longer on speaking terms with: Gates Remington III.

The cab swings onto the wide promenade leading to Criminal Court. Past the steady ticking of the windshield wipers, their blades sweeping aside a thickening flurry of ashes, Nick sees a radical increase in activity. But not of the usual sort. The "smart drug" and gyro vendors who normally occupy the large square across from the columned justice hall are absent this morning, their chrome pushcarts and bright umbrellas nowhere to be seen. Even the homemade brownie stands and strolling dope peddlers have taken a holiday, as have the Krishna revelers and Moonies, the legions of faith healers and guitar-toting troubadours, the runaways, the tattoo artists and petition pushers, the free-lance ecologists, independent political candidates, fortune tellers, stand-up comics, and retired CIA spooks. Even the New Age string quartet which banned Mozart from its repertoire because its members felt he was codependent. The entire muddle-headed circus, in other words. Only the pigeons have chosen to hang around, perched on the ledges of the court's bas relief eaves, cooing, fluffing their wings occasionally, shitting with abandon.

A herding and sorting process seems to be taking shape. Police barricades have been laid out like cattle pens. Each chute funnels into an entrance to the building's underground holding cells. Riot vans, army personnel transports, and city buses commandeered by the urban crisis wing of the force form a long line at the far end of the square. Horse-mounted sentries patrol the area, mirrored shades and white helmets turning their heads into industrial-age death masks. Prisoners step out of the vehicles, hands on their heads, then are directed down chutes by a figure standing atop a patrol car. He is wearing black Special Operations garb, and motions left and right with a riding crop.

For a moment Nick thinks it might be a drug vision, hallucination as news clip. Only there are, oddly, no cameras around. That's a first. Also, the Rasta cabbie is saying, "This is as far as I go, mon," obviously not liking the colonial look of things up ahead. So Nick has to be seeing what he's seeing. Unless . . . he and the cabbie are *sharing* a hallucination. Or, spookier still, it's *history* as collective hallucination.

Which seems possible when the answering machine message begins flowing through Nick's cellular phone. "You have reached the offices of Snuff Productions, where we're in business to make a killing. No one is able to take your call. . . ."

The company is the brainchild of Gates Remington III, onetime entertainment lawyer whose career tanked after it was revealed that he had made sex slaves of his all-nymphet pop-vocal group, Unfondled Booty. Despite a billion dollars in recording revenues, various stages of emotional trauma, drug addiction, and psychosis caused the band to go beavers up. Fleeing the public's backlash, Gates went underground, producing triple-X-rated mock documentaries of serial killers, sex crime offenders, satanic cults, dungeons and dragons fetishists, Asian prostitute farmers—anything he could sell as cinema verité laden with S&M, bondage, torture chamber sex. Porn as investigative telejournalism. Most of the material turned up on the videocassette black market. Until. . . .

An "alternative" cable station with a subscription audience of sixty million featured Snuff/Remington on its weekly "Most Wanted" spot. During it Gates suggested, between film clips, that the pop culture leave behind its didactic/voyeuristic/neurotic attachment to "dramatized or simulated" death, and reembrace the themes of actual pagan sacrifice found in classical antiquity. Dionysus got a mention. Then he screened *Black Virgin: A Puritan Romance,* in which a telemarketer-cum-sorceress is "tried" by a small New England town's city council members, then taken to a football field, tied naked to a goal post, and set aflame. The next day Gates was offered lecture invitations; visiting professorships in film, TV, sexual archetype studies, and cultural criticism; book contracts; talent agency representation; and of course an eight-figure development deal with the alternative cable station's parent network, XXN.

So, with Gatesian products selling quite well, Nick is less worried about Snuff's lingering reputation for sleaze than he is about having his call returned. Hence, his to-the-point message after the beep.

"Gate-man! Nick Wolf."

The cab slides to the curb a block from the courthouse. Eyeing the detainees being herded into chutes, the cabbie raps on the bulletproof divider panel.

"Okay, okay." Nick presses the phone's mouthpiece to his breast. He fishes out his heavy metal credit card and inserts it in the taxi's "payment verification" slot, then puts the receiver to his ear again.

"Don't fast-forward over this. I'm calling to repay my debt—with interest. Also, to expand your tele-empire and already well-deserved reputation as a media genius."

Credit card and receipt are ejected, door lock buttons leap up. The cabbie's dreadlocks snap violently toward the door, his voice rising in some indecipherable Creole patois which Nick, noticing a cop on horseback approaching, decodes as—get the fuck out.

" 'Nother call, gotta go. Call me. I have major product." He leaves his number, then bolts out of the cab, phone and briefcase in hand.

Standing on the street, his limbs feel about as firm as rubber-bands from the pot. He hears the taxi squeal away behind him in reverse. Nick smiles at the cop coming toward him, wondering if his hair is combed, his tie on straight. Also, if he should perhaps pet the trooper's horse, as a gesture of goodwill, when he gets close enough. But with the clip-clop of hooves bearing down on him, Nick is blessed with a momentary lapse into rational thought. Never get intimate with another man's quadruped. Luckily, he is neither too stoned nor too dumb to appreciate the biblical pithiness of this. He is also only passingly concerned with the incarceration process taking place in the square. After all, it's not him. So, rather than saying nice horsey, he simply stops when he can see his reflection in the trooper's mirrored shades, and flashes—along with his trademark grin—some official ID.

"Rough morning." Nick brushes the air in front of his face,

then glances at the sky. The flurry of ashes seems denser, the sun cool and pale as a nickel. Smoke caterpillars across the horizon, spreading into great towering washes of gray. In the high distance, police helicopters circle steadily, cordoning off the square's airspace it seems.

When Nick looks back at the cop, he sees his Death-by-Osmosis credit card dangling disdainfully from the trooper's fingertips. "You're probably looking for something more judicial," Nick says, smile withering. He searches his pockets, comes up with his courthouse pass, and hands it over. While it's being studied, Nick slips a peek past the horse's rump. National Guard troops nudge bodies forward in the chutes with the ends of rifle barrels. "Mind if I ask what's going on?"

The trooper extends Nick's ID between two fingers. "Don't get a conscience."

Nick retakes his pass lightly. "I wasn't considering it."

"I wouldn't think so." The horse bucks its head, and half-turns restlessly. Reins in his black-gloved hands, the cop checks the animal. "Stay off the street. And that's not advice." The horse dancing underneath him, he watches Nick a moment longer, then sweeps the reins back toward the square, and spurs the horse's flanks.

"Fuckhead," Nick whispers. He stares at the maze of rapidly filling chutes. With more transports pulling up, Guardsmen move bodies faster from street level into the cells. Nick flicks the edge of his courthouse pass, darkly thoughtful, then heads for the statue-bounded doors of the hall, fire ash falling steadily now, choppers gliding through the metallic sky like black angels. . . .

Inside, past metal detectors and bomb search crews, up the wide marble stairwell thronging with fast-moving swarms of paramilitary types, Nick spies some kind of computer tracking center being set up in one of the indictment rooms. He isn't able to stop or get too close though. A sentry glares at him, which keeps him walking smartly.

His office is no calmer. Only half the crew seems to have shown up to defend the indigent public today. Phones skirl but go unanswered. At desks, APDs scribble furiously, dashing off courtroom notes, plea bargain options, acceptable jail term limits, bail bond amounts. They fling sheet after sheet into great stacks of paper held in trays marked "Go," "Hold," "Hopeless," "Fucked."

The department head's voice rips through the overhead intercom speakers, summoning assistants to his office where a meeting is in progress. Nick hears muffled shouts coming from behind its glass walls as he steals a glance at the proceedings, then presses on, head down. There's a last-days-in-the-bunker attitude, not to mention a lot of work to be done, sweeping through the place, two things Nick would just as soon avoid.

"Wolf!" a voice cries out, full of surprise and—yes, even though it's Nick—something that sounds like a renewal of hope, a cavalry-arriving joy.

"Got someone waiting," Nick calls over his shoulder, his stride lengthening. In fact, it's all he can do to keep from breaking into an all-out sprint. He hooks around a corner, down another stretch of corridor, not even sure who it was he blew off.

The bustle recedes as he approaches his cubicle which, like everything else in his life, is as far from the epicenter of responsibility as he can get it. Stacks of transfiles, abandoned painting scaffolds, and rolls of carpet have to be dodged to reach his doorway, which he has adorned with signs reading "Wrong Way," "Go Back," and "Achtung," although few of his colleagues and, happily, none of his bosses ever make it back to this still-under-construction wing of the office to heed their warnings.

He quickly slips into his cubbyhole, kicking unrecycled bottles out of his way, sweeping notes, case files, and office memos from the seat of his chair. He swings his briefcase onto the scattered heaps of CD cases, empty cigarette packs, floppy disks, and additional paperwork that mask his desk top, then drops into the chair, wishing he had an office door to close. He is trying to do three things at once—light a cigarette, find the rocks glass he wants desperately to pour three fingers of Scotch into, and program his various phone lines to direct the return call from Gates Remington to him—when his assistant Dan turns up in the doorway.

"You could have said hello as you streaked past."

"And you can drop the passive-aggressive, I'm-a-victim approach which, if I gave a shit, would piss me off." Nick locates the glass in his "Urgent" file, then douses its insides with Scotch.

"You're going to kill yourself."

Nick pulls the smoke from his lips, lifts the glass and drinks. He tosses his head back and swallows some of the Scotch. Alcohol vapors float up through his nostrils, soothing his brain. He exhales, then opens his eyes. The ceiling streams by as if he were the still-point of a carouseling world. Then it stops, blank and unpromising, and the sensation of pointless, purposeless motion—life—descends on him. He breathes deeply, then sits forward, sets the glass down, and takes up the telephone.

"You're also going to miss your eleven o'clock in juvey."

"First of all"—Nick punches buttons on the phone's handset, instructing the unit to "select forward," "page," "identa ring," "prioritize," and basically just find his ass whenever the call from Snuff Productions comes in—"I can't kill myself. There is no death, only insufficient capital. And two: You're right. I am going to miss my eleven in juvey. Fax our apologies. Claim riot fatigue and ask for a reschedule. Also, mention that if there were a waiting period to buy guns—say of, oh, twenty years—we wouldn't have a pre-teen mass murderer to prosecute in the first place. 'Be indignant,' like the T-shirt slogan says. Those in power respond to that."

Nick dials a number then says, "Detective McKuen, please. He's gone? Well could you—well do you—?" He curses, hangs up, slips the portaphone back into its recharger holster, pours another hit of Scotch, then spins in his chair.

Today, Dan's teased, shoulder-length hair is brittle as stir-fried rice noodles. The earrings Nick has seen before, but the gold nostril hoop is new. As are the tattoos. A fan of one-phrase worldviews, Dan's latest body copy reads: "Don't Date Rape, Date Men." "Penis Fuehrer." "Modernation Sucks." "XXN or Death." Nick admires their idiocy-with-an-attitude witlessness. It's cool to stand for something you can't articulate, yet can be summed up in under five words. Nick despairs over the fact that, who knows, if his own IQ had been sixty points lower, he might have become something. A raging success, rather than simply raging, waiting around for a porn-mogul TV slut like Gates Remington to return his call.

Dan, on the other hand, just might be one-dimensional enough to become famous. He's telegenic and weightless. Captivating as a good ad. Who needs meaning, after all, if you can have constant sensation? And who, if he is capable of asking this kind of question, could ever shape a marketing idea simplistic enough to pitch to a TV exec? Thinking limits one's commercial possibilities.

Dan reveals a paper bag marked Psycho Bagel, which he has hidden behind his back. To it, he has taped a red bow. Erotic smirk on his face, he dangles the goodie beyond Nick's reach. If we're all equally lost, Nick thinks, at least Dan is still capable of falling in love. What, beyond addiction, am I capable of?

"Beg."

Nick waves him away. "I'm not hungry." He unlocks his desk drawer and hauls out a nine-inch television.

"Here." Dan drops the gift-wrapped bag on Nick's desk.

"I thought you'd never give in." Nick tears the paper apart and dumps out the deluxe caviar-cream-cheese bagel.

Dan strokes Nick's hair lightly. "Glad you got here alright."

Nick brushes the boy's hand away. "Don't go soap opera on me. Sit down and tell me what's going on."

He bites off a hunk of bagel, then flips on the television. The woman who could change his life, and possibly even alter his drinking habits, is standing there in front of a nationwide weather map. Katrina Quimquerelle, pseudo-meteorologist and exercise-doyenne-of-the-week, is wearing a lace bodysuit, high heels, earrings, and, well, that's it. Despite the regional forecasts—yucky, hellish, acid rain showers, go-out-and-die—Nick's penis throbs. Local weather activity calls for high winds that will fan the riot fires. The *good* news is that the smoke plumes enveloping the city are blocking out ultraviolet radiation, thereby downgrading the metropolis from "immediate skin cancer zone" status.

Mouth full, Nick mumbles, "What's with the *mach schnell* business outside in the square?"

"We're in riot mode. No stops at police stations for booking or bond hearings. Arrestees are being brought here directly for arraignment."

Nick looks away from the TV. "Arraignment for what?"

Dan leans on a file cabinet that Nick hasn't had the key to in so long the lock has rusted shut. "Whatever. Mass arrests, mass lock-ups, mass arraignments."

Nick nods. "I like it. The fast food approach to insurrection. Can't produce jobs, we'll mass-produce criminals." He takes another bite of the bagel. "So, what are we doing about it?"

"We?"

Nick hesitates before switching TV channels to cast a glance at his assistant, this one not so friendly.

"They're having a meeting about it now."

"Anybody looking for me?"

"Creditors have taken the day off."

"You're not fitting my definition of funny. I mean around here."

"Please. Did you see the kid McKuen's holding?"

"Why do you think I just called McKuen? Yes, I saw the kid. Yes, I asked McKuen to send him over. And yes I'm pissed because now how the fuck am I ever going to find him in this mess?"

"You want me to try downstairs?" Dan picks up the phone.

Nick eats restlessly, staring at the tube. "Yeah, sure. Give 'em a call."

While Dan tries to reach the underground holding pens, Nick watches the changing TV images. Riots, riots, panel discussions of the riots, cartoons, and the number-one-rated soap, *The Young and the Well Hung.*

A stud with a pair of tube socks stuffed inside the crotch of his bicycling shorts listens to a sobbing, mid-forties sexpot. It seems her shrimp farming business has been stolen by her husband and the company's sultry head aquaculturist, who in actuality is an industrial spy for an international biotechnology consortium, as well as a member of Feminists Against the Exploitation of Shellfish. He undoes the lace bow of her negligee as the gas fireplace flickers. "I've got popcorn in the microwave," she protests weakly. A moment later she's on the futon, caressing the top of his crash helmet.

Meanwhile, a bottom-of-the-screen bulletin announces that special, not-to-be-seen-anywhere-else riot footage will be available on Pay-per-View later in the day on XXN.

Nick's heart plunges. He imagines Gates Remington, a person he considers less intelligent than himself, cashing in on apocalypse. Licensing, movie deals, product tie-ins—the whole godless enchilada. "Fuck."

Dan holds the phone aside. "What's wrong?"

"Fuck!" Nick frantically searches his pockets, looking for McKuen's card. On the back of it is the name of the kid he's supposed to be defending, representing, exploiting—whatever. "God dammit!" Nick leaps from his seat and strips off his suit jacket. He turns it inside out and fingers the lining's pockets.

"No answer," Dan says, hanging up.

Nick tosses the jacket into a corner, then pops his briefcase open. He flings aside court files, unpaid bills, mail order catalogs, packets of unused, hope-laden condoms. The booze is not so much clouding his thoughts at this point as it is accelerating them, producing a kind of alcoholic psychosis.

"What the hell *is it?!*"

Nick suddenly stops rifling through his things and stands upright. He faces Dan, inordinately calm. "What is it?" he says softly. "It's my fucking life. I hate my fucking life. I am tired of *understanding* everything and *accomplishing* nothing!" He suddenly isn't so calm anymore. "I'm tired of being better off than most, but feeling sorry for myself because that isn't good enough!"

Nick picks up a CD case from his desk and heaves it at the wall outside his cubicle, where it splinters and flies apart.

"I'm conflicted," he says, his voice suddenly light again, bemused, his body at ease. It's as if he's stumbled onto some lovely and inconsequential insight. He presses his fingertips to his chest. "That's it. I'm not crazed. I haven't lost anything, like my mind." He stares at Dan, who looks at the floor. "It's just that sometimes I can't *balance* meaninglessness, horror, and dying with my role as an aging, baby-boom consumer. With my *expectations*. So I think . . . I don't know. Maybe if I made some money off my nihilism. Maybe if I could emcee or co-produce the apocalypse. Maybe then I'd be whole and unconflicted, a fully realized McCitizen. Someone you, as my assistant, would be proud to lie under oath for.''

Nick moves toward his chair, voice softening as it drops into a darker register.

"Only, now I can't remember the name of the kid I'm trying to fuck over. McKuen isn't going to give it to me. And the one sleazy motherfucker who could be my ticket out of this shithole isn't going to return my fucking phone call.''

Nick falls into his chair, then stares up at Dan. "So, you have to ask 'what is it'? Well. If I haven't made myself perfectly clear, let me know. Because in that case, I'll go out and get some *flash cards* when the malls reopen.''

He exhales. His limbs ache, his midsection is soft and bloated. There doesn't seem to be a bright thought or toned muscle in his body. He feels spent, as if he's just come, only without any sense of having rocketed into a state of peace.

He lets his eye fall on the television. The soap opera image fades, half the screen going black. The other half shows footage of a mobile camera streaking past fire, exploded glass, tanks rolling up city streets. Troops engage in small skirmishes along the sidewalks. Then apocalypse fades to grainy black void. . . .

Next image: beneficent blue sky, ocean water beckoning like liquid heaven. Rakish hair and name-brand wet suit gleaming, a vision of male perfection surfs at heart-racing speed, sixties pop music playing on the soundtrack.

Feeling undone by his own meanness and regret, Nick does something unusual. He switches the set off. There's a sudden deadness around him. Closing his eyes, he spins weightlessly through darkness. Off, on. Immanence, image. All distinctions are gone, all limits and bounds with them. It is all a plummeting nothingness. He surrenders to his sense of drift, wishing only that he could remember what it felt like to fall in love, to have there be a limit to his own nothingness that he could touch. . . .

"Are you finished?" Dan asks.

"Yes, I'm finished."

"Then look at your phone recharger sleeve."

Nick opens his eyes, curiosity burning in him softly as a pilot light. He sees Dan staring at him firmly, arms crossed. Nick glances at his desk.

Tucked inside the portaphone's specially designed business card pouch is—guess what?—McKuen's business card. Right where Nick placed it so he wouldn't lose it and then have to turn into a raving lunatic, a role to which, he has to admit, he is readily disposed. He extrudes the card from the transparent pocket and studies it, flipping it between his fingertips. "Darren Adams a.k.a. 'Inch' " is scribbled on the back side. Nick taps the card lightly on the paperwork covering his desk, then looks up at Dan.

"I suppose I'm supposed to feel chastened."

Dan ignores him.

Nick looks back at the card, taps it a few more times. Then someone is climbing over construction materials, ignoring Nick's *verboten* signs, tripping and falling too, which isn't good. Some of the self-righteous moral authority of the mission to find and upbraid Nick is undermined as the guy curses wildly. In the doorway, brushing his pants legs, is Harley von Vaughn, onetime hall monitor, captain of the debate team, winner of his alma mater's "Biggest Wuss" award, and lifelong political wannabe who, given his pedigree, ambition, and net worth, deserves the more accurate title of "willbe."

Nick looks at Harley and thinks, he's Waspier than me, if that's genetically possible. He knows that Harley's tenure in the Public Defender's Office is a calculated, temporary one, a bit of résumé padding. Two years' service. Out into the private sector at twenty-eight. Kazillionaire at thirty-five. Senator at thirty-six.

In his wingtips, pinstriped pants, crisp white shirt, and mallard-duck-patterned tie, Harley does at times strike Nick as his soulless double. The anti-Nick, dweeb leader of the forces of hypocrisy. Not that Nick is holding himself up as any kind of role model. Alcoholic, morally bankrupt, possessor of overdue videocassettes, he's a kind of human toxic waste. Yet he believes that since he's at least *able* to appreciate his own odiousness, he's intrinsically "better" than Harley von Vaughn, who can't. Despite this, or possibly because of it, here he is at thirty-eight, stuck in the power-grabbing world he can neither shake nor conquer.

"Wolf."

"Sterling entrance there, von." Nick shoots a glance at Dan, hoping for conspiratorial appreciation. A smirk, at least. But the kid is still scowling.

"Well if you'd clean this place up."

"Struggle is good for the soul, Har."

"How would you know?"

"Ah, there's that acid wit again."

"Believe me, I don't even want to have to talk to you. They told me you were here, I figured it was a sick joke. But I imagine the world looks pretty much the same to you every morning anyway."

Turning McKuen's card between his fingertips, Nick stares at von Vaughn. He resents the energy he puts into despising pod-people like him. They're everywhere, turning the act of being groundlessly proud of themselves into a crusade.

"I'm here to fight for truth and justice, Har. I flipped on the TV this morning—actually it was on when I woke up—took one look, and said, 'Nick, the city needs you.' "

"Like a hole in the head."

"You're just on a regular roll, aren't you? How does it feel to have your brain out of mothballs?"

"I'm glad you think this is funny. Do you have the slightest conception of what's going on?"

"No, Har, I don't. Enlighten me."

Von Vaughn casts a shifty glance Dan's way, and before he can look back Wolfie is on his feet.

"Could it be the further consolidation of ruling-class power through paramilitary actions? The thought that these riots might be a way of eradicating an entire class of undesirables I find riveting. Please continue." Nick paces in a small circle, ranting at the ceiling. "The last gasp of an empire, imperialism coming home to roost. The final unraveling of Jeffersonian doubt. 'All men are created equal'—*almost*. Fascinating! Prophetic! The stuff talk shows are made of!" Nick stops inches from von Vaughn and looks at him. "I never realized what a deep thinker and caustic social critic you were, Har. It's amazing what an idiotic facade can hide."

"You're insane," von Vaughn says, softly.

"No? Really? Damn." Nick turns back to his desk. "If you're done"—he whisks the air dismissively with one hand—"I have clients to ignore, judges to annoy, work to slough off."

"You're in Arraignment Room 4 as of now, or you're history."

Nick looks at von Vaughn. "Harley," he says politely, "get the fuck out of my life."

Von Vaughn remains in the doorway a moment. Nick picks up his phone and dials. When he looks back, his co-worker is gone.

"Yeah, Chief? Christian Wolf." Nick pauses while his name is repeated with surprise, one might almost say astonishment. "Yup. Just wanted to say I'm here, I think this is outrageous, and I'm with you two hundred percent on everything. Say the word, give the order, I'm there."

Nick lights a smoke, then turns so he can see Dan. "No, I'm not full of shit. I've seen the light. It's taken Armageddon, but I've seen the error of my ways." Nick inhales. "Arraignment Room 4? I'm there. The instant we hang up, I'm there. Just one-on-one'd with von Vaughn about it. But frankly, and I think this is important—the guy's insane. We're all dealing with stress here, but he's not handling it. As a friend, I don't want to see the man go down. He's a good man. But I also don't want to see *our* efforts jeopardized. So if you could talk to him, straighten him out. . . ."

Nick watches Dan's head swivel in disbelief. "Yeah, gotta run here, too. Ar-4, abso— This is not *sudden* concern. It's *ongoing* con— Okay, yeah. Hey, we're on the same wavelength again. For that, I'm happy. Go to work, exactly. See y—"

Nick pauses, then clicks off the phone, pockets it, and takes a drag on his smoke. He looks over his desk, feeling that he needs to take something else with him, but he can't remember what. He's always forgetting things.

"You're losing it," Dan says.

"I've lost it. And you know what? I don't care if I ever find it again." He turns and meets Dan's gaze. "You're talking again. I take it I'm forgiven."

"Would it matter to you if you weren't?"

"No."

"I didn't think so. But I love you anyway."

"Good. Then help me fuck some people over so I can—hopefully, please God—make some money. Try to reach McKuen again. Find out where this kid Adams is. He's supposed to be downstairs—now. I'm going to look. Two: prep bail papers. He's coming in on Rob-1—"

"I thought they wanted him for the cop killing."

Nick heads out of the cubicle. Dan follows. They high-step over rolled carpeting, duck under scaffolding. "They do want him for

1 3 0

the cop killing. Rob-1 is horseshit. But they can't hold him on the other thing. If they do, they have to make a case for it.'' Nick stops and turns. "They don't *have* a case for it.''

He swoops back into forward motion, cruising under a ladder, as always, to tempt bad luck. He figures that his, the city's, the entire love-lost world's can't get any worse.

"I don't know who McKuen's after. *McKuen* doesn't know who McKuen's after. But this kid hasn't killed anybody. They hold him on conspiracy, gang laws, accessory to murder—what's that get them?" Nick comes to a crossroads in the hallway and stops. "Nothing. It means that under the 'Rosario' law they have to give *me* every document *they* have to prosecute the case. You think they want me to know what they know? This whole thing,'' he whispers, sweeping that all-including hand again, "is about secrecy, conspiracy, consolidation of power. And you know what? McKuen is probably the only one who's really *after* somebody. Why? Because he believes it will *mean* something if he catches him. What's going on downstairs, outside, and on the tube. That's what means something.''

Nick turns and begins walking again. "McKuen only sees a small part of the picture. If he charges this kid, he tips his hand. Word gets out—and it will get out—where is he then? His trial's gone. Discordia Sect? Forget it, gone. Coda . . . ? Yeah, right. Good luck.''

They come to a halt in front of a bulletin board. ADAs and secretaries scramble past them, racing down the corridor between the office's power centers. Nick puts a fingertip to Dan's chest. "And who told us Coda exists? Who's given us the Discordia Sect?''

He pauses to watch Dan puzzle it out. "I don't buy that this is a conspiracy,'' Dan says quietly.

Nick spies a TV left on in someone's cubicle. Riot scenes continue to play themselves out, less dramatic in daylight.

"It's just too simple," Dan adds.

"Of course. There's no ultimate conspiracy. Conspiracy implies hidden truth. A single or central truth." Nick's face swivels slightly. "Doesn't exist. There's the marketable manipulation of various truths. . . . And watching. Being tuned in. This." He turns Dan toward the TV. "Executions. Revolution. Rap-apocalypse. It's diversion, surface. Power *always* moves behind what's seen. Trust me, I know these things. I have WASP bloodlines. You want *one* truth? 'The medium is the message.'" He holds up his hands, thumbs and index fingers forming the corners of an imaginary box, a small television. "Our vision is this big. We look at every-thing—city, world, history—through this. Our peephole." Nick lowers his hands. "That's the message. That's the single truth . . . of the moment. Is this bad? No. *It is.*" He turns to the bulletin board, scanning the arraignment court roster that's been posted, checking for his name. "Now I just have to cash in on it."

McKuen has never been a fan of low ceilings. Or the dark for that matter, either. Any dim, cramped space. A holding cell, tene-ment hallways. VC tunnels. Endless snaking mazes beneath vil-lages, sniper nests, and abandoned command posts. Crawling through VC labyrinths, the dark so close it ate up the dim ray of his army-issue flashlight with predatory swiftness, he'd fire his pis-tol straight ahead into whatever it was he couldn't see. Everything inside the flashlight's slim field of illumination was the remains of the vanished or the dead. Spent shell casings, grenade fragments.

Maggots feasting on unidentifiable strips of flesh, bits of bone. Shit. Petrified if Charlie was long gone, moist ripe piles the few times McKuen and company, a.k.a. Zulu 7 on militarized zone radio bands, got a little too close unexpectedly. And oh yeah, blood. He could always count on finding that. Long swaths of it that he would drag himself over, just as the one who had bled dragged himself, or was dragged, over the same stretch of relentless maze. But never a body. It was as if he were chasing ghosts, shadows. His own fears.

Here in the sub-basement headquarters of Special Operations below City Hall, he at least has some headroom. The concrete corridors are poorly lit, but the black tile flooring gives the complex a dance bar's ambiance—end-of-the-world bunker as party pad. Murals depicting the city's pastoral beginnings brighten the walls. Rolling pastureland, the cheerful bustle of the mini-metropolis, white church spires and redbrick smokestacks rising into what then was limitless blue sky.

The Chaos Room, which McKuen is given clearance to enter in order to check out the electronic intelligence map of the city before heading out into the streets, is brushstroked by deep shadows. Police clerks work in the sickly light of computer stations, headphones on. The data they enter instantly light up areas of the map that hovers across the room. Moving into the center of its delicate webwork, riot-indicator lights flashing around his dark shape as chaos spreads through the city, is Special Ops Commander Eschata himself, much-whispered-about riding crop in hand.

It's only the second time McKuen has seen him, Eschata's presence in the department as elusive and legendary as it is to the public. In ghettos around the city many claim to have seen him circling the streets and rooftops at night, black wings spread like a revelation. McKuen doesn't believe or disbelieve the myth. Not after nights in-country when, wet to the bone from fear sweats and rain, visions whirled about him in the black air above the hillsides, VC voices echoing in the bush. He'd turned entire hamlets into bonfire and ashes with a few flicks of his Zippo lighter; summoned Valkyries to char and defoliate acres of jungle merely by the sound of his own walkie-talkied voice. After the night he sprung from a camouflage of underbrush, his M-1 flickering, and wasted five VC, he felt their spirits twist up out of their corpses like genie smoke from a magic lantern, then flutter past him, *through* him—cold and lonely as the last breath in the world. After that firefight, leading Zulu 7 through Pinkville, Tre Banh, My Lai 4, the words "Born to Kill" scrawled on his helmet, dink lore spread the news of his comings and goings, his mercies and wrath. They named him "the Black Angel." Him, McKuen—a myth. So when he hears in barbershops or reads in the barrio's daily underground paper tales of Special Ops Commander Eschata's dark visitations, he rolls with them. Truth has levels way beyond daylight logic. And McKuen has found that, at night, he can believe almost anything.

He looks once more at the grid. It's marked by a six-digit code, the same coordinates system he'd seen in Nam. When he locates his sector, he backtracks his path to Special Ops. Some red lights here and there to indicate street skirmishes, but no concentrated activity. The spookiest kind of stuff. Now you see 'em, now you don't.

In a halo of computer terminal light McKuen spots a recognizable face. Someone he knew vaguely from a stint years ago with PDID—Public Disorder Intelligence Division. Keeping tabs on terrorist groups, mostly. Subversive activities, arms trading. After he moved on, the division got into gangs, cults, all the bad boys of the city. What PDID had on line, no one else had access to.

McKuen gives the guy a moment to place his name, then says it for him.

"Right. McKuen." The microphone arm curled across the guy's face moves up and down as he nods.

"Can I get a check on Sector 247365, and the route between here and there?" McKuen doesn't offer a reason to fill the ensuing silence, though he can see the guy would like one. Instead, he puts a small scratchpad beside the monitor. On it is Darren Adams's address. "The apartment, too. And the kid's gang profile."

The guy removes his fingers from the keyboard and sits back. "You know what you'd have to ante up to some hacker to get in here?"

McKuen remains silent, not offering a deal.

The techie grudgingly calls up the info he wants.

McKuen studies the blueprint of Darren Adams's building, a projects complex named Aslam A Lakem Downs. Several adjacent twenty-story buildings surrounding a huge courtyard. Darren Adams's first-floor apartment is two rooms plus a bath. As the floor plan rotates, McKuen spots a glitch, or blank spot, in one of the apartment walls. He didn't notice anything like that earlier in the day when he picked up the boy. "What's that? Back up."

The guy brushes data input keys with his fingertips and images tumble in reverse. On-screen type reads, "Thank you for using software by XXN." Then the glitch reappears and the guy enlarges it.

It's located on a wall adjacent to the apartment next door. McKuen leans in for a close look, searching for irregularities. He knows PDID gathers this info from two sources: low-income-housing files, and helicopter reconnaissance photos. A draftsman's error or speck of dirt on the camera lens could yield a spot in the image.

"Got anything else on this?"

The tapping of a key brings up another labyrinthine database. A second tap sends the cursor hurtling at hyperspeed through the binary maze. What it yields is a ghost of the building. Shoals of shadowy black walls, fissures in them evanescent as halos.

"X-ray." The clerk peels away the image to reveal a second image. "Heat X-ray. We'll be CAT-scanning by helicopter next."

McKuen eyes the enlargement. Same glitch, same spot. Though now he sees two bodies seated opposite one another in the room, each extending an arm. The image darkens intensely where their hands meet, indicating heat. Something's being smoked. Beside the figures are rifles. McKuen realizes he could be looking at a recon photo of VC sharing a cigarette, terrorists in any city from here to Belfast, or any two grunts from Zulu 7 smoking a joint between barrages of incoming mortar fire. All the bunkers and foxholes have come home.

"Got anything on the place next door?"

Address entered, the adjacent apartment lays itself out on the monitor. "Same deal. Nice and friendly."

"What's that on the floor? Beneath the bed." McKuen is accustomed to finding through-the-wall escape hatches. Gun and drug runners know they're good things to keep handy. But this looks like a trapdoor. An opaque, black rectangle. The computer hack enlarges it.

"Lead. If it's X-ray unfriendly, it's lead. So you want a guesstimate? Whatever you're looking for you're going to find in that basement."

"Who lives in the place?"

Telephone and address registers are run through the system; welfare, SSI, unemployment, and food stamp rolls culled and checked.

"A single woman, Odessa Roberts. Clean, supposedly."

"Uh-huh." McKuen wonders what's beneath the trapdoor. The makings of a counter or anti-city? Or was that clown Wolf right?

There is no on/off, no opposites. If there is a hidden city snaking through an endless underground maze, it's an extension of the city above. "You have either of these buildings red-flagged for anything?"

"I'm looking." Surveillance data scroll up across the monitor's face. Raids, arrests. Mostly narco busts; the kid's playscape handles some heavy drug traffic. All in all, intelligence has a neat little history of Aslam A Lakem Downs. "Some gang powwows, all attended by us undercover. Nothing you're looking for."

"What am I looking for?"

"Terrorist cliques. Sects. Well-financed revolutionaries."

"That so?"

The guy nods. "But you think they'd exist without us knowing about them? You think they'd be here without *him* knowing about them?" He raises his head in Special Ops Commander Eschata's direction.

McKuen looks up and sees the commandant's silhouette. He has moved from the riot grid into the light of a floor-to-ceiling television screen, his shadow embraced by aerial visions of the now-firestormed city. He waves one hand at the screen and the image shifts as a camera descends, silent and invisible as an angel, into the maelstrom.

"Believe me, if this was organized, we'd know about it."

McKuen finds himself wondering if this is the secret meaning of information. Distinctions cease, lines blur. Simulacrum is actuality, dreams are logic.

As Special Ops Commander Eschata leaves behind the televised city's heatless inferno, his shaved skull briefly fixes McKuen with a look as impersonal as a camera lens. Then he's gone, the city burning in his wake. . . .

"Give me the kid's profile, blues of the buildings, everything," McKuen says.

"Whatever." The guy shrugs.

Armed with his tiny piece of the puzzle, McKuen sails out of the Chaos Room, feeling as weightless as the shadows that flicker around him.

Rising through the spiraling underground tunnel, the car's radio crackles, static whispering in the dark. On the street, McKuen swings toward the D.A.'s wing of the complex, going past buses unloading handcuffed people. Ahead, tanks are spread out across the wide boulevard where a checkpoint has been set up. As he glides in its direction, the car's radio automatically scans FM airwaves, now that there are signals to zero in on. It alights on a station announcing that the day's number-one call-in request is Coda's "Hate Funk Jam." Rumors of an any-minute release of his full-length CD can't be confirmed, but if one materializes XXN is going to be the first to have it, so . . . stay tuned. . . .

Coming alongside the checkpoint's sentry box, his police band signal is cleared and over it a voice asks for ID. A digital plaque on the sentry box flashes "Insert Identification Clearance Card Here." Extending his ID tab, he watches cameras mounted on the checkpoint's roof record his movements. He wonders who, besides the sentries, is watching him. How deep *is* the camera's reach? After seeing the files PDID had on line, he wouldn't try to put a limit on it.

Ahead of him, a chute bounded by high corrugated-metal walls curves away from the boulevard toward the plaza.

"You're here to pick up who?" The voice leaps from the car radio's speaker without any preparatory crackle or static.

"Marshall. D.A.'s Office."

He hears the faint cries of megaphone voices, engines revving, helicopters circling overhead. They fill him with a sense of expendability. His actions are monitored, and he's allowed to carry on with his small purpose, but in actuality the world spins along with or without him. His being here—at this time, in this place, at all—is pure happenstance. Or is it? Either way, what does it matter in a world built on anti-actions, cross-purposes, and ghost enemies? If the effect of one's actions is incalculable, then who's guilty, and who's the hero?

The question evaporates when the sentry box spits out his ID tab and announces that he's free to continue, his freedom a blip of information adrift in cyberspace.

Around the first bend of the chute a tank backs into a security alcove in order to let him pass. Checking out the assault-hardened walls that rise a dozen feet on either side of him, McKuen is uneasy about how fast this was all put together. There's being prepared, and there's being *prepared*. This state of readiness seems to border on wish fulfillment. Rolling past a second tank, the final loop of the maze leads him into the plaza area. Its low concrete canopy spreads above him as if the city were evolving—mutating—into a single, sprawling bunker.

Automatic lobby doors part and he sees Julia. She's escorted to the sidewalk's edge by a pair of National Guardsmen who rouse her from what seems to be a daydream. He recognizes something vulnerable in her expression, some intriguing range of emotions. Nothing he can put his finger on, but it does make him want to be quiet, very quiet. When she's in the car beside him, her scent overtakes the odor of burning diesel fuel from the phalanx of tanks streaming past them. He nods at her, and she mouths a nearly inaudible greeting in return, preoccupied. He falls in behind the last of the tanks, then slingshots them down one of the ghost lanes of the city.

They ride in silence. McKuen checks the rearview mirror, City Hall a diminishing gray fortress, helicopters circling it. Julia stares out the passenger window, lost in something McKuen senses is far from where they are at the moment. Reports of "415s," disturbances of the peace, flare through the radio speakers, then fade into pools of deep stillness. McKuen studies her slyly, letting all the unspoken layers of her wash over him. He checks out her legs, a stealthy, one-eye-on-the-road glimpse that lingers, then turns meditative. The leg nearest him is crossed over the other, skirt angling toward her lap, on which her hands lay, crossed. Along the side of her thigh a shadow runs. It's simply a play of light. And yet this contrast is what holds his eye, shadow accentuated by the veil of white stocking stretched along it.

A bus passes them, headed in the opposite direction, back toward City Hall. Windows blackened, its driver and armed guard wear helmets and flak jackets.

"Have you heard anything about mass arrests?" McKuen asks.

His voice isn't what Julia had imagined. It's missing an aggressive edge, the impatience she expected to find in someone who liked to work alone. "Not yet."

"The plaza was filling up with buses as I was leaving."

"On the west side?"

McKuen nods, making a muffled sound of assent. The City Hall complex covers several square miles and contains hotels, restaurants, a shopping mall, a sixteenplex movie theater, courtrooms, the mayor's penthouse, a prison, Special Ops headquarters, the D.A.'s and Public Defender's Offices, even a television studio. A city within the city. So McKuen isn't surprised to find that activities are going on which neither of them knows about.

"I don't think anybody has a handle on what's going on," Julia says.

"Uh-huh." If she picks up the cynical spin in his voice, she doesn't react to it. "What does this do for our kid, Adams?"

"If anything, it should slow things down."

"Or screw things up," McKuen says.

"My boss, Parsons, feels things may get out of hand."

McKuen notices that she doesn't look at him as she speaks, and her voice has a detached, almost automatic tone. "I'd say he's right." McKuen waits, but she doesn't take the bait of his sarcasm. "So what's your theory on this?"

"I don't have one."

"As in, you're not interested?" This remark gets her to glance in his direction.

"I have a fourteen-year-old son who's out in this. Where, I don't know. His school's been evacuated."

"Here? Downtown?"

"Across the river."

"I didn't figure that area would be affected."

"Obviously no one did."

"It was even quiet around here a few hours ago," McKuen says. "You wouldn't know this was lying there, under the surface, ready to blow." The whole feel of the city seems fevered and dream-like to him, and not simply because he's tired. It's the same feeling he had walking into hamlets in Nam, waiting for the firefight to emerge from behind the veil of ordinary day.

"Are you sure you're up for this?" he asks. "I'll take you back to your office."

"The office is mass hysteria. I'm better off out here." She pauses, then adds, "Maybe we'll even accomplish something."

"Are you always this confident?"

"Are you always this sarcastic?"

She's staring at McKuen when he glances at her, the toughness that helped her survive the days in Hate Crimes overtaking the vulnerability he saw in her face, *balancing* her softness splendidly. "Do you want to use the phone, try reaching your son?"

"I've left this number on my answering machine. And at my office, in case he tries there."

"How are they evacuating the school?"

"Shuttle bus, vans, I suppose."

"Well, that could take a while. I'm sure he'll call when he gets near a phone."

"Do you have any children?"

McKuen hesitates. "No."

"Then you don't understand fourteen-year-old boys."

"Why not? I arrest them all the time."

Julia looks at him. "Now I know why you have to work alone."

McKuen understands his defensiveness on the subject of children. He and his wife never got to have any, but explaining his sense of loss is impossible. It's why he makes bad jokes instead. She is gazing out of the passenger window again when he says, "Tell me about fourteen-year-old boys."

Julia watches the chic hotels and boutiques of the City Hall area vanish, as bodegas and pawn shops gradually take their place on the narrowing streets of the barrio. "They need to flex their muscles."

"With their friends?"

"With Mom. A little power game."

"So you figure he's alright, then."

"I'm *imagining* that he's alright."

"Willing it."

"Right. Think good thoughts. Then nothing bad can happen."

Smoke begins to thicken around them. A roiling stream of it spills across an intersection ahead where an abandoned car burns, its hue the dense, billowing, beautiful black of napalm fires. McKuen wants to sail through it into what's now unseeable, the way he hurled himself blindly into the helicopter dust storm last night, pursuing the elusive boy. The way Julia is trying to divine the fate of her son. He senses that the chase is about seeing and not seeing, decoding surfaces and what, if anything, lays beneath them.

"Maybe we should go back," he says, slowing the car.

"For the boy, Adams?"

McKuen nods.

"He's not going to do us any good until we know more about what we're looking for."

"He could get lost in the crowd."

"Well, he can't go anywhere. They have to hold him."

"In the pens?"

Julia nods.

"We can't lose him? He can't be sprung, even with mass arrests?"

"I don't see how."

"You're sure?" McKuen asks.

Habit makes Julia begin to say yes. But she catches herself. She woke up in her own bed, with her son sitting safely in the living room. Now he's gone and she's on the edge of the city's wasteland, encircled by smoke. "I think so," she says.

"Good." McKuen turns back toward the steering wheel.

"I could be wrong."

The vulnerability is back in her eyes, the fear behind them crystallizing. Only McKuen now understands that she isn't afraid for herself, but for her son. "I know," he says, gently. "Think good thoughts."

Then they sail into the smoke as if it were a dream. . . .

We are experiencing technical difficulties. . . .
Please stand by. . . . This is XXN. . . .

. . . .**R**ay dozes in his hiding place as he waits for the helicopters he has been running from to retreat to another section of sky, the drone of their propeller blades slowly fading to silence. He emerges from the ruins of a basement half-buried in rubble, then winds his way along alleys and nameless lanes. A fine dust coats the inside of his mouth, the ashes of the city mingling with his own hangover dehydration and the dregs of crack resin. There are a few greenish puddles lying along the curbs, but nothing drinkable. He pats down his pockets, even the narrow ones on the legs of his fatigue pants, hoping for a forgotten piece of hard candy or cough drop. He finds nothing but lint, then looks up to see where he is.

It's no place he recognizes. Buildings several stories high stand around him in ruins, windowless, hollowed long ago by fire. As he wanders, he notices that all the street signs have been torn down, one intersection as anonymous as the next. Old bus stop benches are covered by faded, unreadable graffiti. Fossilized car skeletons appear every block or so, huge gas guzzler models he remembers from photographs of his mom with dead, jailed, or vanished cousins leaning on them, pointing thumb-and-index-finger guns at the camera. The cars are stripped, the remaining shells dusted by dry, hard soot opaque as the sky.

Ray looks down a wide boulevard. Defaced shop signs hang

above empty storefronts, then give way to a distant horizon. Overhead, phosphorescent glare. Nothing to navigate by. Not even a rifle site. Ray yearns to be Afroman again, even if he is only a stereotype. Anything to ease the pain of being himself, Ray the fuckup. Yeah, you done *real* good, he tells himself. Got your own people to burn themselves out of their houses. Once his shudders pass, he wipes his face. He's about to lick the salty water from the back of his hand when he sees it's a muddy black streak, the tears and soot and fire ash beneath his eyes forming a coal-colored paste.

He sniffs, clearing his nostrils, then is pissed to find himself—after what he's done—out here alone. "Try and do something," he mutters, walking again. A short length of rusted pipe looks like a good thing to pick up, so he does, scooping it from the gutter without breaking stride. It's hollow, and long as a nightstick. Good for cracking someone's skull with. Ray whips it through the air in front of him and his fatigue vanishes. He sweeps the pipe in the opposite direction, backhanded, knocking aside imaginary cops, faceless white folks, TV anchormen. "Stupid motherfuckers." He's surprised when he winds up popping a few homies, Minus Five and even Inch among them. Ray hadn't expected to find himself mad at them too. "D.S., VC bullshit," he says, remembering slogans about the 'hood being Vietnam all over again. Coda rappin' about how you hadda take things into your own hands, be your own leader 'cause that was the only way to bring the white man down. How they couldn't beat you if you was nowhere and everywhere, not like a gang thing where they could nail your ass anytime they wanted, but guerrillas like the Viet Cong. Thinking about it makes Ray angry again. What he did was supposed to *mean something*. Word gets out in the 'hood, homes start writing super dope lyrics about him, everybody knowin' he was down, start lookin' at him with respect. . . . Bullshit. None of it meant dick. His killin's out there, just another thing that happened, lost with, and like, everything else.

"C'mon in here." The voice is commanding, impatient. Ray stops at the last of the intersections, the road ahead cratered, pot-holed, ending in weeds and empty lots. Nobody on either side of the street, nobody over his shoulder. "Yeah, you. Come 'round the side. Need it in writing?" The words drift down from over-head. When Ray looks up an old dude is gliding away from a third-floor window across the street.

The building's doorway is near the remains of an abandoned barbershop. The only things left inside it are two big chairs, burned and rusted down to their frames, rooted to thick metal stumps. Bits of mirror cling in spots to one wall, glinting dully. Everything else is gone.

There is no door in the entryway, nothing to keep Ray out, ex-cept maybe the dimness inside. Still, he checks the street again. Dust, a shattered nightclub marquee, empty warehouses, the odd shack. Patches of old railroad track lie like the bones of the dead where the road has been worn away. Hell, even the 'hood never looked this bad. Ray glances through the doorway, thinks fuck it, maybe they got some water at least, and steps across the threshold.

"Goddamn!" Ray jumps when he steps on something soft on the first landing. It's too dim to see more than a shimmer, as what light there is reflects off scattering mice. He curses quietly, then continues, the floor spongy, pitted with various droppings and molds.

"You coming this lifetime?" The same voice, calling to him from the floor above.

"You got anyplace to go?" Ray yells back. He stops and frowns. When he smells cooking, some kind of sizzling flesh and grease, he realizes how hungry he is.

"This ain't no open-ended invitation," the guy says, as Ray rises into the brightness of the top-floor landing.

"This ain't no palace either."

"Well, you ain't no king."

"How d'you know?" Ray shakes his head, thinking he'd really like to pop this guy one. When he reaches the top of the stairs, the guy is already walking back into what Ray guesses he can call an apartment. It's bright, almost a silver haze—possibly on account of the thing Ray thought was a window turning out to be a missing section of wall. Ray squints as a dome of light opens above him where the roof is gone. Dark wooden beams crisscross, shadowy splotches of plaster clinging to them. As Ray's eyes adjust to the glare, he sees the old guy's thin figure shuffling toward the far end of the space in the direction of the food smell.

"Hey," Ray calls out, but his voice seems to get lost in the air. The place is huge, and being up a few floors makes it like being on a mountaintop, only with the occasional bit of ceiling and no snow. Ray catches up with the guy under an unbroken stretch of roof.

"See that?" The guy points at a Victorian-style love seat—claw feet, gargoyle faces carved into the armrests, faded chintz fabric barely covering the cushions. "Called a seat, named after yo' ass. Use it." He cruises away, then pokes his head around a partition and says, "We got company." Ray watches as the old guy stares curiously for a moment, sniffs, then adds, "You ain't gonna kill that, are you?" He points at something behind the wall.

Ray hears a woman's voice as he sits. "Do I need you in my face? Do I *need* you in my kitchen?"

"I ain't in your face, woman."

"Yeah, what do you call it?"

"I was in your face, you'd know about it."

"Oh, go sit your own behind down."

"I don't have much choice, do I?"

"No."

Ray's eyes roam the surreal—or maybe just hyperreal—layout of the pad. There's a bulbless shaded lamp beside him, electrical cord coiled uselessly at its base like a dead snake. A circular hooked rug riddled with holes and the remains of the words "Home Sweet Home" at his feet. Across from him is an armchair, beside it a nicked side table and cabinet. Behind them a dining table with four chairs. Plastic sheeting falls in long, twisting plumes from places where it has been tacked up overhead to cover ceiling holes, but has come undone. The distant windows and collapsed sections of wall open onto desolate urban plain, the edge of the city; a dead zone, leading, as far as Ray can tell by squinting into the gray haze, nowhere.

"Want a drink?"

The old guy is reaching into the cabinet beside his armchair. He's pretty dapper. Stacy Adams shoes; pleated, pinstriped trousers; matching vest with silk backing. A collared shirt that was once probably white but is now a yellowish-gray, frayed at the cuffs. His tie is held in place by a brass clip going green from oxidation. He wears shades and a satin-banded fedora.

"Some water," Ray says. He watches the guy stand upright with two glasses and a bottle. "What's so funny?"

"Nothing." He pours some clear liquid into one glass and extends it a bit stiffly, as if he were searching for Ray's hand. Ray stares at him, the guy still smirking, then takes the glass.

"I got a pipe in my hand here, you know."

"Yeah? That's good."

"Ain't afraid to use it, I get pissed."

"Absolutely." The guy hovers over the seat of the armchair, feeling for it, then sits and fills his own glass. "To violence, if and when called for, and dinner sometime this century."

"You're gonna be gettin' your own dinner I hear anymore lip," comes from behind the wall.

The old guy hunkers forward as if ducking something, wisps of gray nap visible beneath the fedora's edge when his face comes close to Ray's. "You got a woman?" he whispers.

Ray shakes his head.

"That's alright. Finding a woman is hard. But losin' one's even harder." He taps his glass's bottom against Ray's, then sits back and tosses down the liquid in one shot.

Ray sniffs the stuff, thinking, whatever this is, water ain't a possibility, when he hears, "So, who'd you kill?"

"Say what?"

"Nobody gets this far out 'less they killed somebody. Look around. Would you come here you didn't have to?"

Things *are* kind of on their last legs. Cold and rain could blow right in. Bugs, mice. Turds of all description. No TV. Otherwise, it's not really much worse than the 'hood. In fact it is the 'hood, *except* for TV. And the view, now that Ray checks it again. The view leaves him as empty as it is, lonely to his bones. "It ain't so bad."

"Mm-mm."

"Got mice," Ray offers, sitting forward, the pipe dangling from one hand.

"Hey, mice is alright. Got mice, means you don't got rats. Have to learn to look on the bright side. Go on, drink up."

"This ain't water," Ray says.

"No."

Ray looks down into it, clueless. Maybe it's some wine that's gone bad or something. "What is this?"

"What there is 'cause there ain't water."

"But I'm thirsty." Ray feels naked before the words are even off his tongue.

"Ain't the first, won't be the last. Stuff won't quench your thirst, but it will kill it."

Ray hesitates, then drinks. The liquid tastes briefly of dirty socks and motor oil before it begins to burn, a dry heat cauterizing his throat. He coughs. When he tries to speak, he can't. The old guy smacks one leg, laughing. A moment later the heat, now a warm cloud, curls around Ray's brain. His thoughts turn to melted wax, his vision tunnels and blurs. The weight drifts out of his body, lingers beside him briefly, then floats away through the window, into nothingness.

"A little candy for the head," the old guy says.

Ray's senses seem to stabilize after the rush, which reminds him of a glue high, only without nausea. He feels oddly enlarged, chambered, as if he'd become a big house he could dreamily wander through, quietly opening doors.

"You make this stuff?" Ray asks, his voice returning.

"Only when I have to."

"When's that?"

"Whenever I run out."

"We ain't anywhere, are we?" Ray says, tentatively.

"We're wherever we is."

"It ain't the 'hood."

"Does it look like the 'hood?"

Ray shrugs.

"Maybe once upon a time. But the action's long gone. Barbershop, pool hall, church. Everything. Gone."

"You the only one left? You and the lady."

The old guy leans forward and lowers his voice to a whisper again. "You don't know her, do you?"

"No."

"That's right. You did, you wouldn't be calling her no lady."

"Sorry."

"She don't take offense at what she can't hear." He sits back.

"So you ain't no preacher or anything then."

"I don't hold no offices."

"On account a you killed somebody too?"

"On account of I don't believe in them. What do you believe in?"

Ray sits silently and considers. There is, or was, Coda, though he's never met or seen him. No one has, his one bootlegged tape jacket an anonymous black sleeve. Coda was just words floating through Ray's headphones, exhortations to "bring the hate." Telling how in hate there's love, in apocalypse peace, in the end a new beginning. But here beyond the edge of the burning city, the empty plain and gray sky blank as the old guy's sunglasses, Coda's words feel weightless, impermanent, without soul.

"Gotta think about that one, huh. If what you believed in had done you any good though, you wouldn't be here."

"So. If you so smart, how come you here?"

"I go where you go."

"I ain't never seen you before. And I ain't never been in this place."

"Well if you haven't, I haven't."

"Then how come you was here when I got here!" Ray points at him with the pipe.

"Shouting ain't gonna help."

"Well nothing else seems to be, either."

"If you say so."

Ray slumps against the love seat, shoulders sinking inside his jacket. "Fuck it," he says.

"That's right. Mean old world."

"You ain't made sense yet."

"No, sir. No sense. And don't expect to anytime soon."

"So why don't you just leave me alone then."

"Whatever you say."

Ray pivots on his butt, lifts his legs onto the love seat, and settles his head on an armrest. His cap brim angles down over his eyes, which he closes. "Going to sleep," he says, cradling the pipe.

"Dream away."

"I will."

"Don't let me stop you."

"I won't."

"Just don't ever say Bob ain't never done nothin' for you."

"Yeah. What did you ever do for me?"

"I let you sleep."

"Huh." Ray shudders as a chill races over him, weightless spirit falling into weightless dream. He huddles inside his clothes, making small sounds, then sticks a hand in one pocket, anchoring his drift in darkness.

"Bob'll call you for dinner."

"Mmm . . ." Ray moans, fading.

"Don't worry about poor old Bob." The words float through Ray like a spell. "No, sir. No need to worry." Then they become a mournful lullaby backed by slide guitar.

> I believe, I believe I'll head back home.
> Say I believe, I believe I'll head back home.
> Been mistreated here, Lord.
> Can't mistreat po' Bob at home.

Then a deeper dream is on Ray like a wolf. He runs through the burning city, helicopters streaking after him. Hiding amid a basement's rubble he loses them, falls asleep, then dreams he's wandering, lost and thirsty as he comes upon sprawl's end. He stands at a crossroads, wondering which is the best way back to the 'hood.

Home. A place to puzzle out his—what does he call it? a crime? a sin? a heroic act?

Instead, he gets detoured. Riddles, bad booze, holes in the ceiling. Stretches of wasteland, and not even a TV to animate it. Then the surreal apartment fades. Night falls and Ray finds himself rushing through corridors of a labyrinth, chasing something just beyond his reach. Darkness tunnels around him, riding his shoulder like eternity. Ahead, emerging from silhouette, is a squad car, bullet-riddled, glistening with blood, headless bodies lolling inside it like souls on a ghost ship. A clamor stampedes out of the darkness behind him. Glancing back, he sees a posse of riot troops, TV reporters armed with cordless microphones, and, thundering along with them, Coda himself, the unseen revealed. Above them all, projected against the night sky, a pair of slowly cartwheeling rifle site beacons. Then a third icon—something tribal?—shaped like the letter Z. Ray runs harder, unable to catch the vision ahead of him, yet afraid to stop. The labyrinth brightens as the rifle sites and icon descend. He turns. And as they slowly tumble into a recognizable logo, he's blinded by the letters XXN. . . .

Then he hears his name being called, a voice lifting him into a peace above the frenzy of the maze.

Ray clicks on like a machine. "What?"

"Come on. Time to eat."

Bob's face is there and gone before Ray's panic subsides. Sitting up on the love seat, he eases his grip on the pipe and sweeps a hand across his eyelids. He can't say he feels refreshed. But the edge of his fear is gone, his sense of being composed of buzzing wire diminished. He stands and crosses to the table, leaving the pipe behind.

"How long was I asleep?"

Bob is already seated, six-string acoustic guitar leaning beside him against the table's edge. "Long as you were asleep. Dream alright?"

"I guess." Ray sees a barrel-bodied woman, easily twice Bob's size and couple, three decades—centuries? light-years?—younger, setting down the dinner plates.

"You sit over here," she says, patting the back of a side chair. "Between us, so we can share you."

"He don't have to sit near me," Bob says. "I ain't got nothing to say to him."

The woman nods toward the chair where Ray's to sit, giant earrings dangling on either side of her head. "Don't pay him no mind." She moves gracefully to one end of the table and sits, her ankle-length skirt and scoop-neck blouse making her seem to Ray both dowdy and exotic, a grandmotherly fortune teller. Ray takes his seat, then she clasps her hands and closes her eyes. Not wanting to pray, Ray looks at his dinner plate, the contents of which are as puzzling as everything else in the place.

"What is this?"

"What there is to eat." Bob tucks a napkin inside his shirt collar, then picks up a tarnished fork, and a mismatched knife. He slices something on his plate, then places it calmly on his tongue.

Ray stares at him, squeezing his napkin in one fist. Bob just chews, shaded eyes fixed straight ahead. Ray begins to rock in his seat, half-ready to get up and pound Bob when a soft palm covers his hand. He looks down and sees the woman's fingers patting him, the garish rings she wears rising and falling lightly.

"Now you listen to Beatrice Mae, honey."

Bob snickers, mutters something, then goes on eating. Beatrice grabs Ray's chin to keep him from turning his head away.

"Sulking ain't gonna help you none."

Ray brushes her hand away.

"See?" Bob says to her.

"See yourself," Ray tells him.

"Now there's some advice it wouldn't do you no harm to take," Beatrice says. "Hating everyone ain't gonna solve anything. You want answers, look inside yourself. You're the answer to whatever question you have. You knew to come here."

"I was thirsty."

"Are you still thirsty?"

Ray won't look at her. But he has to admit that he isn't.

"You were tired."

"Yeah. So?"

"You had a nap. Now you're hungry, but you won't be if you eat."

Ray stares at his plate. The food, still lightly steaming, is unrecognizable. He smells gamey flesh, and something onion-like. It glistens, stringy and blood-red. His stomach turns as he thinks of the cop's heart dangling outside his rib cage, viscera sliding down his bones.

Sulfur fills his nostrils. He looks up and sees Bob, a veil of smoke around his face, shake dead a flaming match then drop it onto his empty plate. "Beatrice is a good cook," he says, pulling the hand-rolled cigarette from his mouth. Despite his you-don't-know-what-you're-missing tone, he doesn't look at Ray. Just sits there, one elbow on each side of his plate, deep in some state of peace Ray can't fathom.

Ray turns to Beatrice, her hand still on his. But she doesn't say anything, doesn't even move except for the beating of her pulse, which Ray can feel just above his own. She simply looks at him until he no longer feels separate or distinct from her, some ancestral wisdom or suffering connecting them. Like all them folks he heard about surviving slavery and segregation and all by never giving up their dignity. Insisting on it, quiet-like. Not gangbangers, and not Toms. Just love passed from one generation to the next, each in its turn helping the other get by.

"Do you want to share a meal with us?" Beatrice asks.

"A little breaking of the bread," Bob says, blowing smoke.

Ray looks at her, then says, "Yes."

"Then you can't be lost forever."

Ray doesn't want to be lost forever, but nothing in the world he's from is any help to him. He's without direction. So he waits, hoping the words telling him what he feels, and which way to go, will come. He's amazed to find he even has a choice. That's something new, as is the slowing of his heart, which usually races along. Now its slow rise and fall seems to buoy him, his fear sinking beneath it. He gives himself over to its rhythm, the ebb and caress of his own breathing. The strangeness of the room, halfway between abandoned warehouse and gutted church, no longer unsettles him. Nor does the gray sky, the blank horizon. Instead, he seems to fill *them* with his presence, to be everywhere at once. To finally be at home in the world.

He closes his eyes to let this openness spill over him. It flows in all directions until even the memory of direction loses meaning, falling away as the unnecessary thing it is. A sense of ascension floods him. And through all that is otherwise shapeless emerges the figure of O.C., his long-dead homeboy and brother, whole again and robed in light, his arms spread as if he were waiting for Ray to fill them. Ray hears Beatrice say, "I know, I know," patting his hand, absolving him of a sin long buried and unspeakable. Then O.C.'s figure recedes, dissolving in light as Ray reaches out across his dream for him. But for the moment, he's too late, his reach not long enough. . . .

.... and as the light above him once again becomes city sky, the whop and drone of helicopter units slithering into the distance, Ray awakens, wipes his eyelids, and crawls up from the basement rubble into fading day. On the street he doesn't see a soul. So he turns and begins to loop back toward the 'hood, his step lightening as dream falls away, and he follows the smoke and fire that will lead him home. . . .

We are still experiencing technical difficulties. . . .

In the meantime, XXN would like to announce its latest urban lifestyle complex. This architectural wonder will house twenty thousand condominiums, a high-security school system, an indoor "green" space, and the world's largest discount mall, plus fourteen hours per day of simulated sunlight.

And—for a limited time only—purchasers of "Phoenix Cityplex™" property will receive complimentary passes to XXN's Armageddon Center, the world's first apocalyptic theme park. Be transported through time and space. Watch the destruction of Carthage and the sacking of ancient Rome. Join General Sherman's pyromaniacal march to the sea! Thrill to the firestorms of Dresden!

Visit the terror; buy the T-shirt. Agents for XXN Bank and Realty are standing by to take your call.

We now return to our regularly scheduled program. . . .

The only thing on Nick's mind as he heads for the elevator— besides the chant of "Please make me rich," which is more of a mantra than actual financial game plan—is, how does one sprint effectively without dropping a lot of pocketed electronic para- phernalia. Also, hold the fucking door. This last thought, in fact, turns into a panicky, shouted command, stunning clerks and mili- tary types in the justice building's hallway. Unsure whether to tackle, arrest him, or simply get out of his way, they resort to puz- zled, immobile gaping, which historically is the reaction Nick, free-lance spectacle and bozo-at-large, tends to inspire.

"Thank you," he peeps, daintily, once he's slipped inside the metal doors. They rattle closed behind him, courtesy of Mike E., elevator operator supreme and part-time Sitcom History major at the local community college, who, for some unrevealed reason, prefers to go by the name of Void.

"Hey, dude. Goin' down?"

"Not on you," Nick says, as always.

"All aboard!" Mike E. yells.

"Warp speed, Mr. Sulu."

"Get ready to make the leap to hyperspace."

"Rock 'n' roll."

Void throws the rusted brass lever forward and the ancient freight elevator shudders, then begins its tortured, squeaking descent into the pens. The kid turns to Nick and extends a palm for skin. "Hey man, what's up?"

" 's happening?" Nick passes a suave hand over Void's. Their palms circle one another slowly an inch apart, then withdraw. "No contact, no disease," Nick says.

"No offense."

"None taken. How's the screenplay going?"

Void checks the elevator's progress, one hand on the lever as sublevels of the building scroll slowly past outside the accordion-style gate. Nick can't help thinking the kid has virtually no lips or mouth. There's simply a bit of a nose supporting a tremendous pair of eyeglasses. Above them is an equally tremendous, and shiny, forehead. Void seems to be all frontal lobe and lenses, some new human subspecies: part-man, part-camcorder.

"My writing partner's suing me over the rights to the concept of 'Amoeba Man.' He didn't like the dysfunctional direction I was exploring—binary fission as a form of incest. He also felt repression was beyond the scope of single-celled organisms. So he wants the character back. He says an amoeba is the perfect vehicle for an unconflicted action hero. You think I can sue him under intellectual properties laws?"

"That's not really my specialty, but I think amoebae are public domain."

"That's cool. I'm off movies anyway. They're corporate establishment bullshit. Video, man. Cable access. You don't have a joint on you by any chance? This speed's got me wired."

"No. Sorry."

Void stops the elevator at a video checkpoint, stares at a camera and says, "Hey, man. We're cool." Then waits for permission to continue. "I have a character named A. Biss in this end-of-the-world thing I'm working on. Too blatant?"

"Not at all."

"Anyway, Proletarian Television, man. P-TV. I've got this serial killer sitcom idea. What's cool about it is that I'm deconstructing Cliff Notes of *The Odyssey* to have this mythic subtext cruising right below the surface of it. So basically, the killer's like this modern-day Odysseus, psychically cut off from any sense of home. All his victims represent obstacles to his psychic wholeness. I figured I could hit you up for some background info on psycho killers once I got down to the actual writing." Cleared to proceed, Void waves to the camera. "Later, dude."

As the elevator descends, Nick wonders if the kid, who seems to view him as simply one more image in an endless stream of weight-less images, is suffering from television psychosis, a state in which simulacrum *is* reality. But considering that his own pockets are bulging with duplicators and extenders, all the links to his electronic self, Nick thinks, maybe I'm projecting.

Void continues. "It's all symbol, man. We're all sign readers. *That's* the modern Odyssey. That's why I think this serial killer gig has resonance. I mean, here's a character who's reading a whole *lot* of signs—but he's reading 'em all wrong. That's why it's funny. It's sort of this help-me-I'm-crazy thing. But the key is that this dude *acts* on the input he's getting. It's like he *believes* there's still meaning behind things. So it's like, pathetic, but we're into the dude at the same time 'cause he's trying to impose some kind of order on chaos. It's kind of doomed, but heroic, you know. You have any TV connections?"

"No," Nick lies.

"That's cool. Did you see the executions?"

"Excerpts." Nick thinks he might pick up something to pitch to Gates Remington, besides unmitigated horror. That is, assuming he can pull off even half what he's imagined: Pay-per-View executions; tours of Discordia Sect bunkers and safe houses; grisly footage of ritual torture—hopefully with a little sex thrown in. Even an interview with Coda himself, followed by him in concert at one of the city's underground clubs—Chernobyl, HIV Positive, the Incest Survivor's Lounge. If accused of profiteering, Nick will defend his efforts as a moral wake-up call to a public narcotized by simulated violence. Face up to your voyeurism, complicity, and corruption! Maybe he can even spin this angle off into a talk show, call it *The Jeremiad Hour*. He's capable of imagining any outcome, except failure and continued poverty. So if there's a desperateness behind his plans, who cares? All art requires a proper balance of vision, myopia, derangement, and pure terror. "Were they good? What did I miss?"

"Pure television," Void lows, awed. "If car chases are pure cinema, the executions were P-TV. We *know* movies are about movies, but we've always had this suspicion that TV is about us, kind of into our fate and all, like God before he chilled after the Bible and stuff. Talk shows are kind of Job-like, right? But until this morning, I thought it was a pretty bogus medium to be pinning our hopes on."

"TV as meaning?"

"TV as the vehicle for religious rapture! We finally got the inferno on videotape, man! It was the fulfillment of everything promised by the Oswald assassination, Nam footage, the Gulf. I rarely step outside emotional numbness, but this was the first non-synthetic inclination toward feeling I've had since I flashed in therapy on the memory of my parents abandoning me in a video rental store when I was two." Nick eyes the back of Void's buzz cut as the kid slows the elevator. "All the terror was there, man. It was so purely a vision of the end." Void pauses, then adds, "It was kind of beautiful." He stops the car and yanks back the metal gate.

"There you go. Twenty floors down, dude."

Nick steps off, heading for the pen's first checkpoint.

"A few of us are going to score some Ecstasy tonight, tune in nonstop. Wanna party with us?"

Nick half-spins in the doorway. "Gonna have my hands full," he says, arms spread.

"That's cool. I can still hit you up for the serial killer stuff though, right?"

"Stop by my office." Nick turns, waves over one shoulder.

"Cool." The gate clinks shut behind Nick. "Board!" is the last thing he hears before he is admitted to the registration cubicle by a mechanical door.

Inside the concrete cell, he inserts his ID card, then places his fingertips on a scanner panel, which checks his prints. The faint buzz of metal detectors crests as his hearing adjusts to the monitored stillness. He surrenders his portaphone, flask, keys, roach clip, and Lorcim L-25, a lightweight .25-caliber semiautomatic pistol he carries holstered at the small of his back. The stainless-steel drawer he has placed them in withdraws into its wall slot. He exhales and waits. Clears his throat, slips his hands into his trouser pockets. Then feels the quiet close in. His heartbeat booms in the stillness. Ghosts of his pot high linger, convincing him he's been in this cell for all eternity. How can he prove otherwise? Claim that Void was here a minute ago? His laugh is swept instantly away by the cell's silence. He knows the guards on the other side are pulling his chain, but the thought that this might be the endpoint of his hallucinations, the life he dreamed finally over, terrifies him. *Silence* terrifies him. He prays for distraction to overtake him. And indeed, he is imagining a deal-cutting conversation with Gates Remington when the door slides open. He steps through it, into the guards' rising laughter.

"Very funny," Nick says, collecting his things.

"You'd never hold up in solitary, Wolfman."

"Yeah, well, things get complicated when you have an IQ."

"Ooo, he's testy today," the second one says.

Inside the booth the phone rings persistently, inches from either guard's hands. Nick eyes it as he refills his pockets. He jiggles his flask when he comes to it, testing what seems to be a sudden drop in weight.

"Lose something?"

"Let's see if we can't help you find it."

Nick sees himself on their video monitor, where tape of his brief incarceration in the pass-through cell is being run. Numbers displaying his pulse rate and blood pressure rise with embarrassing swiftness, his face a mask of arrested anxiety above them.

"Looks like the Wolfman could use a drink."

"Gotta keep that brain wet, Wolfman."

When their phone continues to ring one of them lifts the handset from its cradle and immediately lets it fall back into place. The ringing's echo fades. Then there are simply the two of them, almost comically muscled, rolled uniform sleeves tight around their upper arms. They're so puffed up from steroids that Nick often wonders why they don't float, like parade balloons. Maybe there are rocks in their motorcycle boots. Their buzz-cut heads look like chunks of quartz. It's impossible for Nick to tell them apart, except for a single distinguishing feature. One of them has a bicep tattoo that reads "Betty."

"You need to exercise, pal."

"Yeah, do some cardiovascular work."

"And try not to get scared shitless so easily. It's bad for the heart."

"Just trying to brighten your day," Nick says, trading humiliation for speed. "I need to see a kid named Darren Adams. He was sent over from Central Homicide this morning." Nick finishes re-

programming his portaphone—since they always deprogram it—
tucks it inside one pocket, and looks up to find them smiling.
"What's so funny, besides me?"

"Darren Adams," one of them says.

"A black kid, right?" the other answers.

"Oh yeah, now I remember."

"Was he number one thousand, or one thousand and one?"

"Why don't you look him up on computer?" Nick suggests.

"Oh, you mean, like, his record?"

Nick's eyes close briefly; he nods with great patience.

"We ain't got no records."

"Yeah, we're in riot mode."

Nick takes a deep breath, exhales, and acknowledges the fact
that, yes, he is in hell. "Fine, you're swamped. Let me in, I'll go
find him."

"Oh, couldn't do that."

"No, couldn't do that."

"Rules, you know."

"You're in riot mode. Suspend the rules."

"Couldn't."

"No."

There's a slight pause. "Not for anything less than a double-
cheese 'Party Man' pizza."

Nick has his fast food credit card out and is already dialing when
they add, "Plus soft drinks." Which is perhaps why he hears, "You
have reached Dial-A-Nurse. For heart attacks, press one. For
strokes, press—" He redials.

"Apocalypse Pizza, take your riot order, please."

"A double-cheese 'Party Man,'" Nick says, "and—"

"We have an Insurrection Special. Buy one *deluxe* 'Party Man,'
get a second free. Feed a mob, not a frenzy."

"Go for it," Nick says.

"Drinks?"

"Sucro Plus, mega-caffeine."

The guards grow visibly pleased, happy with the order's progress. Nick has to take a moment to remind himself that people outside are dying.

"Address."

Nick gives it.

"You want insurance?"

This is a new wrinkle. "You mean, like on my life?" Nick imagines some interactive, over-the-phone medical exam. Then an unexpected sadness passes through him. In the great jumble of horror and absurdity, he's dying too. Sign-reading his way to labyrinth's end, loveless and alone. He doesn't have a beneficiary, not a soul to leave behind. He briefly entertains Katrina Quimquerelle, the pseudo-meteorologist and video exercise doyenne, as a possibility, but is forced to acknowledge that she's simply masturbation material, and may not even really exist.

"On your order. You're covered in case it arrives with a topping not of your choice. In the event your driver absconds en route with your order after your account has been debited. Or should you or a pizza companion become ill and require medical attention."

Nick ruefully eyes the guards. Even a rockheaded security guard has a girlfriend named Betty, he thinks. Then he makes a spiteful, self-pitying decision and says, "No."

Released, he passes through the checkpoint's iron door and moves quickly along a concrete block corridor. Bare lightbulbs burn overhead. Cameras stare at him; wall-mounted machine pistols electronically track his progress. Lower sections of wall are streaked with scuff marks, blood that hasn't been scrubbed away, clusters of bullet gouges. The air turns distinctly fecal as he approaches the passway's end, a damp heat rising from the pens. He loops around the final corner and approaches a barred gateway.

On the sentry box beside it someone has hung a sign that reads: "You are in a smoke-free zone."

The guard in the booth steps out. A new face, one Nick hasn't seen before. Mustached, pallid, going soft in the jowls. Definitely not Grade-A department issue. Most likely a reserve, some guy who would just as soon be home in the subdivision, watching the whole mess as it's meant to be watched—on-screen, shaped and distanced by color commentary and trainloads of commercials.

"I don't know why you want to get in here." The guy inserts an ID card into the computer lock, and the bars swing open into the chute.

"To see that justice is done."

The guard steps aside to let him pass. "They said you were crazy."

"They just resent my integrity."

Nick walks past the table where his handcuffed clients are usually brought to be interviewed. Behind him, the guard bolts the gate. Nick proceeds, his loafer heels knocking on the concrete floor. The chute narrows and winds, pitching down, taking him closer to the pens than he's ever been. Caged bulbs are spread out along the walls now like torch flames. A murmur rises, enfolding the sound of his footsteps. It crests to a din as he steps around another loop in the spiral, into the central aisle of the pens.

He's instantly blinded by flashlight beams. Dogs bolt out of the shadows, bounding through spears of light, teeth flashing. He freezes as the dogs sniff his loafers and trouser legs. One of them pokes a snout up under his crotch and Nick thinks, fuck, imagining a German shepherd trotting away proudly with his scrotum squashed between its teeth like a field mouse.

"You must be the asshole," a voice croons.

Nick squints through the flashlight's brightness. Above it hovers a face that, when it emerges from shadow, remains shadow. Just eye whites and some ghost letters—S.O./C.D., Special Operations/Chaos Division—floating over them. Other faces—some black, some white—crowd around it. All possess a why-don't-we-kill-him-now look that Nick finds unsettling. They are all clad in dark fatigues and the same lettered cap. Behind them, a flickering panel of bluish light splits the corridor separating the rows of cells.

The lead guard steps closer. Nick thinks for an instant that he's staring at McKuen's double. Same features, but stripped to an expression of mercenary purposefulness, a quality that tells Nick the guy's sole frame of reference is search-and-destroy. "What you want to find this motherfucker for?"

"He has some library books that are overdue."

Nick's arms are spread crucifix style, his legs V'd. He closes his eyes as he's spun about-face and searched. His pockets are checked, his wallet confiscated. When he's turned again, he opens his eyes to see the lead guard, whose name tag says "Sgt. Deacon," being handed his wallet.

"No cash," the guard surrendering it says.

Deacon parts the billfold and peers inside. "My man is right."

"Cash is a regressive medium. A tangible in a world of intangibles. I refuse to deal in it."

"You want to find who you're looking for?"

"You want to barter?" Nick reaches over and upends one of the wallet's inner flaps. "We deal in credit. Pick a card."

There's a stirring among the backup guards. Nick even senses a poignant curiosity coming from the nearest cells, the game, for the moment, absurdly more interesting than their own fate.

Deacon ponders, then says, "Got you a phone, right?"

Nick panics, a sense of doom plunging through him at the thought of missing Gates Remington's one and—he knows how these fucks are—only call. Nick is also forced to admit, pathetic as it sounds, that life has no value for him without call forwarding.

But to his own astonishment, he goes one step further in his spinelessness as he mews, "I'm expecting a call."

The howls are spontaneous and, well, riotous, laughter whirling through the place, spinning into darkness. Deacon says, "Just dial—when I say so." He extracts Nick's small deck of credit cards, fans them between outstretched thumb and forefingers. "Pick one."

"Hm." Nick scans his limited choices. The heavy metal card is near its limit. His environmentally correct accounts are sending testy overdue notices with photos of undernourished pandas. And his XXN credit line, which he maintains religiously with cash advances from other ultimately unhappy creditors, lest XXN cancel his cable service and bonus subscription to its interactive porno channel, is not negotiable. He points out the Human Rights Action Committee card.

Deacon separates it from the deck and eyes it silently. He looks at Nick, who wears his poker face, then jabs Nick's sternum with the card's edge. "You're all heart." Nick leans back slightly as the next jab delivers more force. "Get me a credit line on it."

When Nick accesses his account file, he extends the phone and waits. Deacon receives an approval, then returns the handset. Nick takes it as if he were being offered a lifeline from heaven. "Better not cancel this motherfucker for three days," Deacon says. And with that they are on their way.

The blue light ahead turns silver as they sweep into it. The guards draw their riot sticks and send the dogs bounding toward the first cells to emerge from shadow. Jeers roll through the pens, muting the dogs' barking.

Deacon leans near Nick and shouts, "How long ago this kid come in?"

"An hour, maybe less." He can barely hear his own words above the clamor.

Deacon nods, then taps his second-in-command and points straight ahead, indicating a place way down the line. The guards fan out as they come upon the line of glowing panels. Nick stays with Deacon, the tunnel narrowing around them as it brightens. Rising alongside him and illuminating the faces pressed against cell bars six feet away are not panels of fluorescent sheeting, as Nick suspected, but screens, television screens, one long continuous chain of them. They stand floor to low ceiling, unspooling into the deep distance, their images guttering like candlelight.

Nick seems to glide through televised dream, cruising from channel to channel as if he were flying, then on past the icon repeated every third screen, its halo casting an unflickering ghostlight deep into the pens as it reappears hypnotically, a televised chant and invocation . . . XXN . . . XXN . . . XXN. . . . Nick feels a sense of rapture, wordless peace, as if he himself had become pure television.

He veers penward, a bit of his jacket fabric is clutched, and he's yanked against the cell bars. Hands are on him at once, pinning his ankles and wrists, tearing at fistfuls of hair. The back of his head slams into iron. Fingers rip at his face, voices scream for his dismembering.

Just as suddenly the dogs are leaping at the bars, jaws snapping. Deacon appears inches from him and fires a stun gun directly into a prisoner's face. The other guards break fingers, trying to free him. And suddenly it's all there on-screen, instant live remote. A second later, Nick's released, doubling over as he stumbles blindly toward his own televised image.

"Nice going," Deacon says, patting him on the back.

Silence blooms as they move forward. Guards close ranks around Nick, the pens already no more than clamorous echo. When the ground beneath his shoes turns slick Nick begins to wonder if this maybe isn't such a wonderful plan after all. Then he realizes, he has no plan. He's simply crazy. Which at least puts him on even footing with the world. So he presses on, his desperation linking him to a kind of mad hope.

Deacon disappears around a bend in the maze, then reappears beneath a necklace of torch lamps suspended from a high ceiling. It's a circular vault half the size of the plaza outside the court building above. Detainees are being herded into various corridors. And if Nick isn't mistaken, the figure at the head of an elite guard unit sweeping in dark splendor his way is the black-clad overseer from the plaza, riding crop in hand.

"Hey, it's Dracula," a guard whispers.

"I see him," Deacon says.

"What do we do with slick here?"

Come to my rescue, Nick thinks, imagining some absurd simpatico between himself and Deacon, an unstated mutual respect too elegant for this underling to comprehend.

Deacon barely turns his head. "Cuff him."

Nick's hands are behind his back, his wrists forced up, parallel with his shoulder blades. Cursing silently, he looks up as the dead white skin and shaved skull of Commander Eschata floats past, his black flak jacket bearing his name in gold script above the words "Special Operations/Chaos Division: S.O./C.D." Deacon and company stand at attention and deliver a crisp, simultaneous salute. Then Eschata disappears into the tunnel, vanishing as quickly as he appeared.

"Scumsucker," a guard mutters. Additional low-voiced displeasures are expressed, treasons grumbled.

They approach a command post at the center of the vault. A narrow catwalk ringing its glass walls, it sits on spindly metal legs. Nick is hustled up the short metal staircase. Inside, computer terminal operators are at work, information running through their machines as if it were eternal life.

Deacon whispers to one of them, then summons Nick with his index finger. "Tell the man your kid's name."

"Adams, Darren."

On-screen, grids of the prison scroll by, leaping from sector to sector. Tunnels appear, revolve, tumble into cyberspace. Names are sorted, matched to six-digit ID numbers, sorted again.

"Got any aliases, a.k.a.'s," the computer jockey asks, not looking away from the monitor.

" 'Inch,' " Nick says, remembering the kid's gimpy retreat behind McKuen in Homicide that morning. This morning? It seems impossible, spliff or no spliff. . . . Unless for once Nick truly *is* in the city, living on its time, labyrinth time, multiple and simultaneous, varied and endless as the city itself.

"We got a few possible Darren Adamses."

Nick sees a list of ID numbers. Several names, one being "Darren Adams," are grouped beside each. And on the lower right corner of the screen, "Software by XXN."

"Yours have any distinguishing characteristics?"

Deacon turns to Nick. "What's 'Inch' stand for?"

Nick hesitates, unsure now whether he's exploiting the kid or saving him from this. "A limp. One leg is shorter than the other."

"By an inch."

Nick nods.

Deacon points a finger at him. "I liked the pause before you went for it. Flash a little conscience. Nice touch." Smirking, he turns to the monitor, leaving Nick, a moment later, in an embarrassing position. Handcuffed, his portaphone finally rings.

Heads turn, keyboards fall silent, cyberspace is put on hold. Normally, Nick would be grateful for the attention. Ready to flash teeth, happy to dissipate his loneliness among even the smallest, least receptive of audiences. But, unlucky chump that he is, his longings are never quite in sync with what the unpurchasable things of the world have to offer. So when the phone rings a second time, he grinds his teeth instead of laughing along with the others.

"Want me to get that?" Deacon takes the phone from Nick's pocket. "You are here, right?" Nick realizes this is where the hero spits in the bad guy's face. But he doesn't. He can't. And Deacon knows it, which is why he smiles. "Doesn't feel too good being the oppressed, does it?" He laughs softly as the computer jockeys turn back to information's flow. Raising the handset, he cuts it off in mid-ring and speaks into the mouthpiece. "Wolfman says, fuck you, whoever you are." He doesn't wait for an answer. Instead, he lays the set on Nick's collarbone, then turns back to the computer terminal.

Nick pins the phone between his ear and shoulder. Gates Remington's impatient voice turns from digitalized squealing into an audible signal. "G.R.," Nick tries to say, but his throat is all dust and phlegm. He swallows, cursing to himself. And suddenly, Nick's notion that Gates Remington can deliver him from his situation, his life, reveals itself as desperate, pitiful delusion. Yet he plods on out of sheer meanness. Meanness and fear. "G.R.," he croaks, polite, the mask of confidence back on.

"Wolf?"

"Yeah."

"I could give a shit where or how you are."

"I'm in a meeting." Nick's lie is automatic, a parallel impulse to his urge to self-destruct.

"You're a lying scum in a bind."

"Yeah, well, good to hear from you too."

"Look, screw the lousy seven thousand you owe me. You're desperate, I know it; desperation is something I can exploit. You still at the court thing?"

"Yeah."

"Good. Close to the blood. So. You got ten seconds. Pitch me."

Nick is startled into brain-void. He hasn't prepared a pitch. He's been too busy being strangled, handcuffed, crotch-sniffed, and laughed at to fine-tune a marketing plan. So, after all this, his poor organizational skills, a flaw since his earliest schooldays, catch up with him. Here, in hell. I'm here because I didn't do my homework? Fuck everything, he thinks. Fuck it all.

Gates Remington takes an accusing stance toward Nick's silence. "Don't tell me you don't have anything. I've got seventeen channels here, they all bear the name of my various production companies. And you know what I'm seeing? Badly dressed people in cheap shoes, running around with stolen televisions. Everything's on fucking fire! Yet all I've got is ninety goddamn million aerial shots of police helicopters. If I'm lucky—if I'm lucky!—a couple of people a minute get beaten senseless. And you know what I'm beginning to think? I'm beginning to think, this blows. It's starting to look like a movie they shot, then remembered they forgot to write the fucking script. I have a Pay-per-View audience tonight that's going to make Super Bowl numbers look like the Nielsens for a PBS rerun. We've got apocalypse, and we can't get twenty-four fucking hours of programming out of it. We *deserve* to be the largest debtor nation on earth! This is the Trojan fucking Wars here, where's my Homer? Taking a goddamned screenwriting course!" Gates Remington's voice mellows, revealing a bit of an entertainment CEO's longing. "Give me character, give me story," he pleads. "Give me heartbreak, give me love among the ruins."

"Hey." Nick is pulled out of the cave of Gates Remington's voice by Deacon. "We found your boy." Nick stares at his guide, extorter, and, for the moment, master, then turns away without acknowledging the news. In his ear, Gates Remington is still waxing nostalgic over the death of narrative drive.

"I need mystery, yearning. I could even accommodate cannibalism. You going to tell me it doesn't exist? If it exists, I want it. You understand me? But with a story. With a *human angle. . . .*"

On that asinine utterance—is there cannibalism that *doesn't* have a human angle?—Nick decides he wants some of Gates Remington's money. No, lots of Gates Remington's money.

". . . but there has to be something uplifting in the horror. That's why I called you back, you useless fuck." Soft sell over, Gates is back in abusive-mode overdrive. Nick remains amazed by the number of executives who equate yelling with accomplishing something. The world sucks. The world really sucks. "You're in deep shit, I can smell it. I need an execution, you can maybe get me one. Gimme an answer. Yes or no?"

Nick hesitates. Not out of a sense of compunction. No sudden nostalgia for scruples overwhelms him. If he were a little nearer to dying, maybe. But he's only handcuffed, so cynicism rather than remorse still rules. It's simply that if he is going to enter the business of selling people's souls, he'd like to have a strong opening hook. So when he does speak he says, "I can give you Discordia Sect access; a cop-killer member of the sect, who I'm going to defend; and, if the deal is right"—revealing this last detail in the most tempting of whispers—"Coda himself. In other words, yes." Nick is trembling from the sheer amount of lying he's done by the time he's finished. But the brief silence that follows tells him he has a deal. Also that he doesn't have much phone time left. Deacon is wrapping up things behind him, awaiting only final confirmation of ID and location.

"The sect as sect is uninteresting," Gates says, mulling aloud. Nick understands a producer isn't satisfied until he's trashed a proposal, then resurrected it intact as his own, thereby stamping it with genius. He only hopes Gates Remington is quick about it. "Does the cop-killer bastard have any tragic human qualities, or are we dealing with a piece of sirloin that has an Uzi and limited powers of speech?''

"He's a sympathetic figure," Nick says, inventing without regard for the truth. Just like defending his clients in court. Reality? Reality is whatever you delude yourself it is. Success is simply getting people to subscribe to the same delusion.

"So we're supra-political then?" Gates asks, for assurance.

"The killing's an identity thing."

"Good. Motivation."

"And we've got a childhood friend as accessory." Nick's wrists are beginning to chafe and ache, so he takes little pleasure in the fact that he and Gates Remington are now speaking as "we."

"This is what I'm talking about. Story. Camera angles and bullets are fine—as camera angles and bullets. But don't give me carnage without character, then plead verisimilitude. What else?"

Else? Nick combs his filmic memory files for a plot twist, some essential element of all movies, then says with deal-clinching authority, "I get the girl."

"There's a girl?"

"A blond assistant D.A." Wistfully, he thinks of Julia's face, her legs, legs he might, with any luck, one day be able to name as beneficiary on his pizza-chain life insurance policy. Then adds, "She loves me."

Gates begins doing his alma mater's third-and-goal chant, which goes something like, "Yes, yes, yes, yes," though the sounds are indistinguishable from barking.

Over this, Nick hears Deacon calling him. "Look, I'm going to have to book."

Nonetheless, Gates continues. "Coda is the key, though, the synergy figure. If he's got any image charisma at all, we can go book, video, and feature film in addition to the music. Provided, of course, he lives."

Nick feels a finger hammer his unoccupied shoulder. Deacon is there, looking all business.

"Hang it up. We're out of here."

"A minute," Nick suggests, softly.

"Is that the asshole from before?" Gates asks.

Meanwhile, Deacon reaches inside Nick's blazer and pirates Nick's favorite lighter, plus a pack of imported cigarettes. He lays one between his lips, lights it, pockets the pack and lighter, then says, "Thirty seconds," and moves off toward the door.

"You're not a hostage or anything?" Gates wants to know. "You do have creative control?"

"Yes," Nick says.

"I am going to be able to reach you continuously at this number, correct?"

Nick eyes Deacon out on the catwalk, smoking contemplatively, watching the ongoing lockup. "Yes."

"You'll need a crew. Smaller is better in this case."

Deacon puts one boot up on the catwalk's black steel railing, bodies herded along below him. After another drag, he flicks ashes out over the crowd.

"Van, couple of techies," Gates continues. "Speed—and I can't impress this fact on you strongly enough—is paramount. Audience drop-off by tomorrow will approach critical mass. Everybody'll go back to the shopping channel—crises always jump-start consumer spending—or else tune into the nature network. Bozos sitting around with herbal tea and mass-produced homemade biscuits."

And this, the fact that even apocalypse has a short tele–life span, brings on in Nick an even deeper sadness, a sense of detachment and numbness. Everything is disposable. Yet transcending it there's . . . what . . . ?

"So you are going to have something for me tonight, right?"

"Yes," Nick says, with absolutely no conviction.

"Good."

"Provided I have a contract."

"I'll send a standard one with the crew."

"Fax it."

"I'll fax it."

"And a cash retainer."

"What?"

"Cash. The thing that operates without faith."

"Nick—"

"Don't call me Nick."

"Asshole. Real people—gentlemen!—get paid at the back end."

"You're going to fuck me at the back end."

Nick watches Deacon take a final drag on his smoke, then jettison the remains into the preterit masses.

Gates Remington exhales. "All right. Fifty thousand."

"A hundred."

Another aggravated sigh. "A hundred."

"Against future royalties. Plus co-producer status."

"Fuck you."

"I'll get tape, sell it myself anyway."

"When we're done, we'll sit down, work out the details."

"Five percent of gross revenues, all media," Nick hurries. "And bail for my client."

"Cocksucker! Luck like this shouldn't happen to a piece of shit like you. You don't even have a videophone. I feel like I'm talking to someone from the Stone Age." Nick waits. "All right, all right, yes. Gimme your fax number, tell me where and when for the crew."

Nick does and Deacon is at the door, eyeing him through the glass.

"Gotta go. Include an authorized line of credit for bail in that fax." Then a ghost sound is on the line, a whisper in an abyss— "This is XXN" . . . and just as suddenly it's gone. "What was that?"

"The audio ID on my fiber-optics line."

"Your *phone* line?"

"Phone, cable, computer, TV. What's the difference? Get with the program." Gates Remington cackles at his own bad pun. "But first get me some videotape."

With that the phone is stripped from Nick's aching ear. He barely hears Gates Remington's closing sentiment, which is basically, "Then drop dead," a pale, electronic curse. Business.

An instant later he's out the door, Deacon pushing him down the stairs, into the traffic of souls. As they sweep out of the plaza into even deeper shadow the pace is swift, the guards silent. Deacon squeezes Nick's arm tightly, dragging him forward. Nick studies his profile and notices Deacon's fierceness intensify as a new tunnel closes around them. The tunnel opens onto a wide, dark basement. Thick pillars support a low ceiling, the dirt floor soft beneath Nick's damp shoes. The sewery wetness of the pens gives way to a gagging warmth, the air oppressive with the odor of shit. Nick's stomach clutches, half-digested food and booze spurting up into his throat as Deacon slows the pace. They come to a stop several feet from the nearest pillar. Nick swallows, vomit burning his Adam's apple. When Deacon shines his flashlight, the dark movements around the bases of the pillars leap out of shadow. Bodies are chained to stakes driven knee-high into each of the pillars. It takes Nick a moment to register this. Faces look up, squinting into the beam Deacon sweeps over them. Whispering floats through the shadows. Some of the figures seated on the ground jackknife their legs, folding themselves into less vulnerable positions. The place seems fantastic, unimaginable. Yet when Nick accepts the fact that it is not illusion, he understands the silence.

Deacon slips behind him, taking hold of the short chain linking his handcuffs. He raises it till Nick bends forward. "Keep an eye out for your boy. Wouldn't want to come all this way, then leave empty-handed."

Nick steps over a pair of legs. Deacon simply kicks them, the guards behind him adding several more boot-blows. Nick knows not to glance back.

The next gathering of bodies looks the same as the first. Stained, blood-spattered clothes. Their hands cuffed behind their backs, just as Nick's are. The final line blurred. Real, unreal; guilt, innocence; preterit, saved. All is illusion. The only distinction is a deferral of pain.

Nick's revelation doesn't bring on a flood of empathy, though. What he feels is revulsion, loathing. He resents being included with this lot. He hates it. And the thought that Gates Remington is his passport to salvation only makes him angrier.

"Think anybody'd ever find you if I left you here?" Deacon whispers in his ear.

Nick doesn't want to think about it. In fact, he's ready to give up on Inch when he spots a familiar face. "There." His eyes follow Deacon's flashlight beam over a series of faces, brown, a smattering of yellow, some white. Even one in the dim light that appears to be American Indian. Most are bruised and cut. All are dressed in tatters, cheap rags. Nothing like Nick's suit, or Deacon's crisp uniform.

Deacon's beam alights on Darren Adams a second time and Nick feels a stillness open around him, the noise and clutter of the city no longer a distraction or a sanctuary. He is face-to-face with his sins.

"Him?"

Nick doesn't answer and Deacon whacks the side of his head with the flashlight. Nick sees black, his temple throbbing. When his brain stops rattling, he opens his eyes, stares at the dark ground, and without looking at the boy says, "Yes."

"Welcome to hell, motherfucker," Deacon whispers, his breath warm on Nick's ear. He pops the handcuff locks, freeing Nick's hands.

A moment later they are retracing their path with Darren Adams in tow, his hands bound behind his back as Nick's were. Beyond the guttering light of the television panels, the two of them are delivered into the final loop of the maze, and released. Deacon and company retreat instantly, turning only once to call the dogs before they're gone.

They stand there, Nick rubbing his wrists, the boy breathing hard, the corridor desolate around them.

"I didn't do nothin'," Darren says, voice quivering.

"I don't care what you did. I care who you know."

"I don't know nobody."

Nick backhands the boy near the temple, where Deacon struck him, and the boy stumbles against the concrete wall. Nick's breathing eases. He offers no apology, feels no remorse. His swings from rage to kindness are over. He feels tension bleeding out of him. He feels pure, unredeemable. Dead.

Taking the boy's arm, he leads him away from the wall and back into the blaring city, toward release, and then on, toward whoever it is they are chasing. . . .

The words "Black boys go to prison, white boys go home" are the first thing to catch Julia's eye as she and McKuen emerge from the veil of smoke. They appear on an abandoned storefront, then drift away behind them. Julia notices him check the rearview in silence.

"What do you expect we're going to find at Darren Adams's apartment?" she asks.

"You mean, is this whole trip futile?"

"Something like that, I suppose." She is surprised to hear herself admit this. She didn't realize it was what she felt, even fleetingly.

McKuen exhales. He isn't as young as she at first thought. There's some gray in his beard stubble, pouches beneath his eyes. He's nearing the age where exhaustion drags at every feature of his face. "I don't know. It's a step, the next step." He pauses as they look at one another. He's thinking that he likes the way she looks when she's concentrating, lost in thought. He's also thinking that plodding along step-by-step in this case may not help them find who they're after. Another sort of movement seems to be afoot, the city's fate beyond the reach of an ordinary police procedural. "I don't know," he repeats. "It's the best we can do, at the moment."

They cross an intersection, its traffic light out, the streets deserted. Julia sees the interstate's elevated roadway, her path home. Then it's gone, the shells of buildings once again enclosing their route. Whatever momentary elation she felt vanishes.

"We'll see," McKuen mumbles. "We'll see."

To Julia, he seems to have a strange capacity for going with the flow. She feels it in him, almost as if it were a kind of electricity.

Ahead, a corridor of flames appears. A mob of people crowd a wide ghetto intersection, then move toward the curbs as McKuen slows the car. Women hold infants in their arms, and reach for children's hands. Everyone, except the few men trying to hose down a church that hasn't yet caught fire, watches them approach.

"Leave everything, get out of the car." McKuen cuts the engine and removes the keys from the steering column. Some teenagers drift toward them. "And look people in the eye."

He gets out of the car, his door closed before Julia even has hers open.

The air outside makes her eyes tear. She feels an instant tightness in her chest, a soft burning beneath the spot where she clips her bra closed. McKuen looks up at the dead sky. Hovering in the distance is a lone helicopter, its underside marked XXN.

"You an anchor lady?"

A black boy, a year or two younger than her son, stands in front of her. Some other kids come up beside him, forming a half-circle around her. "No. I'm not."

"You're dressed like one of them XXN ladies."

"She don't have no microphone, though," a girl says.

McKuen appears, then tilts his head in the direction of the church. For an instant, Julia thinks he might take hold of her arm. The impulse seems to be there, but quickly retreats.

"Why you with this white lady?" the girl asks him.

"Because it's my job." This time, McKuen does reach out. Not quite touching Julia's hand, but coming close as he beckons her.

"That's no excuse," the girl says.

"Wasn't lookin' for one," McKuen says over his shoulder.

The mob ripples around them, allowing a narrow passage. Julia hears murmured obscenities directed her way, whispered threats. McKuen meets every eye with the same impassive expression.

Ashes fall lightly around a group of older men gathered outside the doorway of a restaurant called Slim's Joint—Get Yo' Own. They watch as others try to keep the small clapboard church from going up in flames. It's the one building in the area with a spire.

Rows of low, flat-roofed bunkers and block-shaped high-rises stand around it like tombstones.

A man in a baseball cap looks their way. The other men seem to cede him some kind of authority, watching for him to validate their comments on the state of things. McKuen heads straight for him, excusing himself as he pushes through the mob. When they reach him, the man shows cursory interest in Julia. She's a white woman operating in one official capacity or another. To her, that's all his glance seems to imply. His hands remain in the front pockets of his chinos, a hefty clump of keys, a sign of responsibility in these parts, dangling from one belt loop.

"You mind helping us out?" McKuen says.

The man wears a shirt that identifies him by the stitching above the breast pocket as "Slim." He checks McKuen out silently. "Depends on what kind of helping."

McKuen hands him a Xeroxed Discordia Sect flyer. "Looking to find anybody connected to this."

Slim studies it impassively through his eyeglasses. Some of the others lean toward him to get a look; the rest eye McKuen, trying to assign him a rank in their universe. Slim looks up and returns the Discordia Sect piece. "Haven't seen it till you give it to me."

"Not even on TV?"

"Don't watch TV."

"Haven't heard about it, either?"

"Not interested in what some people have to say."

McKuen looks around, then waves a hand toward the church. "Who started the fire?"

"Things is always on fire." Slim is seconded immediately, heads nodding around him. "What's burning just moves from time to time."

"What goes around," someone says, "comes around," another answers, the pair trading open palms.

"Can we ask you to call us if you do hear anything?" Julia asks him.

Slim's eyes meet hers. "You new in the neighborhood?"

The crowd gathering around her laughs. She tries to block everything out of her mind, to not think, not feel, as if somehow she were less vulnerable this way.

"Yeah," a voice in the crowd shouts, "she's getting a chauffeured tour of the *ghet-to.*"

"Yo, that's right. He's *ridin'* her!"

More ugly laughter.

"You see," Slim tells her, "you got to be from *around* here, to ask me a question *about* here."

A male voice close behind her says, "Maybe she needs to get better acquainted with us."

No laughter follows the remark. The spooky silence and fire ash swirling through the air suddenly vanish, sucked into the dead sky by the convection of chopper blades. Julia looks up, deafened, closing her eyes as street soot spins and rises around her. The hem of her skirt flutters. She places one hand between her legs to hold it down, the street's dry heat rushing over them. Suddenly she feels a sense of ascension, a lightness capable of lifting her above the city's viciousness. When her eyes open, an XXN helicopter bursts into sight, ashes spinning wildly in its wake. Then it's gone, rushing away like the echo of a bomb blast.

Flames leap from a building to the church in its backdraft and spread over the church's white clapboard. Stained-glass windows melt, their images distorting, and finally bursting from their sills. The spectacle draws the crowd's attention.

"Come on," McKuen whispers. "Let's go." He takes her hand.

As they turn, someone in the crowd calls out, "Where they think they're going?"

McKuen stops, the mob hushed around them. He glances at Slim, who says, "Can't help you out. That's why my place is called 'Get Yo' Own.' " He pauses. "You'd know that if you hadn't been out of the neighborhood so long."

Then McKuen feels Julia's hand slip from his. When he turns, he sees her moving through the crowd, bodies spinning slowly to study her. McKuen starts after her. The crowd reminds him of the dead zone he chased the boy through last night. He isn't a part of these lives; he isn't a part of anything. Maybe chasing the boy is an extension of his confusion, his sense of exile. And perhaps his hope is that if he finds the boy, he finds his own way home.

People milling around the car drift away as Julia and McKuen approach, violence's flashpoint sidestepped, for the moment. Last to leave are the young boys. They peer through the car's tinted side windows and study the dashboard technology—radio, fax, computer, mini-monitor—hungry to understand their functions, their curiosity a kind of loneliness similar, Julia thinks, to her son's. They argue about the instruments' capabilities, jostle and shove one another as if defending the merits of absent fathers. McKuen moves them away from her door, his voice a whisper, and the few who look up at him seem stunned to find a gentle hand on their shoulder.

He holds the door open until Julia is in her seat. The last thing she hears before he locks her inside the car's musty quiet is the whop of chopper blades. Then they're gliding through the city again, searching for another route to Aslam A Lakem Downs. They don't look at one another. Julia turns and stares out the window. Fire, gray sky. Hate. Yet how close we are to Eden. We inhabit it already, the city of God not even a whisper away, but here, behind a veil, with no borders except those we carry around inside us.

She turns to McKuen. "I want to find my son."

McKuen takes his eyes off the road, allowing his gaze to linger on her before it returns to the empty street ahead.

"You don't know where to look."

"I want to start."

"What about our kid?"

Julia hesitates. "I'm not asking you to come along." She pauses, then adds, "I can only protect one boy at a time, if that. So if this is abdicating professional responsibility, if it's selfish, fine, you've got me. Only I don't care at the moment. My life's unraveling."

The city streams by as solitary figures dart across deserted lots, moving from condemned building to condemned building. What has he protected, McKuen wonders. Not the villages he sacked and burned in Nam. Not his wife, found dead in their living room, McKuen always there in the room with her in his dreams, but still unable to save her, his movements too slow, weighed down by forces he can't see. And certainly not the city. He used to believe his wife's death was bad karma for the hamlet in Tre Bahn. That he'd lost his home in exchange for the villages he overran. But now he knows it isn't simply his karma playing catch-up. All our ghosts have come calling. And like the phantom boy he's chasing, there's no choice but to go forward and meet them. "Which way?" is all he says.

Tonite on XXN, City of God TV
Apocalypse '99—A Gates Remington True Life Movie.
Be there. It isn't safe to go out.

Daylight passes swiftly into night. In the distance low planes of sky glow and flicker, illuminated by fire. Ray feels a chill pass over him as he cuts through a fence hole, his sweat turned to sheets of ice by the dirty breeze. Grit lifts from the ground and swirls around him, empty cans and junk food wrappers tumbling past his ankles. When the gust dies away he unties the jacket sleeves looped around his waist and slips the jacket on, then wraps himself tightly, tucking one flap inside the other. His Kaos/Peace T-shirt clings to his skin like mold, hangover fatigue and steady-falling dusk bringing on a case of dread to go with his sickly exhaustion.

He could eat something, he thinks, crossing his arms over his chest. His hands nest like birds beside each breast. He could listen to some Coda rhymes too, hear 'em breaking over the darkness, phones clapped to his ears, eyes closed, stretched out on his bed. Coda's bassy voice, rough with pride and rage raising him above the sirens and gunshots of the terrordome, out of his loneliness into something beyond fear, something Ray wants to call love. But a love full of in-the-world anger, carved out of hate. Different than the soft melting into the infinite he felt when he saw O.C., open-armed, beaming with forgiveness. That felt open and permanent. It felt right.

He surveys the wasteland ahead of him. Aslam A Lakem Downs is silhouetted against the horizon a good five miles away. He exhales, a tired calm coming over him. Little Do-Ray, he whispers. The name is strange on his tongue, distant, the fear and self-hatred attached to it finally over. Time to track down O.C.'s mom, tell her it was him who killed O.C., atone for the one sin he's sure is solely his. No blaming Coda, the white man, revolution, anything. Then, if he's still living, slide by Inch's place, explain how he got amped thinking of being a hero to Coda and all, but that he don't feel proud no more with people burnin' their homes, and why maybe the cops might be looking for Inch on account of the C-4. He stands there under a dead tree, getting his head right about what he has to do, then moves on, alive in the face of the night to come.

Rats scatter along the ground where more trash has collected. Food tins, microwavable containers, Styrofoam boxes, waxy drink cups with advertising logos Ray recognizes, their shapes instantly familiar even in the dim light. He climbs a short rise and finds himself beside a long stretch of railroad tracks. Ahead he can see a cluster of dark shapes, square patches of gold light opening and closing near the center of them. He starts in their direction, the ties passing solidly under his feet, as if he were walking on the back of passing time. A few dogs stop to take note of him, then turn back to their scavenging once they've decided he's too big to eat but nothing to worry about. Field mice are seized by hawks swifter than the helicopters that have pursued him. One hawk streaks up from the basin floor, its prey clutched to its breast. Then the sky enfolds both hunter and hunted, and together they are swallowed up by oblivion.

The smell of food cooking draws Ray's attention. The tracks have multiplied, parallel sets of them laid out around him. Against the dark ground they seem to glow, more vapor than metal as they swirl into deeper darkness. He sees a window of light open again, the shapes recognizable now as boxcars. Bodies emerge from shadow and soon Ray is walking among them. Voices call from the freight cars, gathering people in to the abandoned rail yard.

"How we know why they be calling us?"

Ray looks to his left. Moving step for step beside him is a boy his size. When his face is close enough for Ray to see it clearly, he notices something familiar in his features. Nobody he knows from the 'hood, and the tiger-striped wool cap pulled down over the boy's ears doesn't drop him into one set or another. It's a stranger kind of familiarity, as if the boy were some presence Ray knew from TV, or another life. "We don't know," he says.

"Well, when we gonna find out?"

"Soon."

The boy watches bodies hurry past them before he says, "How you know they ain't gonna be sellin' us into slavery, or lynchin' us?"

"I *don't* know."

"You know they sayin' Coda is maybe a white man. Or 'least, hooked up with the white man. The killings ain't true or nothing, either. They made 'em up—"

"Wait a minute," Ray says. "Who's saying this?"

"—the TV, XXN, like the moon landing and shit. Never happened. Just want us to riot, burn ourselves out. Get lost, go away."

"But what if it is true, the killings and all? Somebody tried to do something, make things better."

"Don't matter. They made AIDS to wipe us out. Crack, same thing. Either way, we still dyin'."

Ray thinks about the policemen he's killed. The act *changes*, or loses, its meaning when he tries to grasp it as something absolute, his crime merely another spectacle in the city's ongoing series of spectacles. All his expectations have resulted in reversals. His people haven't been liberated, but dispossessed. Do-Ray isn't a hero, he's lost. And Coda's vision of an end and new beginning, his City of God, is ashes.

Voices rise through the dark, enfolding him. People angle across sets of tracks, coming out of the shadows. As they converge, Ray senses an absence of menace and fear in the crowd, as if they were united by mutual dispossession. The pace slows to a shuffle as a line forms between two rows of boxcars.

"Smells like food," the boy whispers.

They edge forward, Ray finally placing a hand on the boy's arm to stop his nervous fidgeting. "Slow down."

"I think we should cut outta here."

"It'll be alright," Ray tells him.

"Yeah, it'll be alright till it ain't alright. Then what? I just wish they'd hurry up. This waitin' stuff makes me nuts. Kill us so we can get out of here already." He breathes softly, then sniffs the air. "Man, I hope this food ain't stuff needs cuttin'. They call it meat, you can bet yo' ass some cats ain't going home tonight." The boy glances at Ray. "You sure a quiet motherfucker."

"I'm thinkin'."

"We on line. What's there to think about? Always complicatin' things. That's why folks is going insane."

A woman's voice cuts through the dark air. Bodies in the doorway of the next boxcar lean out into the shadows, arms extended. People on the tracks reach up with their hands, take something, then move on, the woman waving them along as she gives them a blessing and directions.

"Oh man, I don't like when they be mixin' food with religion.

Like they gotta feed you if they want an audience."

"You don't trust nobody."

"Besides you, uh-uh."

"Why you trust me?"

" 'Cause you let me walk wit' you."

As they step forward into the field of light, Ray sees propane lanterns hanging from nails along the car's back wall. Working over makeshift cookers and tall stainless-steel pots are men and women dressed in gray uniforms. They pass plates toward the doorway where others hand them down to the people on line. The lady blessing everybody is the only one talking. She distributes pamphlets and points everyone toward a car on the opposite set of tracks where there's the sound of voices chanting.

"Sound like a slave ship," the boy says, his voice low.

"They praying is all."

"More craziness. Fix somethin' here for a change. Know what I'm sayin'?"

"It don't hurt nobody."

"Then why they always be groanin'?"

"Come on, children," the woman says. "People's waiting."

The boy steps to the boxcar door ahead of Ray, then pokes his head inside for a look around. "Got anything besides food?" he asks, ignoring the man trying to hand him a plate. "Blankets, clothes, anything like that."

"Got places to sleep just up ahead," the woman tells him.

"Don't need me and him a place to sleep. How's about—"

"Sister just wants you to take this and—"

"You a nun? Man, I knowed it."

"Hey." Ray places a hand on the boy's shoulder to calm him.

"Hey nothin'."

One of the boy's wrists is grabbed by the guy trying to serve him food. "I think you should take your food and do what sister says."

Ray covers the man's knuckles with his own hand. "He just gets excited. We're goin'."

The boy tries to pull his hand away. "We ain't sleepin' here neither," he shouts, his tone somewhere between hysteria and defiance. "Come in the middle of the night an' kill us!"

"Nobody's trying to hurt you, child."

Ray glances at the woman, expecting the man's grip to relax at the sound of her voice. But it doesn't. "I'll take the food for both of us," Ray says.

"I ain't eatin' that stuff."

The man yanks the boy's arm sharply. "Then what you get on line for?"

"He's hungry," Ray says.

" 'Course he is." The woman leans forward and touches one side of the boy's face. Closing her eyes, she mutters something Ray can't make out, a kind of baritone dream babble.

"Get offa me with that voodoo shit."

The boy jerks his head away from her hand. Then the plate of food is on the boxcar's floor and the boy is spinning, his arm twisted behind his back as he's pinned against the doorway. He shrieks, his cap falling from his head. The man catches him under the chin and snaps his head back. "Shut up!"

Ray instinctively grabs the man by his shirt front and somersaults him to the ground. People step away with no offers of help, no outstretched hands.

Then Ray starts toward him, but all his streetfight impulses are gone. He doesn't try to kick him, or look for something to club him with. Instead he has the sense that he himself doesn't matter, if this man on his knees does not matter to him. It's as if his heart and his actions were connected for the first time. As if with no 'hood, creed, fear, or city in his way, all that remains is mercy.

Then the boy flies past him and hits the man square in the chest with his shoulder, catapulting him backward. They go down to-gether, arms and legs entangled, each flailing blindly at the other. Footsteps come up fast behind Ray and his breath vanishes, kicked out of him by a blow between his shoulder blades. He falls, every-thing going black. The weight leaves his body, as if he were shed-ding some dead version of himself. When he pushes up off the ground and opens his eyes, figures swirl dizzyingly around him until one appears and holds fast. Dazed, all Ray says is, "Mama?"

"Come on, child," the woman says.

Ray looks past her for the boy. The man has him in a headlock, as the boy flails at him, helplessly.

"John Lee, you leave that boy alone," the woman calls out. "Let him go."

Freed, the boy tears away from the man. "Was gettin' ready to kick your ass," he shouts. People shuffle away from him. He touches the top of his head with both hands. "Where's my hat?"

"Don't be yelling at people," the woman tells him. "John Lee, fetch the boy his hat."

"Yes, ma'am." He passes the boy his hat without looking at him, then takes the woman's hand. "Sorry, sister," he says. He kisses her fingers lightly.

The boy looks at Ray. "You wanna sit for a bit? Chill? Look like you died or somethin'."

"He's tired," the woman says. "Come on and get your plates. Then go on down to the next car and find a seat."

"Yeah. We goin'."

"God loves you," she says, then turns away.

"Then God shoulda thought twice 'bout putting my ass here," he mutters. He leans close to Ray and whispers, "Gotta dis 'em like that, but don't wanna piss 'em off too much till we eat." As they walk the boy shoulders his way between bodies clustered around the head of the food line. "Come on, man. Organize your asses."

He steps to the front of the crowd and places his hands on the boxcar's floor. "Got our dinner?"

One of the cooks comes forward with two plates. "Better never let me see your ass again," he says, squatting in front of him.

The boy looks over his plate of food. "What's this next to the rice?"

"Beans."

He picks one up, holds it to his nose, sniffs, then pops it in his mouth. "Yeah, alright. Got stuff to drink?" He drinks the cup of grape juice he's handed, then extends it for a refill. He turns to Ray. "You got enough?"

"Yeah."

They move away from the food line, staying close to the darkened boxcars ahead. "You hear that?" From the other boxcar comes the sound of voices. "Praying. Man, I knew it."

The woman calls to Ray and the boy. "Come on, children. Over here."

"Shit," the boy whispers. He stops and points ahead, cup in hand. "Yeah, we just gonna sit up here while we eat."

"There's plenty of places to sit inside." Some dude steps forward, decked out in gangbanger regalia—beltless fatigue pants, the elastic waistband of his boxer shorts showing, doo-rag tied around his head pirate style, tattoos on each arm. But as he steps closer, Ray notices the slogan on his tanktop. *Stop the Killing.* Between his pectoral muscles is a small bright cross.

"Them fools told us it was full," the boy says.

"Get your butts on in there 'fore I kick 'em back to your sorry-ass mamas."

"Yeah? God tell you you could do that?"

The guy swats the back of the boy's head.

"Hey. Quit hittin' me. Tired a this shit."

"Then go sit your ass down, and listen for a change."

Walking beside Ray the boy whispers, "Man, I hate it when mo-therfuckers get saved."

Inside the car people are seated on crude benches and over-turned crates. Lanterns burn, their halos splashed across the wall. Painted between them are images of trial, crucifixion, and salva-tion, the wounds so vivid Ray imagines they're blotches of actual blood. Up front there's a small platform with rusted folding chairs along the back of it. Lighted candles burn at the fringe of the stage.

The boy sets his plate on his knees. "Damn, it's like a tomb in here." He leans forward and looks at the old man next to Ray. "Hey, you wanna shove over. Half my butt's hanging off this thing."

Ray gets a strong whiff of urine as the man's coat opens.

"Eat up so we can get outta here." The boy shovels rice into his mouth with a plastic spoon. "I bet this food is poisoned, too. Make us crazy, go 'round killin' each other."

Stepping to the edge of the stage, the woman begins clapping her hands, gangbangers standing behind her as they join in.

"Aw shit. I knew it. They gonna make us sing."

The far end of the sackcloth is pulled aside and a man wearing a black suit and tie enters. He's flanked by two other black men dressed in the same cut of suit and immaculate white shirts. They move to the back of the stage and stand there, hands clasped, wait-ing for the hymn to end.

"Kill everyone, get it over with. That's what I say," the boy whis-pers. "Coda knows."

"Coda don't last," Ray says.

"Nothin' does." The boy looks up as the hymn concludes. "Here comes rent-a-rev. Maybe he's gonna tell us what's what."

Nearing the front of the platform the reverend takes the sister's hand, then bends to kiss it. One of the men motions for ushers to dim the lanterns. Light sinks into shadow.

"They turn down lights at the circus too," the boy whispers.

At the foot of the stage, the man removes his eyeglasses and places them inside one of his jacket pockets. Ray pictures Coda pacing the floor of some dim, underground studio, gathering his thoughts, getting psyched to kick some rhymes, one black voice against a background of sirens, chopper roar, gunfire, all the chaos of the unholy city. Only where Coda emerged unseen and raging from the killing fields, this man fills the room with stillness, as if he could stop time by the sheer force of his will.

"Now I ain't going to preach to you," he says softly. "Mm-mmh, no. Don't believe in it. Last thing you need is more rules. More laws. Somebody *else*"—his hand snaps as if he were cracking a whip, the pitch of his voice trembling—"telling you how to live." He stares into the crowd, head swiveling lightly from side to side, his voice gentle when he resumes speaking. "Don't need it. Got enough *rules,* got enough *laws,* out there in the city." Someone in the crowd seconds him. "Got *laws* from sunup to sundown, from Monday to Sunday." He flicks one hand through the air. "Got enough laws that if they didn't write another one from now till *doomsday* we couldn't break all the ones we already got!" His pitch drops low again and he stops moving. "But I'll tell you one thing we ain't got, and that's justice." There's a great quiet in the air, and he allows it to hover before snatching it back. "No, don't have that. Don't have much in the way of mercy, either." He flicks a hand to one side. "And compassion? I ain't even going to mention that."

"I thought he wasn't gonna preach," the boy says, tossing his empty dinner plate onto the floor.

Prowling the stage, the man says, "Tell you why we don't have these things. You can't *legislate* justice. You can't *legislate* mercy. And you sure as hell can't *legislate* compassion. Go on an' tell someone, love your neighbor. Know what the answer gonna be?"

He swats the air, his voice squealing. "Man, get the fuck outta my face! Love your own neighbor."

The crowd laughs and he laughs with them, the others on stage nodding behind him.

He points down into the pews and says cheerfully, "You know I'm right. That's why I ain't gonna preach to y'all."

"Promised you wasn't!" the boy shouts.

"That's right, I did." He aims a finger in the boy's direction.

"Why don't you just shut up an' listen?" Ray whispers.

"Just 'cause you need this shit don't mean I do."

"How you know what I need?" Ray finds himself suddenly angry, then understands why the boy looked familiar to him. The boy's features match his own. He's as adrift and terrified as Ray ever was. Lost. And on his own. "Sorry," Ray whispers, as if he were forgiving the ghost of himself.

The boy offers a sulky grunt in reply. Then Ray reaches over and lays one hand on his knee, which goes calm under his touch, and neither of them says a word.

"I can't be lecturing you an' all," the man is saying as Ray becomes conscious of his words again. " 'Cause I don't know nothin'. Come from nowhere, got nowhere, expect I'll probably go back to nowhere. Dust unto dust." He flashes the palm of one hand. "That's alright. No problem. 'Cause I been low. I mean *low*. I'm talking"—he leans forward and pretends to pick something up from the floor—"people be lookin' under the carpet, saying, 'Where is that motherfucker?' " There's a faint sweat covering his forehead now, and it shines like a flame in the candlelight. "I don't know," he says, mimicking a second speaker. "His lazy ass was on the couch a minute ago." He laughs, then shifts gears. "I been *high* though, too. If you low, you just got to get high! No way around it. So I been *high*," he draws this last word out, then pauses, "but I ain't never been . . . to the mountaintop! Not many of us been''—his voice booming, then followed by a miraculous return to gentleness—''to the mountaintop. So I'm gonna tell you a story.''

''Alright,'' sister's voice says from the darkness behind him.

''Alright,'' he repeats. ''It's the *story* someone who *has* been to the mountaintop . . . told me.'' He pauses, and when he speaks again his words explode like cannon fire. ''It's the story of an angel!'' His hand clenches into a fist above his head, then slowly descends. ''And it's the story of a devil,'' his voice like the hush after a storm. ''Got to have one of each, otherwise—there's no story.''

''I know all this stuff,'' the boy whispers, head down. His tone is apologetic, as if he's failed Ray in some way.

''We'll go in a minute. We go now, they'll just catch us.''

The man is pacing when Ray looks up. ''And this devil just wouldn't let the angel be. Angel's trying to chill an' all, devil's in his face. I mean like *constantly*. Come on over here'n do this. Don't sit there. Want some a this? Can't have it. Tellin' the angel the whole time, God don't love him. That's why you living with me, motherfucker. God don't want nothin' to do with your sorry ass! You're lucky you got me. Other motherfuckers ain't gonna put up with your shit. And on like that till, finally, you gotta ask yourself.'' He stops pacing and looks up. ''Why? We know people always trying to get something for nothing. Man ain't no prince—we *know* dat! But with this buggin'-the-angel stuff, we're getting into, like . . . craziness. So you gotta say to yourself—why. What's the point? Leave the dude alone, you know. Get a life.''

Low laughter ripples over the benches.

''Then it hits you. Without fuckin' with the angel's behind twenty-four zillion hours a day . . . the devil wouldn't have nothin' to do. And with nothin' to do, the devil would lose his whole *purpose* in life.''

The room is still enough for Ray to hear the thick tubercular breathing of people sitting several rows away. No coming attractions or blaring commercials. No brain-crushing helicopter whirlwinds. Just grave, timeless silence. Peace in the heart of the eternal city.

"You alright?"

Ray turns and sees the boy staring at him.

"Look like you in a zone or somethin'."

"I'm here."

"Yeah but you somewhere else, too." He glances at his knee. "Go on and get your hand off my leg." Ray lifts his hand and they sit there silently.

"—till finally the angel say, That's it. I'm gonna whup yo' ass."

"Amen."

When Ray looks again the boy is gone, sackcloth flapping, footsteps thinning to silence in the distance. . . .

"So they fought. Then they fought some more," the man says matter-of-factly. "They fought a thousand years."

"Yes," sister calls out.

"Ten thousand years!" His voice grows louder.

"Keep going."

"They fought for what seemed like all eternity! And when the smoke cleared," he says quietly, "the angel had won."

Ray can hear the boy's voice in his head. *Bullshit.* But the pressure in his chest, the clenching of his throat is not because the story is right or wrong. He's beyond the story. It's time to get home, face his own devil.

"So one voice is tellin' the angel, leave, cut bait, get your behind outta here. But this other voice is tellin' the angel—stay. Hold on, *think* about what you doin' here. . . . And the angel turned back. He saw that devil *down on his knees!* . . . where he'd wanted him to be for so long. And his heart was filled all over again with bitterness! With callousness! And with hatred. Yeah, all these things. Things he wanted to be rid of now and forever. . . . And while he's standing there, figuring out what he's gonna do, he hears this voice. And it's the devil's voice. And it says—you believe this?— Help me. Just like that, Help me.''

Silence.

"Help your *mama!* is what the angel's thinking." The man laughs, as do others, though Ray remains quiet. The story's outcome is already running through his veins, bringing a kind of ecstasy, the sense that he inhabits this moment yet all of eternity, this flesh and yet all that does not distinguish itself as flesh, this place as well as the city of God. He has run the labyrinth and found it to be a circle, sin leading to compassion, hate to love, blindness to sight, the maze no more than the ghosts of human fear and confusion. He mourns all that is done and cannot be undone, then surrenders to all that is unfathomable, yet is. The unspeakable.

"So the angel went back. Not because he had the strength to carry his devil, no. But because he saw that if he was ever gonna forgive himself, he had to forgive his devil too. See, they're the same. One and the same, angel and devil. And the angel *saw this*. And *seeing clearly*—without hatred, without bitterness—is all there is. You may *whup* your enemy, but you better never stop *lovin'* your enemy, 'less you wanna stop loving yourself. 'Cause then where are you? . . . *Lost* . . . lost. . . . So the angel went over and *picked up* his devil! Probably wasn't too gentle, more like get your ass up, motherfucker. Then told him, alright we goin'! We goin' now, you and me!''

Ray stands.

"Ho." Ray glances at the stage and sees the man pointing at him. "Don't mean 'we' going, like *you* and me. Workin' with what you call a parable here."

"I know."

"That's good you know."

"I just need to get on is all."

"Oh." The pitch of the man's voice rises. "You ain't got nothin' to learn here? I see. Well then, maybe you wanna get on up here and tell us where they headed."

"No."

" 'Cause they goin' to the Promised Land! You ever had your skinny little ass to the Promised Land?"

"No."

"No, I didn't think so! So why don't you go on and put it back down?"

Ray pauses, then says, "It's just a story."

"Oh, it's just a story." The man turns to the crowd, incredulous. "Listen to the little motherfucker." The usher beside him whispers something, the man tilting his head to listen. "Where's your friend?" he asks, straightening up.

"Runnin'."

"Running where?"

"Just from."

"Ah, I see."

Ray wonders how he can make the man understand what he feels. He doesn't want his words mistaken for mockery. "See, I killed some folks," he begins. "So while I like it an' all, it's just a story."

"Uh-huh."

Ray gropes for impossible, nonexistent words, a language of miracle. "It's like that cell," he says.

"What cell?"

"In the Afroman game. It's way up. And it's like I'm here *and* there. In two worlds." Ray's eyes study the man's eyes. "You killed, ain't you?" he asks.

Silence. "Maybe." Then silence again. "You know where you're going?" the man says.

"Home."

The man nods, and Ray sees that he's no longer being judged but acknowledged. A presence, not a shadow. "We'll see you around, then."

Ray pushes aside the sackcloth but the man's voice stops him. "Little man." Ray looks up. The reverend points at Ray, eyes opening wide as he becomes animated once again. "We goin'. Oh yeah, that's right. We goin' to the Promised Land!" He spins toward the opposite side of the stage. "Like it or not! And we not only goin', we gonna get there!"

Alone, Ray's high-tops crunch on the gravel as the voices fade behind him. Beyond crumbling warehouses the plain rises again, distant office tower windows jeweling the night sky. The graceless silhouette of Aslam A Lakem Downs appears as he reaches the crest of a hill. Searchlight beams sweep through the dark above it. Fires turn the concrete fields into a sea of burning candles. And the red logo that crowns the city's tallest building flashes in sync with the beating of his heart—XXN, XXN, XXN. . . .

Darren Adams's three-page-long confession is typed, spell-checked, passed through a computer's grammar-rite software program, then run off on a laser printer by Dan, who has been covering Nick's behind in Arraignment Room 4 during the ninety minutes it took Nick to locate the boy. The crimes dreamed up by Nick include: Robbery 1 *and,* with extreme prejudice, assault (of Nick himself—lie), conspiracy (with the Discordia Sect), aiding and abetting (Ray), incitement to riot, treason, illegal possession of a handgun, speeding (all pure fabrications), the sale of narcotics, participation in a hate crime, and attempted murder.

"Sign it," Nick says. They are back in his office cubicle.

"What's it say?"

"It says you're totally innocent of all charges."

"It don't say that."

"I thought you couldn't read."

" 'Cause that's what I wanted you to think."

Nick exhales, sits quietly, then takes out his Lorcim L-25 pistol, which is no bigger than his hand. "You want to go back down to the pens?"

Darren doesn't answer.

"If I don't spring you, McKuen's going to tie your ass to a pair of executions. You know what the sentence for cop killing is?"

"I don't know nothing 'bout that stuff."

Nick checks his watch. He has six hours to deliver Gates Remington a TV mega-event, or else he gets to work for Harley von Vaughn for the rest of his life. He leans close to the boy and puts the gun barrel to his head. "Well then, pretend you do. . . ."

". . . Your Honor, every apology to the court for the brief yet essential recess." Nick leads Darren Adams into the room he was supposed to be in two hours ago. "But I could not in good conscience, having this signed, astonishing, and utterly criminal confession in hand, simply sit by and see justice ridiculed."

Though the halls outside throng in pandemonium, the interior of the arraignment room is snug, hushed, and virtually empty. There's only Nick, Darren Adams, one bailiff, a stenographer, the judge, two long tables facing one another, and some chairs. It's so quiet Nick can hear the judge's phlegmy, asthmatic breathing as he studies the confession in his trembling hands. So quiet he can hear Darren's muffled crying behind him.

The judge, however, can't. His hearing aid seems to be on the fritz and Nick finds himself having to scream into the man's face in order to be heard.

"Your Honor, the people being locked up today are, by and large, petty criminals charged with looting, public disorder, spitting. My client, and this in no way reflects negatively on his person, is a major felon. A terrorist, in my opinion, with links to a worldwide revolutionary underground."

Nick watches for some sign that his words are registering with the ancient magistrate. He estimates the judge's net worth at three million, seventy percent of it accumulated through bribes while he was serving on the bench. Nick bristles at the thought of someone who has only two needs in life—an adjustable mattress and a bedpan—having all that cash. He has a sudden urge to bash the man's head in, then go live in his house. Just as suddenly he understands the riots. It isn't even a verbal sensation, more like an electric shock. For a moment he's tapped into the fury of the dispossessed. It passes when he remembers that he hates them, too. He isn't a revolutionary, simply a failed megalomaniac. Fuck solidarity. Raise my credit card limit.

"Sir, we in the Public Defender's Office are aware of the tacit intent of the District Attorney to avoid setting bail for defendants in order to detain people as long as they wish. I state that this is not only illegal, but morally loathsome." Nick stops and clears his throat. "However, it is, as I'm sure you know, not without precedent. Chicago, 1968. L.A., 1992. Miami. Detroit." He feels pretty good pacing in front of the bench. His peculiar mood—part remorse for hitting the boy, part wealth-anxiety, plus the Percodan is starting to take the edge off his Benzedrine rush—allows him to relish a certain false professionalism. If he could only persuade himself that the law wasn't all a huge crock of shit, he believes at times that he could actually be a good attorney. Carry on a spunky courtship with Julia from Hate Crimes. Argue the exclusionary rule over cartons of ethnic takeout. Fuck her gloriously every night. Why am I denied these things? Why do I only know people who make documentaries about satanic gangbangs?

"Judge, sir, I want you to know that what I witnessed outside on the plaza this morning, a mass incarceration, the very beginnings of a total descent into fascism, troubled and frightened me profoundly." He gropes for a properly sincere expression. "Therefore, I urge you not to besmirch the sterling record of your fifty years on the bench by falling prey to the trendy allure of a police state. Distinguish between terrorism and jaywalking." Nick points at Darren. "My client is evil incarnate! Don't let him escape on a technicality. I beg you—look into your heart. Then crucify him!"

The man is immobile.

Nick rolls his eyes in the direction of the Latino bailiff, a short, extremely muscular woman in a skintight uniform. She's pretty, if a bit stern-looking, her moussed crew cut giving her a teenager-about-to-go-bad attractiveness. Nick flashes his patented, sex-meister smile at her—no teeth showing, just pursed lips and irresistible dimples. She mouths the words "Fuck you."

A rumbling emanates from the judge, who seems to have shriveled even further. His bald head and hands are pale as jellyfish and crisscrossed by bulging scriggles of blue vein. He looks like an anatomy class specimen. Nick still isn't sure the sounds he's making qualify as language.

"Excuse me?" Leaning forward, Nick waits on a response. Then the judge raises his head. His eyes, obscured by cataracts, look like a pair of raw oysters.

"Five hundred thousand dollars bail," he croaks. He scribbles his signature on the arraignment petition, then tosses it onto the table. "Next."

The line at the cashier's window is short—just prostitutes, stock fraud specialists, and serial killers accompanied by their literary agents—but it isn't moving very fast. The computers are down.

Nick tries to call Gates Remington and is told by a recorded voice that the phone number has moved outside its area code's transmission halo. Please try your XXN call again later.

How can a phone number move *outside* its area code? Nick severs the portaphone's connection with a tap of his thumb. He presses "memory dial 1," his office cubicle's extension. Beside him, Darren Adams has stopped crying, though his eyes haven't once looked up from the floor and his breathing resembles extended sighs. "Look," Nick says, tempted to lay his free hand on the boy's shoulder. Instead he lets the hand drop away, brushing the air in a gesture of futility. The boy flinches as Nick's hand moves past him. Nick exhales. He's sorry for hitting him, isn't he? He didn't *want* to put the gun to his head. How long is he supposed to grovel and apologize?

Nick's thoughts are interrupted by his own voice on the answering machine at the other end of the line when Dan doesn't answer. The beep is extremely loud.

"What is the point of underpaying you if you're not there to screen calls? Call me when you finish applying your eyeliner. And order me some Chinese. I'm depressed." Nick sees that Darren Adams still hasn't looked up from the ground. "Get a lot of stuff. And extra chopsticks. And put it on Gates Remington's credit card number! It's on my desk." Then he's off, just as the computers come back on. The criminals in line creep toward the teller's window. Nick's phone rings. It's his call-forwarding system giving him his own message. He curses and hangs up.

Nick stands shoulder to shoulder with the boy. He's a head taller than him and can read the initials etched onto the back of his nappy buzz cut: *D.O.A.* Dead on Arrival.

"Listen, you're not going to jail for murder. Would you rather be back downstairs? Or with that lunatic who almost took your head off at the police station this morning? No. I had to say those things in the arraignment room to get you booked. If I don't get you booked, they don't set bail. If they don't set bail, you don't get out." Nick doesn't add, get out so you can help me make a small fortune, though he assumes that the boy understands the concept of enlightened self-interest. He even decides to donate, provided he makes half a million or more on the Gates Remington deal, one percent of his after-tax earnings to the community center at Aslam A Lakem Downs. If they have one.

"Believe me. This is the system. They don't want you. *You* don't exist. They want any anonymous bad guy, and a good show. That way they shape it, they control it. Why? Two reasons: one, so the truth never has to be faced; and two, so history and dream merge, creating the illusion that there's a future. We can forget for a while the fact that we're doomed. But hey, you know." Nick tosses his hands up, helpless. "When the end is near, who needs due process? Revelation! A New Jerusalem. That's what we want."

Nick lets the speed in his system finish wiring together a pair of synapses. Revelation in pill form. Pharmaceutical Jerusalem. The techno-city of God. A new thought comes to him, some daydream bulletin from the city's unconscious. It's tough to say whether he simply has spliced together a lot of information, or heard the voice of a knowing angel. Does it matter? It matters deeply. It's the difference between being bound to one another by reason, or by mystery and faith. Linked by law, or linked by love. So yeah, it matters. But whether Nick channeled his new idea or pulled a Sherlock Holmes, he is convinced of one thing. There is no Discordia Sect. There is no single, objective truth. There is no Coda. Or if Coda does exist, he was quite possibly dreamed up by some demon programmer on the fast track at XXN.

This revelation might not be of any comfort to Darren Adams, though. "Look," Nick says, "elevating you to the status of terrorist-murderer is the best thing anybody's ever done for you."

"But it ain't true!"

"That's why it worked! Whatever isn't true, we own. And manip-
ulate." Nick catches stares from the military brass scurrying past in
the corridor. He feels energized by the sense of crisis in the hallways. It's as if a good action movie has come alive with him in it.
Illusion as existence.

He surveys the wide hall, checking for Harley von Vaughn or
anyone else who might dampen his spirits by having him arrested.
Skinheads sweep past, so close he can smell the beer on their
breath, indistinguishable from their uniformed guards except for
the handcuffs and swastikas. Beyond the crowd a high arched window looks out onto the city: helicopters, smoke, a snow of ashes.
To Nick, hopeless and speeding his brains out, the scene does
seem kind of beautiful. His elevator operator acquaintance was
right—the end is sublime. And necessary, Nick thinks. Apocalypse
had to come because God wouldn't. The struggle to impose meaning never ceases.

Nick sees the boy studying him. "What are you worried about?
This is good. No truth means you're free. If there were an absolute
good or evil, you'd be on your way to the gas chamber. You're out
because everything's hollow and corrupt; also because I'm one of
the few people brave enough to admit that the world is a barbaric
sinkhole, without holding a grudge. You're free because I, your
attorney, believe in absolutely nothing."

"Ray believes."

"Who's Ray? The one we're chasing?" Darren nods. "See?
That's his problem. He believes, he's going to death row. You?"

"I didn't do nothin'."

"Inch, Inch." Nick puts his hands up to calm the kid.

"Darren."

"What?"

"Call me by my right name."

D.O.A. Darren O. Adams, idiot. "What's the 'O' stand for? Clue me in."

"Do I got a choice?"

"It's up to you."

Darren makes a sound that's part laugh, part cough. "I'm in handcuffs." He's silent as the line shuffles forward, then he says, "Ogun. The Nigerian god of war. His mother was the mother of gods." He pauses. "Had him a good dog, too."

Nick looks at the boy, pondering his rap sheet. A long list of petty offenses, shoplifting, curfew violations, some low-level dope peddling. But he really *is* innocent. Or at least right. He didn't do anything. "How did McKuen hook you to Ray?"

"I don't know."

"Think."

"I don't know."

"I'm not going to tell anybody. I'm your goddamned attorney for Christ's sake!"

"Oh, you mean like a protector an' all?"

Nick has an instant understanding of the boy's petty criminal career. Ray killed two city policemen. He's the one who's after something. This kid wavers between helpless self-pity and what-we-gonna-do-next? As unmoored as I am, Nick thinks. Only I have a twelve-hundred-dollar suit and WASP genes. "Yeah, like your protector and all. You think your friend's gonna waltz through this like Oswald?"

"Oswald?"

"Sirhan Sirhan. James Earl Ray. Lone assassins. The world is sane, except for one crazed individual. We don't buy that anymore. Things have gotten *too* random. So we have cults, sects, small groups with organized, destructive purposes. That way the insanity makes sense again. We need conspiracy theories no matter how irrational they are. You follow? They defer the truth, promise revelation. They're what we have in place of God. So don't tell me you don't know. Your friend is uninteresting on his own. If he's uninteresting, he's unmarketable. And if he's unmarketable by virtue of not being hooked into some secret terror organization that'll hold an audience past the first bowl of popcorn, you'll be one dead Nigerian. Do we have the power balance of this relationship worked out now? Hm, Darren?"

Nick doesn't hide from the boy's stare. "So you want to kill me. What else is new? Want to know how I live with it?" At the cashier's window Nick presents the automated teller with Gates Remington's credit card number. "You're a confessed terrorist-murderer, and they're letting you go because you have Visa." He takes the approval slip as it's spit out of the machine, hands Darren Adams the indictee's copy, and keeps the outgoing security checkpoint's copy himself.

"See, you're at large again. The slip even says 'Have a nice day.' I take a pill, twenty minutes later I'm profound. Believe me, there's no right and wrong. There's only the avoidance of suffering." He nudges Darren in the direction of his office cubicle. "Belief in *anything* is unwieldy. All to be explained in my new book, *Meaninglessness Made Easy.*"

They turn a corner, moving out of the fray.

"Belief is the reason we're going to catch your friend. The *real* players go whichever way the money's flowing." Nick stops the boy so they're facing one another. "So tell me. There isn't any Discordia Sect, is there?" Silence. "Darren, as your *attorney,* I have to know these things."

"You gotta ask Ray."

"Were the executions on TV this morning staged or real?"

"I don't know nothin' 'bout that stuff. I was *there* with you!"

"So why did McKuen bring you in?"

"I don't know."

"We can go ask him. Then find Ray, lock your ass up with his."

"What'd you make me confess all that stuff for?"

"I told you. Now is now. Later you'll disappear."

"I ain't got no place to disappear to."

"Then you'll deny it. The sect threatened to kill you so you lied. Give up your friends from TV this morning—"

"I don't know 'bout that!"

"So you give up Ray, he sells out the others. *That's* the Discordia Sect, right? Ten guys who couldn't make the NBA find God. There's no Coda either, correct?"

"Ray got his tapes."

"Tapes! Great!" Nick slams the wall behind Darren Adams with the palm of one hand. He stares at the ceiling in disgust, and doesn't notice the boy warily bracing himself for a blow until he lowers his head. "I'm not going to hit you," he finally says. Out of habit, he lights a cigarette, something to help him scheme, calculate, think—all of which he finds annoying. Why does there have to be cause-and-effect, logic? Why can't everything be disconnected sensation, like acid trips and movie trailers?

"He could exist," Darren says. "Coda an' all, I mean."

"Yeah, yeah, yeah." Glancing at the boy, Nick wonders if he could kill *him* for the TV special. Better yet, have McKuen kill him. That way he co-opts McKuen's blackness for the forces of good— i.e., people with property and taxable income—and demonizes Darren Adams. It's an elegant idea, not to mention commercially viable. A patronized character (McKuen) confronts and overwhelms a scapegoat character (Darren Adams). Racial identity vs. allegiance to the good; order vs. chaos; father vs. son; undoubtedly a good chase scene. It's biblical *and* banal, simplistic *and* gaudy; and, above all, as morally reprehensible as it is untrue. In other words, perfect television. Who needs reality? Invent!

"Come on," Nick says, flipping his cigarette in the direction of a recycling bin. "Whoa, hold it." What if, and this is a big *what if,* but let's just say intrepid, fearless, city-saving Public Defender Christian Wolf, on the trail of the underground forces plaguing the metropolis, is saved from escaped Discordia Sect zealot Darren Adams by the ultra-noble detective Dennis McKuen, who kills the boy, *and* the secret that there is no Discordia Sect along with him. Nick tries to determine whether he's possessed by some screenplay writer's hallucinations, or an exquisitely Shakespearean sense of narrative possibility. He hasn't thumbed a Cliff Notes version of the bard since sex was safe, so he graciously decides to accept his own genius on faith. "Alright, let's go."

"We gonna look for Ray?"

"Yeah. Shortly."

" 'Cause he's the one who could tell you 'bout the killings an' all."

"That's the only way I'll be able to help him."

"I ain't saying he done any of 'em."

"Everybody's innocent until proven guilty." Nick hears the phone in his cubicle ring one and a half times, then stop. Incoming fax.

"Ray's just really into this apocalypse stuff, like somethin' could come out of it an' all. You know?"

"We all live in hope."

Darren takes the seat Nick has pointed to. "I am gonna get these handcuffs off, right? I mean, I am out on bail and all."

"Technically." Nick eyes the page slithering out of the machine. Bold print at the top of it reads "Gates Remington Entertainment." He can't make out the fine print. "We have to be out of the building, maybe a little farther."

"I let you lie 'bout me and didn't say nothin'!" Nick looks at the boy. "Now I'm helpin' you so you could get what you want." The only sound is a slight squeaking from the fax machine's printer wheels as page two emerges. "I ain't like Ray," he mutters.

"No," Nick says. "Obviously not." He finds himself wondering if McKuen could actually kill Darren. Once we're crisscrossing fiction and reality, might as well be morally instructive. "Crime Doesn't Pay." Nick's simulated, live-action docudrama will be lauded for its unflinching realism. Who knows, with the proper "spin," he might even walk away with the first Pulitzer for TV journalism. After all, the lie he's selling seems poised for immediate, widespread acceptance. The deeper the lie, the greater the hype. "Later," Nick tells him. "The cuffs will come off later."

"Just don't wait too long." Darren stretches his legs out in front of him. "Chained up like this, I could forget things." Nick turns away from the boy, who dreamily studies the mess and clutter of the cubicle as if he were alone. A moment later, he even begins to hum.

Nick reaches for the contract, now three pages, and sees a note from Dan sitting atop his desk litter.

"Harley is looking for you and he's *not* happy. Film crew arriving one hour, approx. 3:30 base of steps by plaza. *What* are you doing?!" He hasn't even ordered dim sum yet. Dope. Attached is a memo from Harley von Vaughn, which is unflattering but pithy. "Expect disbarment." Nick checks his watch: 2:45. Five hours to prime time. He drops into his armchair and pulls open a desk drawer. He scrounges through debris, comes up with a Zantac anti-ulcer tablet, then locates a half-buried can of warm Coke, which he figures will help settle his stomach.

"I get a sip of that?" Darren says.

Speedreading the contract, Nick holds the can to the boy's lips.

"... and whereby for the purposes of a joint venture responsible for the creation of live docudrama events based on the ongoing citywide riots, up to and including speculation as to their point of origin, ideological genesis, possibly unverified yet nonetheless videotaped acts of sex or violence of a pagan, satanic, or other deviate religious nature, let it be known to all the parties involved that this contract constitutes the formation for said purposes a subsidiary of Gates Remington Entertainment, herewith known as Apocalypse Productions & Enterprises (A.P.E.), co-producers Gates Remington III and Christian Nicholas Wolf."

Yes!

The rest of the fine print outlines licensing, royalties, world rights, sequels. Then comes a clause that makes Nick nervous. "The sum of one hundred thousand U.S. dollars or its equivalent is to be paid. . . ."

Its *equivalent?* Fuck, cocksucker, and other contract negotiation phrases come to mind, but Nick's vicious memory-dialing only gets him the same out-of-area-code message as before. He claps the cordless phone down into its recharger cradle and seethes, his eyes closing. He's startled by Dan's panting voice.

"Get out. Von Vaughn left AR-4 thirty seconds ago with half a SWAT team. You're being arrested."

"Disbarred."

"Disbarred *and* arrested. Harley read the arraignment log as soon as it came on line."

"Doesn't this guy have a fucking life?"

"They were headed toward the cashier lines."

Nick is already packing. Swearing like a maniac, but also packing. Into his briefcase go drugs, electronic equipment, gun, and the contract forming Apocalypse Productions & Enterprises. His free hand waves the boy out of the vinyl armchair. "You have a number for the film crew?" he asks Dan.

"No."

"Get one."

"Before or after I'm taken into custody?"

"Harley's not going to arrest you. Fire, yes. But not arrest. Get a number, tell them to call me."

"If not?"

"I'll be at the plaza steps at 3:30." Backing down the corridor, Darren Adams at arm's length ahead of him, Nick watches Dan recede and senses that he's at the end of something. Whether he's free of his deadening, loneliness-crazed past or simply lost, he doesn't know. He feels only sadness. If it were a perfect, sentimental TV-movie world, Dan, the one soul Nick has been loved by, would be Danielle, long hair falling around her shoulders, the office partition a white picket fence, the stained ceiling a blue sky filled with ozone and radiant sunlight. She would be pregnant as he goes off to save the city, promising he will come back for her, even if it takes forever. . . . But here in the blighted city their love is fated to die, unless it lives on as a gay fairy tale of unrequited devotion. *Leather-ring Heights,* set in a gay condo complex on the Pacific Palisades. Nick is Heathcliff, who dies of a drug overdose, which is becoming a distinct possibility. As he nears the fire exit, he raises one hand, forming a viewfinder with thumb and index finger. "Reverse tracking shot. Dolly back slowly. Time stretches. . . . Bittersweet silence. . . ." He twists his hand quickly. "Reverse angle. The hero is gone, a door swinging closed in his wake. . . ."

The stairwell is streaked with shadows once the metal door booms shut behind them. And quiet, which makes Nick uncomfortable. The Benzedrine he took makes his pulse race and the Percodan does not quite lull his anxiety. He can hear his own heartbeat. He prefers the city's distracting blare and noise. Clubs, traffic, the sounds of chaos.

Studying the initials at the back of Darren's head as they hustle down gritty concrete steps, Nick wonders if, as a corporate executive of A.P.E., he's ultimately responsible for the boy's death if he's killed during the Revelation-TV special. What if Darren's death is the catharsis the city needs to sate the chaos-gods within it? Isn't that the same as ancient sacrifice? Isn't that . . . sacred? Is Coda responsible for Ray's actions? Someone gets crushed by a tank, you going to blame the guy who invented the wheel?! Where do we draw a line on responsibility? And do we move the line individually, or do we move it together?

"Hold it, slow down." Nick tugs on Darren's shoulder, then leans against a cinder-block wall.

"I can't move too fast, bein' I'm handcuffed and all," Darren says, turning to look at Nick.

"Funny." Nick takes a deep breath. His forehead is covered by a greasy film of soot and sweat. He imagines that if he saw his pupils in a mirror they'd be the size and color of black beans. "Is my skin yellow or . . . gray or something?"

Darren takes a close look, his face tilting from left to right. "White folks never look too healthy to begin with, you know."

"You're a big help."

"Says I'm supposed to help you?"

"Fine, get another attorney. Go to the electric chair."

"Don't sound to me like you're no attorney no more."

Nick pushes away from the wall, woozy yet alert in a paranoid kind of way. He stares at Darren until his eyes focus. "I'm still an attorney. Blacks join gangs and shoot each other; whites go to law school then make hollow threats. Don't be impressed by Harley. He never got over being hall monitor. And don't use double negatives." Nick exhales. "I look alright?"

"You'll live."

"Lucky for you." Nick nudges the boy forward again. "You say something?"

"No."

"Because I thought I heard something like a snicker."

"It could be the echoes in this place."

"Not wiseass mumbling?"

"No, nothin' like that."

"Good." Nick raises his chin, indicating the direction they're headed. "Go."

The passageway leads past parking lot doors and freight elevator shafts. Exit signs posted along the walls begin to change from judicial markings to commercial ones. Small televisions set in the cinder-block walls advertise Mondo Burger, an all-nude juice bar called Squeezed Lemons, the Discreet Strumpet, Mantras to Go, and Karla, the Brutal Masseuse.

"You know which way you're goin'?"

"Yes, I know which way I'm going."

Nick doesn't have a clue. All he knows is that they're in the walking-mall section of the complex. He's not even sure what level. Businesses set up, half of them to launder drug money, then disappear into oblivion two months later.

"Hold it." Nick watches the next liquid-crystal television screen they come to. Nothing is advertised overtly, which Nick instantly understands as *très chic*. He presses the "menu" sensor at the base of the protective Plexiglas casing. The screen's buzzing colors and shape-shifting images, a kind of Day-Glo video lava, become a set of instructions: "You must have a minimum available credit line of one hundred thousand U.S. dollars in order to enter. Please insert your ID now." The information also appears in German, Japanese, Italian, Spanish, and Arabic, with corresponding currency amounts.

"Turn around."

"What for?"

"So I can shoot you in the back, that way you're totally useless to me. I'm going to undo the handcuffs. Or have you been begging me to do something else for the last two hours?"

"Undo away."

Nick whispers. "Don't even think about my gun. Think about mall security. Think about the white taxpayer subdivisions you're going to have to limp through to get home." Nick springs one cuff. "You have heard about skinheads stomping skulls till they crack?" Free, Darren Adams turns, rubbing one sore wrist at a time. "Nasty stuff. Unpleasant world," Nick says. "And it's all the fault of television."

Nick enters Gates Remington's XXN credit account number into a computer-coded locking system. Three seconds later, the account is approved and compression deadbolts disengage inside a pair of steel slab doors. They open onto pristine brightness, perfumed air, New Wave classical Muzak. Nick extends an ushering hand. "Onward."

The floor is café-au-lait-colored marble with a gold tile border. Above, the atrium ceiling reaches three stories, then converges in a Gothic arch. Chandeliers brilliant as sunbursts dangle from mahogany buttresses. Cherubs float through blue sky and clouds white as the cotton stuffing of pill bottles. Nick figures he's hallucinating because the red-cheeked imps do seem to be moving. Then he realizes they are. The entire mural scrolls in continuous motion, heaven by the yard.

Boutiques line the long, deserted gallery. Down its center are Louis XIV cherrywood tables, topped with vases of long-stemmed roses. Delicate gold trays hold engraved business cards for shops with additional locations in Paris, London, Rome, Tokyo, Berlin, Rio de Janeiro, Hong Kong, Melbourne, and fashionable Saigon. Behind the polished brass of locked doors, merchandise rests in almost sacred repose. Linen slacks, three-thousand-dollar loafers, ropes of pearls. Two-story-tall Persian carpets, Ming Dynasty pottery, colognes in cut-crystal bottles, Mozart's first piano. It occurs to Nick that he actually may be dead and in consumer heaven. Although, he has to admit that he feels defeated, more worthless and inconsequential than he did before he stepped through the gallery's doorway. When he looks up, Darren Adams's cap, fatigue jacket, and stained baggy trousers make the boy seem almost unreal. He's staring through a window at swirls of thousand-dollar silk shirts.

Nick checks for security guards. He can't believe they're not being monitored. Where there's wealth there's high-tech security. He sidles up alongside Darren and touches the boy's arm, breaking his trance. "Come on. No loitering in public." Then Nick realizes there isn't anything public about the place. Public space is gone. There are places for consumers to graze according to disposable-income levels, and there's wasteland, war zone, terror central. He tugs on the boy's arm and together they move away.

"Them's some fly shirts," Darren says, voice hushed. "You know they don't bag with plastic here."

"Well, stay in school, study hard, and one day all this can be yours."

"Ha. Right."

"Look at me."

Darren laughs. "You're a thief."

"Nietzsche would call me the superman. You shoplift, right?"

"Yeah."

"So, same concept. Only why steal a sneaker when you can mass-market human tragedy? This"—Nick sweeps the scented air with one hand—"is the reward for elegant, ruthless pillage. Faith wanes; wealth persists."

"You on your way to gettin' some cash, right?"

"I am. And this is what separates me from you."

"Ain't you worried I'm gonna run on your out-of-breath ass?"

"Where could you possibly run to?" The question goes unanswered. Searching for a place for them to hide, a pair of lizard-skin cowboy boots catches Nick's eye. The fifty-five-thousand-dollar saddle above them he can probably do without.

"Who's this Nietzsche dude, anyway?"

"The first skinhead," Nick answers, distracted. He's found them sanctuary.

A smooth face of black granite appears beside a display window holding a diamond the size of an apple. Its doorway is a diagonal incision in the facade. If you were in a hurry you might walk past it, thinking it was shadow. Inside, a bracelet of glowing light appears at the end of a short passageway, bright letters hovering magically in the dark. *Nettwerk.* A luminous electronic field bearing multilingual entry instructions materializes. Nick recites Gates Remington's credit account number as if it were an incantation, then waits.

"You sure like tossin' this guy's money around," Darren says.

"We're old friends. Thrown out of prep school together." Approved, Nick says yes to a cover charge of two hundred dollars each. "Social contacts are everything. Trust me."

Almost imperceptibly, the floor begins to slide forward. Soundproof doors part, synthesized din and flickering, bomb-blast light engulfing them. Low ceiling peels away and they glide through a black veil, weightless as angel's wings, into a vault of flames. It's a heatless inferno, a hologram of the burning city. An escalator lifts them above it. Overhead, Nick sees a dance floor, silicon-treated glass two feet thick and supported by black steel struts. People dance barefoot, a few clutching champagne flutes. Outfits range from tuxedos to lingerie and combat boots. Nick wonders if he has time to put some moves on a six-foot blond wearing a cheerleader's skirt, silver dollar pasties, and nothing else. But she seems content to dance with her own reflection in the mirrored ceiling, not even acknowledging Nick's exceedingly resistible grin as his reflection floats past hers against the backdrop of burning abyss.

At the top of the escalator they step directly into the lounge, every detail done in black and gold. Nick makes his way along the bar, Darren trailing him. The strobe lights dim to a pale lightning, the frenzy on the dance floor muted by a glass dividing wall which grazes the fifty-foot ceiling. Pressed snugly against its black marble base are matching tables. Nick studies the faces brightened by the shaded brass lamps. He even recognizes a few he knows from magazines, a model or two he has lusted after while watching the fashion channel, someone dying famously of AIDS. He hears German, people arguing excitedly in French about *les riots*, something that sounds like hip-hop lyrics sung in Russian. Tables are cluttered with Euro-beer bottles, platters of half-eaten sashimi, carpaccio, tapas, and dumplings with lemony-green and plum-colored dipping sauces ringing them. Notebook-sized TV screens play at the head of each booth. When Nick sees an ad for an Apocalypse Productions Pay-per-View special—ghostly letters emerging from black to spell out "Revelation"—he stops. But no other information appears, except the seductive command to stay tuned, and the logo XXN.

"How much for the boy?"

Looking up at Nick is a smooth white skull containing a pair of arresting blue eyes, or else very convincingly tinted contact lenses. The man's navy silk shirt is buttoned to the collar, his hands clasped placidly, a leash grip between them. At the other end of the leash is a shirtless boy with greased black hair and nipple rings who appears perfectly happy to have the studded noose around his neck. Opposite them, a young woman with lifeless blond hair and tattooed arms camcords Darren Adams.

If there was ever a time to experience moral revulsion, Nick guesses this would be it. But in a universe of infinite contingency, this is only another channel. "He isn't for sale," Nick says.

"Too bad."

Nick is waved aside, the man turning away as if neither Nick nor

Darren had existed. Walking toward a pair of stools, Nick understands that you can't deny someone interested only in new sensations what he wants, when new sensations are mass-produced
every milliminute. Desire requires limits, if it's to be transcendent.

Nick checks his watch once he's in his seat. Three o'clock.
Thirty minutes to find McKuen, Gates Remington, the film crew,
an excuse for Harley von Vaughn in case he needs his job back,
and a game plan for the Pay-per-View special. He also wouldn't
mind locating something close to a normal pulse rate, as well as a
bite to eat. Maybe a little food and grog will chase away the inky
black blobs cruising the edges of his vision. He tosses cigarettes,
lighter, portaphone, and handcuffs onto the bar, then autodials
McKuen's number.

"I ain't puttin' them suckers back on," Darren says, indicating
the handcuffs.

"I'm not asking you to. Anybody's curious, you're my sex slave,
not an escaped terrorist. And I'm not an ex–public defender and
nouveau felon. We're just two weenie rubbers into interracial
bondage, out for a mid-apocalypse cocktail." Nick continues au-
todialing, waiting for an open line into the Homicide office.

"I must be putting some serious change in your pocket," Darren says.

"Why? Because I didn't sell you to someone who wants to put a
poodle collar around your neck?" Nick shakes his head, disappointed. "Darren. Are we sitting opposite one another? Are we
going to have a drink together? Yes. Why? Because even though
the culture is at the end of the Romantic period and a new age of
overcrowded techno-barbarity is at hand, my philosophy is pure
Age of Enlightenment. Inalienable rights, exaltation of the individual, harmony, sweetness and light. And you are the link between these two worldviews, which I intend to explore in my docu-

drama sometime in the next eight hours. Ray executed two cops, right?''

"He did?''

"Why do you think we're chasing him? Why do you think McKuen hauled your ass in in the first place?''

Someone picks up in Homicide and Nick motions to Darren for silence. When he's told that McKuen is in the field, whereabouts undisclosed, Nick tries to wheedle McKuen's mobile phone number out of the desk sergeant. Failing to, he mentions that McKuen isn't going to be happy and the guy admits that he couldn't give a shit, Nick still isn't getting the number. "Fine. The message is: Nick Wolf. I have your boy.'' He looks at Darren, then adds, "Call me if you want the other one.'' Nick leaves his number. Darren is questioning him before the line goes dead.

"When was this with Ray?''

"Late last night. Don't tell me you didn't know about it?''

Darren remains silent. He wants to say he didn't know, but he doesn't want to risk renewing Nick's anger.

The bartender arrives, shirtless and predictably well-built. Broad chest and shoulders, tapered midsection plunging into a pair of low-riding spandex shorts. His hair, which he sweeps into a long ponytail, is the color of fresh ginger.

Nick picks up the gilt-edged menu. Juices, power shakes, "smart drug'' combos. "What's Orange Sunshine?''

"Tang and liquid Prozac. Anti-depressant and a brain booster.'' The guy has a British accent, and the husky, working-class quality of it comes across as sexy. Back home he'd be just another unemployed yob on the dole. Here he's attractive and probably over-tipped.

"What do you think?'' Nick asks Darren. "Want to get smarter?'' The boy shrugs. "Fuck it,'' Nick says, "I'm wired enough. Gimme a French '75, and some dumplings. Couple of dozen, assorted. Sauces, chopsticks, etcetera.'' He looks back at his, well, prisoner, though he doesn't like to think of Darren that way. "What about you?"

"Same." Darren looks at the bartender uncertainly. "What he's having."

Nick surrenders Gates Remington's credit code once again, receiving instant approval and a receipt for drinks at twenty-five bucks a pop, plus four dozen dumplings at nineteen ninety-five per. With tax and tip there goes a quick hundred and seventy, or what Nick makes, or used to make, in a ten-hour day, including benefits. Good thing he's getting into the pop culture biz. The end of the world is expensive.

"Now lemme hear this," Darren says. "Ray killed two cops?"

"Yes."

" 'Cause of what?"

"Coda. The Discordia Sect. Revolution. That's the theory."

"You said they don't exist."

"Am I right?"

The boy shakes his head. "You know, guys be talking about revolution and stuff, but that's like . . ."—he tosses his hands up helplessly—". . . forever. And we still here, nothing different."

"Except half the city's on fire."

"That shit just happens. Always been happenin'. Always gonna happen."

"So the whole thing exists in Ray's head? He listens to a few tapes, gets deranged, ten other guys do the same thing at the same time—maybe it's even loosely planned, according to Coda's lyrics—and, bang, revolution? That it?"

"You know more than me."

"Why didn't Ray tell you about the executions?"

"Ray's . . . strange. He's out there. You know what I'm saying?"

Nick shakes his head as their cocktails are set down on the bar, sparkling platinum liquid swaying inside each snifter.

Darren gulps half his cocktail, then makes a face like a firecracker just went off in his throat. "What is this stuff?" he croaks, hoarse.

"Brandy and champagne. Velvet for the brain." Nick considers that it might not be a bad idea to have Darren under the influence when they reach Aslam A Lakem Downs. Conveniently malleable, his reflexes muddied and off by a beat. "Drink it slow. Watch. Your hand heats the snifter, warms the brandy, so when you raise the glass the rim of it covers your nose, and the vapors go straight to your head. Rush number one. Rush number two is letting the champagne caress your tongue like a thousand little kisses." Nick sips some of his cocktail. "See? Rush number three is that after two of these, you see deities from your favorite religion or music video. Go ahead." He watches Darren lift the glass to his lips and sip tentatively. "Better?"

"Definitely."

Nick taps his glass against the boy's. "To mass-market terror." They drink. "So, Ray's strange. You mean like crazy, burnt from drugs, clinically depressed, epileptic?"

"Naw, not like that. He does his smoking and drinking an' stuff, like everybody. But he's just kind of . . . to himself."

"You mean obsessed?"

"I don't know. It's like he's mad at the world an' he don't know why. Ray's like, things gotta *mean* something. Add up, make sense. Be something you could hold on to."

"Out of belief comes terror."

"What?"

"Revolutionary fanaticism. Serve God with guns. What about you?"

Darren shrugs. "We here, we fucked, get what you can."

"A man after my own heart."

The dumplings appear on gleaming black platters. Blades of lemon grass lay crossed over small pools of sauce. Accompanying each serving are chopsticks in disease-proof cellophane wrappers, and bright gold damask napkins.

"Most likely the computer lines are jammed," the bartender says, "but since you gave only the credit account number, I need either the card for an imprint, or the personal security code."

"Hell," Nick answers, eyeing a pink-veined shrimp brushed with caviar. He snaps his napkin open, looking up. "The security code is Hell. And can we get another round. Plus, do you have a car service?"

"Limos. Four hundred an hour."

Nick checks his watch, which looks pretty cheesy given the surroundings. "Twenty minutes?"

"Same account?"

"Why not?" Nick says grandly.

He eats quickly at first, then slows, his eyes wandering to the shifting TV images behind the bar. Mixed in with abstract computer art are faint replays of this morning's executions. The clips are light as ghosts, therefore difficult to separate from the images laid over them. They fade and rematerialize, absorbed into the lexicon of pop culture. So it isn't any surprise when the music playing over the speaker system glides from industrial rock to Coda's "Bring the Hate," which has been doctored for maximum danceability. Nick bites into another dumpling, tuning in to Coda's banal lyrics. "I'll tell you one thing, your friend Ray's gotta be out there to believe in this horseshit." Nick turns to see if Darren agrees. But the kid's having a tough time with his dumplings.

"Here." Nick sets his chopsticks down and takes the pair from Darren's hand. "Like this, thumb here on top. Index and middle fingers like so. See?" He scissors them open and closed. "Forget the pinky. Except for data input clerks, it's an obsolete append-age. Our great-grandchildren won't even have them. Try. You're not a lefty, are you?"

"No."

Nick lays the sticks over the boy's fingers. "Fold your thumb over." He bends it into place for him. "Fold it. Now, these fingers here and here. See?" Darren lowers the chopsticks and clamps a dumpling. "Same three fingers as a TV remote control unit." Nick pretends to have one between two fingers, thumb pressing an imaginary channel changer. "Same three fingers you hold a slice of pizza with. Natural selection. Think about it."

They eat together in silence, the bedlam of the club comforting, already familiar. The food brings some blood back into Nick's face and stabilizes his pulse. He feels flush, warm, his chills and perspiration subsiding. Rather than feeling restored, though, he has a very arresting sense of being unreal, barely anchored to the world. Some people have God or love. I have TV. But twenty generations from now it will seem as if television always was. God will have vanished from our vocabularies like myths of the Earth Mother. Then the notion that television *is* existence won't require even the slightest leap of faith. And this tele-apocalypse will be only one among many available from the infinite files of the XXN video library.

Nick looks at Darren, who is handling his chopsticks nicely. Brow furrowed, he eats with total concentration, oblivious to the rest of the world. "How did we get here?" Nick says.

"Huh?" Darren turns his head, puzzled.

"Us. How did we get here?" Nick looks around the club. "I mean, we brought you people here in chains for this?"

Darren shakes his head and exhales heavily through his nostrils. "All you guys always get around to feeling bad sooner or later.

Then you can't wait to tell us about it. And when you get over it, we's where we always was.''

Chastened, Nick reaches for a cigarette, upset with himself for even entertaining the notion of human solidarity. Master/slave. Viciousness/power. They're eternal. Compassion depends on a booming economy, and more naïveté than any one human should be allowed to possess. Nick blows smoke at the dumpling making its way to Darren's mouth. "So, fuck Utopia. Great. Your friend's a murderer and a terrorist. He's going to be lynched on satellite TV. If you don't want to join him, tell me how McKuen linked you to him."

Darren slowly sets down his utensils. "We had some guns and stuff."

"You and Ray?"

He nods.

"Like how many?"

"Like . . . a lot. Ray was into it. Coda said load up, Ray loaded up."

"Said when, where?"

"On the tape."

"There's just one?"

"Far as I know."

"You bought the guns with drug money?"

"Some. Stole a few."

"From where?"

"Police armory. Houses. But you know, there's a lot of dudes more than happy to give you guns. If you gonna use 'em for the right things an' all." Darren pauses. "Ray needed this C-4 stuff, though—"

"And you got it for him."

"Well it wasn't like I knew—"

"And McKuen traced the C-4 to you."

Darren nudges a chopstick around the edge of his plate, silent for a moment. "You know how you could sometimes think you could be ready to die an' all? Without feelin' scared, I mean. Like it was somethin' you could handle."

The question hangs between them, undiminished by the swirl of noise and images. "Look," Nick says, then he stops. He doesn't want to know; he can't afford to care.

"Forget it," Darren says.

"Yeah, well, all you guys get around to self-pity sooner or later, then can't wait to tell us about it." Nick flicks an ash onto his platter. "I mean, you expect me to take you seriously?"

"I don't expect nothin'. Who gives a fuck! Ray's crazy. Now I'm in up to my ass. Sittin' here an' all, eatin'. Man, I ain't nothin' to you!"

"I told you I would get you off!" Nick's lie blends perfectly with everything else in the unreal city. He is so used to lying that he can't stop himself. But then, what would be the point in stopping? Context changes from millisecond to millisecond, frenetic sensation follows frenetic sensation. Go with the flow. If by some miracle his lie turns out to be the truth, some happy new unreality, then this unmoored moment in time will be long gone, absorbed into the blur and flux of the city. Information travels and mutates too quickly to worry about the truth. "Listen, we were having a good time," Nick says.

Darren flashes him a stern look. "You're crazy."

"No, I'm not. Insanity is belief in reason; enlightenment is complete surrender to illusion. Total immersion in the unreal moment. And when you're there, in it . . . dying isn't terrifying." Their eyes remain fixed on one another until Nick feels himself being drawn toward an intimacy that frightens him. He reaches for his cigarette. "So when I say I'll get you off, I know what I'm talking about. But I need answers. Now, where are the guns?

Where does Ray live?'' The boy is silent, thoughtful. "Trust me,''
Nick says.

"We going to Aslam A Lakem Downs?''

Nick nods.

"Then I'll show you.''

Minutes later they cross the dance floor, a montage of riot images and ads carouseling around them, the designer inferno lap-
ping at the soles of their shoes from below. They are met at the
club's drive-up doorway by a gleaming limousine. Nick ushers Darren in ahead of him, then follows, the sweet hush of wealth enveloping them.

"Money's nice,'' Darren says, staring out his window.

"Yes,'' Nick says. "It is.''

Then they are spiraling through the maze of parking ramps,
headed for the film crew and Aslam A Lakem Downs.

The car's dashboard fax monitor flashes the word "receiving,'' and Julia's heart catches, hoping it's word of her son.

McKuen keeps his hands on the wheel. Around them, the landscape has changed. Wasteland gives way to crumbling industrial
zone. Surrounded by tanks and scatterings of sandbagged foxholes, power plants stand against the gray horizon, smoke from
their stacks blending with the ashen veil of sky. Rail lines connect a
few factories and warehouses. From the high center of the bridge
they're crossing, McKuen can see raw sewage spilling into the
dead river below, the slow current carrying it past the abandoned
harbor and out to sea. Ahead, National Guard groups cluster at a

roadblock, their fatigues dark smudges against the sudden Astroturf green of subdivisions in the distance.

Julia tears the fax transmission along its perforated edge and reads the message.

"Any luck?"

"No. It's from Nick Wolf. Says he has your boy. Call him back if you want the other one."

"How could he have Darren Adams? I thought the kid couldn't be sprung."

"I don't know."

"Well can you find out? Call your office?"

"I can try. Just don't yell."

As they coast into the single lane of the checkpoint, McKuen exhales. "Sorry. I wish it had been better news."

A ticktocking electronic arm waves them to a stop. He and Julia step out of the car, hands above their heads, as the megaphone voice instructs. Guards wearing flak jackets and helmets with shatterproof visors appear, weapons drawn, from behind rows of tanks. Pistol barrels are put to McKuen's head and he's forced facedown onto the car hood while the car is searched. One guard removes McKuen's wallet from his pocket; another takes Julia's purse and hands it to a man emerging from behind the mud-colored bow of a tank.

He freezes, puzzled. "Julia?"

It's a guy from her food co-op. They met once at a wine tasting she had been dragged to by her divorced aerobics friend. He found the Merlot puckish, if she remembers correctly. He had reminded Julia of an ad for hiking equipment. Masculine, sanitized, macho-lite. Now he was spot-checking her for terrorist intent.

"What are you doing out here?" The guards lower their weapons and back off, not even waiting for his absentminded flapping of one hand.

Julia tries to recall his name, but his eyes leave her to study McKuen. "Sam, right?"

When he looks at her again, an eager cheerfulness returns to his expression. "Right."

Despite the riot gear, he's angling for a date. "Please, let him up." Julia takes her purse from his hand, then turns to see McKuen, palms flattened on the hood. He stares at her in a way that says, so this is how fast we go from predator to prey. Just travel a few blocks in the city if you want a new identity.

McKuen's wallet is tossed over the car to Sam. "He's a detective, homicide," a guard yells.

Julia watches Sam study McKuen's ID, then notes a touch of disappointment in his voice. "Alright, go ahead. Let him up."

Some guards wander back toward the tanks, others light cigarettes. One even removes a sandwich from his flak jacket and begins unwrapping the clear plastic covering it. The scene reminds Julia of a factory yard during lunch hour, before the city's plants closed and jobs vanished. Women, blacks, Latinos, Asians, whites. The police state has become a multicultural growth industry.

McKuen stands and brushes off his palms. It's obvious that he's considering hopping into the car and abandoning her. Yet something makes him stay, though Julia can't say what it is.

Sam holds McKuen's wallet out to her. "You heading home?"

"No. I'm going to the high school."

"Oh, good," he says, as if this is happy news. He eyes McKuen cordially, then suddenly remembers something. "But hasn't that been evacuated?"

"Yes, but my son isn't home yet."

"Well, maybe they moved him to a security shelter. You know, the old civilian defense bunkers by the ball fields."

Julia hasn't thought of these since she was a girl. Underground rooms stockpiled with canned goods and potable water, theoretically enough to last until the fallout blew away, or evaporated like rain. Her father, a ham radio buff and Korean War vet, had constructed a small shelter in the basement of their ranch-style house, equipping it with blankets, cots, lawn chairs, a card table, even a collapsible commode which dissolved human waste. His generator would provide power for several days, by which time, assuming a Russkie ICBM hadn't landed on the rusty swing set in the yard overhead, they could reemerge to sunshine, cotton sheets snapping on clotheslines, and the poor reception of three channels their black-and-white console TV received. Now, in the distance, armed subdivisions cling to the valley floor, everyone wired, plugged in, the enemy no longer out there, but here.

"It isn't a good idea to wander around," Sam warns her.

"I'm not wandering." Julia has no desire to hurt his feelings, but it is a little late to expect the pose of strong, protective male to be taken seriously. "Are the roads clear?"

"Yeah. You shouldn't have any problems. Things are still bad, but so far we're containing it to that side of the river."

Julia looks down the rows of military vehicles. "You got this set up pretty quickly."

"Yeah, well, we're ready. This thing's been in the pipe and ready to smoke for a long time."

"You knew it was coming?" She sees her reflection distorted in his visor.

"Not this specifically."

"You mean the sect, Coda?"

"I heard the song, saw the flyers and TV stuff. Coda's one figure. The *threat* is what we're prepared for. That's permanent, that doesn't change. Do you know what'll happen to property values if they come across the river?"

Julia can see that Sam would like some indication of understanding. Perhaps even thanks, the way her father expected appreciation for his obsessive work on the family's bunker. It always gets down to dominion, she thinks, rather than inclusion. "Can we go?"

Disappointed, Sam turns and waves to a tank crew, which backs the vehicle out of the lane leading off the bridge. Julia doesn't glance in Sam's direction again until the car is gliding downhill and his figure recedes in the passenger-side mirror, above its warning that the objects reflected are closer than they appear.

"Do you want to call Wolf, or do you want me to call my office?" she says, handing McKuen his wallet.

"You call. You obviously know the people in charge."

"He called me for a date once. Okay?"

"Let me guess. Target practice, right? Go out, snap off a few hundred rounds, then back to—what's the bar called? Jim Crow's Joint?—for a couple of longnecks and some country music."

"You can't be serious?"

"Yee-hah."

The pitch of his voice is sultry, as if he were teasing her. When he turns, he's smiling.

"I am heading the right way, correct?"

She notices his lips pucker as they close. "Yes. And I suppose you want to tell me how you knew?"

"No."

Julia thinks, I can't possibly be flirting. My son is missing, the city is in chaos. It's definitely not the time to wonder how my hair looks. But also, maybe, the best, most sublimely right time. Who knows? Reach the end of things, begin again.

They pass strip malls protected by armed Citizen Watch groups and private security forces. Business is brisk, if spotty, the wide commercial roads empty but for the few shoppers loading up on groceries, liquor, and videos.

"It's all become normal so quickly," Julia says.

"Mm."

"Think it'll disappear as fast as it came?"

"Don't know."

"So what do we gain by catching this kid?"

"We get to hold on to our hope a little longer."

The area around them turns quasi-residential, a mix of housing, clinics, and cookie-cutter professional buildings. Ahead, the manufactured village square appears, a patch of Astroturf embellished by nineteenth-century streetlamps, cast-iron bike racks, concrete-and-pebble benches. Surrounding it are espresso and wine bars, automatic teller machines, a health club, an herbalist's office. Boutiques called Ur-Sweater and The Deconstructed Jock. Outlets that sell fresh pasta, organic vegetables, hydroponically raised fish. Restaurants operated by Thai, Cambodian, and Eastern-European refugees. The sandwich shop her son Paul liked when it was The Antihero is now The Cloned Cold Cut. Plus there's her transcendental meditation chapel, which she hasn't visited in quite a while. Usually Saturday afternoons. She would release Paul with fifteen dollars for a trek to the multiplex with his friends, then pace herself through a workout, sauna, shower, maybe some shopping for ginseng, rose hips, and valerium root after a "lite" lunch. Finally, she'd spend an hour on a mantra mat, barefoot, stripped down to her tights, chanting until she either saw the light or fell asleep. Afterwards in the wine bar, the gray sky beyond the picture window looking like hammered pewter, she would fantasize about the bartender, a twenty-two-year-old with curly, gunmetal black hair and screen idol blue eyes. He was paying off his student loans while trying to decide whether to go to law or film school. He would steer her through the maze of California whites there was to select from, explaining the ratio of chardonnay to pinot blanc grapes in a particular vintage, whether the wine had been fermented in oak barrels or stainless-steel drums, what hints of fruit and spice the vintner had been trying to accentuate. She would answer his questions about law school, the glut of attorneys, entertainment law as a possible plus in the film world, all the while wondering if it was time for her, at thirty-eight, to be the older woman. Inevitably, around sunset, the sky over the square infused with a sickly salmon afterglow, a man her age would appear at her elbow, wearing seriously creased trousers and some kind of outdoorsy pullover or pre-stressed canvas jacket. Some were discreetly self-centered, a bit like her ex-husband, others job-obsessed or boring. In any case, they drove the bartender away and, after one more glass of wine, her too. Out into the semi-toxic dark, across the unnaturally bright carpet of fake grass, and home. If Paul was in, they'd order a pizza and watch late-night television. If he wasn't, she'd thumb through catalogs with the CD carousel on, drink some more wine, and even once or twice watch a cable channel's soft-core porn offering until she was lonely enough to masturbate before sliding into bed, emptied by what was there to fill her up.

At the far end of the deserted square McKuen drives past Express Mail boxes and a giant satellite dish, which rests close to the fake grass carpeting. It reminds him of some kind of ancient altar, the place locals congregated to watch a lamb or a virgin being sacrificed.

The road winds uphill past art and collectibles galleries. Private homes hide behind eight-foot-high security walls. Trees, "No Parking" signs, and electronic eyes perch above "Do Not Enter" notices.

"So, how did you guess the way?" Julia asks him.

"Private school, right?"

"Uh-huh."

McKuen pauses, glancing at the surroundings. "I just followed the money. Anything you're looking for can be traced by money."

"The boy we're chasing?"

McKuen shakes his head. "He isn't in it for money."

"How do you know?"

"If he was, he wouldn't have killed the cops himself."

"Maybe he was hired."

"Then why didn't he pay his friend Darren to disappear after he lined up the C-4?"

"He didn't expect you'd trace it."

"A pro would."

"Well, if he isn't linked to money, how do we find him?"

McKuen looks at her as the car reaches the top of a hill. "Wolf's going to lead us to him."

"Why?"

"Money," McKuen says softly. The hushed force of the word seems to dissolve the distance between them, as if all along they had all along shared some secret intimacy, something primal, and totally disconnected from the artifices of wealth. "Go ahead. Call your office. Find our friend."

"You have to make a left," Julia says, lifting the phone.

"Where?"

"The corner you passed ten seconds ago."

"Just checking it out. One drive-by for safety."

"Uh-huh."

"The School on the Hill," McKuen coons. "What's your son studying?"

"The history of country-western music."

"Ooh."

The high school's grounds overlook the factories and dead river below, then the grayish-black ruins of the 'hood beyond. From this far away the projects resemble abandoned temple cities, the sweep they make across entire city blocks diminished in the mottled dusk.

Except for a few idle vans with school markings on their sides, the parking lots are deserted. Instead of athletic facilities there's a greenhouse, some kind of bunker roofed with solar energy panels, and a small, concrete amphitheater. McKuen pulls into a space and cuts the engine. Its ticking makes him aware of how far they are from the blare and steady panic of the city's killing fields.

Julia slips the phone back into its recharger cradle after speaking with her office.

"Well?"

She hesitates, as if what she had to describe were almost too ludicrous for words. "Wolf delivered a signed confession. The boy confessed to murder and . . . ." She's momentarily astounded by the fact that devious, chronically deranged people like Christian Wolf are not only capable of operating in the world, but of manipulating it.

"And," McKuen coaxes.

". . . treason, terrorist acts, conspiracy. . . ."

"Jaywalking?"

"He's insane!"

"And the two of them are gone, whereabouts unknown."

"He got some senile substitute judge on crisis duty to set bail."

"How did he raise bail?"

"He charged it to a credit card." She watches McKuen's expression change. "I'm glad you think this is funny." She opens her door and gets out of the car.

McKuen catches up with her on the walkway. She moves nicely, he thinks. Nothing affected or self-absorbed. Just someone with things to do, a clear sense of purpose. "I'm not supposed to think it's funny? I catch 'em, you people let them go."

"If that's what you think, quit your job."

"I can't."

"Why not?"

"You're the good mother, right? Always trying to prove yourself, but you never quite make it." Julia doesn't slow her pace, but she does look at him. "Well, I'm the good cop. Serve and protect."

"Only you never quite make it."

"Right." They reach the base of the entryway's wide staircase. "So how'd your office know all this so quickly?"

"Harley von Vaughn, Wolf's boss, called the D.A.'s office."

"So Wolf is gone with our kid, presumably off to find whoever it is we're chasing."

"Right."

"What does your office suggest we do about it?"

Julia reaches the top step, then glances at McKuen. "Nothing—since we're not good enough to hold whoever it is you catch."

McKuen stops on the landing, letting her glide away from him. "Att-i-tude," he whispers.

"I heard that."

"I'm glad." He follows her past an unattended metal detector and into the bright gray halls.

Skylights run the length of the thirty-foot-high ceilings. A second-floor-balcony railing is draped with slow-turning mobiles dangling the words *truth, ennui, abyss, heavy,* and *pseudo-Freudo.* Bulletin boards announce TV detox workshops and something called the Break with the Future Society. Graffiti is multilingual. Copies of the school's student paper, *News for the Numb,* litter the floor and occasional tattered couch. They pass departments marked Soap Opera Studies, Gender Politics, and Image Manufacturing. A seminar on Effective Public Lying is being offered. The "Art Is Dead" area displays giant comic-strip panels featuring "Retro-Chick," the chronicles of a girl whose clothes are always ten years out of date.

"So this is high school?" McKuen says.

"Private preparatory school. Admission by invitation only."

"Like gangs."

Julia gives him a long look. "Nobody likes to be excluded."

From down another long hallway comes the faint sound of what Julia calls Bacchanalia music, dissonant guitar riffs dished out like electroshock, and laid over a bass line indistinguishable from volcanic activity. The music's point seems to be to encourage the people listening to lose their minds. She has read that it's best danced to after a hit of Ecstasy, or with an extremely high fever.

A sign reads *Go Away. This Area is Off-Limits to People Who Can't Handle Their Computer Dependency Problems.*

The first student to notice them standing in the doorway swivels away from his computer monitor and says, "Hi. Adults. Wow. Wild," in a soft, plush voice. Julia takes him to be roughly seventeen, a senior. Although, he may look older than he is because of the fuzzy goatee and mustache. His companion is manifestly adolescent, and totally oblivious of the fact that anyone has entered the room. Wearing Walkman headphones, tanktop, pleated black skirt, and motorcycle boots, he continues doing some kind of Egyptian let's-party-with-the-pharaoh shuffle. The body in the tanning coffin on the far side of the room is female, bikini clad, and bright as a new penny. All Julia can think is, melanoma.

"It's quite safe," the boy at the computer says.

Julia sees that he has noticed her staring at the girl in the broiler. "Cancer is safe?"

He lifts a thin brown cigarette from the ashtray beside his monitor, flicks the ash, then takes a drag. "It's not our generation's disease. We'll die of other things—AIDS, mutations of hepatitis B, extravagant jungle viruses, television sickness. Cancer was twentieth century. Our diseases will be synergistic, almost multimedia. Disease mirrors the technology of the age. I expect most of us will die on camera."

He crosses his legs and sucks on the cigarette, gazing at her alertly but, Julia feels, vacantly, as if there were no continuity to his thinking. "I'm looking for my son."

"Uh-huh."

"Well, he goes to this school. May—"

"Cool."

"Maybe you know him."

The boy shrugs. "Sure."

Julia moves toward the boy while McKuen loops around the room for a look. Computers, TVs, telephones, all marked "Property of the Communications Lab." Scribbled on the equipment are notes saying "Take this and Die." The "No Smoking" sign has been surrounded by suggestions to also refrain from driving, using a microwave oven, producing toxic waste, causing a nuclear power plant accident, selling biological warfare toxins, launching ICBMs, snowmobiling, or investing in mutual funds that facilitate any of the above activities for profit. Turning, McKuen sees the boy in the skirt staring at him, headphones lowered.

"Terrorist?"

McKuen shakes his head. "Detective. Student?"

"Consumer. I'm double-majoring in Pop Culture Demographics and Chaos Theory. I believe there's a relationship between meaninglessness and high sales volume. Can I ask you something? If the universe is amoral and irrational, then when you 'solve' a crime—'crime' being a subjective cultural contingency, okay, like it's cool to kill in war and things—what do you really solve?"

"The problem of how to keep faith alive." McKuen doesn't even have to think about his answer. This part of the equation is always right there. But *meaning*? Ultimate truth? He knows better than to speak of that. "Let me ask, what do you solve if you establish a relationship between the things you're studying?"

"The problem of how to get rich. What sells is the only question left. The ethics of selling are irrelevant."

McKuen listens closely to the tinny, minuscule sounds coming from the boy's headphones. Among the crackles and static he picks up a familiar beat. "What are you listening to?"

" 'Bring the Hate.' "

"Coda?"

"Um-hm. The heavy metal mix."

"When did that happen?"

"I don't know. An hour ago?" Slipping his headphones back on, the boy closes his eyes and drifts away.

Across the room, Julia is seated beside the kid at the monitor, whom she seemingly has convinced to lower the boom box's volume. Her legs are crossed, skirt angling higher toward the back of her thigh. As she leans forward, her hair falls past her ear and across the profile of her face. McKuen can hear her speaking, the sound of her voice drawing him forward. She doesn't notice him until he's beside her. "Any luck?"

"No. He's sending E-mail to all the possible shelters Paul may have been taken to."

"It's my guess he isn't at a shelter," the boy says. He watches the monitor note the stages of message transmission, raising one hand to readjust the tilt of his wire-rim glasses.

McKuen waits for the boy's reason for thinking this, but doesn't get it. He looks at Julia, who seems to have decided not to expect anything. "I didn't get your name."

The boy looks at McKuen as if just awakened. "Zed."

McKuen repeats it, quizzically.

"Final letter of the German alphabet." He exhales, seeming frustrated by the business of explanation, maybe even with the idea of human communication. He's polite and attentive, but there's a quality that makes his actions seem automatic, programmed. "It's an appropriately apocalyptic name. Twentieth century, Germany, last things. Also, at the end there's always a new beginning, which is the true meaning of apocalypse—crisis, purge, rebirth. An elegant pattern, despite the grotesquerie of Revelation, Nostradamus, millennial panics, etcetera. Apocalypse is just a rhythm. Inelegance stems from one thing only. The hope for transcendence."

"You chose the name yourself?" McKuen asks.

Zed blows smoke in the direction of the monitor, eyeing the computer's progress. "My parents gave me the name. I would never be so obvious."

"Why are you three still here if the school's been evacuated?"

"Why?" He seems perplexed, as if the question made no sense. "We opted to stay."

Julia says, "But you don't think Paul went to one of the shelters?"

He turns to her. "My contact with Paul has been minimal. But as you can see on the screen, two shelters have already replied negatively. I've posted his name on a number of electronic bulletin boards to give us the widest coverage possible, so we may turn up something there. But if I were to chart a graph of Paul's probable actions, the shelters would factor in as a very low potentiality. Watch."

Swiveling toward the monitor, he drops his cigarette butt into a coffee cup and begins speaking to the computer. "Mr. Chris, may we have a new folder, re: Paul. Save all incoming E-mail and fax responses. Alert upon affirmative response, please." He manipulates the mouse with one hand and hurtles through function choices. A color-coded graph appears. "Paul strikes me as being cold, distant. Yes? You have a difficult time expressing affection, whatever that is, toward him, correct?"

Julia doesn't answer.

Zed clicks on Yes. "Absent father, if I remember correctly." He pauses, fingertips drumming lightly on the edges of the keyboard.

Julia whispers, "Right."

Zed inputs responses to psychological and demographic queries, which appear beneath the graph. "Tell me if any of this is incorrect," he says, continuing to make accurate assessments of Julia's age, income, education, religious affiliation, political leanings, reading habits, TV dependence, even the catalogs she receives by mail and personal computer.

"What is this?" McKuen asks.

"Behavioral software system. Developed by the XXN media lab in conjunction with the military. Mostly used to track terrorists and arms dealers. Predict what they'll do next."

"Can you use it to tell me where the kid we're looking for is?"

"What did he do?"

"Killed two police officers, started this whole thing."

The boy chuckles softly.

"What?"

"I doubt *anybody* started this. All the elements were simply in place. The progression of events follows the pattern of catastrophe theory precisely."

"Don't know it."

"René Thom. He demonstrated that the evolutionary cycles of societies do not move forward smoothly, but in fits and starts. Lull, decay, oppression, revolution. Massive, violent, catastrophic upheavals. Then a new plateau. Two shootings would not have set any of this off if all the other conditions were not ripe, or unstable. A minor traffic accident and ensuing fistfight would most likely have produced the same results."

"I find that hard to believe," Julia says.

Zed shrugs. "That's the trouble with belief. It's limiting. So we frantically try to back up one narrow view with force, authority, reason. Paul has some deep problems with authority, doesn't he?"

"He's fourteen. All boys have problems with authority at fourteen."

"Yes, but in this case Dad, with a capital D, is gone, and Mom, cap M, is a criminal prosecutor." He indicates the screen. On it, Julia's credit, medical, and domestic intelligence files scroll upward. "In the Hate Crimes division, no less." Zed lights another cigarette, then opens a computer line and says, "Megan, turn ninety degrees for maximum lateral exposure."

In the tanning coffin the girl rolls onto one side, her back to the room.

"You pay tuition for this?" McKuen says.

Zed glances at him. "I'm on full scholarship, straight through graduate school."

The computer says, "Excuse me, we have an affirmative response."

Julia sits forward, hands on her knees.

"Go ahead, Mr. Chris."

The E-mail is from a student who saw Paul slip out of the building with a group of other students.

"Send 'smart' messages to all in the group, and alert upon receipt of response." Zed leans close to the computer's mouthpiece. "And thank you, Mr. Chris," he whispers.

"Do you know these students?" Julia asks.

"Somewhat. They're on the aesthetic side of things. Not really my fetish."

Julia doesn't recognize any of the names on the screen. But then, Paul has been drifting away from his elementary school friends for some time, becoming more private, she almost wants to say withdrawn. But should she pay any attention to the theories of a quite possibly disturbed seventeen-year-old? "Thank you, Mr. Chris"? We've reached the point of homoerotic relationships with hard drives now? Maybe she has lost her son; she isn't sure. It's as if logic no longer applies, Paul's absence a part of the larger pattern of the city's chaos, which is finally too complex for her to trace.

"What are 'smart' messages?" McKuen asks.

"Messages designed to find the party you're tracking by exploring all the transmission options available. Phone, computer, fax, pager. Just an extension of the notion that everywhere is here."

"Electronically?"

Zed shrugs. "If you still need to make that distinction."

"Why would they have pagers," Julia says, "unless they're dealing?"

"Exactly." Zed notices differently colored lines begin to inch across the probability graph. "See?" He points to a squiggle near the base of the screen. "Less than a one-in-twenty chance that Paul went to a shelter. Why would he? Low self-esteem would prevent him from seeking personal protection. He definitely doesn't want to return to the womb. And finally, there's the figure of the spectral father hovering about shelters. They're built to protect the father from his own phallic impulse for self-destruction."

Julia notes that home is one of the places where Paul is least likely to turn up. It ranks below malls, jail, fast food restaurant, virtual reality arcade, a friend's house, dance club, or cruising the city in a car. The place he will most probably be found, however, she has never heard of. She's not even certain if it's a location.

"Running raves. What are they?"

Zed inhales, then holds smoke in his lungs as if considering the dated forms of intelligence Julia and McKuen possess. "Essentially, mobile parties."

"How mobile?" McKuen asks.

"They move about every seventy minutes. Depends mainly on the length of the CD, and, of course, the condition of everyone participating not being arrested."

"For drugs?"

"For generally violent behavior. Lots of body slamming. Drugs aid and abet, but there's simply a lot of pure rage involved. Bones are broken all the time. Fights." The boy adjusts his glasses, staring at McKuen passively.

"So where would we start if we wanted to catch up with one of these things?"

Julia begins to tell McKuen that questions are useless, the hunt at its end. But then decides that he may see or understand something she doesn't, and that together they might figure out which way to go.

"Well, that's the point. There is no probable or logical coordinate that denotes origin. Like the riots. They take shape quickly, gather momentum, then dissipate. Raves move from empty house to abandoned church to unsecured factory. People fall in along the way. The event peaks when it reaches a state of mass incoherence, bodies flailing, puddles of drool and beer on the floor, no one capable of forming a sentence. It isn't a social event, if that's what you're wondering."

"I wasn't," McKuen says.

"It's about negation. *Pure* negation requires stasis and silence. The only thing achieved by raves, or riots for that matter, is exhaustion. But I never said the less gifted don't resort to crude methods."

Mr. Chris announces that none of the shelters can account for

Paul. Also, there is no answer at Julia's condo.

"I took the liberty of calling." Zed pauses to stare at her. "You seem crestfallen," he says, puzzled.

Julia understands that what she assumed to be his vacancy is actually emotional deadness, the incapacity to feel anyone else's pain.

"Why? You came in clueless, you're leaving with a fairly enlightened sense of Paul's probable whereabouts. What could you possibly want beyond that?"

McKuen notices Julia's hand squeeze the chair cushion tightly.

"Certainty and security are illusions. If you don't think so, consider Paul growing up fatherless. Not in the original game plan, right?"

McKuen pins Julia's hand to the chair before she can slap the boy. He stands, leading her up with him. "If you get any responses from those pagers, let us know." He gives the boy a card with his various numbers printed on it.

"Sure. Cool. I wouldn't expect it, though. I also wouldn't worry."

"No," McKuen says, "you wouldn't."

"I've got it all graphed out according to Thom." Zed hits a keyboard function button and the behavioral graph is replaced by a catastrophe theory chart. A line rises then falls at dramatic angles. Virtually pure ascent, followed by a symmetrical plunge. "See? The riots will be over by tonight. Brief, chaotic upheaval, instant normalization. Listlessness, a routine sense of confusion, and lack of purpose resume tomorrow." Zed studies the line as Julia slips from McKuen's hand and drifts toward the door. "No Aristotelian movement toward crescendo and denouement here." He makes tiny stabs at the screen with his cigarette. "Just sensation surrounded by ennui." He swivels toward McKuen. "Like life. No dramatic unity. Just a few ashes, some dead, and everyone else on the electronic sidelines watching."

McKuen regards him in silence.

"The person you're chasing is a young black male, no education, obviously violent, most likely obsessive, isolated, and suffering from some form of hero or martyr fantasy, correct?" McKuen doesn't answer. "You'll find him at home."

"Why?"

"It's the only place his actions have any meaning. The rest of us don't care." Zed flicks an ash. "Besides, where else can he go?"

"Yeah, well, pray he never finds your ass."

"If he does, he does." Zed waves his cigarette hand once.

"You won't be saying that then."

"That's why it's called revenge *fantasy*. We don't live in a morally just universe; there are no consequences. I accept only the concepts of chance and irony."

"Well add privilege to the list, peckerhead."

"In my case, I consider that a given." Then he's tapping at the keyboard once more, no longer curious about McKuen's receding presence.

Julia is on the walkway when McKuen reaches the front entrance. Only she isn't moving in the direction of the car, but drifting along a path that climbs past the greenhouse and amphitheater. Stepping through the tinted-glass door, McKuen notices that the smoky light doesn't change. It's dusk. At a distance, Julia floats against the deep greens and pockets of shadow among the steroid-fed hedges and shrubs, almost as if she were an apparition.

Below, early night swirling moonlessly above it, the city lays like a child, a soothing, motherly dark descending on it. Silence rises around him as McKuen moves higher on the school's grounds, away from the main building's generators and buzzing power lines into a kind of crystal stillness. Deep in the shadows the air changes, smoke giving way to a sweet mist, greenhouse sprinklers hissing softly as they make tender rain.

Ahead, Julia disappears where the path winds through science project plantings of non-indigenous orchids, blossoming vines, lush and fragrant jungle—*everywhere is here*—all breathing silently around him. The scent of her perfume trails lightly in the dim air. At the end of the maze she reappears, then is just as quickly swallowed by darkness again, inside the mouth of a small pyramid or temple, its moonstone walls glowing in the dusk.

Inside, electric candlelight and a hush that cleaves him from the city draw him forward, Julia's scent a sweet incense. She has drifted to the center of the temple where its smooth, monochrome walls rise in flushed grayness around her like a dawn with the faintest rose of sun stirring, so that to him it seems they are suddenly adrift in some pale, continuous mist. The only thing above them, where the walls converge, is shadow, then a deeper, finally impenetrable dark.

As she turns McKuen steps inside a ring of low curved benches, which encircles them the way the veil of walls envelops them, shutting out the city and its endless whorl of images, its siren light and fire. *I used to come here with my son,* she hears herself saying, but his hand is already reaching up to touch her face, his voice no more than the softest of whispers as his fingers trace the outline of her mouth. He waits at arm's length, fingertips trembling lightly over her lips, her chest shuddering as if a small bird were trapped there, beating its wings. Then their eyes close and they're wrapped inside one another, the room around them diaphanous, everything a kind of weightless ascension, her body floating until he comes inside her, reaching up until they are joined bone to bone at the loins, clutching, like root to earth, at the still center of the world. And there, in the luminous spinning dark, he bleeds sweetly and slowly into her, no difference between them, no difference at all. One. Only afterwards does he sink to his knees, cradling her as he lowers her to the soft dust, where they lie together, silent and peacefully adrift. . . .

.... this is XXN. ....

McKuen strokes her brow, kissing the top of her head lightly. She lingers on his shoulder, one hand over his heart, the beating of it anchoring her to the world. They are outside on the path once again before they speak, darkness now lying over the fire-lit city below.

"How did you know it would be alright?" she asks.

"I didn't. I trusted you to know."

"I needed . . . I don't know what I needed." She drops onto one of the molded fiberglass benches along the walkway. "Something. To be out of myself, out of the world? Hope? I don't know." McKuen sits beside her. "What did you need?"

He pauses thoughtfully, then says, "Oh, any big old desperate woman."

She nudges his shoulder. Smiling, he caresses her knee, watching his hand gently move over it. "You. I needed *you.*"

They sit until the fullness of night has drifted out over the planes of earth and sea surrounding the city. Held there like a lighted altar in the dark, it waits on them, their lovemaking not a cleaving from it but a celebration of its grace. *Everywhere is here.* Love this place, if you expect love in return.

"Come on." She rubs McKuen's shoulder. "Time to find Wolf." And even though she doesn't tell him—it would sound foolish, superstitious, although he might not think so—she feels that if they complete the circle, McKuen will find the boy he's chasing, then lead them both out of the labyrinth and home to her son.

. . . . all ways, all days,
This is XXN, your until the end of
time network. . . .

The streets become familiar once again as Ray reenters the 'hood. He looks down a wide avenue, the scene lit by the flare of headlights, burning cars, and, high above in the blackness, city police choppers. A few avenues away, Aslam A Lakem Downs looms, its block-long roof veiled by smoke. He crosses into a narrow lane, concrete tenements pressing in on either side of him. All the streetlamps are shot out. Bodies drift through crack-house doorways. Others slide close enough for Ray to see their faces. They hit him up for spare change, dope, sex, whatever they're selling or trying to buy. Except for the deeply stoned and delirious, his silence is enough to back them off. The rest fall by the wayside after trailing him briefly.

At the corner a car cruises past, hooded shadows inside it pointing a gun muzzle at him through an open window. Ray stops, moving only his head as he tracks the slow glide of the rifle's barrel. When the shot comes there's a sudden empty stillness in his chest. He feels himself plummeting. Then his heart trips back on, the first beat punching blood against his breastbone. As he opens his eyes and sees the rifle pointed toward the sky, laughter inside the car fades, along with the gunshot's echo. Ray remains where he is, ashamed. He thought he was ready to die because he had already died. But it turns out not to be so easy. Coda's lyrics flit through his head, plenty of info on bomb-building, soldiering, hate, but nothing for this lonely fear burning inside him. And maybe his fear of dying will always be there as a lifelong payback for killing O.C.

He walks on, past pawn shops and convenience stores, their metal gates drawn, security lights bleaching the graffiti sprayed across them to ghostly shadow. Outside his grandmother's church, a crowd spills from the main door. Two large TV screens are set up on either side of the wide steps. Parked at the curb and guarded by private security is a van marked XXN News and Enter- tainment.

Ray recognizes faces from the neighborhood as a camera pans the congregation inside the church, but he doesn't see his grand- mother. Then he's on-screen himself, people crushing up against him once they notice the street scene is being televised. Above him on the TV scaffolding, a ponytailed cameraman directs the lens barrel of a camcorder at him, and for an instant Ray feels it wants something from him. An expression of guilt, defiance, shame, regret. Then it's gone, sweeping away from him, its sudden indifference confusing. Things seemed on the brink of making sense. He might have confessed if the camera had stayed on him long enough. Told about Coda being his inspiration. How black people were slipping farther away from where they ought to be, nobody caring enough to stop it except me. Coda said bring the whole thing down so I tried. Made the flyers myself, the bullets too, with C-4 Inch got me. Only this isn't the way it was supposed to go. Everybody in the 'hood on TV. It's just another ghetto. We only *look* connected up there on the screen, but it's just dots, disconnected dots. Nothing sticks, the camera moves on. In order to be connected, you have to forgive and be forgiven. You have to remember.

On-screen, a man with a headset sits inside the church on one side of the altar, a panel of black men and women across from him.

"Yo, Do-Ray!" Ray turns, his street name distantly familiar, something he responds to almost by instinct. Ray recognizes Cootie Mac standing near the back of the crowd, one hand in the air. "Get your behind over here." Ray angles past people who shove him, or tell him to get the fuck out the way, as Cootie Mac edges away from the crowd. "Why you ain't been around all day? Been lookin' all over for your scrawny ass." In a whisper he adds, "Inch killed some cops or somethin', man. They hauled his ass off this morning." Cootie Mac stares at Ray. "You hear what I be tellin' you?"

Ray looks past him. "Yeah." He pauses. "How you know about Inch?"

"I saw him get in the car with the Man. Way early too, before it got crazy an' all. And the Man was a brother, no less." Then Cootie Mac mutters, "You was gone for that."

Ray fixes his gaze on the other boy, the old craziness kicking up inside him. "So?"

"Kinda early, that's all."

"I can't drag my butt out the house now? I gotta be answerin' to your ass?"

"I ain't sayin' that."

"Well you makin' me *think* it."

Behind them, people shout at the televised panel discussion. On-screen, folks wearing suits and dresses, others in street garb— caps, dashikis, shades—disagree about the day's events. Ray feels all his hate for the place springing back to life, his flesh aching under the iron weight of it. Back ten minutes and it's got him wanting to smash things.

Ray blows air through his nostrils, then briefly shuts his eyes. "Look man, I don't want to argue wit' you."

"You doin' a good job though."

"Well don't be gettin' in my face like I ratted on Inch or some- thin'."

"I wasn't—"

"Yeah you was. Now bury it. It's over. That's how come we always fightin' one another. Tired of it." Ray sees tanks moving along the street several blocks away. National Guard troops leap from cov- ered transport vehicles in the dim streetlight. Some revolution. Do nothing, things get worse. Do something, things get worse faster. He glances at Cootie Mac, but his friend has turned his at- tention to the television screens. A man old enough to be Ray's father sits forward, pushing up the sleeves of his turtleneck sweater.

"Look," he explains to the moderator, "all I want to know is why you don't have me on a show about high blood pressure, or paying bills, or raising kids, or teaching for a living. Because these are things I am *expert* at. Being *black* is only a part-time gig for me."

"Oh, now you too good to be a black man," a young sister half his age says.

"I wear a lot of hats is all I'm saying."

"Big, tall, pointy one?" This draws a laugh from the street crowd when the gangbanger on-screen says it.

Ray doesn't laugh though, not even when Cootie Mac turns to him, smiling. "Sorry for jumping on you like that," he says.

"Man, why you so intense all the time?"

" 'Cause this ain't funny to me no more." Ray raises a hand toward the television sets and the crowd. "Just us arguing. Only time we get on TV is when we fightin' or killin' each other."

"Ball games."

Ray starts to walk away. "What do I have to know you for?"

"Why do you gotta be such a cranky motherfucker?"

Ray stops and turns. " 'Cause I'm tryin' to do something, and nothin's getting done!"

"Nigger, nobody does things. Things get done to them. Look at this turtlenecked motherfucker on-screen. You think he *did* something to get intelligent an' all? Fucker was born that way. Got lucky nobody was hittin' him in the head all the time. Some other motherfucker come along an' say, Hey, you's a smart little homie. Before he know it, he wearin' glasses and reading—writing his ass off, thinkin' it's him doing it." Cootie Mac huffs. "It's what been done *to* him. And that kind of luck passed our asses up a long time ago. So why don't you just chill your behind on out and give the rest of us a break? Wearin' me out."

"Inch didn't kill no cops," Ray offers softly, as Cootie Mac turns away.

His friend looks at him. "Man, I know that. He's handicapped, but he ain't mentally handicapped. Some fool just got crazy. Too much wine or something." He snorts. "Discordia Sect bullshit. Any fool knows we been down that road. Shit don't work." Cootie Mac removes a pint bottle of gin from his jacket pocket, takes a sip, then offers the bottle to Ray, who shakes his head. Cootie Mac shrugs, then screws the cap back onto the bottle. "Inch ain't dumb enough for it. You maybe," he laughs, "but not in-it-for-a-dollar Inch." His voice trails off as he adds, "He's fucked now, though. *C'est la vie,* home."

Cootie Mac turns toward the TV screens, where one of the panelists is attacking the turtlenecked guy for being smug.

"I'm not smug. I'm building on the past. The last generation got us some things. Integration. Good. I'm gonna honor them by taking advantage of the rights they fought to get us. And one of those *implicit* rights . . ."

Ray waits on the magic formula he senses is out there, commanded by people like this older brother, but just beyond his understanding.

". . . one of those implicit rights, is the right to put the color of your skin *behind* you, back there with the past, which we *never forget,* but which we also move beyond." Before the others can shout him down he adds, "And until we stop sitting around arguing what it means to be black, as if there were a recipe, we're never going to get around to the two basic problems—*economic* slavery, and man's inhumanity to man, both of which cut through skin color like an axe through cornbread."

With that, the man stands and begins to leave the church's makeshift talk show set.

"Sir? Are you leaving, sir?" the moderator asks.

" 'Course he's leaving." Ray recognizes the guy speaking as Nervous Rex, so called because that's what he claims to make all white people. He's a rapper whose fan club Ray once sent thirty dollars to for membership privileges, which included concert and bomb-building info, monogrammed Nervous Rex condoms, a prison survival guide, and a countdown-to-Armageddon newsletter. "He kissed enough white ass for one night."

Hoots from the crowd on the street quickly subside when the man stops and points at the younger man.

"You're the house slave, with your record contract. Kicking street bullshit to kids and making a profit for the man you *say* you hate."

"Makin' a profit for me too, a black man. Spend it in the black community, and not be takin' it off to no vanilla condo complex."

"You want to live in Soweto, cut yourself off from people who want to make things better? You're doing a good job, man. *Bring the ghetto to the world*. Go ahead. Only don't expect my help. I'll tell you something. I'm middle class and I dig it."

"Better? Man, you dreamin'."

A woman at the end of the dais says, "Perhaps we could find some way to avoid casting every conversation in the framework of confrontation."

"Yeah, shoot the sucker," someone on the sidewalk calls out.

Inside, the man ignores her suggestion. "You want to be radical?" he says to Nervous Rex. *"Earn* the right to be confident, and *strive* to be excellent. Inferior is inferior, criminal is criminal." Then he spins and descends from the stage, moving through the crowd and off-camera.

Nervous Rex says, "Oh, I get it. Niggers be in the shape they in 'cause they don't eat enough wheat germ. Get that fiber in the diet, watch some public television." He wipes his brow. "Phew. For a minute there I thought it was, like, somethin' critical."

Several parishioners stand amid the pews and hurl accusations toward the stage. Their voices and the moderator's, his tone emotionally flat except for a faint edge of distaste, muffle the woman's words. All Ray can make out is, "Hasn't anybody noticed that burned-out areas of the 'hood are now owned by Phoenix Cityplex." Then the audio/visual signals both announce, "This is XXN," as the turtlenecked man bursts through the church door.

People in the crowd taunt him, but move quickly out of his way. Ray senses something about the man, an intensity or kind of force field that backs people off, as if to touch him meant you also had to confront yourself. No masks, no disguises, none of the amped rhetoric and boastful posing that carried you the rest of the time.

"That's it. Walk away," someone shouts at him.

"Hope yo' bedsheets clean and white!"

"Yeah, get some sleep, 'cause you sure ain't awake, sucker!"

Even Cootie Mac jumps in. "He just don't know what time it is! Maybe he needs his clock punched!"

The man seems not to notice Ray at first, as he hurries toward him. But there's an instant with the crowd perched and still, primed for a signal to tear loose, when the man's glance cuts toward him. It's a look Ray has seen before in people's eyes, a naked terror. It was there in the expression of the first policeman last night. Perhaps that was his reason for killing. To one time *justify* the expression. If all you see me as is a threat, a killing machine, then that's what I'm gonna be. No sense trying to fight it. But now, as tired of brutality as he is of being misperceived, Ray stands still and allows the man to pass. He watches him walk down the street, then hop into a waiting car which sweeps him away to another world, one Ray no longer hopes to enter.

Cootie Mac catches Ray as he leaves the crowd. "Man, why didn't you jump his ass? Arrogant motherfucker."

"He didn't do nothin'."

" 'Cept come down here and dis us on the TV. Uncle Tom lowlife peckerhead."

Ray ignores him, shutting out the blare and frenzy of the street. Overhead, helicopter blades slap and pock at the siren howls floating through the air, their infrared tracking beams circling him.

"Where you rushing your ass to now?"

"I gotta see somebody."

"You seeing me." When Ray doesn't answer, Cootie Mac slaps him on the arm. "Come on, you can't go home and shit. Let's get fucked up, find some hootches."

"Why can't I go home?"

"Why? Cops. Inch killed a couple. You think they gonna say, Oh well, that's cool. We fuck them suckers up all the time?"

"Thought you said Inch didn't kill no cops!"

"I did. But that don't mean they ain't going to hang him for it."

Ray stops. "They ain't gonna hang him."

"No, they'll let him hang hisself, then say it was a fuckup. What do you care?"

"How'd you like none of us to give a shit about you?"

"Man, you don't! I know that much." Cootie Mac takes the pint bottle from his pocket again and drinks from it, not offering Ray a taste this time. "Solidarity. Brotherhood." He looks at Ray. "That's fantasy, man! Coda. Revolution. They's all as far away from us as that guy on TV. Be excellent. Yeah, right, gimme a minute. Just the same old same old."

"It can't just go on," Ray says.

"Oh yeah, it can. It does." Cootie Mac nudges Ray. "Come on. Bitches'll be scared tonight. They'll *want* some huggin'."

Ray closes his eyes, and gradually, there on the street, he experiences a sensation of floating, as if he were leaving body *and* soul behind to be extinguished in a crystal nothingness, weightless and blissfully dead. *Nothing matters.* My actions are meaningless. I can't even atone for my skins. Accept it, make the leap, then drift into the city as it is, the purposeless quest over, the labyrinth home, now and forever. . . .

"Come on, man, 'fore all the streets is closed down."

But his weightlessness fades. Ray has brought grief into the lives of others, and he just can't let that go. So grief leads to meaning. And meaning, possibly, to hope. "Maybe I'll catch up with you later," he whispers.

"There ain't no later."

Ray hears the loneliness in Cootie Mac's voice. "Then come with me."

"Why? An' sit in your grandmother's house?"

"I'm goin' by O.C.'s place."

"O.C.?" Cootie Mac straightens. "Man, you *are* outta your mind. He's dead long as Elvis."

"I ain't going to see him."

"He got a cuzz or sister I don't know about that you fuckin'?"

"No."

"Then there ain't no point in being there."

"Well I'm going."

"Well fuck you."

Ray clenches his fists and Cootie Mac's eyes brighten. He backpedals slowly, without turning away. Ray watches, motionless, arms at his sides. When Cootie Mac reaches the corner he flips Ray the finger. "Hope some cops *kick* your ass!" Then he vanishes behind a building.

Ray starts up the street. Graffiti unspools into the distance on either side of him, the painted scrawl a kind of dead, surreal foliage. Garbage sacks spill into the gutter and give off a sharp, ammoniated vegetable smell like a garden gone to rot. The entire street feels diseased.

Ray picks up an empty bottle and heaves it through the first window he sees. At the corner he smashes a trash can with the sole of his foot, its contents spattering across the pavement. The city begins to feel familiar again, his rage carving him a place within it.

He bashes in the window of a parked car, unlocks the door, and springs the glove compartment looking for a pistol, smokes, reefer. He scoops everything out onto the floor, then reaches around the driver's seat and pops the trunk hood, unaware that he's talking to himself. He feels a demented sense of release. "Just a crazy nigger, that's me. Uh-huh. Ain't happy 'less I'm fucking with somebody." The trunk contains only a few greasy rags, some plastic antifreeze and oil bottles, and a set of battery cables. He rips up the trunk's carpeting, sees a spare tire and yanks it loose. Beneath it lies a tire iron, one end tapering to fit inside the jack's lever, the other topped by a lug wrench the size of a snake's head. He watches his hand take hold of it, feeling as if he were observing his actions from another place.

He slams the trunk hood closed, then finds himself in a fight with it, kicking and pummeling the hood senselessly when it pops back at him, hammering the car's body until his arm rings from palm to elbow.

Yet none of the numb clarity he felt killing O.C. or the police overtakes him. Killing told him who he was, only he can't kill any longer. Something has gone out of him, and now he's lost. He doesn't know a thing about himself. Where is his father? He doesn't know. Why did his mother kill herself? He doesn't know. How can his grandmother have faith? How can someone love when everything conspires against love? He doesn't know. He answered the heartlessness of the city with his own heartlessness, only to come to grief. Saw the fever of his hate set the city aflame, only to have that which promised peace bring despair. Come full circle in the labyrinth, and yet everything he would know, but does not, hovers above him like an angel.

. . . and finally, knowing himself to be lost, the angel becomes his. The video game's prison cell, long a mystery, reveals itself. His fate is *this* place. Not just the city or the skin of Afroman, but the skin of man, stumbling blindly ahead, frail and filled with terror. The mystical prison bars evanesce, and all that was imprisoned by them, Ray sees, is himself. Ray. Flesh of Ray. Ray who bleeds as others around him bleed, feel as Ray himself feels, in the city of their own making, the city of their longing and despair. And when his compassion for himself reaches out saying, you are forgiven, you are loved by me, he feels himself to be forgiven, to be loved. In the end, the city exiles no one. And so he allows the iron bar to slip free of his hand. And when he looks up, he's home.

The wide plaza is deserted as he passes beneath the entryway's arch. Benches are toppled, trash cans overturned. A smashed television set lies near one wall, as if it were dropped from a high window. Even the Discordia Sect flyers Ray had pasted to walls have been defaced, his faith in Coda unreal to him now, and slipping quickly into the past. He bypasses the annex building where he and Inch live, heading into the tower at the center of the project. In the shadowy glare of the lobby he steps into the one working elevator. The car shudders as it ascends, its fluorescent light making a dull buzz, then shorting out and plunging the car into darkness. The flickerings pass weightlessly at first. Then they become denser, heavier with each recurrence, as if Ray were being born over and over again, his soul springing back from eternity only to reappear here, instants away from having to look into O.C.'s mother's eyes, and tell her he killed her son.

In the hall, a single bulb burns at one end of the long corridor. Voices murmur behind doors and walls, inaudible except for the words "This is XXN." He finds the door and knocks, and a soft brilliant light falls instantly upon him. In the doorway is O.C.'s mother, LeShawna, standing there as if she had been awaiting him.

"Didn't I tell you to keep your little no-good asses away from here?"

"I ain't been here," Ray says, confused.

"Well, if it wasn't you, was one of your waste-of-life friends. William and Lissa are *not*—do I have to repeat myself?—not setting one foot outside this apartment."

Ray sees Lissa appear behind her mother, the young girl's features familiar to him from the courtyard's playground. "It's Ray," she says. "He ain't here for William or me."

LeShawna's stance softens. Her shoulders sink, bare feet shifting on the floor. "Ray?" she says, as if testing his presence. The sternness in her eyes fades, overtaken by wariness and fear. "Yeah, Ray." He tries to blot himself out, to speak without inhabiting his words. He closes his eyes, his body shuddering. "I come about O.C.," he says.

Then he's in a screaming darkness, as LeShawna hits him hard with something he doesn't see. Lissa is crying when he opens his eyes. The floor seems to be close to his face, its tile cool against one temple. One side of his head is numb, as if part of his brain were gloved. He lies there, remembering LeShawna saying, Oh God, like someone had just let all the breath out of her, her voice dying in her chest, the light around him blood-red, the texture of it no longer clear but mucousy. LeShawna falls to her knees, down with him on the floor. Ray has no desire to protect himself. And, gradually, her blows soften, slowing until they beat against him like the seconds of his life passing, hammering at time and loss, and he hears her crying.

Voices swirl around him, apartment doors opening as Ray is dragged to his feet. LaShawna's son William whispers, "It's alright." He leads Ray into a room which brightens until Ray feels as if he were being swallowed by light. LeShawna tells Lissa to go fetch a washcloth. Ray can still hear the girl weeping softly. LeShawna comes back into the room with a metal box as William eases him down into a chair. She sets the first aid kit on the table beside Ray, springs the top, then wipes the tears from her eyes.

"Damn, Mama. What you doin'?"

Ray looks up out of one eye and sees William studying his face. He has the impression that O.C. is standing there beside his brother.

" 'Damn, Mama' nothin'. Out of my way."

LeShawna pulls Ray's hand from his face, but O.C. isn't where Ray sensed he'd be. There is only a blurry redness, foregrounded against the light. The silhouette coming toward him is Lissa, bearing a damp cloth. LeShawna takes it from her and brusquely wipes Ray's face with it, using little caution near his bad eye.

"Close the door." The young girl does so quietly, as if in shock.

"Why'd you go beatin' on him?" William asks.

" 'Cause he's been lying to me a long time." LeShawna pauses to glare into Ray's clear eye. "Boy, the only reason you breathing is 'cause I ain't figured out how I want to kill you yet." She scrapes blood off Ray's eyelid, turning his head with the force of her hand.

"Ah!" Ray's body jerks.

"I'll give you 'Ah.' William, turn off that television."

"Yo, Mama. They got that thing where they're gonna hook up with Coda coming on."

Ray glances at William and realizes that he doesn't know about Coda's terror not being out there, but carried around inside us. Or about himself and O.C., either.

LaShawna dips cotton in peroxide, then cleans Ray's cuts. "Don't I have all the criminals I need in my house right now *without* the damn television on?"

"Well what's he doing here?" William has O.C.'s features, though he's lankier. He's wearing a tanktop with a college insignia, and the tails of the shirt drop straight past his narrow hips. He doesn't seem really tall until he comes up behind his mother. Then Ray sees a resolute quality in the boy's face, heightened by his gold-framed glasses. There's a sense of determination, but also a constant, low-level fear that he projects. Here his similarity to his brother vanishes. O.C. had been innocent, trusting, happy. Confident about belonging in the world. Even when Ray approached him on the bus, O.C. was grinning, like, what's up, home? Ray envied O.C. for living with no sense of being an outcast. He envied O.C.'s joy. And for that he killed his friend. Jealousy, a pitiful meanness of spirit. Two other men were also dead. Stripped of rhetoric, Ray's crimes appear to him as what they are: stark, brutal, inexcusable, and his alone.

Ray sees LeShawna studying his face, as if she were asking herself what heartlessness in him could have led to the killing of her son. A reason. Something logical, or redeemable, in Ray's actions that she can hang on to. Then it's gone, her urge to forgive him cooling inside her like a dying ash.

"I'm waiting," William says. "Why's he here?"

LeShawna stares at Ray. "I promised his Mama I'd whup his ass if it ever got outta line," she says.

"What?" William's voice rises. "When'd you make this promise?"

LeShawna exchanges the cotton swab for a bottle of iodine. "A long time before you started backtalking me. Lissa."

"Yes, Mama."

"Turn that thing off." Then the room is quiet except for a hushed, spooky music. Bells, chimes, and a flute which sounds to Ray's ears like a lone human voice. It drifts up the hallway from one of the far rooms. And Ray thinks that, beneath all its fantastic terrors and electronic links, this is the true city, the vulnerable hearts of a few people together in a single room.

William's gaze shifts to Ray. "Seems like you should have started correcting his ass a long time ago."

LeShawna looks at her son. "Oh, now you the authority on what I gotta do?"

"Didn't say that."

"Funny. That's what I heard."

"It's just . . . It's Do-Ray. Why you waste your time?"

Lissa runs out of the room. Down the hallway a door slams, muffling the music.

"You happy with what you done now?" LeShawna says. She turns from William, then dabs iodine on the places where her nails cut Ray's face.

"What I done?" William says. "She was crying her touchy twelve-year-old butt off when I come out here and find you going crazy. First you kick his ass, now you're nursing it."

"Yeah, well, why don't you just go quiet your sister down."

"Why'd he show his face anyway?"

"His grandmother sent him." The sting of iodine coincides with LeShawna's lie, making Ray jerk backwards. "Stealing out of her house money. I said, 'You send his ass on over here. I'll talk to him.'"

William exhales, hands on his hips. "He ain't blinded or anything, is he?"

"You worried about him now?"

William huffs. "Yeah, right. Only now I gotta be watching my back double-time."

LeShawna whirls and points at him. "He ain't never gonna come anywhere near you, you understand?" She looks at Ray. "Tell him." Ray hesitates. "I said tell him. Now!"

Through Ray's good eye, the distance between himself and William seems greater than it is. But somehow this feels right. They are wholly unlike one another, something Coda, with his cries of injustice for all young black men, blindly overlooked.

"You gonna go anywhere near him?" LeShawna says.

"No."

"You even gonna look at him?"

Ray presses his lips together, then quietly says, "No."

"Good. Start right now."

At first Ray resists. Coda's voice urges him to surrender to nothin'. But soon, he closes his eyes and bows his head.

"See? He ain't gonna come near you."

"Yeah, saying that with one eye bleeding is one thing. On the street, it's something all over again."

"He ain't gonna be on the street. Mr. Ray done decided it's time to move on, get a long way away." Ray feels LeShawna's fingers around his jaw. She's looking at him when he opens his eyes. "You're gone, aren't you?"

He says, "Yes," not only to please her, but because he feels it's true.

LeShawna releases him. "See? So you can put worrying out of your mind. Now go calm your sister."

"Yeah, alright." William sulks, though Ray detects a sense of relief in his voice. "Didn't have to miss this Coda business on account of this jive, though."

"You seen enough criminals for one day. There'll be plenty more tomorrow. Now get."

LeShawna tilts Ray's head back and leans over him with a threaded needle curved like a quarter-moon. "What you gonna do with that?" he says.

"Pluck your eye out." A bolt of fear shoots through Ray's body. "Gonna stitch that cut. What you think I'm gonna do?"

"It's that bad?"

"You want it to stop bleeding?"

Ray nods.

"Then don't be moving your head."

"It gonna hurt?"

"Oh nigger, please." LeShawna exhales, then places a knee on Ray's thigh. "Now hold still."

His vision clears for an instant as she tugs on the skin at the corner of his eye, blood no longer pooling inside his lower lid. He sees the needle slide past his pupil. Then it pushes through his skin, the shadows of LeShawna's hands all he can see out of that eye, the rest of the room bright and clean out of the other. This feeling of being torn in half makes him close his good eye. In the dark, the needle hooks through his flesh a second time. The dryness of the thread trailing behind is gentler now, slicked by his blood, and he is drawn down into his breathing until he feels himself swimming in it, separate from the lacerations of his flesh. A soft musk rises from LeShawna's breasts. He feels her hips swaying over him. Between his legs the tingling of an erection begins, though all Ray wants is to put his arms around her, curl around her darkness and musk, and find a place of stillness where he can't fall the way he feels himself to be falling.

"There." The weight of her body is suddenly gone. He opens his eyes to see her cleaning the needle with alcohol. The redness has diminished in his bad eye. In its place is a watery distortion of shapes and depth. "Those stitches will dissolve in ten days, you don't have to worry about having 'em out. Here." She hands Ray a ball of cotton. "Dab at it with this. Gently." He takes the cotton from her hand and places it against his eye. "The blood'll clear up, but that eye's going to tear for a while." She strips a Band-Aid of its wrapper, then turns to him. "Move that hand."

As she's pressing the Band-Aid to his temple, he says, "Why you doing this?" Her hands fall still. He waits, then she smooths the bandage and turns to the table. Ray watches her repack the kit carefully, each item tucked into a designated spot. "It's alright," he says. "I don't have to know."

"Boy, don't you pity me." She flings what she has in her hand into the box. "You don't feel *nothing* toward me. You got that?"

"Yes."

"You lost any right to think about me a long time ago. You dead to me." Her voice drops as she seems to speak only to herself.

"Grieved over this more than enough for one lifetime. Ain't about to be swallowed up in that again." She looks at him. "Who sent you 'round here anyway?"

"Nobody."

"Oh, so you just got it in your head six years later to come and tell me who you really are."

"No, it ain't like that."

She slaps the first aid kit shut. "William don't know about you and O.C., and he ain't *ever* gonna know. Lissa figured it out herself, when you came to the door, she's smarter. So I done what I done because I'm not about to let him be touched by any of this." She glances at Ray. "You're evil, and I can't ever forgive you. Don't care how hard your life been. It's hard for everybody. That don't make 'em murderers."

Ray tries to coax the words he wants onto his tongue, which is as dry as the cotton she handed him. "Did you, I mean . . . did my mother ever really ask you that? 'Bout me."

Ray watches LeShawna, feeling as if his fate were being weighed. It occurs to him that she might lie in order to kill off the last of his hope, to extinguish him forever in this life the way he extinguished O.C. Then she sinks into the chair beside his, drifting down into it like a leaf after it ceases to cling to what for so long held it in place. On the table are a set of keys, a hospital tag with LeShawna's nursing title etched on it, a stack of bills set atop a small computer. She reaches for the name tag, studies it, then taps it against the table's surface. "She asked me to look out for you, case anything happened to her. Guess I ain't done such a great job. Look what it got me."

"It ain't your fault. You can't be thinking that." Ray sits forward so she has to look at him.

LeShawna laughs softly. "She always warned me she was a

witch." She pauses, then says, "You know you think, as a black woman, that it might be easy for something to happen to you. So you plan. But you never expect that it's gonna wind up. . . ."

Ray lays one hand over LeShawna's when her voice cracks. "It's okay. It's okay. You had your own blood to worry about. The problem ain't with you, it was with me. I was crazy out of my head all the time. I know you came around to check on me. I remember. But there wasn't nothing nobody could do." Ray rocks her hand, trying to make her look at him. "You ain't to blame for this. All the mess, from my mother and all, wound up in me. That's why I. . . ."

LeShawna's eyes are reddened except for the pupils, where Ray can see tiny reflections of his face on their dark surfaces.

"See, O.C. ain't the only one I killed." He's aware of a small, almost imperceptible jolt inside her. He begins to speak quickly. "This other stuff with the riots, and Coda an' all. You gotta understand when my mother . . . after she took herself . . . I was nothin'. I mean, how could she. . . ." He begins shaking.

Then LaShawna's voice comes to him as if she were in another room, saying, "Ray . . . Ray. . . ."

Slowly he falls back inside himself, into the clean bright room with LeShawna now holding his hand. He can hear sirens on the street below, yet this moment feels peaceful, as if he'd arrived at some final reconciliation with the world. He clears his throat. "You don't have to hold my hand if you don't want," he says. LeShawna leaves her hand on his, though. "See, I was empty for a long time. Like . . . how could I be worth anything if my mother could go leave me like that. I didn't. . . ." His voice vanishes.

"It's alright," LeShawna whispers.

". . . it's just I couldn't, you know, see that the pain was hers too. That she felt these things in herself."

" 'Course she did. We all do."

"Well I didn't know that!" Ray's voice rises slightly. He presses his lips together. "Sorry."

"Ray." LeShawna forces him to look at her. "I ain't saying your mother killing herself shouldn't have had any effect on you. It did, I know. And I'm sorry I wasn't there for you when you needed me. That's my grief, and I have to live with it. But you can't use her dying to diminish my boy's death, or excuse yourself for whatever else you done. *You* done what you done. Nobody forced you."

"I know."

"Well maybe *now* you know. But it's a little late." LeShawna's jaw tightens. "So you telling me you got mixed up in all this Coda business?"

Ray hesitates. "Yeah."

LeShawna shakes her head. "When are you gonna learn? Do you have to die on the streets before you get some sense?"

"That's what I'm saying."

"Don't whine at me, boy. I'll hold your hand, get you right in the mind, but don't you sulk to me."

"I wasn't. . . ." Ray doesn't know how to explain what he can see in his head. Coming toward O.C. on the bus, slinking up alongside the cop car. "It's like, I wasn't even there."

"But it ain't *like* my son *isn't* dead."

"I'm only tryin' to explain is all. I just. . . . I was lost. Evil didn't have no meaning to me. It's like, I was nothing, so everything I did, everything around me, was nothing too."

"And you see that now?"

"Yeah."

"So if you was lost, why you turn to some life-hating, second-rate 'revolutionary' for advice? Being lost mean you have to be stupid too? We're all lost! Only some of us don't take it out on the rest of the world! Discordia Sect! Macho bullshit. You know how you get through the world? You don't accept it as it is."

"That's what I was doing, following Coda an' all."

"That's destroying the world. Hate leaves you nothing to build on. You want to be lost forever, keep on hating." She pauses. "Only maybe now you've grieved enough to start loving the world. Ain't enough to just love yourself. Though maybe you see that now. After all," she pushes away from him and sits up straight, "you came here on your own."

While they sit in silence, Ray feels the peace in the room slipping from him. A dizzy weakness passes through him, as if his veins had been sliced open and he could do nothing but sleepily watch his life leak away. After the electronic highs of Afroman, the chaos of the streets, and the dislocations of watching the city and his crime within it through the eye of XXN, it is hard to fathom that beneath the clatter this is still all that matters—two people, naked before one another with their grief.

LeShawna pats his hand. "So. I made my peace with your mama. Now you're on your own."

Ray sits there, staring at her hand over his.

"It's good you came. Not knowin' for sure about O.C. caused a lot of sleepless nights. And now you know your mother *was* thinking of you, all the time. So a lot of ghosts got buried. But now you gotta go. And once you leave, I never want to see you again. We done with each other in this world."

Ray rocks gently in his chair, though he can't bring himself to raise his eyes to meet hers. "You check on my grandmother now and then?" he says.

LeShawna is slow in answering. "I can do that."

Ray's head bobs. "Appreciate it. Those other folks I killed—"

"Ray." Her hand releases his. "I can't help you with that. I won't. Nobody was there to hold my hand for O.C., and now we going to let him be. But this other business." LeShawna brushes the air in front of her as if she were whisking him out of her life. "That's your own lookout. You had a lot of grief in your life, but now you gotta answer for the part of it you made yourself."

Ray feels the connection between them wither. He stands, then leans down and places a kiss on LeShawna's forehead. Through the window behind her he sees a car pulling into the courtyard below, its headlights off.

Crossing the bright room, he's aware of the blind spot in his eye. He fumbles with the door locks, his hands shaking. LeShawna comes alongside him, softly opens it, then Ray walks into the dim hallway without looking at her. Behind him the apartment's light holds for several moments, laying his long shadow across the tile floor. Then the brightness vanishes, only the faint clicking of the door's lock audible in the hall's reclaimed darkness.

Riding the elevator, he watches the blurred floor numbers tick by. At the basement level, he heads for the tower's rear entrance, then slips out into the building's shadow, toward the light burning in Inch's bedroom window.

The van bounds along potholed streets as night falls and the arc lights come on, drenching the air with a jaundiced glow. Everything in the cab clatters. Camera equipment, loose videocassettes, empty soft drink cans. Plus the contents of Nick's open briefcase: portaphone, CD Walkman with assorted CDs, video camcorder, palmtop computer, backup flask, pill bottles filled with Benzedrine, Valium, Quaaludes, multivitamin supplements, and, for nostalgic reasons, chewable orange-flavored aspirin for children. The Lorcim L-25 pistol, however, he has slipped into one of the case's side compartments where it rests snugly, and easily accessible.

The noise is good, actually. At least, Darren thinks so. Because ever since surrendering the lovely hushed splendor of the limousine and sneaking into the idling van parked outside the Criminal Court Building, Nick has been, to put it delicately, out of his mind. For stretches of fifteen to twenty seconds, the sounds making their way out of his mouth would be hard to classify as coherent. Darren has witnessed transformations like this in sci-fi movies. Some guy drinks smoky serum out of a laboratory glass, loosens his tie, then begins quaking and sticking his tongue out three feet past his lips. The next time you see him his clothes cling to his body like strips of torn newspaper and he's got a bad case of tarantula head.

Darren is reluctant to call Nick's ranting to his attention, though, fearing that the ex–public defender might pitch his defenseless behind out the panel van's sliding door. Judging by the number of spotlighted Virgin Mary lawn grottoes they've passed in the last few minutes, they're in the heart of Mafia Land, known in the 'hood as "the black hole." 'Cause a black dude gets anywhere near it—*arrivederci*, homes.

The driver, who has deftly bypassed roadblocks and other riot delays since they left downtown, doesn't seem unduly upset by Nick's tantrum, though. In fact, since passing Nick the envelope, which seems to be the source of his psychosis, the driver has been content to run red lights, drink numerous jumbo containers of what smells like some very strong coffee, and whistle along with tunes on the digitalized radio's country-western stations. His assistant, a Chicano youth about Darren's age who is wearing low-heeled cowboy boots, jeans, and a "Viva Nada TV!" T-shirt, is actually snoozing on the van's rear bench, his face buried beneath an open paperback with a fighter jet and a woman wearing nothing but a scarf on the cover.

Darren checks the dashboard's TV screen. Electronic numbers flash across huge lightboards. It looks like ball-game scores, only he doesn't recognize any of the team abbreviations, and the point totals are crazy—½ pt., ¾, ⅝, with some teams even scoring in *reverse*. Darren leans forward, noting the frustrated calculations Nick is making on his palmtop computer in the front passenger seat. "What kind of sports channel you got on, anyway?" Nick ignores him. Spread over his briefcase are legal-looking documents tattooed with rubber-stamp marks and illegible signatures. Beside them are sheets of ornately decorated paper that resemble gigantic, phony dollar bills. "You gonna break that machine in your hand, you keep whacking it like that."

Nick stops poking keyboard numbers, then slowly turns his face toward Darren's. "Oh, you know about electronics now?"

"No, I just—"

Nick offers Darren the mini-computer. "Maybe this is a model you've stolen in the past. Here, show me how to use it. Tell me why no matter how I punch these figures in, I come out financially screwed." Nick sees the driver's huge oval belt buckle glowing like a moonstone as it reflects the dashboard's panel lights. Above the collar of his checked shirt, his lips move in sync with the song lyrics playing on the radio, a faint, off-key mewing. "Trampas, are you sure this is all you were supposed to give me?" Nick clutches his contract and shares of Apocalypse Productions & Enterprises stock.

"Yup."

"There weren't any one-thousand-dollar bills or money orders clipped to the contract at some point?"

Trampas exhales, his first sign of deep feeling. "This is going to go a whole lot smoother if I don't have to kill you," he says, in a plaintive twang. The grease in his buzz cut gleams like fresh tar. "And had you done business with G.R. before, you'd know the man does not have any affection for cash disbursements."

Darren taps Nick's shoulder when he sees the A.P.E. logo from the stock shares on-screen, right above XXN. "Hey, that's us."

Nick eyes the 9 × 12 television. An Apocalypse Productions ad offers "otherwise unavailable" riot-related information, as well as comments from revolutionary leaders. Call 1-900-Dis-Cord. Calls are $9.95 per minute.

Nick stares at Darren. "Us? Us?"

"Yeah, like them things right there in your hand. A.P.E."

Nick raises his eyes and scans the padded ceiling. "Has socialism overthrown our technopoly without holding a press conference? Or did I miss it, due to an alcoholic blackout? I thought we were still capitalists, like the rest of the world." Nick looks toward Trampas.

"I ain't heard about any changes."

Nick turns to Darren again. "There's no 'us.' There's *me.*" He offers the boy a look at the stock shares. "Do these say Nick and Darren?"

"No."

"Thank you." Nick turns away from him.

"If them's yours and they so hot, then why you cursing like a wild man?"

"Trampas?"

"I guess he was counting on a harder kind of currency. Tell you, I like them yen. Whenever I can get my hands on some—you know, under the table—I grab all I can. Gatesy steered me into some pretty good deals. Rice paddies in China? Boom, gone! All factories, warehouses, and huge industrial plants now. Don't have to worry about environmental regulations, so you keep costs down."

"What kinda stuff they make?" Darren asks.

Trampas thinks, momentarily stunned. "Hell, I don't know! Everything! *What* ain't the point. It's *how* they make it. And there's only one correct answer to that question—cheap." Trampas looks over his shoulder at Darren. "That's why the poor ain't got jobs, then have to go around shootin' up half the damn city. You expect wages." He shakes his head, looking at the road ahead. "Corporations *hate* to pay wages. Independent contracting, the wave of the future. Service. Hell, that's what I do. And Hector?" Trampas indicates his assistant. "He's got that wetback work ethic, you know. Do whatever to clear a field. Fuck heat, sun, rattlesnakes. Only he's working the high-tech end of the fields nowadays."

Trampas leaves one road, arcing across the communications belt of the city. They pass glass pyramids and stainless-steel cones which house microchip labs, electronic publishing facilities, spatial imaging shops, and simultaneous-interpretation telephone stations. The troops surrounding them wear odd uniforms. In the silvery floodlight that seeps from each building out to its fenced perimeter, they appear to be made of supple tinfoil.

"Them is some weird cops," Darren says.

Nick grunts, then returns to his calculations.

Trampas checks the scenery beyond the shadowed fringe of the interstate loop. "Private security. Corporate police. Those are Mylar uniforms. Makes night vision goggles useless. In that light, hell, those guys look like sunbursts. Mostly ex-CIA, FBI types working the security field nowadays. Clipped the technology from their old employers, so they eliminate R&D."

"What's R&D?"

"Research and development. Big nut. Eat up a serious chunk of your profit."

It takes Darren a second to catch on. "Oh, like wheels. If you gotta have wheels to move a load of crack or guns or VCRs, you gotta lay out for 'em."

"That's overhead. But still, that's what I'm talking about. Do it yourself. Those guys design, distribute, install, *and* service their own hardware. So, wham!" Trampas whacks the steering wheel. "You hit the consumer at both ends. Sweet deal."

Darren studies the security troops and the pristine temples glowing serenely behind them against the city's outer dark. Strangely, his fear of the area lightens. The veil of speculation separating it from his life in the 'hood vanishes. The place is about money, nothing else. And with the mystery dissolved, he knows it is possible for him to cross over, to belong here.

"This is XXN" filters through the television's speakers. Otherwise, they are all silent, allowing the city to stream by. Trampas dreams of some ineffable product to successfully mass-market. Nick, trying to fathom the potential gain hidden within clauses, subclauses, and riders contained in his contract, wonders why his thirty-eight years feel as if they have been built on nothing, drugs and booze only a gloss laid over a deep emptiness. Darren imagines a bridge leading to this zone of the city, the 'hood no longer visible as he sails away from it, his one fleeting thought of Ray quickly fading.

Darren leans toward Trampas. "Say. You been to college?"

"I have," Nick mumbles. "I've been to many, many colleges. Let me assure you, it's the path to success. Not simply in an economic way, but on cultural, social, and spiritual levels as well."

Darren can't tell if Nick is mocking him. He was mellow in the limousine, but with the booze wearing off he seems sullen, sadder.

"I did some time at a Vo-Ag school," Trampas says. "Agriculture-type stuff."

Darren shakes his head, not understanding.

"Agriculture is the stage where they actually grow the pot, the coca leaves, the poppies," Nick explains.

"Yeah? I grew some herb one time. Lame shit. What's that other stuff, though? Cocoa and poppies?"

Nick stares at Darren. "Cocaine. Heroin."

"Yeah? I thought that shit was like . . . powder."

Pausing first, Nick says, "What college are you going to attend, Darren?"

"That's just it. I'm askin' you to help me out."

"This goes okay," Trampas says, "Gatesy might be a good connection. He does stuff like that so he can tell himself he's not a total shit."

"You don't like your employer?" Nick's voice rises a sarcastic octave or two. "Yet you're telling me to relax when he sends me shares in a corporation which hasn't even gone public yet."

Trampas shrugs. "G.R.'s a snake, but he's always done alright by me income-wise. Take Hector. He's one smart little cockroach. Figures out all this camera shit, transferring video by computer, you name it. Me, I can't barely find the trigger. But he does everything I say, so we're partners"—Darren eyes Nick, who ignores him—"eighty/twenty, long as he don't give me no shit. G.R.'s putting him through M.I.T. by E-mail."

"So this guy is, like, major rich?" Darren says.

Trampas eyes Darren in the rearview mirror. "G.R.? G.R. owns the world. TV is just a way for him to get stroked. Video's sexy. It keeps him near the celebrity crowd. Otherwise, he's just another fat ugly fuck with a lot of cash. G.R. basically needs to purchase affection. That's why he's backing me in this brothel deal over in

Tokyo and Saigon. Hell, maybe even Hanoi and Beijing, if it shakes out right. We're bringing in U.S. beaver. And not just street scags, either. These are gonna be college coeds. Work for us one summer, earn next year's tuition and board. Payment is piped directly into your university's Vax hookup. Sure beats flipping burgers and wearing a stupid paper hat. And man, those Jap and Vietnamese guys love the idea of fucking our pussy." Trampas falls silent, then adds, "In a way, I kind of hate to do it. But," he shrugs, "that's the market."

"So you gonna live over there?" Darren asks.

"Hell, yes. Already got me a spread, good for raising cattle. That ties in with the other idea, which is for a small, exclusive chain of barbecue joints. Dance floor, longneck bottled beer, satellite country-western hookups. Them dinks really go for the shitkicker number." Trampas stares through the windshield. "I just hope we ain't fucking too bad with some of that karma."

"You mean Nam, Hiroshima?" Nick says.

"Nah, wars don't mean dick."

"What then?"

"You know, the rice spirit. In the land, in the water . . . or it was." Trampas shakes his head. "Shit, we stole their God."

As the beltway horseshoes toward downtown, Darren watches the 'hood reappear through the van's observation window. From this distance it is no more than a small fire surrounded by a grid of lights which spread across the basin and low hills of the city.

Trampas points out his window at the fires. "Hell, that's some primo real estate. You can bet somebody's got plans for it already. Just like burning fields and rotating crops. The trick now is to make it *look* like the apocalypse for your basic cable audience."

Nick looks at Trampas. "Gates isn't getting a single frame until he and I have a serious financial powwow."

"I got two messages: give you the envelope, and bring back live footage of some dead people. And I mean to do both." Trampas glances in the rearview mirror, then takes an empty cola can off the dashboard and flips it to the rear of the van. "Hector! Enough *el sueño. Trabajo* time."

At the crest of an exit ramp is a brightly lit oasis of gas stations, fast food outlets, and convenience stores. Short lines of cars trail away from the canopied islands where the pumps stand. National Guard troops check arriving vehicles and direct traffic, rifles in hand.

"I need some coffee and a piss." Trampas glances at Nick and Darren. "I also need to know *exactly* where we're headed, and a map of the place we're headed to." He slows as they approach a small posse of guards, several of whom have one palm raised. "Hector." The young cameraman sits up, wiping sleep grit from his eyes. "Make me up a shot list, *también.* I want to know what the hell we're doing once we get there."

"Are we broadcasting live?" Nick asks.

"That's the general idea. Terror-TV: death coming to you live— every day, every way. Tell you one thing. I like working close to home. Some of those Third World countries seriously suck." He turns to the guard moving warily toward his window. "Hey, good buddy. XXN-TV. Stopping to gas up and rinse a kidney."

Darren sits perfectly still as the guard's flashlight beam sweeps through the van's interior, pausing when it reaches him. He is only dimly aware of Trampas surrendering identification and saying, "Nick Wolf, producer, Hector Veracruz, cameraman, and Darren . . ."

"Adams," Nick says. "Creative consultant."

The light lingers on Darren, blinding him. Then it's gone, purple spots spinning before his eyes.

"How do you fit in?" the guard asks Trampas.

"Hell, I'm the brains!"

Their ID is cleared by a guard who runs it through a handheld computer. "What was all that stuff?" Nick wants to know, once they've pulled away.

"Shooting permits. Curfew exemptions. Shit, everybody but us, cops, troops, and criminal types have to be off the streets in an hour. Nationwide. G.R. says the president is going to announce a state of emergency tonight."

Nick surfs the airwaves, checking each of XXN's news channels until he finds the coverage he wants. Streets in other cities are deserted except for the occasional police or National Guard presence. TV voices say, "The nation braces for disaster." "Sympathetic rioting breaks out around the country as night falls." "Links to any sect have not yet been established." There are images of window smashing and scattered fires.

"Is this going to kill our audience share?" Nick asks.

Trampas pulls up beside a gas pump and twists the ignition key. "If there's one thing G.R.'s good at, it's cornering a market. Twenty-four hours, we might have some competition. But hell, we got Armageddon *now!* That's what being a product leader is all about—timing." Stepping out of the van, Trampas looks back at Darren. "You people sure got a knack with this entertainment stuff. Wish I could bottle it and sell it."

"You are," Nick tells him.

Trampas stares into space for a moment, holding the hat he is about to put on. "Hot damn, you're right!" He slams the door shut, slips a credit card into the gas pump's "Pay First" slot, then waits for the day's price per gallon to appear on-screen. The message that returns with credit approval reads: "Due to rioting, our prices have temporarily risen to reflect anticipated cost increases." The price of super unleaded with gasohol and a cleansing agent known as "the Carburetor's Friend" has tripled since morning.

"Madre de Dios!" Hector leaves the van's sliding door open behind him as he stares at the fuel pump.

"And them ain't pesos, either." Trampas inserts the gas nozzle and locks its handle. "Looks like I'm going to have to pass some of these cost overruns on to you, *pobrecito.*"

Hector shrugs. *"Que hay de nuevo?"*

Trampas heads toward the convenience store. "And rock 'n' roll on that shot list," he yells. "Time's *dinero. Comprende?"* Trampas tips the brim of his Stetson as he passes the Guardsmen near the electronic door, then cruises into the building's bright interior beneath the eyes of surveillance cameras.

Nick punches Gates Remington's number into the van's cellular phone. Its digits materialize on a vacuum-fluorescent display beneath the radio/CD player, as the speaker system automatically switches to phone mode. After a high-pitched squeal, an electronic voice states that the call cannot go through. The system has reached overload.

"I been thinkin'," Darren says. "All this stuff costs a lot of money. Limousines, cameras, fancy drinks."

"It's called decadence."

"Yeah, well. I think I should be gettin' me some of it."

Hector appears in the van's doorway, a notepad computer in one hand. Sensing he has arrived at a less than ideal moment, he remains silent.

Nick fixes his attention on Darren. "In exchange for what? What are you selling, Darren? What product are you marketing?"

"Information."

Nick studies the boy. "Maybe you *should* go to college. You're good at picking up buzzwords that make you sound almost intelligent." Nick turns. "Hector."

"Yes?"

"How do you earn your money?"

Hector shrugs, then holds up the computer. "This. The cameras."

"You make things, figure things out," Nick says, leading him.

Hector nods slowly. "*Sí.* Sure. I guess."

"Well, what would you say about someone who sells his best friend to earn money? You know, overlooks the ethical imperative that should be motivating his contribution to the capture of a criminal mastermind, in order to secure personal financial gain?"

"*Repételo* . . . ?"

"You think you ain't doing the same thing?" Darren says. "Selling me."

"You're going to hold *me* up as a moral guideline? Or maybe you have a short-term memory problem from smoking so much weed, and have forgotten that you're supposed to be incarcerated!"

"I ain't forgettin'."

"Oh no? What then?"

"Negotiating. If everything's for sale, I'm sellin'."

Hector extends the computer's display screen. "We should really. . . ." He makes a handwriting gesture. "You know. The shot list. *Ahora.*"

Darren folds his arms over his chest, and turns away.

"Fine. You think this is worth anything?" Nick slaps his pile of stock shares, then flips the TV back to the financial news channel. Numbers from round-the-clock global funds flow across the screen, thin bands of bright, contrasting colors. "Let's see, we've got twenty thousand shares of Apocalypse Productions stock which—since the company doesn't appear to be *listed* on any of the exchanges!—I feel confident in assessing at a total net asset value of *zero.*" Nick flings the stack of laser-printed paper at Darren as if he were winging a Frisbee. The boy jerks to one side, paper bouncing off his shoulder and fluttering to the floor.

"Then there's *this* handsome addition to our portfolio. One thousand shares of G.R.E. preferred stock, obviously an industry leader, trading in, if memory serves me correctly, high *single*-digit territory." Nick throws this next set of financial instruments at the van's ceiling in mock celebration. "Nine thousand pre-tax dollars to split two ways, Darren. Think of it! With this windfall our financial horizons are *boundless!* Why, you can buy that shirt you liked, and still have pennies left over for a college education!" After glowering at Darren, Nick slumps against the van's passenger door.

Darren watches the compact cars, Guardsmen, and the brisk business at the crossroads mall. Ray wanted an end to injustice; all he brought on was panic buying and a few TV specials. Turning toward the dashboard screen, he sees stripes of glowing color, lulling and hypnotic. There's even an upbeat soundtrack playing in sync with the data, the kind of let's-get-happy stuff they play on phone lines and in malls and burger joints. Everything is information *and* entertainment. Everything wired and empty. For the first time, Darren glimpses the world Ray wanted to escape. Coda and the sect were only links to a deeper emptiness he must have felt. Ray wanted justice; the world gave him bright, floating numbers. "Take me back," Darren says.

Nick lowers the flask's nipple from his lips. "We are taking you back."

"I mean to jail."

Hector makes a soft mooing sound.

"I didn't do all them things you said. They can't lock me up when I didn't do nothing."

Nick laughs. Just stares at the van's ceiling and laughs, his feet on Trampas's bucket seat, the back of his head against the tinted, bulletproof window.

Hector taps Darren on one knee. "If it's the *dinero,* don't worry."

"You going to pay us out of your cut?" Nick asks.

"No, but—"

"It ain't just the money," Darren says. He exchanges an unfriendly glance with Nick, then looks back at Hector but says nothing more.

"It's only the money as far as I'm concerned. But I'm not giving away anything for a pile of worthless stock. Not this public defender."

"You ain't got no job," Darren says.

"Yes I do. You took me hostage. I was kidnapped by terrorist revolutionaries. Luckily, I shot you and escaped before I could be executed by Coda himself. The book and film rights alone will make me rich."

Hector sets the computer down, then reaches into his pocket and withdraws several certificates of Apocalypse Productions stock. "This is good, as money," he says, holding the shares out so Nick can see them. "It's new, that's all."

"A little too new."

"No. *Mira.*" Hector picks up the computer and requests customized information on A.P.E. and G.R.E. stock. The numbers on the TV flip into data limbo, replaced by up-to-the-millisecond reports on both subsidiaries of Gates Remington Entertainment.

Nick sits up. "The TV's wired to the computer?"

"*Sí.* It *is* the computer. Cellular linkup." Hector calls up the latest share price quotations, as well as abridged analyst forecasts for each. Since announcing exclusive broadcast rights to special riot footage, G.R.E. stock has doubled in value. Sweetening the deal are licensing arrangements with video-game manufacturers that have obtained Coda and the Discordia Sect as entertainment properties. "Good growth stock," Hector says.

"You own shares?"

"Yeah. Sure. *Seis, siete mil.* Reinvest *automático.* You know?"

"Of course," Nick lies, dumbfounded. Why is he always the one to get in on the top floor?

Darren silently watches the screen. The images are dead and beautiful. And maybe Ray understood this, his sense of dispossession extending to the synthetic world. Against the processed, stainproof leather and plastic of the van, Darren can smell his own grubby funk. His teeth are rotten, he limps. There are holes in his socks and underwear. He is never going to college. The level of the city where everything is pristine would never have him. Even the television reception is better here, the screen image brilliant and smooth, lush with electronic perfection.

"Yes!" Nick climbs over his bucket seat and begins scooping up the scattered stock certificates.

"The money is good," Hector says. "No?"

"The money is *muy excelente!*" Nick shoves Darren's leg aside to get at a stock share lodged under the boy's foot.

Darren kicks at him absentmindedly, annoyed at not being able to decode the financial information on-screen. He doesn't know what "small cap stock" means, or "public offering." The latter sounds religious, like a kind of sacrifice. He can pick up the fact that A.P.E. stock, for some reason, doesn't go on sale until tomorrow. But in other parts of the world, it *is* tomorrow. And a lot of foreigners seem amped about the stock. Nevertheless, what is perfectly clear is that the number attached to the stock has quickly gone from 4 to 12.

"So we should, you know, do the layout." Hector extends the computer to Darren.

"*Escribe.* Absolutely." Nick clambers off the floor into the front passenger seat, then looks at Darren. "Unexpectedly high earnings have boosted quarterly dividends. I'm happy to announce I'm laying a grand on you." Darren turns away, then refuses to answer when Nick calls his name. "Oh, now three thousand isn't enough?" Nick says, after raising his bid.

"I changed my mind is all." Darren stares into the Kwik Shop. The glass windows make Trampas seem strangely unfamiliar, a figure from a dream. Under the store's bright interior lights, the cowboy inserts his credit card into a checkout payment slot. He looks the clerk behind the thick glass in the eye, moving his lips as he thanks him. Striding toward the electronic door, Trampas keeps his chin up, smiling at everyone he passes as if he owned the place.

"Five thousand," Nick says. "Five thousand, plus ten percent of net profits from the sale of all stock valued at fifteen dollars or higher."

Darren looks at Nick. On-screen, numbers continue to stream, music piping softly through the speaker cones embedded in the van's plush roof. The cellular phone's automatic call light flashes incessantly, like a heartbeat. The city's breathless webwork holds them all, as if the streams and flashings of information were the bright lights of stars bleeding into an otherwise infinite dark. And with oblivion so palpable to each of them, Darren sees that Nick, in his despair, and Ray, in his unholy blind rage, had to flail against it, the two of them united by fear. "You would have sold me to that guy in the bar," Darren says. "If I'd a been worth much, you'd have sold me."

"Not true. *No es verdad!* You're just feeling guilty for being smarter than your idiot friend, Ray. And now you're looking to blame your problem on me. Grow up."

"I ain't blaming nobody."

"Then name your price. What's it going to take to get you out of the 'hood?"

"Somethin' besides money."

Hector sees Trampas come through the automatic door. His boot heels pock hollowly on the pavement as he approaches the driver's-side window, a six-pack of soda dangling from one hand, a shiny bag of chips from the other. "Uh-oh. *Estamos muertos.* We haven't done the layout, or the shot list." Hector holds up the blank computer screen.

The driver's-side door flies open and Trampas tosses the chips onto his seat. "Twelve bucks for a six-pack of Coke. Can you believe it?" He notices the G.R.E. stock reports on the TV. Seeing the price hike, he makes a fist then jerks his arm backwards as if yanking a lasso to cinch its noose. "Whoo-oo-whoo! Paid for that six-pack in a hurry." He tears a can loose, pops its tab, then raises it and offers a toast. "To caffeine, the stock market, and my dick— things that are always headed up."

"You mixed your metaphors," Nick says, swiping a Coke for himself. He instantly begins blending it with Scotch.

Trampas sucks his can dry nonstop, crushes it in one hand, then hurls the squashed remains at Nick, clipping him above one eyebrow as he ducks. "Don't care what I mixed." He pauses to belch loudly, a rolling, multi-tiered exhalation that spirals up from his balls and out through his mouth like a weird saxophone solo. "You're a piss-ant. And now you got a stain on your pants."

Nick has, indeed, spilled his cocktail on one trouser leg. He doesn't mind, though. The clarity of thought brought on by being angry with Darren is fading. Even his elation over the paper wealth he holds in his hands feels distant, made unreal by time's refusal to grant it any permanence. In the harsh electric glare of the security lights, Trampas appears to him with all the odd, disorienting force of a hallucination: American history on the head of a microchip. Nick realizes he's riding in a fiberglass-covered wagon with a cowboy, his vaquero, a slave, and a camcorder, past tribes spread across the great plain of the city, ever westward into new financial frontiers. He laughs while Trampas glares at him, which only makes Nick laugh harder.

"You're out of your mind."

Nick spikes his Coke with another hit of Scotch, then toasts Trampas. "No. *Yo soy Americano!*"

Without taking his eyes off Nick, Trampas says, "Hector. Tell me you have the directions and layout we need, so I don't have to get deranged."

"We're working on it. So, you know, as we drive—" Hector grips two sides of the laptop computer and tilts it from left to right as if he were steering the van.

Trampas goes cyborg before Darren's eyes, all the cowboy's human fluidity freezing inside of him. Replacing it is a kind of automatic fury, the out-of-his-skull hate Darren has seen in the eyes of cops. He remembers McKuen and wishes he had not been so slick with him this morning. He should have trusted him, compromised, saved himself. Being brave, pushing to find what he's after, that's Ray. Just as Ray is now the only person who would care enough to save him, if he could.

"We'd know *exactly* where we were going," Nick says, "and have a shot list and map of the place in hand, if his lowliness hadn't decided he was no longer interested in honoring our agreement."

Trampas screws his gaze slowly toward Nick. He looks at the strands of hair messily draped over Nick's temple, his loosened tie, the sweaty pallor of his skin, and sees in him one of the private-school types he hated in high school—rich, arrogant, and hollow.

All of them are jarred by a sharp rap on the driver's-side door. "Let's move it," a guard says. He glides alongside the van, twirling his black nightstick, then passes out of sight.

Trampas examines the door for bruises, muttering to himself. Coming back to the interior of the van, he swats the bag of chips off his seat, then shoves the rest of the six-pack onto the floor. "Hector! *Cierre la puerta,* goddammit!" Both van doors whoosh closed. Trampas strips the ignition motor trying to start the engine. He releases the key and tries again. This time it catches.

"The gas cap," Hector says.

"Goddammit!" Trampas strangles, then pounds the steering wheel. He hops out of the van, whacking a side panel with the palm of his hand. When the hollow boom sinks away, the only sounds are Trampas's cursing and the gas nozzle knocking against the metal throat of the tank.

Slumped in his seat, Nick chuckles softly.

Hector offers Darren the laptop, its blank screen glowing brightly. Darren nudges it away. Trampas leaps back into the van and yanks the door closed. Darren can see his eyes searching for Hector's in the rearview mirror.

"Now what the fuck is the address we're headed to?" Trampas shouts. "And what is the layout of this goddamned place so I don't open the wrong door and get my head blown off. There's two thousand apartments in them fucking projects!"

"I'll take care of it," Hector says.

"No you won't," Nick says. "Darren has discovered his conscience."

Trampas's eyes cut away from Hector's, and Darren meets them rather than looking away.

"Well we're going to undiscover it." Then Trampas pops the van into gear and darts past cars and tanks, ignoring the hands motioning for him to slow down. The light from the oasis fades, and the speeding van's interior falls into the dim gray glow of the dashboard TV.

Intent on his laptop PC screen, Nick is blissfully, drunkenly, unaware of the uncivilized dark at this far edge of the city. There are no subdivisions or high-tech outposts. Just the shadowed edges of the airport's runways, their flashing lights lined up like cadets, radio tower and a halo of terminal light in the distance. Otherwise it's unwired brush and plain, and abandoned agricultural roads, crossed only by insects, small game, and the invisible movement of satellite signals.

Darren, however, is well aware of the unlighted ditches and trees. For him, it is a different kind of dark. And when he looks out at the open fields, he sees something other than development property.

Nick stares at the Terror-TV voice-over copy he has been tinkering with. "What you are about to see is the rot at the worm-eaten core of our tele-society," he types, straining to think clearly. Between elation and drunkenness, he forgets from moment to moment that he is among others. All that exists for him is the linking up of his visions with the net of shimmering data on his color monitor, his electronic cocoon. Studying his latest entry, he finds it too British, too public television. He doesn't want to come across as socially responsible. Deranged would be fine. Deranged plays. So he is going to have to project an edge of mockery. "Technology leads, humanity bleeds." He scans it numbly, then says, "I've got it! The closing line for our docu-pocalypse. I'm a genius."

"You're a pinhead," Trampas tells him. "This here's Gates Remington TV. Scream 'Horror,' shove your way to the bleeding corpse, we splice in nude scenes later. Stereotype, goddammit!" He pounds the steering wheel again with the heel of his hand, then points at Nick. "You give me one original idea, that laptop's gonna be sandwiched between your hemorrhoids."

Trampas veers off the paved road and onto the shoulder without slowing down. Gravel kicks up, sounding like tin rain as it pelts the insides of the wheel walls.

Nick ruminates on the state of television and has to admit that Trampas is right. Stereotyped sex and gore. The medium is beyond parody, beyond vilification. There's only plugged and un-plugged, and even that distinction is passing. Everyone is wired: techno-myth's time has come. We see through liquid crystal, walk through virtual landscapes on bionic limbs, our pains and mad-ness tempered not by the cool hand of God but by amber-bottled pills and co-insured magic elixirs. Why resist? The new myth is waiting, a bliss ready to be slipped on like new, electronic skin . . . or a very expensive designer suit, which is what a reserved Gates Remington is wearing on-screen. "It's him! It's Gates!" Nick shouts, jarred out of his reverie.

Trampas stomps on the brake pedal, bringing the van to a skid-ding halt. He rams the gearshift into "park," then flings his door open and hops down onto the dusty fringe of the road. Only when he is on the ground and searching for something beneath his bucket seat does he show any interest in his employer's satellite TV presence.

Hector crouches forward, one eye on Trampas, the other on the interview-in-progress. XXN's financial news network is beaming a chat with porn-and-gore-meister Gates Remington III live by mi-crowave link from G.R.E.'s "Sky Studio."

"That's why I couldn't get through by phone," Nick says, hyp-notized by the screen. "His office is airborne!"

Es verdad. The site is a converted army transport helicopter, now hovering six thousand feet above the city. A quick tour by hand-held camera reveals a newscaster's desk, banks of televisions and computer hookups, a cockpit, and a sunken lounge area, its curved black leather couch lit by soft gold spotlight beams. Seated on it is a red-headed woman whom Nick instantly admits he could marry and divorce, and the Gateman himself, in full-tilt financial guru mode. Nick listens, adrift, stoned.

"The nineties were all about mergers, building the electronic highway, wiring the world. It was about the control of information delivery lines. That's accomplished. Now the focus is, once again, on software, product. And the financial markets have been very receptive to A.P.E.-TV, I believe, due to the fact that they recognize interactive terror as the wave of the immediate future. The future, in telemarketing terms, being the next six minutes—excuse me, months. The next six months."

"Why isn't he the bastard-of-the-universe he was to me on the phone?" Nick wants to know.

"Haven't you figured out by now," Trampas says, "that the prick knows how to make money?"

Darren can't see what Trampas's hands are doing, but he seems to hold something in one, then yank with the other, as if disengaging a pair of objects.

"Hector." Trampas suddenly seems to forget that he's angry. His voice is calm. "Hook up the Betacam. I want to get some footage from out here. Darren?" Trampas waits, immaculately still. "Don't you look away from me, boy."

"Listen." Nick raises the TV's volume. "He's talking about us."

Trampas shifts his gaze to the television in grudging, angry silence.

". . . We now have primetime riot coverage throughout the U.S., plus mid-morning programming set to go across Asia. With a few more ads we'll have most of Europe stumbling out of bed before dawn to tune in. The overseas response has been phenomenal. Why? Because we represent the last moral struggle on earth. America is paradise lost. End and beginning, darkness and light, black/white. The dichotomies are all here. We fascinate *and* repel. A.P.E.-TV has several crews out at this very minute, making sure we bring it all to the world. Why, do you know that our Asian footprint, the XXN satellite signal, reaches forty million households? That's a huge chunk of the world's population in some of its faster-growing economies—"

"That's it," Trampas says, facing Darren. "You gonna tell me where we're going?" Darren remains silent. "Alright, out of the van."

"What does he mean, 'several' crews?" Nick asks blankly. The world seems to be splitting up into separate cells. Maybe because he's high. But all the continuity is gone. Gates is one thing, the shares of stock another, and neither is connected to him or to the others in the van. Nothing is connected. It's all a random flashing of images, the mute spaces between them dizzyingly black.

"Hector, goddamnit! Rig the camera." Trampas moves out of the arc of his door, then slams it shut. He reappears out of shadow a moment later, the upper half of his body lit brightly by the van's headlights.

"Don't think I'm only into the gore," Gates explains. "We're developing very sophisticated communications equipment to make this possible. The camera, for instance, is actually a modified Betacam that plugs into a portable computer worn on the cameraman's back. The images are stored as an electronic imprint on the computer's hard disk, then digitized, compressed, and fed directly to the audience by microwave link, cellular phone, or modem. So in one way, this is a communications laboratory as well as a national tragedy."

"And profitable," Nick reminds Gates, his face close to the screen.

Darren watches the sliding door pop onto its track and sweep open. Trampas stands there, framed by darkness. The long barrel of a pistol shines at arm's length beside his hip.

"Get out. Now."

Darren nudges Hector's leg. "Go 'head," he says softly.

Hector looks at him, then climbs out of the van. Trampas doesn't take his eyes from Darren as he shoves Hector away. "Get the camera."

"You should be watching this," Nick announces, his tunnel vision fixed on close-ups of the Sky Studio's communications gadgetry, all of it developed by the military and entertainment industries.

"You, let's go." Before Darren can get off the seat, he feels the cowboy's hand on his shoulder, dragging him forward by his jacket. "I said get the fuck out."

Nick half turns to see what's going on in the back of the van, and in the deep, vivid part of his high where each glance or thought is an entirely new universe, he hears Gates Remington explain that one possible benefit of the inferno sweeping through ghetto areas is the sudden freeing up of developable real estate near the lucrative downtown market. Particularly in the Phoenix Cityplex vicinity.

"The devastation will provide an opportunity for us to rebuild. I mean, destruction is a part of progress, correct? But I also understand the need for healing," Gates adds. "So even though we'll be showing some necessarily graphic and violent material during our special, we plan to follow it up with panel discussions by serious intellectuals. Also something with artists. Poets and painters responding, in their work, to the horror. And, of course, placing these events in a religious context goes without saying. So I expect to be seeing clergy. I mean, if there was ever a time for God to show up. Right? So, if He's listening, and He wants to—hey, the crews are out, we're ready. . . ."

The bench Darren was sitting on is abandoned. Nick sees only the sad uselessness of unattended objects which litter the van's interior. Hears nothing but the whistles and roar of an idiot wind. He wonders if Darren and the others were ever here with him, or if he hallucinated the entire trip. When he looks for Trampas all he glimpses is a sleek leather holster lying on the driver's seat. On TV, Apocalypse Productions' share price has risen to 14½. And for an instant, Nick feels exactly like one of the numbers on-screen: discrete, adrift, attached to nothing but currents in an immense pointless flux. He has the sense that he might never see Darren and the others again when they miraculously reappear, half-shadowed, at the edge of the headlights' dust-whirling brightness. Trampas, his hat lifted off his head and bounced into darkness by the wind, drags Darren forward, then stops on the tips of his boots and flings the boy to the ground. There's shouting but no intelligible words, just a lone human voice railing in the tempest. It's a strange movie, Nick is thinking, when Trampas suddenly stands over Darren and kicks him in the ribs. "Hey," is all Nick says, one hand blindly groping for the door handle.

Nick is weaving past the headlights, the tails of his suit jacket fluttering when Darren sees him, before Trampas moves toward him again.

"Get up, goddammit. Hector, *venga aqui!*" Then Trampas's breath is on Darren's face, gun tip pressed to his temple. On his knees, Darren hears Nick's voice calling out to him over the beating dust. "You want to *be* my fucking documentary?" Trampas screams.

And as if the act already existed and he was only playing it out, Trampas feels that killing the boy is not beyond him. Voices like drumbeats in his head urge him on until his hand is no longer his own hand. The boy, the shadowed plain and battering wind, all are vivid and disconnected as dreams. Not even Nick's voice coming up behind him, or Darren's eyes, which now look at him, possess the fierce rootedness of the gun. It holds him there on the chafed ground, both he and the boy he is about to kill trembling, burning in time . . . until Nick comes between them and the instant passes, forcing Trampas beyond the rush and blindness urging him to pull the trigger . . .

. . . And if Gates Remington were looking down from his Sky

Studio he would see four human forms moving about on a patch of lighted dust. One in boots, kicking the ground in disgust; one kneeling; another placing his hands on the kneeling one's shoulders as if shielding him; and on the edge of darkness, camera dangling from one hand, a witness who waits until a tentative peace has been made. Then, slowly, they all retreat to the vehicle. The van half-circles on the empty road, sweeps the dark with its headlights, and begins to creep through the vast blackness, back toward the shimmering city. . . .

Gliding down the elevated beltway's exit ramp, McKuen watches flares light the bombed-out buildings like X-rayed bone, the inner city nothing but patches of glare and blackness. Cherry-red tracer bullets necklace from rooftop to rooftop, then appear here and there along the streets. He slips on a pair of night vision shades, and kills the headlights. The world around him goes gray-green, tinged by a granular, dirty light, the kind he imagines the dead must inhabit. His exhaustion, and the Benzedrine he took to counter it, turns the city into a dreamspace. To assure himself that he's conscious he passes one hand over his mouth. Julia's scent lingers on his fingertips where they reached up inside her, her taste there when he slips one finger between his lips.

He has been quiet since they recrossed the river, Julia thinks. With night falling, it seems there is less to say. She finds a kind of peace in this, though. The world was born in darkness. We dream in darkness. Darkness is mother to light. To interrupt the cycle is unholy, a word she hasn't used in a long time. The firelight is terrifying, yet strangely beautiful, the citadels in the distance filigreed by the crossfire of tracer bullets. She feels a sense of awe before the fury of the world.

"This is the spot where the squad car was last night," McKuen says. They cruise past a glass-speckled patch of pavement, close enough to see glistening stains, slick as open wounds. McKuen wonders if it's leaked motor oil or blood. Beyond the yellow police ribbon looped around silver streetlight poles, the fence is rent where he burst through it in the squad car. Tonight, the lot is un-lighted by helicopter search beams, no boy running across it sur-rounded by bright swirling dust. "We got lost one time, lost radio contact with base," he says softly.

Julia watches him, the night vision shades bringing out an inhu-man aspect in his face, as if sediment had been stripped from an archaeological find to reveal the burnished war mask beneath.

"We weren't even in Nam. Cambodia maybe. Wandered for days. Our radioman was dead, killed in a firefight. So we were just . . . running. Everything the same, like we were walking in cir-cles. The same circle."

Window lights appear in the high distance, the broad western expanse of the projects slowly sweeping closer.

"You go numb after a while. Begin cutting deals with yourself, like—dying would be okay if it got me out of here. Then you say, no, maybe just a limb. I'll give up a limb." He pauses. "Of course, you don't want to give up any of those things. Then you look at the guys around you and realize you've been sacrificing them, too. Like, if five of them died and the rest of us got out, that'd be okay. This one for that reason, that one for this. Sick, huh?"

"No."

He nods, unconvinced.

"So you think the boy we're chasing is lost, too?"

McKuen looks at her. "Maybe."

"You found your way out, though. Obviously."

McKuen studies the street ahead, wishing he could continue along it straight out of the city, out of time, beyond himself. "There was this clearing. Maybe we'd circled the edge of it already, but there was just that extra foot of brush to keep us from seeing it. You know? That close." He raises his hands on either side of the wheel. "Then suddenly, there it is. And inside it is not a temple really, but a city. A small city. The walls reaching above the treetops. Bones half-buried in mud. Statues, icons. Rooms built into the walls. The roof is the sky. The city *is* the temple. From the top of it we can see base. Home." He pauses. "Somebody sends up a flare, so we'll be seen. After all, we're only a few clicks away. Up where it's clear, that's nothing."

The empty lot McKuen chased Ray across vanishes, hidden by the fringe of the projects. "How many died?" Julia says.

"Three. Charlie reached us before the choppers did."

"All on your list."

McKuen hesitates. "Two new guys. Crazy. Torched a village, shot a kid. You don't leave that stuff behind."

"And the other?"

McKuen turns toward her, his eyes dead black circles. "He didn't know any better. He shot the flare. Everyone else got out by helicopter. Out of the temple, into the machine."

The projects' archway slips over the car's roof as the dead garden of Aslam A Lakem Downs opens around them. McKuen pulls the car into the center of the courtyard, close to the tower that holds the boys' apartments. He cuts the engine, the faint radio static and police band messages as quiet as their breathing. Adjusting to the hush, he can hear the light *pop-pop-pop* of automatic weapons fire in the distance. The scents in the air—exhaust fumes, smoke and cooling ash, Julia's perfume—are to him ghostly doubles of napalm fires, burning huts, and the jungle's sweet fertile indifference. He feels as if he still *is* in the temple city. Even his muscles seem young again, his fear-adrenaline dissolving time.

Removing the night vision shades, he reaches into the back seat and collects two armored vests, then hands one to Julia. They remove their jackets and slip the Kevlar vests around themselves. While Julia holds a small elastic loop between her teeth and gathers her hair into a ponytail, McKuen checks his pistol's cartridge clip, then stuffs another half dozen of them, ninety rounds, into the vest's zippered pockets. He enters their location on the dashboard computer, checks the time—a full day since he was last here, on virtually the same spot—and transmits both via cellular code to the department's mainframe.

"It's quiet," Julia says.

"For now."

"Wolf isn't here yet."

"He will be."

McKuen checks a flashlight to see that it's working. "The action on the streets—those tracer bullets—seemed to be house-to-house searches. These things die down, flare up. It might be a lull; it might be burning itself out." He curls one hand around hers, her pulse as faint beneath his fingertips as the tracer fire echoing softly along the streets. "Stay till I call you. I'll go partway, then you follow."

Then McKuen is through the door and out of the car. Around him, the city is softly alive. The dirty breeze caresses his face, sirens arc overhead, spotlights streak the low curtain of marbled sky. He stands there, waiting, expecting, in a way, it all to end. "You don't hear the bullet meant for you" drifts through his mind, seeming less like a superstition than a prayer, words passed between the living and the dead.

Ray watches the familiar figure stare at the high rooftops as if checking for snipers, then leans back into the building's shadow when the man walks across the courtyard. Seconds later, the car's passenger door opens and a lady steps out. Her shoe heels pock on the concrete before she, too, disappears behind the base of the tower. Waiting to be sure they've gone inside, Ray listens to the city howling beyond the small sound of his own breathing. Faintly, in music from a passing car, there is, and then just as quickly there isn't, Coda's voice. The swiftness with which it appears and vanishes mirrors dreamspeed, the weightlessness of shadow.

Ray tries to recall what it felt like to believe Coda's words, to walk inside that halo. He remembers copying the spelling of "Discordia Sect" off a wall onto a sheet of paper. Not even Minus Five was able to tell him what the first word meant when he slid by the arcade to use the machine that photographed pages for a nickel apiece. It's like watching some other life he led.

He hears the building's metal door quietly clap shut. Edging the tower's rear door open, he listens for their voices inside the maze of first-floor corridors, but hears only the hum of power lines, the dull tangled harmony of machines. The hall smells of urine and cooking oil, a close, overheated scent which reminds him of rotting flesh. He remembers feeling sickened and trapped by it. That was the sweetness of Coda, his promise to destroy everything, to wipe it all away. And yet as Ray softly presses the door back into its frame, he can feel his heartbeat. And even though he's afraid, the cold sick fear that drains the marrow from his bones, he feels as if he were being carried by this elemental force. In a way, it isn't even *his* heart beating, but something eternal. He puts one hand to his chest to still it. A moment later, when his shudders pass, he turns and heads toward the light in Darren's bedroom window.

McKuen's light rapping on the apartment door goes unanswered, though he can hear the sound of a TV inside. When a second knock brings no one, he grips the knob and twists it. With a light push, the door floats away and the sounds of the city bloom. Clear, hollow miniatures of the real thing. All of it linked by the brief announcement that this is XXN. . . .

Over news commentator babble comes a deep, animal breathing. McKuen smells the stale apartment air waft into the hall, dead scents of old smoke, grease, and a sourness as if sewage had backed up and been left standing. Crack resin filters through, charred and synthetic. He waits, then swiftly flashes one arm in front of the threshold to see if it draws gunfire. Nothing. He crouches slightly, breathes, empties himself of thought. Then he's moving quickly inside the dim living room, past bags of trash and empty aluminum cans heaped inside the door. He takes aim at the curled form lying beyond the litter of ashes, bottles, and cigarette packs on a dark couch. The TV flickers like electric candlelight, an impalpable gray that makes McKuen feel nearly bodiless. The figure on the couch takes the shape of a woman as he approaches, her back to him the way his wife lay when he found her. Only this woman's side rises and softly falls under her sweatshirt as she breathes. Her body is tucked, knees to stomach, her hands balled into small fist and crossed over her breasts. Rolling her toward him, the heat of her body seeps through her shirt and takes McKuen's hand as if it were his wife clutching him all these night-fevered years later, waiting to be led back from the land of the dead.

When he studies this woman's face though, McKuen sees the sweaty face of a skeleton, wrapped in the deep black of drug-sweetened sleep. She barely stirs, a single moan drifting through her before she slips back into dream. As he lays her down, McKuen feels released, the woman's warmth—and with it his wife's ghost—passing from him as if a long fever had broken. Saving everyone isn't possible. Time to let go.

Julia sees "This is XXN" floating amidst the fires on-screen.

Across the room is a kitchen. Sink, narrow stove, small refrigerator. Cans, pots, and dishes scattered over them. A barred window. No softness, nothing to make a boy feel wanted in the world.

McKuen moves out of the room through a darkened archway. When his flashlight turns the interior of the next room into a bright cave, the face Julia thinks she sees outside the barred window vanishes. There is only a god's-eye view of the city and the letters XXN reflected there, as the television burns steadily at the opposite end of the room.

McKuen squats beside a thin mattress and bedcover as she steps across the threshold. He pulls Discordia Sect flyers, several boxes of 9-millimeter cartridges, and a T-shaped submachine gun from under the bedding. He stands quickly, hauling the mattress with him, dust devils swirling in its updraft. Nothing. He searches the milk crate beside the bed, a few pairs of socks, underwear, and sweatshirts tumbling out of it. He pops the compartments of the boom box sitting atop the crate, then pries apart the few CD casings surrounding it, including Coda's. Just some lyrics printed on an insert, nothing more. He turns the flashlight in the direction of the room's one small closet. Two or three items of clothing and a few bare wire hangers dangle above a pair of scuffed high-tops. On the walls are posters of sports heroes and celebrities.

Ray watches the movement of light through Inch's bedroom window, listening intently for their voices as he crouches below it. All he can make out are the different tones—hers smooth, almost like the ringing of a bell, his muddy and much deeper. A sharper sound obliterates them with its harsh buzz. Ray sees a light arc past the high upper floors of a far tower, then wing toward him. It looks like the cell in the Afroman game. Bright center, four spokes of light extending from it. A rifle site. He creeps past Inch's window, heading for the pistol tucked beneath his bedroom's windowsill twenty feet away.

Inside, McKuen hands the flashlight to Julia, then lays the apartment's blueprint on the floor. His fingertips skim a low section of wall until he finds the seams he's looking for. Then he tears away the poster covering them. Strips of duct tape hold a cutout square of Sheetrock in place.

Julia doesn't mention forfeiting whatever evidence they may turn up if Wolf arrives and discovers them. She thinks of Parsons trusting her to keep it honest, the rumors of mass detention, the official and unofficial visions of the city. The illusion of a reasoned world seems to be vanishing, her vision of the city shifting and uncertain, every quest, including her own, doubled by a counter-quest, until every last distinction, the meaning behind every action, threatens to blur, and confuse, and paralyze. Silent, she just lets McKuen go.

Lifting the slab of loosened concrete from its window casing, Ray sees a veil of light spill into his bedroom. He ducks as it sweeps past the window, then squats motionless, the windowsill resting on his knees. His heartbeat seems absent for a moment, then explodes as if he'd just rocketed back from the dead when a helicopter's dry thunder falls over him. In the sky, a second searchlight beam appears opposite the first. As they approach, a third drops from the clouds, dim as a falling star. Rising, he leans against the tower's wall. The light bobs inside the window, inches from his face, while he tries to guess when he should reach for the gun.

McKuen lights the crawl space between apartments until Julia is through it, then slips the flashlight into her palm and whispers, "Be right back." He disappears into an unlighted hallway outside the room.

Julia moves the light over a neatly made single bed. A plain wooden crucifix hangs above its headboard, a small night table topped by a shaded lamp set close to one side. There's a chest of drawers with framed photographs of people with their arms around one another. Julia lifts one off the chest's crocheted runner. A young woman smiling at the camera holds a scowling five-year-old boy close to her, their cheeks touching. Another shows the two of them on what appears to be the same day. Trees in the background, him in a tanktop, the woman kneeling, bare-armed in a summer dress. She has her lips pursed and is trying to kiss him, while he keeps his hands stuffed in the pockets of his shorts, looks at the sky, and laughs.

Julia wanders past championship pennants, and caps suspended on wall hooks, their colors clashing like a motley flag. The room could easily be her son's room. "Aslam A Lakem" is carved into the top of a small desk. Surrounding the words, etched so finely into the veneer that Julia has to pass the light closely across their pale outlines to see them, is some sort of private dream language. Backwards letters, barely phonetic spellings, primitive human figures. Bones and open mouths in poses of attack, surrender, open-armed resurrection. They've found the boy they're looking for, but his motivation is no longer incomprehensible to her. He has simply been wandering in darkness, looking, like us all, for his way home.

McKuen enters a second small bedroom. He peers into its closet and runs his hand blindly over soft dresses, lingering among them as if their touch was a kind of bliss, a safe mothering warmth, and he wonders what it takes *not* to get lost in the world. He sees neatly stacked envelopes lying on a dresser. Pay stubs, a small lined pad. Thumbing through the slips, take-home pay of one hundred and fifty-four dollars ticks by without change. Odessa Roberts works for less than welfare would put in her pocket. On the pad he sees dollar amounts for rent, electricity, groceries, carfare, laundry. Under some long addition where her hand has carried small figures from one column to the next, the amount remaining is divided between church, two dollars, savings five, and pocket money for Ray, the boy he's chasing, who for the first time has a name.

Nick already knows Ray's name, though it no longer seems important. He can hear Trampas radioing in coordinates to Gates Remington's Sky Studio. He can see by the dashboard screen that the upcoming Terror-TV special is being linked by satellite to markets in Eastern Europe, and huge audiences in Brazil where it is being presented as a *telenovela,* or nighttime soap, taped news footage instantly converted to melodramatic background material for fictionalized love scenes and shoot-outs. In India, the riots have already been turned into the opening chapters of a miniseries. The main plot, which concerns a real estate conspiracy, is quickly overshadowed by dance numbers, soft-core enactments of the Kama Sutra, elephants, men eating fire, clips of American gangster movies, the sudden intercession of a god. Deepest Mexico has even purchased, as part of the licensing deal with A.P.E.-TV, the rights to Nick's life. And in a moment during which hallucination, revelation, media illusion, and reality all dissolve into the weightless force of dream, Nick sees on-screen the slick-haired, mischievously attractive, caballero film star who is to *be* him for all of Latin America, *El Lobo Hombre!,* his tele-double.

So as the van descends, Aslam A Lakem Downs just ahead, a wireless microphone is placed in Nick's hand. The dashboard clock tells him they will be on time, they've made it. Apocalypse Productions will happen. Its stock share price doubles as new markets sign on. He understands the instructions Trampas is barking at him. Talk slowly and clearly, yes. Look into the camera, yes. Nick is finally plugged into the vast sprawling electronic web of the world, whatever they capture on camera beamed across the streaming etheric night.

And yet, all that matters to him is Darren Adams's dark quiet presence on the bench behind him. No longer on his knees, no longer whipped by the furious dust. Running toward him, Nick seemed to slip out of his own skin. First into the long, wavering shadow his body cast over the ground, then beyond it, into the skin and pulse of the boy himself. With that, his own life no longer mattered quite so simply. It lived through the boy, as well as through himself. The states of stoned rapture and electronic higher ground he chased suddenly felt like the surface distractions they were. Nice surface distractions, ones he plans on keeping. But pale and depthless compared with this deeper clarity and grace, this sense of communion.

As the van pulls into the courtyard, Nick sees McKuen's squad car. Then, converging high above, three searchlight beams. He opens his door and steps out into the night air, the city luminous and alive, and he knows that the wired world is only a yearning for and reflection of an absolute, unfathomable connectedness. He knows, too, that before an audience of billions, he must speak briefly and universally of mercy, then deliver a sequel-worthy happy ending by standing back, and letting Darren Adams escape. He can't believe he's going to get rich *and* do good. It's a miracle. Ecstasy-TV! God is on the air.

. . . "This is XXN" appears on screens across the city, across the dark plains beyond it and the teeming constellations of cities burning 'round the world like seas of fire. . . . It even materializes raw and unfiltered, without the standard seven-second delay, on the private screens of Gates Remington's Sky Studio and Special Ops Commander Eschata's Night Wing command post, both of which are tapped into the same central computer bank, the same modem lines and microwave links, patiently waiting.

Nick wonders where McKuen is when Trampas gives him a thirty-seconds-to-air signal. The cowboy has been largely silent since the roadside stop, as if he were disappointed with himself for not having been able to shoot Darren Adams. He doesn't even look at the boy. Instead, he addresses his remarks to Hector who dutifully carries them out, answering softly in Spanish.

Hector runs a final check on his power pack connections, computer jacks, and camera settings, then looks up, ready.

Holding the microphone to his mouth, Nick waits for Darren to look at him, then whispers, "Oh Kimosabe? Amigo?" When the boy turns, he sees Nick grinning like a maniac, one hand extended, as he croons into the microphone, "It's showtime!"

McKuen kicks a throw rug aside and shoves Ray's bed away, revealing the lead rectangle exactly where the surveillance blueprint told him it would be. He lifts the crude slab from its frame, then takes the flashlight from Julia and sweeps it over the narrow section of tunnel below. A shallow sub-basement, forty inches deep, into which McKuen lowers himself.

Ray wonders why their voices have faded. Shadow falls over the window and he realizes they've found his weapons tunnel as one of the city's Night Wing pursuit helicopters swoops by low enough to shake the suddenly bright ground beneath his feet, grit and dust sucked along in its wake. When the whine of its propellers drifts away, all that's left swirling is Ray's rekindled fear. He reaches for the gun, as startled by the woman whose eyes meet his as she appears to be, before he grabs it and vanishes.

McKuen feels a tremor in the tunnel's walls as the helicopter passes overhead. Nothing like the earth-muffled vibrations in dirt tunnels, their soft stillness like a grave. No spiraling path to Coda's lair, either. Just a small stash of guns, ammunition, and explosives stacked where the sub-basement dead-ends. He sifts through Xeroxed copies of the manifesto he peeled off the battered squad car. A hand-drawn map of the execution site notes the squad car's pattern of arrival and departure. A few failed efforts to construct crude bombs lie beside a pencil, check marks descending halfway down the step-by-step instruction sheet. He opens a small cardboard carton and finds dumdum bullets, their tips split to resemble the crosshairs of a rifle site. C-4 putty forms a crust around each cartridge's mouth. McKuen sits back on his heels and closes his eyes as Ray's stark hopelessness gathers inside him, until Julia's voice reaches him, shouting, "He's here."

The alleyway's darkness bursts from around Ray as he sprints into the glare of the courtyard. Darren is the first to spot him, or so he thinks, the others busy with the final countdown to electronic linkup. In the harsh light, Darren feels he's not seeing Ray but phantom tracings of him, which is what R.F. Tillinghast, Night Wing Private Fourth Class, sees on his heat-seeking surveillance monitor, high overhead. The image of the streaking figure is beamed simultaneously to the airborne screening room of Crash's superior officer and bestower of the long-promised, nose-mounted .50-caliber machine gun, Commander Eschata, who dines alone in plush electric candlelight, riding crop on the smoked glass table beside his champagne flute, as he watches Gates Remington's Terror-TV special, which has begun, and, in the nature of things, passes as quickly and lightly as dream.

Ray hears his name echo off the high walls of Aslam A Lakem Downs, then sees Darren break away from the startled figures laden with camera, microphone, and headset around him. In the apartment, McKuen and Julia retrace their steps past the sleeping woman, pausing to watch Ray's ghost-like figure projected out into the city, into the signal streams and satellite waves, Darren Adams and Nick Wolf closing in behind him.

His pocket calculator and computer dropping to the pavement, Nick sprints after the boy, gaining on him, Darren's limp slowing his uneven strides, which must be why Ray is waving him away, Darren thinks. His body is too slow. He hates it and wants Ray to wait for him near the base of the tower, which Trampas is praying they don't go into. He doesn't want to lose the open field where Hector and the camera can capture everything, even the piercing lance of searchbeam light that appears as Wing Private Tillinghast, country-western music blasting from his radio, rips past the arched entryway and begins firing a dozen rounds per second at the silhouette everyone below is running toward. He recognizes Ray as the same target he chased the night before only after he yanks the nose of the copter into pure vertical ascent, thinks uh-oh, then clears a tower's roofline by a pin's width and checks his telemonitor, which is tuned to XXN.

Gates Remington goes to split-screen instant replay, the Sky Studio's digital-imaging system editing, enhancing, and rebroadcasting the assault sequence while raw pursuit footage continues. Ray waits, his fear passing in the near silence that follows the helicopter's whirlwind. Darren is running toward him, the man in pursuit no longer shielding his head from the rain of bullets. Behind them, a crew from XXN follows, ready to bring his death to the world. And emerging from the door to the cell Ray for so long called home is the man who chased him and is chasing him still, as if his world depended on it. Ray watches them come, knowing they will always come, will always be there when he turns to stop, and he no longer wants to feel the malevolent rush of the world, its formless overflowing furor. Still, he can't let go. Something holds him in this place. And then he knows that there is no forsaking this world. There is only being torn from it—unfinished, afraid, and wanting, in the knowledge that you have not loved enough, more.

His hand closes around Darren's when his friend comes close and suddenly the two of them are running side by side, Ray's speed seeming to lift Darren out of his body as they race through the dead zone of the courtyard, Darren unaware that to Ray his hand feels like the hand of O.C. hurtling back from depths of the underworld to forgive him.

A light comes up behind them, reaching first the others, then Nick, who sprints as if through a stretch of dream landscape, alone with the sounds of his footsteps beating against the ground and his deep, eager breathing. Adrenaline courses through him as a tempest of street grit, glare, and noise engulfs him, driving him deeper into the rushing chaos of the world. And he thinks, I'm high, on TV, *here*, I love it!, the faint tapping against his back just before the wind and clatter and light are swept away feeling like fat, soft drops of rain. Crash Tillinghast is unable to make out anything of his second pass until he vaults the tower's block-long rooftop, then bursts through the low halo of cloud cover and checks his XXN hookup. He sees a guy holding a microphone drift to a stop and stare down at his shirtfront, which Nick sees has gone from white to a deep slick red. There are tears in the fabric and a trickling sensation, as if something tiny were crawling across his midsection before numbness and chills overtake him and he begins spinning, Trampas and Hector appearing and disappearing like figures on a carousel, their voices faint and excited. And if Nick could watch television he would see himself, blood-soaked and dazed, an expression of bewilderment on his face, which is how the rest of the world sees him. But he's lost and can only think, I gotta dry out. It isn't until he hits the ground—he thinks he's hit the ground—and finds the camera lens spinning above him, Julia descending out of nowhere like an angel or dream presence as McKuen passes quickly by, that he thinks, I'm dying. Or no, I'm going to wake up, I'm asleep. That's why I can't hear their voices and the world is like water. Nick's eyes search the sky, not even noticing when Trampas drags Hector away, or the warmth of

Julia's hand around his own. He's trying to remember something, but the world is falling away, his memory a small bright receding shape in the dark. It isn't Darren Adams, though Nick holds the image of the boy in his mind for a moment, or Gates Remington, whose name he can no longer place, or the meteorologist he lusted after, who provides only an instant's peace before he sees Dan's face close to his own. And he realizes that Dan will know what he wants to remember. He will say, I've forgotten something, and Dan will tell him what it is, and hold him, and then every-thing, everything, will be alright. . . .

Julia doesn't look at the figures drifting toward her from the homeless camp, or see where the chase has gone, or even wonder if the city is still here, wheeling into night. Eyes closed, she is cry-ing as McKuen bounds through the tower door, Ray's and Dar-ren's footsteps and breathing growing louder ahead of him. Only tonight, the dim halo of his flashlight bores a narrow passageway through the darkness, and when he bursts through the roof door, his lungs on fire, the city's glittering expanse stretching around him like an exploded star, Ray is there, running. From the air-borne cameras of the Sky Studio, the three bodies on the long rooftop seem to move in slow motion. Darren tires, stumbles, then releases Ray's hand. McKuen passes him without a glance, un-aware of the camera's eye above him, or XXN's claim that Coda is being chased toward the edge of a city rooftop, as Wing Private Tillinghast, hoping to redeem himself for Nick, sweeps skyward into the narrow canyon between the towers of Aslam A Lakem Downs. The helicopter rises as Ray jettisons his gun. His legs turn to water, the parapet blurring as he races toward it until the sound of his breathing is swallowed by helicopter bedlam, McKuen's voice not reaching him as he steps up and off, the city opening around him like the vision in the video game. And now, plummet-ing, arms spread, the secret cell opens. He is ready to reenter the labyrinth, the circle that has no beginning and no end, and to which he simply says yes, the helicopter blades passing through him as if he weren't there, scattering him so quickly over the city that to McKuen, slowing near the rooftop's edge, Ray's body seems to vanish. The Night Wing helicopter pirouettes, spun as if some invisible force were rewinding the hand of time, then explodes against the wall of a crumbling tenement, a bright crown of flames one moment, a hushed spire of softly billowing smoke the next.

Above it, the searchlight icons of the Night Wing station and Sky Studio are already sailing toward opposite horizons, red warning lights flashing as the droning of their engines falls to silence. And with the camera crew creeping through spirals of darkness, there is only McKuen watching as the city grows quiet, a dreamy stillness spreading over it.

. . . . Centuries later, legend may claim that Ray's body, regathered and united once more with his spirit, was borne heavenward through the night by those he had slain, leaving behind all allegiance to illusion, all attachments to the dissonant surfaces of unfinished things, and returned to his mother, the moon. Or legend may not, every trace of the city forgotten, lost in dust and time, buried within dream-visions and the long impenetrable night. . . .

But for now the only witness is McKuen, staring into the sprawling candlelight, his deep breaths rising out of the city's stillness and peace until there is nothing else he can hear, or feel.

CODA

The first sound Julia and McKuen hear other than the soft hum of the car's engine is an XXN DJ announcing the morning's most-requested track, as power stations come back on line. There's light traffic as they recross the bridge. Below, a pair of refuse barges skim the brown surface of the river, heading out to sea. Roadblocks are dismantled, planes rise and fall over the airport, deliveries are made. And along the beltway's service road, people hurry in and out of Quik-Marts and fast food outlets, the effects of the chaos virtually traceless in the distant reaches of subdivisions and corporate techno-parks. The sky is dull silver, just the usual pollutants swirling through it, the pall of smoke dispersed. Even the day's pop chart sensation makes the day seem dreamlike. For as it rises above the silent flashing of the car phone's all-circuits-busy signal, the voice sounds faintly reminiscent of Coda's, which has quickly drifted down the request lists into oblivion . . . along with Do-Ray Roberts, Christian Wolf, Crash Tillinghast, and any number of unnamed others. And though Darren Adams was released, Dan testifying that Nick held a Lorcim L-25 to the boy's head and forced him to sign a confession, the fates of the dispossessed swept from the city's streets, and the real estate conspiracy theories surrounding Phoenix Cityplex . . . they pass from rumor into history, and finally recede in the labyrinths of myth. . . .

The security gate's electronic eye decodes Julia's passkey signature and its two sword-like arms swing inward as Coda's voice-double and XXN artist-of-the-day, D.P. MOH, a.k.a. the Definitely Pure Master of Hope, sings about love and universal chillin'. McKuen follows the winding path past flower beds, and timed sprinkler systems misting lawns and greenish-black hedges, beautiful and dense with shadow. He glides into Julia's assigned parking space, then follows her up the terra-cotta walk to the garden apartment's doorway through which, once she's pushed it open, drifts the same song that was playing on the car's radio. Only this is the music video version, images of clouds and ethereal bodies drifting through computer-generated spacetime, in front of which Julia's son, reeking of stale beer and wearing a millennium party T-shirt under his fatigue jacket, lies sleeping, home safely from his all-night rave. He opens only one eye when Julia leans over and kisses him, then says before dreamily falling back to sleep, "I saw you on television."

McKuen stands on the landing outside the doorway until she returns. "You'll be alright?"

Julia puts one hand on the door's edge, the threshold separating them. "Yeah. I'll be alright."

"Yeah, well. Okay, then. I'll see you."

"Yeah. I'll see you."

McKuen turns and walks down the sloped path, removing the car keys from his pocket. He stops at the curb and stares at the irregular shapes the teeth of the keys make. When he raises his head he looks east toward the smoldering city, west toward the new subdivision lots under construction, then twirls the keys on his fingertips, slips them into his pocket, and walks back up the path and through the door Julia is holding open for him. The final image of it closing behind them holds for an instant, then blossoms into burning glare and nothingness, before that too fades, and black screen yields to credits and the letters XXN. . . .

. . . . So, that's it, homes, outta-here time. We goin', but we *will* be back. Just want you to know that from up here in the satellite streams and ether, the great wastes of iced blackness and super-nova fires, things down there ain't looking so bad, kinda cool blue and green, once you get some distance. So until next time, thro-win' one last shout down to all y'all, sayin' this has been, is, and forever shall be—XXN. Aslam A Lakem, Shantih Shantih Shantih, and yeah baby, that's right . . . peace. . . .

Fade out. . . .

<XXN>